MERCY

David Kessler dropped out of school at the age of 15 and was self-educated from then on. After struggling for 25 years to become a published author, he courted controversy by co-writing *Who Really Killed Rachel* (about the Wimbledon Common murder) with Colin Stagg, the man who was falsely accused of the crime. The book is now out of print, but since then, the real murderer – who was named in the book – has been convicted of the crime.

D1148808

Dorset Libraries
Withdrawn Stock

DORSET COUNTY LIBRARY

205073744 W

DAVID KESSLER

Mercy

Dorset Libraries
Withdrawn Stock

DORSET LIBRARY SERVICES	
HJ	16-Nov-2009
AF	£6.99

This novel is entirely a work of fiction.
The names, characters and incidents portrayed in it are
the work of the author's imagination. Any resemblance to
actual persons, living or dead, events or localities is
entirely coincidental.

AVON

A division of HarperCollins*Publishers*
77–85 Fulham Palace Road,
London W6 8JB

www.harpercollins.co.uk

A Paperback Original 2009

Copyright © David Kessler 2009

David Kessler asserts the moral right to
be identified as the author of this work

A catalogue record for this book is
available from the British Library

ISBN-13: 978-1-84756-182-4

Set in Minion by Palimpsest Book Production Limited,
Grangemouth, Stirlingshire

Printed and bound in Great Britain by
Clays Ltd, St Ives plc

All rights reserved. No part of this publication may be
reproduced, stored in a retrieval system, or transmitted,
in any form or by any means, electronic, mechanical,
photocopying, recording or otherwise, without the prior
permission of the publishers.

Mixed Sources
Product group from well-managed
forests and other controlled sources
www.fsc.org Cert no. SW-COC-1806
© 1996 Forest Stewardship Council
FSC

FSC is a non-profit international organisation established
to promote the responsible management of the world's forests.
Products carrying the FSC label are independently certified
to assure consumers that they come from forests that are managed
to meet the social, economic and ecological needs
of present and future generations.

Find out more about HarperCollins and the environment at
www.harpercollins.co.uk/green

I should like to thank Robert Burka Esq. for his advice on US criminal law and Roberta Burns for her advice on the California vernacular. They have not, however, reviewed the final draft of the manuscript and in any case I have taken literary license where I deemed it expedient. Therefore any remaining errors are the author's alone.

One example of the aforesaid literary license is that I have chosen to disregard a moratorium on the death penalty that at the time of writing exists in the State of California and the whole of the USA. This moratorium is due to rulings in both the state and federal courts. The precise details of these rulings may be found in various articles available on the internet for any readers who are interested in doing further research into this fascinating and contentious issue.

How this will pan out remains to be seen. Suffice it to say that we are living in interesting times . . .

For Mai, Shir and Romi

Author's Note

The times stated at the beginning of each chapter (usually in Pacific Daylight Time) refer to the time at the *start* of the events in that chapter. Thus chapters may overlap chronologically with subsequent chapters. This should be borne in mind in the reader's understanding of events.

09:30 Pacific Daylight Time
(August 14, 2007)

It's hard to sit still when your client is scheduled to die in fifteen hours.

Alex Sedaka felt gripped by that all-too-familiar urge to stand and pace up and down like a caged lion. But he knew he couldn't do so. It would be undignified – and hardly befitting the governor's office. So instead, he sat there tensely in the brown leather upholstered mahogany armchair, as his client's life hung in the balance.

'I know he had a fair trial, sir. That's why I can't get the courts to reconsider the case. But justice isn't a game. It's a search for the truth – at least it should be.'

Alex felt the gaze of suspicious eyes upon him, his shoulders hunched against the strain of the task that awaited him. Since hitting fifty, he had become somewhat self-conscious about his appearance, despite the fact that tennis and rock climbing had kept him lean and fit, as well as tanned.

But it was not the ravages of time that had aged him: it was his work. Three decades of professional cynicism, defending scum and lowlifes, had worn away the youthful charm from the face that Melody had fallen in love with

– or given it character, as she liked to say. Only this very morning, he had stared at his wedding picture with a mixture of joy and pain and had been surprised at how much he had changed.

But right now he was self-conscious, not about his looks, but rather about what he was going to say next. He had held the *freedom* of other men in his hands on numerous occasions. But this was the first time he had been entrusted with another man's *life*.

As if on cue, the governor's voice came back at him with quiet cynicism.

'It's not my duty to second-guess the courts now, is it?'

At the back of Alex's mind, a question was nagging away at him. *Do I plead for justice or mercy? Do I place the emphasis on the lingering doubts or argue about the ethics of 'a life for a life'?* And he had to think on his feet.

'No, sir, of course it's not your duty to second-guess the courts. But sometimes an unusual case can slip through the system. And *you* have the power to make a difference.'

He monitored the governor's face for a reaction to the obsequious flattery. The face remained neutral. Alex took it as the green light to continue.

'The courts are bound by a rigid code of rules. But sometimes the rulebook goes out the window. Every case is different and this case is a classic example. The whole trial took place in an atmosphere of anger and vengeance. All those comparisons with *Carrie*—'

'Carrie?'

'The book by Stephen King . . . about the girl with psychic powers who was bullied in high school.'

'Oh, right,' the governor replied suppressing a smile. 'I saw the movie.'

Alex squirmed.

'Well anyway . . . The press kept making comparisons. They just didn't let up.'

The governor scratched his head, looking puzzled. He had rejected Alex's written request for clemency a few days ago, but agreed to this eleventh-hour, face-to-face meeting at his San Francisco office, the location chosen by mutual agreement over LA, San Diego, Fresno and Riverside because of its proximity to San Quentin.

'I don't mean to sound like I'm making fun of you – 'cause I ain't – but you're contradicting yourself now. You said before that Burrow got a fair trial.'

'Yes, sir, in the courtroom. But what about the media circus beforehand? It poisoned the atmosphere. By the time the trial opened, people had already made up their minds. Folks were baying for blood. But vengeance isn't the same as justice.'

He had used the term 'folks' deliberately, hoping that it would click with the governor's populist vocabulary. But the governor was one step ahead of him.

'Are we talking justice for the murderer here or justice for the victim?'

Over the past few days, back at the office, Alex had practiced pitching various arguments, with Juanita and Nat at the plate, striking the kind of counter-arguments that he would inevitably face. But the more he had practised, the more banal it had all sounded. There was nothing more to add to the fossilized debate. All he could offer was a mind-numbing replay.

However, he had a few things going for him. Perhaps the strongest of these was that the incumbent governor – Charles Dusenbury – was himself an opponent of the death penalty. Not many politicians would stick their necks out by going on record with such a politically unpopular sentiment. 'Chuck' Dusenbury was one of the few. Even with public opinion divided on capital punishment, supporters of the death penalty were more likely to be one-issue voters on the subject.

But this didn't matter to Dusenbury. He was a lame duck, serving out his final term of office. His public position was that he had no plans to extend his political career at either the state or federal level and wanted to retire to a lakeside log cabin and spend his golden years playing golf and catching fish. This might have been good ol' hometown politicking. Some people – 'the media cynics,' Dusenbury called them – suspected that he still harbored aspirations to catch bigger fish than you can find in a lake. You could never tell with Dusenbury.

Alex took a deep breath and tried a different line of attack.

'Okay, there's something else that I'd urge you to consider: there's still reasonable doubt.'

'You mean the fact that they never found the body?'

'Exactly.'

'So why didn't you argue lack of corpus delicti before the courts?'

The governor was teasing him – his smile said it all.

'Corpus delicti means the "body of the crime," sir, not the "body of the victim." You know that.'

'Of course I know it,' the governor snapped. 'So why are you feeding me this line of bullshit?'

Alex recoiled from the anger. But he gathered his wits and recovered his nerve quickly.

'Because even if there's corpus delicti in the formal sense, it's still possible that the alleged victim is alive. Can you send a man to the death chamber with these lingering doubts still hovering over the case?'

'Well let's see now. They found breast tissue from the victim in a plastic bag at the back of the freezer at Clayton Burrow's home. They found the victim's blood-stained, semen-stained panties, hidden beneath the floorboards in Clayton Burrow's bedroom. They also found a blood-stained knife with a perfect set of Clayton Burrow's fingerprints in the same place. They used DNA to establish that the blood belonged to Dorothy Olsen and the semen came from Clayton Burrow. I don't know what *you* call that, but *I* call it corpus delicti!'

'Don't you think it was just a little bit too convenient? The cops finding all that under his bed after an anonymous tip-off?'

'You think they planted it? How would they get such evidence in the first place?'

'I don't know. From the body?'

'Which they never found!'

'But why would he keep all that stuff?'

''Cause he's a sex killer and he wanted to keep a trophy – that's why! Like countless sex killers before and since!'

'But would he be stupid enough to keep it under the floorboards of his own room?'

7

'Sure he would! He's a peanut-brained redneck!'

Alex shifted uncomfortably. He was flogging a dead horse. Time for another shift in his arguments.

'Well what about her trust fund? Eighty-six thousand dollars that she just liquidated a few days before she vanished?'

'The defense already tried that smokescreen at the trial. It was *her* money. She'd just turned eighteen and she wanted to get her hands on it.'

'And what about all that jewelry she bought with it?'

'What of it?'

'Well why would she suddenly do something crazy like that?'

'How the heck would I know? Maybe she wanted to make an impression at the prom!'

'Then how come they never found the jewelry afterward?'

'Maybe Burrow stole it! After he killed her!'

'Then why didn't they find any of it on him? Or in his house?'

'Maybe he sold it. He had seventeen months between when she disappeared and when they arrested him.'

'So where's the money? He didn't exactly lead a lavish lifestyle.'

'How the heck should I know? Maybe he lost the jewels! The point is, they found incriminating evidence on him and he had no explanation for it. It was an open and shut case.'

Alex Sedaka let the air out of his lungs. This was going nowhere.

He had only recently learned these details. He had not in fact had anything to do with the original trial. Burrow had been represented by an overworked Public Defender. After the guilty verdict, Burrow's cause had been taken up by a liberal-leaning law firm, which had tried to base its appeal mainly on allegations of incompetent representation by the defense counsel. When these efforts failed – and with the execution date looming ever nearer – they hinted to Burrow, in no uncertain terms, that he might like to consider hiring new counsel. They had no desire to be associated with a failed attempt to save a murderer from execution, hence their eleventh-hour retreat from the battlefield.

The upshot of all this was that Alex had been called in six weeks ago to try and save Clayton Burrow from death by lethal injection.

'He'll see you now.' A hard-edged female voice cut through Alex's imaginings.

Alex had been so wrapped up in his mental dress rehearsal of his pleadings, that he hadn't even heard her enter the room. He looked up to see the same lean, prim and spinsterly woman who had politely told him to wait here a few minutes ago. He hoped to God that he hadn't been talking out loud while alone in the room.

She led him down the corridor, turning back to give him a disapproving stare through her horn-rimmed spectacles when he stopped for a moment before a perspex-fronted painting to pat down into place his gray-tinged, black hair. Alex sensed that she was the kind of woman who didn't suffer fools gladly.

When they arrived at the meeting room, the woman

opened the door, holding it for him to enter. He looked at her expectantly, but she made it clear with her body language that she had no intention of entering the room herself. As he stepped into the plush, mahogany-panelled room, the governor – a smiling, hulking figure in a check shirt and extra large jeans, part fat, part muscle – rose from the conference table to greet him.

It was at that moment that Alex was struck by an unexpected sight. On another chair on the far side of the conference table sat a lean, short, frail, middle-aged woman with gray hair.

'Alex Sedaka,' Chuck Dusenbury's voice boomed out. It was a politician's tone – that sort of 'I'm a man of the people' twang that Alex associated more with the Midwest or Rocky Mountains. Dusenbury followed through with a firm handshake. Alex was grateful that it wasn't a bear-like hug.

But instead of meeting the governor's eyes as their hands gripped, Alex looked past the big man at the frail, familiar-looking woman beyond. She *looked* about sixty, but Alex sensed that she was somewhat younger, as if tragedy or illness had added years to her appearance.

Alex was mystified by her presence here right now. It wasn't merely the fact that this was supposed to be a private meeting between himself and the governor that left him so surprised to see her. It was the fact that he knew only too well who she was.

This sad-eyed lady was the mother of the very girl that his client had been found guilty of murdering.

09:38 PDT

Inside the blue Lincoln, the small man was sitting tensely. He knew that waiting was an inherently tense activity. Inactivity breeds a kind of stress that the most vigorous of purposeful action can never match. But there was nothing he could do about it. Waiting was part of the job.

The car was parked and the engine was off. But the key remained in the ignition, as if inactivity might give way to dynamism at any moment.

He touched the Bluetooth earpiece in his right ear, nervously. There was nothing particularly conspicuous about him. No one would pay attention to a twenty-seven-year-old, blue-eyed, brown-haired man in a dark blue suit nursing a Styrofoam cup of coffee from the Midway Café a few yards ahead. Strictly speaking, he wasn't wearing a suit: his jacket was off, his blue tie loosened and the collar button of the white shirt opened.

From his attire and demeanor, he could almost have been an off-duty G-man. But his modest height and slight build detracted from that, giving him an innocuous aura. If he had been a Washington spook, he would have been a pen-pushing bean-counter, not a field agent. There was no way anyone could have felt threatened or intimidated by him, even though his close-cropped hair hinted – misleadingly – at a military background.

Poised well above the horizon, the sun's warm glow was filtered by a thin veil of cloud. To the man in the car it had all the appearance of a giant wound in the sky, with blood still oozing through the bandage – not a new wound, more like an old one that refuses to heal.

He lifted his coffee cup out of the holder and took a single sip. Then he put the cup back down and looked round. Golden Gate Avenue looked normal, neither calm nor exceptionally busy. There was no sense of anything important going on twenty yards from where he sat.

He stared at the lacquered, grainy wood of the dash-board, admiring its elegance. It was a trivial thought – but it helped to stave off the boredom . . . for a couple of minutes at least.

The day was warm – not hot, just warm – hence his decision to take the jacket off. He tended to sweat in any sort of cumbersome clothing.

Finally the Bluetooth earpiece crackled to life.

'You know Mrs Olsen, I presume.'

'We've seen each other briefly,' Alex's embarrassed voice came through the earpiece. 'But we've never actually been introduced.'

09:40 PDT

Alex walked over awkwardly to the chair where Mrs Olsen was sitting. He held his hand out toward her, not expecting her to rise. She took it limply and he made sure that his own handshake was suitably gentle.

But when he opened his mouth, a polite 'How do you do?' was all the lawyer could muster.

What *did* you say in a situation like this? Do you belatedly express condolences for her bereavement? Apologize for the fact that you're representing the man convicted of murdering her daughter? Or keep your own counsel and remain silent?

For a few seconds he hovered, unsure of what to do next. The normal procedure was for the lawyer for the condemned man to meet the governor either alone or, more usually, with one of the governor's staff present. But the sight of Mrs Olsen in this room had thrown his entire game plan out the window.

'Well sit down, sit down,' said the governor amiably, pointing to a chair.

Alex shuffled awkwardly toward the vacant chair. He sat down and looked straight at the governor – anything to avoid meeting Mrs Olsen's unforgiving eyes. Dusenbury spoke again.

'I've been following the Burrow case closely. I was most impressed by your work.'

'Most of the work was already done. I only came in on it six weeks ago.'

Dusenbury, Alex remembered, was a lawyer by training, and by all accounts a wily old bastard.

'Well all I can say is that you've been pretty busy in those six weeks,' said Dusenbury. 'If the press reports are anything to go by.'

'Mr Governor—'

'Chuck,' the governor interrupted. '*Everybody* calls me Chuck.'

'Sir . . .' He couldn't bring himself to address this man as Chuck. 'I know this is going to sound rather rude, but I was expecting this to be a meeting in which I could plead the case for clemency for my client. This isn't usually the way it's done.'

Alex gave Mrs Olsen a quick glance to make sure that she hadn't taken offense at his remark. Her eyes remained neutral, but there was the merest hint of a nervous smile, as if she were reaching out to him in a way that he couldn't understand.

'I know, son, I know,' the governor responded. 'But this is an unusual case, ain't it?'

Alex couldn't argue with that.

'I'll put it to you real simple,' said the governor. 'The reason Mrs Olsen is here is because she's asked me to offer your client clemency.'

09:43 PDT

There are things I have done in my life that I'm not proud of. There were things I shouldn't have done. I was a product of my upbringing. I wasn't always taught right from wrong. And I was taught to hate people for things they had no control over or for things that I thought were bad because that's the way I was brought up.

But whatever wrongs I am guilty of, murder is not one of them. I may have been a bully in my youth, but I was never a murderer. Dorothy Olsen suffered at the hands of many people, myself included. But I did not kill her.

Clayton Burrow stopped writing and put the pen down, his hand aching. He opened and closed the hand several times to alleviate the cramp. But it was nothing compared to the pain inside: pain . . . fear . . . guilt? He didn't really know. He just had this constant urge to cry. He wouldn't do so of course – at least not now. Crying was unmanly and, with a prison guard stationed outside his cell twenty-four hours a day, he wasn't going to let

15

the bastards see him broken. But at night, when the lights were dimmed (they never switched them off altogether on death row) he would bury his face in his pillow and give in to the weakness that he managed to hide from others in the light of day.

He looked down at the letter and scanned the words. At the time of writing, it had felt like the right thing to say and the right time to say it. But re-reading his words now, all he could think was how pathetic it all sounded. This was to be his final letter, to be read out before his execution. Or was it? Maybe it was to be his final plea for clemency to the state governor. Maybe it was to be his letter to Mrs Olsen if his request for clemency was granted. He wasn't really sure.

Was it meant to be a letter of appeasement or a letter of defiance . . . an apology or a denial? What did he *want* to write? He didn't even know *that*. All he knew was that he was feeling bitter and angry . . . and afraid . . . and . . .

Alone.

That was the worst part. In all his twenty-seven – nearly twenty-eight – years on this earth, he had always been one to surround himself with friends. Or perhaps 'cronies' was a better word. He liked to surround himself with people who cheered him on and told him he was an okay guy. Never a *great* athlete, he was nonetheless a *good* one, with a muscular build, defined rather than developed. He was also blessed with a smooth, 'golden boy' handsome face that belied his rather spiteful nature. And he had enough puerile wit and energetic sporting prowess to be popular with the girls and the guys alike. He was always on the right side in the high school clique, always with the majority in any lynch-mob situation, always in with the in-crowd rather than the geek or freak on the butt end of the bullying – be it verbal or physical.

He was very rarely alone. And that meant a lot to him. It meant more than he ever realized, because he was actually quite afraid of being alone. But he never knew this until he found himself in a situation in which he was unable to avoid it. Throughout his happy, time-wasting, fun-loving years at high school, he had never even had to think about it. Because he was never alone, he never knew how badly it would affect him when he was.

Looking back on it now, he probably had an inbuilt defense mechanism against solitude. Whenever he was alone he would rush to find human company. He was always the first to stride up to a friend or a group and stick his face into the conversation. He was always the one to approach the new kid in the class and size them up as friend or foe: friend to be used as a sounding board, foe to be bullied, or at least harassed.

Even in his own home he avoided solitude. He was an only child, but he always had friends over for sleep-overs. More often than that, he slept over at friends' places. He preferred that because he was embarrassed by his mother. He didn't know who his father was – neither did his mother.

Now, he had to dwell in solitude for the first time in his life, he had to confront his fears. And this was a young man who had never known fear before.

But his fear of solitude – the fear that had always

been there but that he had concealed from himself for so long – was now confronting him like an inner demon who would let him have no peace.

His mother didn't visit. She had written him out of her life. And his old school friends – the ones whose lives he had brightened up with his antics – seemed to have no desire to share a moment's company with their fallen idol.

But it wasn't solitude as such that he feared. Solitude merely opened the door to his own personal Room 101 – that secret, terrifying inner chamber where one's worst fears become a reality. It forced him to engage in *introspection*. And it was introspection that he feared the most. Human company had merely been a way to stave off the need to look inside himself at the miserable squalor of his own soul. But stripped of that shield, introspection was all he had. Now at last, in the deafening silence of solitude and living under the shadow of death, he had to take a look at himself for what he really was.

And he didn't like what he saw.

He saw a man who had wasted every opportunity that had presented itself. He saw a man who had been needlessly cruel toward the weak. He saw a man who had achieved popularity with the mob at the expense of the frail and the vulnerable.

But most of all he saw a man who had no chance to redeem himself.

He knew that Dorothy Olsen must also have had inner demons, probably far worse than his. But he had just trampled all over her. And for what? For some cheap puerile thrills that meant nothing to him now.

He wished he could have his life over again. He wished he could have those moments back so that he could make wiser – and kinder – decisions. But God grants no second chances . . . if there even was a God.

He looked down at the letter and realized how little it really said – how little of what he really *wanted* to say.

Seized by anger, he picked up the letter and ripped it to shreds.

Through the bars, the cell guard watched with an implacably neutral look on his face.

09:45 PDT

Alex sat there in stunned silence. Whatever he had expected, it had not been this. Clemency? Before he had even put his well-rehearsed arguments? And the mother of the victim had specifically *requested* it.

Then reality kicked in.

'She's asked me to offer your client clemency.'

The words had been chosen very carefully.

'When you say "asked you,"' Alex said cautiously, 'does that mean you haven't decided yet?'

'You know my views on the death penalty.'

'Yes, sir, I do. And I've always respected your courage in taking that position.'

He regretted saying this as soon as the words were out of his mouth. It sounded sycophantic, and the governor was too shrewd a politician not to see right through it.

'And you also know that I'm pretty much my own man, especially now that I'm quitting politics.'

Alex nodded. Like many others, he wasn't quite sure if he believed this, but now was hardly the time to give voice to his skepticism.

'Nevertheless, it would be inappropriate for me to set

myself up against the will of the legislature and the courts.'

Alex panicked at the thought of this opportunity already slipping away.

'But you said—'

'*Unless* . . . there was some compelling reason. You see, son, even though I have the luxury of being able to *ignore* public opinion, I believe that I have a duty at least to *respect* it. Remember the words of Thomas Jefferson: "a decent respect to the opinions of mankind requires that they should declare the causes which impel them." The people who elected me may not *agree* with my decision. But I owe it to them at least to *explain* it to them. History will judge me harshly if I fail in my duty to put my reasons on record – and those reasons had better be good.'

Alex took a deep breath and regained his composure, trying to read the governor. He wasn't sure if the governor was really thinking about his place in history. But now was not the time to get diverted down a blind alley of speculation over his motives. Dusenbury was throwing him a lifeline – or at least waving it in his face. That was all that mattered.

'So you need reasons,' Alex edged forward hesitantly, 'and as yet you haven't got them.'

'That's right.'

'And you want me to supply them.'

'No, I want your *client* to supply them.'

Alex was beginning to understand.

'Is that why you said "*offer*" my client clemency . . . rather than "give"?'

Dusenbury smiled.

'You picked up on that real quick. That's just what it is, son: an offer.'

'So presumably,' Alex pressed on, 'there's a quid pro quo?'

09:48 PDT
(17:48 British Summer Time)

The clinic was quiet as the late afternoon melted into early evening. But the spacious TV room, with its well-scrubbed pale blue walls and clean gray leather furniture, was sufficiently sound-proofed and isolated from the wards to have the TV on. They had it on all day and all night. The nurses on night duty especially liked to take short coffee breaks there, flopping down on the armchairs and watching late-night TV. They preferred the all-night news stations – British or American – to the late-night quizzes, which were little more than premium line rip-offs.

Susan White, a middle-aged nurse of the 'old' school, flopped down in front of the TV with a cup of coffee and started skimming through the channels, trying to catch up on the news. While surfing, she caught the tail end of a report about a clinic in America being picketed by hordes of anti-abortionists, or 'pro-lifers' as they liked to call themselves, and realized how lucky she was to be here in Britain.

She liked her coffee strong but milky and the machine never quite got it right. She also liked it sugary, and that the machine usually *did* get right. It was often hard for her to get a coffee break, even though she was entitled to three per shift, because the other nurses frequently came to her with their problems, both personal and professional. So she made sure to get her caffeine fix before her shift started.

Using the remote, she turned the sound down, mindful of the fact that at this time most of the in-patients were sleeping. On the screen, a well-groomed, thirty-something woman, with somewhat underplayed oriental looks, was talking to the camera. She was wearing a smart blue suit, with a mid-length skirt and slightly tight jacket, designed to emphasize her firm, athletic figure, without *over*-emphasizing it.

But then a face came on that caught Susan's attention. A photograph of a young woman, almost like a mugshot. Susan felt an uneasy stirring as her eyes focussed on the screen.

She picked up the remote and turned up the volume. The voiceover of an American female reporter could be heard. It was one of those generic, female anchorwoman voices, the kind that all sound alike, the trained confident voice that always carries a trace of sarcasm or bitchiness, but only the merest hint. Or maybe it was just the hard edge that was required to make it in what once had been a man's world.

'Dorothy Olsen never had a happy life. She was bullied at school, her parents broke up when she was in her teens and she never had any real friends. Just over nine years ago, on May 23, 1998 – the day of her high school prom – Dorothy Olsen disappeared, never to be seen again.'

The picture changed to that of a man whom the nurse didn't recognize. This one was definitely a mugshot.

'Clayton Burrow is the man convicted of murdering Dorothy Olsen. At the time she first disappeared, she was classified as a missing person. It was widely assumed that the harsh treatment she received at the hands of her classmates, which drew comparisons with Stephen King's famous novel *Carrie*, prompted her to run away. There was speculation that she had committed suicide, although no body was ever found.'

Susan White raised the Styrofoam coffee cup to her lips with a growing sense of unease. The picture of Burrow disappeared, to be replaced by the reporter.

'Foxy news' was how one of the young male nurses had described it, whenever he saw her. The joke was wearing thin now.

In the background the grim, bland entrance to San Quentin State Prison was visible.

'However,' the reporter continued, 'all that changed just under eight years ago, on October 19, 1999, when the police, acting on an anonymous call, found parts of Dorothy Olsen's body in Clayton Burrow's freezer. They also found other incriminating evidence hidden under the floorboards, which Burrow was unable to explain, such as a blood-stained knife with Burrow's fingerprints and blood-stained panties with semen traces. DNA matched the semen to Clayton Burrow and the blood to Dorothy Olsen. There was also evidence that Dorothy Olsen had bought some expensive jewelry with money from her trust fund shortly before she disappeared. But none of it has ever been found.'

Nurse White felt something wet and hot on her wrist and fingers. She realized that her hand was shaking and she had spilt the coffee. She put the cup down and wiped the front of her uniform. But she didn't take her eyes off the screen.

'Despite his protests of innocence, Burrow was unable to explain away the evidence against him and, on February 20, 2001, he was found guilty of murder with special circumstances. Just over a week later he was sentenced to death. Now he is scheduled to die in just over fourteen hours. Martine Yin, *Eyewitness News*, San Quentin.'

Nurse White gripped the arms of the chair tensely, her heartbeat picking up speed.

9:50 PDT

'As you say, Alex, a quid pro quo.' Dusenbury turned to Mrs Olsen. 'Esther, maybe you'd like to explain.'

Esther Olsen sat up slowly. It was a struggle, but she forced herself. Alex sensed her difficulty as he watched her painful movements. He adjusted his chair to face her, moving slightly to make it easier for her to look at him.

'Mr Sedaka,' – her voice was shaky – 'I do not know you, but you are a good man. At least, I have been *told* that you are a good man.'

Alex nodded. There was not much he could say really. To agree would be arrogant; to disagree, ungracious. In any case that was clearly just the preamble to what she wanted to say.

'I know that you only came in on this case recently and I know that you have a duty to help your client.'

Again he nodded, trying to make it reassuring. Whatever she was about to say, he knew that it must be painful. It must have cost her a helluva lot to reach the decision to ask the governor to grant clemency to the man who had murdered her daughter.

27

'Mr Sedaka, in Hebrew your name means both "charity" and "righteousness" and I hope those are ideals that you live up to.'

Like Esther Olsen, Alex was Jewish and, although he had long ceased to practice the religion of his childhood, he still remembered much of what he had learned about it in the first fourteen years of his life. He knew about the meaning of his name, or rather the Hebrew word 'tsedaka,' from which the family name Sedaka was derived.

'I am dying, Mr Sedaka. I have cancer of the pancreas and the doctors have told me that I have at most a few months left to live. I was estranged from my daughter, for reasons too complicated to go into. One of my biggest regrets is that we never got the chance to make it up.'

'Was this disagreement shortly before she died?'

Alex didn't know why he had asked it. But he knew that it was more than just idle curiosity.

'No, this was several years before she died. I always thought – I always *hoped* – that the passage of time would heal the wounds. But it was not to be. We were never reconciled.'

She took a deep breath, struggling to speak.

'To outlive one's own child is a terrible thing, Mr Sedaka. But if there is one thing worse than to outlive one's child, it is to part from those we love on bad terms. And that is the pain that I will carry with me to my grave.'

Her eyes were welling up with tears now and Alex felt a lump in his own throat.

'It is too late for me now to be reconciled with my

daughter and I do not know if we will be at peace with each other in the next life, because I do not know if there is a next life. But there is one thing that I want to do in this life and that is to give her a proper burial . . . or . . . at least to know where she is buried.'

Now, at last, it was all falling into place.

Alex turned to Mrs Olsen.

'So let me see if I've understood this correctly. You want me to get my client to reveal where he has dispo— where he has *buried* the body. And in return for this, you have asked for Burrow to get clemency and to serve a sentence of . . . what?' He turned to the governor. 'Life without parole?'

Dusenbury nodded. Obviously the governor wasn't going to give Burrow a complete amnesty. Alex looked to Esther Olsen.

'That is all I ask, Mr Sedaka. That is a mother's dying wish.'

Alex lowered his eyes, overwhelmed by his own emotions. How, he asked himself, could my client have been so evil as to do what he did? How could he be so cruel as to put a mother through this?

But he quickly cut off the thought. It was not for him to judge his client. It was not even for him to believe that his client was guilty as long as Burrow maintained his innocence. Of course he had a duty to put the offer to his client. Maybe now at last Burrow would come clean. Alex had never really believed that Burrow was anything other than guilty. Of course as a lawyer, Alex had a professional duty to act on his client's instructions and to argue that his client was innocent as long as that was what the client maintained. But there was no authority on earth that could issue a formal ruling that is binding on human nature, much less on human thought.

Alex had assumed that Burrow was guilty before he had even taken on the case, if only from the news coverage when the original trial took place and through the long and tortuous appeals process. By the time he was asked to take the case, he was pre-disposed toward the idea of Burrow's guilt. But he was persuaded to take the case by the pleading of his ambitious legal intern and by the formal personal request of Burrow himself, for reasons which Alex had never quite understood.

Although Alex had speedread the trial transcript, working in an intense pressure-cooker atmosphere as the execution date loomed up ahead, nothing he had read had in any way changed his mind. Although the case was too complicated to be described as 'open and shut' it was certainly sufficiently overwhelming. There was no doubt in Alex's mind: Clayton Burrow had murdered Dorothy Olsen.

The only question was, would he now come clean, now that he had a chance to save his miserable life in exchange for something so small? There was no chance of him being re-tried and acquitted, no chance of him being released from prison, so it would cost him nothing to tell the truth. And if there was a God, it might even save his soul.

Alex knew better than to approach the matter with anything so presumptuous as expectation. He would approach it, instead, with cautious hope.

But first he had to be sure that he had understood the terms of the deal correctly. He turned toward the governor.

'So let me get this straight. The deal is, if Clayton Burrow reveals where the body is buried, he gets clemency and will serve a sentence of life without parole.'

'That's right,' Dusenbury responded with a nod of his patrician head.

Alex considered for a moment asking to have the terms set in writing. But from the look on Esther Olsen's face he knew that this would be needlessly cruel. And, from the governor's firm handshake, it was also unnecessary.

10:03 PDT

'Life without parole,' Alex had said. The man in the car couldn't believe it.

There was no doubt. The offer was on the table.

The man's mind was reeling. When the governor had invited Alex to come early for the meeting, he had wondered about what was going down. He had known that it was likely to be something unusual. But he hadn't expected *that*.

He kept running over the conversation in his mind.

Nathaniel Anderson was not a G-man. Neither was he a cop, nor a journalist, nor a hired assassin. He had recently graduated from law school and was working as a legal intern while preparing for his bar exams. He had done a lot of Public Defender work in his final year of law school, helping indigent clients plea bargain down their sentences in the proverbial meat-grinder that was the criminal law system.

It had taken time to win their respect. They saw him as a stuck-up white boy, like most lawyers. But he had worked like a dog and won them over through his sheer tenacity and hard work. And because he worked for the

Public Defender he had also built up a powerful list of contacts in the criminal community. It was a list that had come in very useful.

So the governor was offering Burrow clemency in return for revealing where the body was located. He wondered how the public would react to that – not that the governor or Alex would reveal it until it was a done deal.

Nathaniel looked round at the traffic on Golden Gate Avenue. Parked a few cars down the road was a limousine. He looked up. The sun was higher now: the day was wearing on. Just under fourteen hours till Burrow was due for the lethal injection – unless Alex could save him.

He looked back at the limousine and wondered if it was the vehicle that had brought Mrs Olsen here. Her proximity left him feeling uneasy. But that was all right. He knew that they would both be gone in a minute.

Keeping his eyes on the rearview mirror, he waited while the next couple of minutes went by. Finally there was activity from the entrance to the building and several people emerged at the same time: Mrs Olsen, the limo driver and Alex Sedaka. Alex watched while the limo driver led Mrs Olsen back to the car, opened the door to let her in, closed it behind her and went to the driver's seat. He continued watching while the limo drove off past him, heading east toward Larkin Street.

As Alex turned away, Nathaniel strained to see the look on his face in the rearview mirror.

As Alex approached, Nathaniel pulled out the earpiece and put it away in the glove compartment. He reached forward for the ignition key as Alex opened the front passenger door and got in.

'I assume you got all that, Nat?' said Alex, pointing to Nat's cell phone.

'Every word. So what's it to be? The office?'

'No, I think we'll pay a little visit to San Quentin first.'

10:05 PDT

A shrine.

That was the only way you could describe it: a shrine that radiated outward from the mantelpiece above the mock fireplace.

The picture sat there in the center of the mantelpiece – a teenage girl smiling at the camera, or at least trying to smile. With Dorothy you could never tell if the smile was real, because she had learned from an early age to wear her face as a mask. Was it a smile of joy? Or the painted greasepaint smile of the clown who had to go on and perform even when she was grieving on the inside?

The picture was flanked by a pair of candles and the surrounding area of the wall was adorned by her tennis certificates and poems. Round the room trophies were liberally distributed across several coffee tables and glass-fronted cabinets.

Apart from the memorabilia, the only furniture in the room was an armchair and a small TV set.

The young man stood before the picture, staring into Dorothy's eyes, trying to decipher the enigma. Were they happy? Had she ever been happy? Had she ever had the chance to be?

She had always treated him with love and kindness, however badly she was treated herself. He felt the tears in his eyes. Why couldn't they have loved her as she loved him?

He felt himself choking and he switched on the TV to distract himself. There was bound to be rolling news about the impending execution of Clayton Burrow. He looked at his watch. It would all be over in less than fourteen hours.

10:08 PDT

'Do you think he'll bite?' asked Nat, keeping his eyes on the road. He had just taken the first left at Larkin Street and was about to take another at Turk.

'I don't see why not. He wants to live . . . I think.'

'Even if it's behind bars? For the rest of his life?'

'He's a narcissist,' Alex explained. 'He likes to be the center of attention and to be told what a great guy he is. He wants to be The Fonz.'

'The Fonz?'

'Fonzie . . . from *Happy Days*.'

'*Happy Days*?' echoed Nat, betraying his youth, as they hung a right at Van Ness.

Nat was half-pretending. In truth, he enjoyed watching the re-runs of it and he knew perfectly well who 'The Fonz' was. But he still didn't see what it had to do with his question about Burrow taking the deal.

'The Fonz was the local school drop-out who didn't care about anything except being *cool*. That was his trade-mark phrase. The thing was, everybody liked him, the guys and the dolls.'

'And this is relevant because . . . ?'

'Because that's what Clayton Burrow always wanted to be. Cool. A hit with the clique. Numero Uno. Mister Popularity. In with the in-crowd. Like I said – a classic narcissist.'

'I know that type. But I still don't see what that's got to do with taking the deal.'

Alex smiled. Nat may have got top grades in law school, but he had a lot to learn about the real world.

'The thing is, Nat, that what a narcissist wants most is attention. But the next best thing is to live. He wants to live – even if it is behind bars. He'll still be the center of attention for a while, with the press . . . and the public . . . until the novelty wears off.'

Nat thought about this for a moment.

'He's never admitted it . . . killing the Olsen girl, I mean.'

'I know. But until now he's never had a reason to. In fact he had every reason *not* to.'

They were taking a left into Lombard Street now and a tense silence settled over them. Strangely, Alex found himself thinking not about Burrow, but about Nat. The truth was that he hadn't originally planned on hiring a legal intern, his law practice was just too tiny to warrant one. But Nat had badgered his way into Alex's professional life with an enviable dedication and tenacity. He had started off the campaign while still a student, with an impressive résumé and a series of letters praising Alex's work. At the time, Nat was doing a pre-graduation internship with the Public Defender's office.

But the coup de grâce was an impromptu visit to Alex's office. When Alex had politely offered a referral to another firm, Nat replied that he didn't want to work for the 'whores and heathens' of the legal profession. He wanted to work only for a true believer in justice. Alex wasn't sure if the student was a genuine *meshigena* or just a younger incarnation of himself, with the ideals still intact. But the clincher came when Nat silenced Alex's attempted rebuff by saying that he wanted to play St Peter to Alex's Jesus. It was the kind of killer line that a lawyer would give his Rolex – if not his Rolodex – to come up with. And it caught Alex from left field.

Nat's arrival at the firm had been most opportune in terms of the caseload. Alex had been getting a lot more business in the wake of a major success in the appeal of a drug baron's girlfriend on accessory charges. And this heavy workload had culminated in Alex's biggest case of all when the *California* v. *Burrow* file landed on his desk. There had been so much material to read through, so much ground to cover. Alex still wasn't sure that he had truly come to grips with the facts of the case.

But the execution date had been set and the court had refused to give him any more time.

'You want me to copy the recording?'

Nat's voice punctured Alex's cogitation. They were on Doyle Drive, heading north toward the Golden Gate Bridge.

'Oh, er . . . yes. Upload a copy on the mail server and lodge a CD copy with the bank. Get Juanita to do a transcript. We'll compare it to the official transcript when we get it.'

Throughout Alex's meeting with the governor, they had maintained an open cell phone connection, with Alex's brand new iPhone on silent and Nat listening in and recording the conversation.

Originally the plan had been for Alex and Nat to go in together. But Nat had suggested that Alex might be more effective alone. Two on one would seem like bullying and might serve only to harden the governor's attitude. One on one and it would come over more like a genuine plea for mercy. Alex would be like a stand-in for Burrow, making a straightforward appeal from the heart.

Alex liked the way Nat thought. He had the knack for bringing a fresh perspective to the situation.

10:17 PDT (18:17 BST)

'Are you all right, Sue?'

Susan White had been daydreaming. She was barely into the first hour of her shift and her mind was a million miles away. She became aware of a young nurse looking at her.

'Oh yes. I'm fine. I was just thinking about something.'

The young nurse was dark-haired and pretty, with a smile that reminded Susan of some young British actress who had made it big in Hollywood after several appearances in British movies. She couldn't remember the name of the actress. It was all she could do to remember the name of the nurse.

Danielle. Yes, that was it. Danielle Michaels.

'You sure?'

Susan White could sense Danielle was genuinely concerned.

'Yes, I'm fine. Don't worry. Really I am.'

Danielle smiled again and walked off, glancing back over her shoulder briefly, with a look of concern. But right now, the thing that was uppermost on Susan's mind was that news report about the man who was about to be executed.

41

Were the cases connected? She didn't know. But she had to be sure.

The first thing she did was head for the records room. The room was unlocked but the cabinets were not. It was out of hours and the records manager wasn't there. Then she realized that she didn't actually need the whole file, just the index. The hard copy files were filed by consecutive number and physically stored by date. But every file had a matching card in the card index and these were arranged alphabetically. The index card would have the date.

She found it in less than a minute and a chill went up her spine. The file had been opened on May 25, 1998. Nine years ago, just like the TV reporter had said.

There was no getting round it: the dates matched.

10:36 PDT

When they arrived at San Quentin, Alex again went in alone, while Nat waited in the car. He had been in many prisons before, but never in death row – not even the relatively calm North Segregation block.

'It's just too depressing,' was all he had offered by way of explanation.

'What are you talking about?' Alex had responded. 'It's just like the rest of the prison.'

'No, it isn't. Not to me. It has . . . I can't explain it. It's like the place has the smell of death about it.'

Alex had found this attitude incomprehensible.

'How do you expect to work as a lawyer on cases of your own if you're afraid that you can't compartmentalize your emotions?'

Nat had just shaken his head and turned away, as if struggling to contain those emotions.

'I can't do it,' Nat had almost cried. 'Not yet.'

Alex remained mystified but realized that he had to accept it. Whatever psychological baggage Nat was carrying, he couldn't shake it off and wasn't ready to share it with anyone else.

So on this case at least, Nat was functioning as little more than a driver. It was hardly a way to get ahead in his chosen profession. But in fairness to Nat, he had done a lot of background research. You couldn't fault him for effort or enthusiasm. If Nat needed to keep Burrow at a distance to maintain that enthusiasm, then so be it.

It took a few minutes to process Alex through security. But it seemed to be getting quicker. They knew Alex now and he knew the drill, so less had to be explained to him about what he could and couldn't bring in. Also, as the execution date drew near, they realized the urgency of these meetings and there was an element of sympathy for even the basest and most evil of murderers. Years on death row humbled and mellowed a man and even those prison guards who believed most strongly in capital punishment were ready to admit that by the time the condemned man is about to meet his maker, he is a very different man to the one who was sentenced to that fate.

Whatever they said about capital punishment being the ultimate *individual* deterrent, it was a punishment that eliminated the need for itself. It was living in the *shadow* of death that reformed a man's character, not death itself. But for collective deterrence, the death penalty served no purpose, Alex felt. But there were others who were all too ready to argue the point.

When Alex was finally in the cell with Clayton Burrow, the condemned man appeared to be struggling to read the lawyer's face.

'What did he say?' asked Burrow, a tremor of fear creeping into his voice.

'It's kind of complicated,' Alex replied hesitantly.

'What do you mean?'

Burrow's breathing was heavy, as if not daring to hope.

'He's offering you clemency – but it's conditional.'

'What does that mean?'

'It means he's ready to commute your sentence to life if you 'fess up.'

'That's it?' said Burrow, letting the air out of his lungs.

'No, there's one more thing. You've got to reveal where you buried the body.'

The smile vanished from the condemned man's face.

'Fuck it!' yelled Burrow, pounding his left palm with his right fist. 'Goddamn fuck it!'

Alex looked at his client, puzzled.

'Why, what's the matter?'

'I can't *do* it! I can't fuckin' do it!'

10:39 PDT

It had been most kind of Chuck to lay on a limo, Esther Olsen thought.

The overpass drifted away behind them. But Esther was past the stage of admiring the view. On the way there it had been a distraction from her worries. She didn't drive and illness had left her pretty nearly housebound. So any journey like this was an escape, both mental and physical. But the novelty soon wore off.

The same was true of the limousine. The luxury of its leather upholstery and lacquered wooden paneling raised her pleasure level by a microscopic degree. But such petty pleasures were short-lived when ranged against the quantum of suffering that had borne down upon her in recent years. First a murderer's unbridled malice had claimed her daughter. Then the ravages of disease had selected her at random and struck her down with a death sentence of her own.

She had had her fair share of life and although it hadn't always been a smooth ride, it was at least a fair crack of the whip. She could accept being singled out by the Grim Reaper. But it was the loss of her daughter that had been unforgivable: for that was the work of human agency. And she blamed not only Burrow but also her husband.

Yet it was precisely from this anger that she wanted to escape. That was why she had approached Dusenbury and persuaded him to offer clemency to Burrow. As her own fate loomed up ahead, she needed closure more than revenge. And that was also why, as she closed her eyes, she now felt herself drifting back to a happier time.

She couldn't understand why, but of all the memories that flashed through her mind, the one that lodged itself and lingered at the forefront was the one-night stand.

They were both students: he celebrating the end of his tentative first year at law school; she celebrating completion of her finals for her bachelor's degree in literature. It was one of those drunken frat parties where everyone knows someone but no one knows everyone. Even now she didn't remember how they had ended up in the sack together. Yes, the drinks had been flowing freely. Yes, he was handsome. Yes, they had both been sitting in the corner, trying to withdraw from the rowdy celebrating and wild carousing that had long since lost its appeal for both of them. She wasn't cerebral like him, more the free-spirited romantic type. But she *was* the quiet type. That much they had in common.

She was also engaged, to a decent if somewhat boring – not to say cold – man whose family was 'well to do' and who had 'prospects' according to her pushy mother. Was it an attempt to escape from an engagement that she never really wanted? Or a final celebration before she lost her freedom forever?

Whatever the reason, the memory of that night of passion reminded her of a phrase from the end of Hardy's *Mayor of Casterbridge* about happiness being an occasional incident in a general drama of pain. It was a line that Dorothy had talked to her about for many hours, after reading the book in happier days when mother and daughter could still talk to one another. Esther had thought that Dorothy was too young to read such a book. But Dorothy had lapped it up with her unquenchable thirst for literature that she had inherited from her mother.

But the line lingered with Esther now. Had there been *any* truly happy moments in her life after that? Her marriage to Edgar certainly hadn't been happy. She wondered if the blame had been hers . . . if the marriage had been tainted by that one fleeting indiscretion before they had even solemnized their union.

And yet she felt no guilt, not even when her thoughts rolled on through the years and settled on that image forever frozen in her mind – the image of her husband lying there with a bullet hole in his head.

10:43 PDT

'We're talking about your *life*!' Alex practically shrieked. 'When I went in to meet the governor, I thought you were a dead dog. And now he's throwing us a lifeline – against all the fuckin' odds! Are you just gonna fling it back in his face?'

'You don't understand!' Burrow replied, sobbing into his hands. 'I can't tell you where she is because I don't *know* where she is!'

'What do you mean "don't know"?' asked Alex, looking round to make sure that the guard outside was out of earshot. 'Are you gonna carry on with this innocent act even now, when you have a chance to save your neck?'

'It's not an act! Look, I'm telling you I never touched . . . I mean, I didn't . . .'

He broke off, seeing the look of disbelief in the lawyer's eyes. For a few seconds, neither of them spoke. Alex tried again.

'Okay, so what do you think happened? You think someone else killed her? You think she just walked off the edge of the earth?'

'She set me up!'

'*What?*'

'She framed me!'

'What are you talking about?'

'Why do you think her body was never found?'

Alex realized that this was no time for pussyfooting round – not if he wanted to save his miserable client's neck.

'Because you buried her?'

'Because there *was* no body! She's not dead, I'm telling you. She's sitting in a room somewhere, watching the TV, laughing her head off at this whole cornball sideshow!'

'You think so?' Alex practically sneered.

'Goddamn right, I think so!'

'And have you got anything by way of . . . evidence?'

Burrow looked at the lawyer like he wanted to hit him.

'If I had evidence d'you think I'd be in this shit hole?'

Alex was breathing heavily, trying to restore calm.

'Okay, I'm sorry, that was a stupid question. But just tell me one thing . . . *why would she frame you?*'

'What?'

'Motive? What's her fucking motive?'

Burrow's face showed how hard he felt the full force of his lawyer's skepticism.

'You think I'm bullshitting, don't you?'

Alex sighed.

'I think you're clutching at straws.'

But he knew that this didn't make sense either. Why would Burrow be clutching at the straw of a crackpot theory, when the governor had just thrown him a rope?

'I think she did it because I . . .'

He trailed off. But Alex could see in his eyes that he wanted to say more. He tried an encouraging tone.

'You . . . what?'

But Burrow's mood had changed.

'Look, forget it, okay? Let's just forget it. You've done your best for me. I can't say you haven't gone the extra mile. Now let me just prepare for the inevitable.'

Alex was looking at Burrow with an uneasy thought going through his mind: this was not the response of a guilty man.

10:52 PDT

Martine Yin was checking her makeup in the trailer outside San Quentin prison preparing for her next report. It was a hot day, and she decided to swap her blue jacket for a man's waistcoat – the one that she wore as a semi-professional snooker player.

Her mind was focussed on the matter in hand. She had spotted Burrow's lawyer going into San Quentin and had been hoping to get an interview with him when he came out, but she found herself caught in a media scrimmage and was unable to get anywhere near his car before it broke through the line and receded into the distance. She knew that the lawyer had been scheduled to meet the governor that morning, but that was just a formality. Besides, if anything had come out of that meeting, it would have been announced by the governor's office.

Nevertheless, she did want to talk to Sedaka, if only to get the low-down on how his client took the inevitable bad news. But she had missed the opportunity. Aside from that, she assumed that Alex didn't want to talk about it. In fact he probably *couldn't* talk about it. But still, it would be nice to get an exclusive.

The problem was how to contact him. All she had was the number of Sedaka's office. The secretary had been polite, but consistently refused to give out Sedaka's cell phone number.

So now Martine just had to sit tight outside the penitentiary awaiting further developments. The report this morning had gone well. Of course as the execution time approached, things would hot up. The closer to midnight they got, the bigger this story would become. There was no chance of the governor granting clemency – notwithstanding his own unpopular views on capital punishment. Indeed the only thing that could upstage the execution itself would be if Dorothy Olsen walked in off the street and said: 'Surprise, surprise! I'm alive!'

Martine smiled at the thought. It reminded her of all the urban legends and conspiracy theories about the Lindbergh baby, complete with several people claiming to be the dead tyke – including one who was black and female!

There were a few doubts about the case against Hauptmann, who had been executed for the murder of the baby. Some said his trial was unfair – not least the atmosphere of vengeance amid which it had taken place. But it was a strong case nevertheless. Likewise the case against Clayton Burrow.

The cell phone cut into her thoughts.

'Martine Yin.'

'Hi, Marti, it's Paul.' Paul was an eager kid who worked

at the station. 'We've just had a tip-off about what's going down in the Burrow case. You're not gonna *believe* this.'

In response to what he said next, her jaw dropped.

11:04 PDT

'And he didn't say why?'

'No. He just claimed she framed him and then pretty much clammed up.'

Back in the car, Alex hadn't even bothered to tell Nat about Burrow's response at first, and Nat hadn't asked. Alex realized that the look on his face must have said it all. Only when they hit the road and found themselves back on Sir Francis Drake Boulevard, did Nat ask.

'So what are we going to do?'

'Not got a fucking clue.'

'Why would she frame him?'

'That's what we've got to find out.'

'And how are we going to do that? With our client refusing to play ball?'

'We've spent the last few weeks arguing the law. Maybe it's time for us to take another look at the facts.'

'You believe him?'

'Not really. The most likely explanation is that he can't *remember* where he hid the body. It was nine years ago, don't forget. He probably just buried it somewhere in the hills. He wouldn't necessarily have any reason to remember the exact location. Now it's probably just a faded memory.'

'He could tell you that. He could admit the killing and say he doesn't remember where the body is after all this time.'

'He could have done *that* ages ago. But maybe he doesn't want to come clean in case I lose motivation.'

Nat shook his head.

'He obviously doesn't understand lawyers.'

'He understands jackshit!'

'So how is looking at the facts going to help us *now*? We need to come up with a point of *law*.'

'We need both. A new fact to convince them there's a strong chance he's innocent and a point of law to give them the leeway to act on it.'

'And what are we supposed to be looking *for*?'

'I said I *think* he killed her. But I'm not sure. What if I'm wrong? What if we're *all* wrong?'

While Nat was thinking of an answer to this conundrum, Alex put in a call on his iPhone to the office. Juanita answered.

'Hi, Alex,' she said, as his number popped up on the display. 'How did it go?'

'Not good, Juanita.'

He had phoned her on the way to San Quentin and told her about Dusenbury's offer.

'He refused?' she asked incredulously.

'He said he didn't know.'

'But how—?'

'Listen, I haven't got time. I'll fill you in when I get

56

back to the office. In the meantime, I need you to do a couple of things.'

'That's what you pay me for.'

'I want you to go online and find out everything you can about the feud between Clayton Burrow and Dorothy Olsen.'

'We already looked into that, boss.'

'I know, but all we found out was that she was the butt of his jokes. What we need to find out is if there's anything behind it.'

'What's to find out? He was a bullying jock and she was the smart, geeky girl with glasses. What else *is* there?'

'Okay, I know it's a long shot, but I got the impression that Burrow was holding out on me.'

'How do you mean?'

'Well it's just that none of it makes sense. If he's guilty, why the hell did he reject the deal?'

'So now you think he's *innocent*?' Juanita asked incredulously.

'Until today I never even considered it. But innocent or guilty, I think there's something he's not telling me.'

'And you think it's something to do with this high school feud?'

'It's a good place to start – the relationship between the victim and the accused.'

'Are we looking for anything in particular?'

'Let's start off with motive.'

'I thought the feud *was* the motive?'

'No, I mean the *cause* of the feud. Was it just a culture clash between the male jock and the female geek? Or was

57

it a case of hell hath no fury? Maybe some of the other students know something.'

'It's gonna be hard to track down the phone numbers. And I can't leave the office, can I?'

'Use the internet. Maybe there's discussion about it online. We also need to know who her friends were. And if she had any enemies – other than Burrow, that is.'

'It's going to be hard. You know how it works on the web. You do a search and it throws up a million irrelevant items.'

'Do your best, Juanita. I'll be back in fifteen.'

Nat smiled. Twenty-five was more realistic. He'd have to floor it.

Alex put in another call, this time to Information. He asked for Esther Olsen's number, adding that she lived in Sunnyvale. Fortunately the number was listed. He followed up by putting in a call to her.

'Yes?' The voice was weak . . . nervous.

'Mrs Olsen? It's Alex Sedaka here.'

Her mood seemed to brighten.

'Oh, hallo, Mr Sedaka.'

Alex was embarrassed. He didn't know how to continue.

'Listen, I'm afraid I have some bad news.'

'He . . . he wouldn't tell you?'

She sounded sad, but not angry or bitter as he'd feared.

'He said he didn't know. He still maintains he's innocent.'

'Can I ask you a question?' Esther Olsen's voice was croaky now.

'Yes.'

'Do *you* think he's guilty?'

This was a question that Alex couldn't answer. Not that his own private thoughts were privileged. But a lawyer's view of his client's innocence or guilt is partly based on what his client tells him, and this could be a slippery slope.

'I don't know, Mrs Olsen.'

This was the diplomatic response if not an altogether truthful one. Alex pressed on.

'But can *I* ask *you* a question?'

'Yes?'

'Do you know anything about the relationship between them? I mean, I know they hated each other, but do you know why?'

There was a moment of hesitation.

'I don't know. She never really confided in me. Like I told you, I was estranged from her before she . . .'

'Did she confide in anyone? A friend? A relative?'

'Not really. I mean, she got on well with Jonathan, but—'

'That's her brother, yes?'

'Yes. But he was younger – five years younger. She probably didn't talk to him about it because he wouldn't have understood – and also, she wouldn't have wanted to put the burden of her problems on him.'

'So you're saying she kept her problems bottled up?'

'That's right.'

Alex's mind was racing ahead. A girl with problems and no one to talk to? That was a perfect recipe for suicide. But there was no body. And how did all that incriminating evidence end up in the apartment where Burrow and his mother lived?

'Could I ask you another thing, Mrs Olsen? About Dorothy liquidating her trust fund and buying that expensive jewelry. Do you have any idea why she might have done that?'

'No.'

Esther Olsen sounded tired, as if she had been through all this many times before – which she probably had.

'Was she the sort of girl who was interested in jewelry?'

'No, not really.'

'And you don't have a clue where the jewelry is?'

'I . . . I thought that maybe Burrow stole it . . . when he killed her.'

'But now?'

He was prompting her, picking up on her hesitance.

'I don't know.'

'Do you think she may have been planning to run away?'

'She . . . might have been.'

'Could she have been planning to run away with Clayton Burrow?'

'Certainly not! She hated him! And he hated her!'

'Are you sure it wasn't just an act?'

'No, Mr Sedaka, *it definitely wasn't an act*!'

Alex had been speculating that maybe Burrow had tricked her into thinking he was going to run away with her and persuaded her to liquidate her trust fund and then killed her and stolen the jewelry. But Esther Olsen's reaction had pretty much quashed that theory. She may have been estranged from her daughter, but a mother's perceptions counted for something. And if Esther Olsen said that Dorothy wasn't planning on running away with

Clayton Burrow, then Dorothy Olsen was *not* planning on running away with Clayton Burrow.

'Can you think of anyone at all that she might have spoken to? A friend that she might have confided in?'

He waited a while for an answer.

'There *was* one thing,' Esther Olsen's voice came out of the silence.

'Yes?'

'She had a computer that she was always working at – an old laptop. She used to spend hours in front of it, either online or just writing.'

'Writing what?'

'I don't know, but she treated it like an old friend.'

'You think she might have confided in her computer?'

'I don't know. She never let me see it.'

'Do you still have it?'

'Yes. But why do you think this will help?'

'I just think that if I can unravel what was going on between Clayton— my client and your daughter, I might be able to make some progress.'

He didn't add that he was also still mindful of the possibility that his client might actually be telling the truth, despite the long odds.

'I still have the computer. I haven't switched it on since the day she vanished. I don't even know if it works. But I still have it.'

'Look, Mrs Olsen, I know this might sound like real *chutzpah*, but would it be possible for me to borrow the laptop? To take a look at what she's got on it? Just in case I can find anything that might help.'

'We haven't got much time.'

61

'I know. I'll send a courier round right now . . . if it's all right with you?'

There was a short pause and the sound of a sigh.

'It's all right, Mr Sedaka. You can send a courier as soon as possible. Just please . . . bring my daughter home for me.'

11:09 PDT

'Slow down a bit! My fingers keep missing the goddamn keys!'

'You told me to make it fast.'

The TV van was winding its way through the mid-morning traffic, following the same route that Nat and Alex were taking. Martine was sitting at the front with the driver. The cameraman and soundman sat in the middle row of seats, while the spark and boom operator sat in the back, holding on to the equipment every time the van swerved.

But Martine was trying to make a call on her cell phone at the same time, and the constant swerving wasn't helping.

'Governor's office,' the friendly female voice came through her Bluetooth earpiece when she finally keyed in the right number.

'Hi, my name is Martine Yin from *Eyewitness News*. I'd like to interview the governor regarding the Clayton Burrow execution.'

'I'm sorry. Governor Dusenbury won't be making any comments on this matter.'

The friendly, sunny voice had become somewhat clipped.

'Okay, well, can you just tell me, is there any truth in the rumor that the governor has offered Clayton Burrow clemency in return for Burrow revealing where he buried the body of Dorothy Olsen?'

'Just a minute please.'

She was put on hold and noted with wry amusement that the music they were playing was 'California, Here I Come.' After what seemed like well over a minute, the clipped voice came back on the line.

'I'm sorry, but the governor is unable to comment on such rumors.'

'So you're not denying it?' persisted Martine.

'The *governor* is neither admitting nor denying it. As I have said, we do not comment on rumors. If and when there is anything to announce it will be announced in the usual way, Miss . . .'

'Thank you very much,' said Martine. She pressed the red button and smiled.

'No go, huh?' said the driver.

'He doesn't want to talk about it.'

'If it's true, he'll have to talk sooner or later. Maybe he's waiting for Burrow's answer.'

'He must have an answer by now. We saw Sedaka driving into the pen.' Her voice became irritable. 'I just wish we'd followed the shyster when he left the building!'

'You weren't to know,' the driver replied. 'All the signs said the action was at the pen.'

'Yeah, well it looks like it's still that way.'

'What do you mean?'

'Well Sedaka didn't make any statements to the press.'

'Maybe he has to report back to the governor first. I mean, they're going to have to check out whatever his client tells them. If he told them where the body is, they're still going to have to dig it up and test it to make sure.'

Martine's eyes lit up.

'And wouldn't it be nice to be there when they do?'

11:17 PDT (19:17 BST)

Susan White had been agonizing over the report on *Eyewitness News*. It was all too much. It couldn't just be a coincidence. She thought that the face looked familiar. But it was the name that made it impossible to ignore.

Dorothy Olsen.

Dorothy had been a sensitive girl but not too talkative. She had never made it clear why she came to England for a procedure that could be done just as easily in America. It wasn't as if she was a health shopper, seeking free medical treatment under Britain's National Health Service. This was a private clinic and she had paid a lot for the procedure.

Susan had asked her about it once, but she had just clammed up. It wasn't that she was shy or secretive, it was just that she had made it clear that she found it too painful to talk. Of course she may have told the doctors, but Susan doubted that she told them more than she had had to.

The nurse speculated that it might have something to do with opposition from within her own family. And also,

Nurse White reflected, there might be some very complicated background to the whole case.

But none of this was what was troubling her now. It was the timing. The news report hadn't specified the exact date but the reporter had said nine years. That was about right. Could it be the same person? The reporter had also said something about Dorothy disappearing on the night of her 'high school prom.' According to the records, Dorothy had first approached them in *May*. Was that when high school proms took place? Susan White didn't know.

Maybe it's someone else with the same name . . . or maybe someone deliberately took her name.

The trouble was, there were just *too* many things in common: the name, the face, the date. It was too much to dismiss as a coincidence.

Her mind was racing into unfamiliar territory. Maybe there was another explanation. Like what? Twins? An identical twin using her sister's name? Not very plausible. There was nothing in the *Eyewitness News* report about a twin sister – something they would surely have mentioned if it had been the case, if only for the human interest angle.

There was no getting away from it. Susan knew that she had to act. Time was of the essence. She found a set of master keys and used them to open one of the offices. She wanted to use the phone without anyone else overhearing. The person she called was Stuart Lloyd, the Chief Administrator who had gone home for the day.

'Hallo.' She recognized the voice of Elizabeth, Stuart's wife.

'Oh hallo, Mrs Lloyd. It's Susan White from the clinic. Is Stuart – Mr Lloyd – there?'

'He's eating dinner.'

'Oh I'm sorry.' Susan didn't know how to play it. 'Look, I know this . . . I mean . . . would it be possible to have a quick word with him?'

There was a tense silence.

'Can he call you back?' The voice was sharp, showing the irritation even while trying to hide it.

Susan White knew that this might mean in five minutes, two hours – or never. And she couldn't take a chance on that.

'It's rather urgent.'

'Just a minute,' said Elizabeth Lloyd, even more stiffly.

In the silence that followed, the nurse strained to hear the voices in the background. But she didn't need to strain for long. Through part of the brief exchange at least, the voices were somewhat raised. When silence returned, the nurse tensed up, anticipating a possible storm.

'Yes, Nurse?'

It was her boss.

'Stuart, listen, I'm sorry to bother you at home like this. But I've just seen a report on one of the American news channels. It was about a murder over there.'

'What on earth has that got to do with us?'

'The victim's name was Dorothy Olsen.'

'Good God!' Lloyd muttered under his breath.

'We have to do something. We can't just ignore it.'

Stuart was silent for a few seconds.

'We have to be careful. We're not just talking civil negligence or malpractice here, don't forget. There's also that small matter of fiddling the dates.'

11:28 PDT

'We're bringing you this special report from outside the building that houses the state governor's San Francisco office for a special, exclusive report about the latest developments in the Clayton Burrow case.'

Martine Yin was delivering her usual smooth, polished performance. Not a strand of the glossy, jet-black hair out of place, the skin smoothed and softened by foundation, the eyelashes defined by just the right amount of mascara, the man's waistcoat that made her look professional yet sexy – the whole picture perfectly crafted to tell the story and sell the story-teller.

'This station has learned that Governor Dusenbury has offered clemency to Clayton Burrow on the condition that he reveals where he buried the body of eighteen-year-old Dorothy Olsen, whom Burrow murdered some nine years ago. The governor made the offer in a private meeting earlier today with Alex Sedaka, Clayton Burrow's lawyer.

'However, this station is now in a position to reveal that this meeting was not quite as private as it was supposed to be, because also present at the meeting was Dorothy Olsen's mother, Esther. But the most surprising aspect of this whole new development is that it was Esther Olsen who convinced Governor Dusenbury to make this extraordinary offer. It is not entirely clear what motivated Mrs Olsen to make such a generous request on behalf of the man who murdered her daughter. But there appears to be evidence that Mrs Olsen is suffering from a serious, potentially life-threatening illness and she wants to be able to give her daughter a proper burial while there is still time.'

Martine stopped and held the nation in her gaze.

'What is also not clear is how Burrow responded to the offer. His lawyer visited him in San Quentin this morning immediately after his meeting with the governor. But Mr Sedaka was tight-lipped when he left the penitentiary after relaying the offer to his client. Since then, neither Mr Sedaka nor the governor's office has been ready to answer questions.

'Martine Yin, *Eyewitness News*, the state governor's office, San Francisco.'

11:33 PDT

'How the *fuck* did she find out!'

Alex had barely got through the front door of the office when Juanita told him about Martine's broadcast. In the face of Alex's explosive response, she didn't so much as bat an eyelid, let alone flinch.

Juanita was a dark-haired, super-fit Latina beauty, with penetrating eyes that would have made her a good interrogator. She had only known Alex Sedaka for a few months, but that was long enough for her to realize that on the rare occasions when he showed anger, it was not directed at her – even if it might seem that way to an outside observer.

'I don't know,' she replied coolly. 'I called *Eyewitness*, but they weren't saying . . . something about "protecting their sources." The usual press freedom bullshit.'

Alex took a deep breath. He hadn't meant to yell. When he could trust his voice to hold at an acceptable level of calm, Alex spoke again.

'They probably don't even know themselves.' Nat looked at him blankly. 'Anonymous tip-off,' Alex added.

'You look like you could use a cup of coffee, boss.'

Juanita was already striding energetically to the kitchen, followed by Alex's eyes, by the time he replied: 'Thanks, Juanita.'

Nat was looking awkward.

'What next?'

'Conference time. We need to work out a strategy.'

Alex followed Juanita into the kitchen, leading Nat the same way. Juanita was putting fresh coffee beans into the DeLonghi Prima Donna, and pressing the button.

'So what happened?' she asked over the rumble of the machine.

Alex quickly filled Juanita in on the events at the penitentiary while the grinding in the background stopped and gave way to an orchestration of burping and frothing.

'So what are we going to do?'

'Well as long as Burrow insists he's innocent there's nothing much we can do regarding Dusenbury's offer.'

Juanita frowned.

'You just had me spend a lot of time online and now you're just going to give up?'

'Did you find anything?'

'Not yet.'

She sounded frustrated.

'The thing is, as I was saying to Nat, we've all been assuming that he was guilty. But maybe we've been overlooking something.'

'Like what?' asked Juanita.

'Well maybe he's protecting someone,' Alex ventured.

Juanita screwed her nose up.

'That doesn't make sense. If he was trying to protect

someone then why not just confess to the murder and say that he doesn't remember where he buried the body?'

'Or maybe he's telling the truth. Maybe he *was* framed.'

This time it was Nat who made a dismissive gesture. 'Ah, come on. You're not buying that, are you?' He put on a redneck hillbilly tone, gesticulating at the same time. '"She faked her own death and framed me." That's just a crock of shit straight out of a comic book.'

'Maybe it wasn't Dorothy who framed him. Maybe someone else *killed* Dorothy *and* framed Clayton.'

'How did they put his fingerprints on the knife?' Nat wasn't letting up.

'He slept with a knife under his pillow,' said Alex. 'Why shouldn't it have his dabs?'

'With her blood on the blade?'

'Maybe she got some of her own blood and wiped the knife on it – using gloves and being careful not to leave any fingerprints of her own.'

'So we're back to blaming Dorothy,' Juanita chimed in, handing them their coffee mugs.

Alex realized that his theory didn't stand up. As they made their way to Juanita's office, he shifted back to his earlier line.

'Well maybe it *was* her. Maybe Dorothy set him up for some kind of revenge.'

'And presumably she also planted the blood-stained panties?'

Nat chuckled when Juanita said this. But Alex wasn't ready to give up just yet.

'She *could* have done.'

'And Burrow's semen?' asked Juanita.

'Maybe they slept together.'

Juanita was trying very hard not to roll her eyes.

'So let's see,' she said. 'Dorothy Olsen sleeps with Burrow, gets his semen, stains her panties with blood and his semen, plants them under the floorboards in his apartment, takes the knife from under his pillow, wipes her blood on it and plants that too, then calls the police using a voice changer device and tips them off.'

'That's the theory,' said Alex, realizing how absurd it all sounded.

'Now all we need is motive,' Juanita suggested, echoing Alex's own comment at his meeting with Burrow at San Quentin.

'There's also the small matter of breast tissue in Burrow's freezer,' Nat chipped in.

'Technically it was his *mother's* freezer,' Juanita shot back.

'Whatever,' Nat replied.

Alex was shaking his head.

'What sort of DNA comparison did they do at the time?' he asked.

'How do you mean?' Nat replied.

'There are different types of DNA test. Short Tandem Repeat? Low Copy Number?'

Nat and Juanita looked at each other blankly.

'I'll get the file,' said Juanita, getting up and heading for the broom closet that doubled as the file and records room.

File wasn't exactly the word. It was several boxes full of files and ring binders. But Juanita's filing system was so efficient and well-organized that she knew exactly where to look for it. It was the forensic evidence file, with the lab reports. There were several of these, but she found the right one almost immediately and brought it back to the office.

They huddled round it as she flicked through the file.

'Okay, here it is,' she said with delight. 'They did a standard nucleic DNA test on the breast tissue.'

'Remind me who they compared it to,' said Alex.

Juanita's eyes skimmed the page.

'They compared it to . . . ah, yes, here it is: both to Mrs Olsen *and* Jonathan.'

'That would be Dorothy's younger brother,' Alex said.

Juanita was reading the summary of conclusions at the end of the report.

'Yes. Now there's a note here that says that the test concluded that the breast tissue came from a *half*-sibling of Jonathan Olsen.'

'Wait a minute,' Alex perked up, 'what does that mean?'

Juanita flipped over a few pages and carried on looking.

'It means that they share only one common parent? They decided to make sure by doing a separate test using *mitochondrial* DNA. That's DNA that's not from the cell nucleus, but rather from non-nucleic material in the mother's ovum. And in that test, all three of them matched exactly.'

'But I thought mitochondrial DNA was only passed on to girls,' said Alex.

'No, it's passed on to boys too,' Juanita corrected, 'but *they* can't pass it on any further. That's because it's contained in the somatic cells and female germ cells, but not in the nucleus of either. Sons have their mother's mitochondrial DNA in their somatic cells, but not in their sperm. So they can't pass it on to the next generation.'

'So if Jonathan, Dorothy and Esther all had the same mitochondrial DNA,' said Alex, 'it means that Dorothy and Jonathan are blood siblings and that Esther Olsen was their mother.'

'That's right,' Juanita confirmed. 'But the differences between Jonathan and Dorothy with the test using nucleic DNA imply that they had different *fathers*.'

11:39 PDT (19:39 BST)

Stuart Lloyd was still frozen with indecision. He had told Susan White that he would look into the matter and get back to her. She had accepted it reluctantly and put the receiver down. But he was still unsure of where to go from here.

It could just be a coincidence. The name was uncommon, but in a country of three hundred million people more than one person could have it. But Susan had said more than that. She had said that the picture they had shown on TV had looked like Dorothy. She hadn't been sure, she admitted. It was, after all, nine years ago. But the similarity of the face *plus* the name? And the fact that this girl in America disappeared *nine years ago*.

It was too strong a coincidence to dismiss.

'Is anything wrong, dear?' his wife asked, entering the room.

'Nothing,' he replied. But he knew that his tone was unconvincing.

Elizabeth sidled up to him and put a comforting arm round him.

'What's the matter?' she asked gently.

He couldn't tell her – not yet at any rate. Maybe when he was sure. But not yet.

'Just a bit of trouble at the clinic.'

'Complications?'

She meant medical complications. The worst thing that could happen to any private clinic was medical complications leading to death or serious damage. Even if it was covered by the insurance, a successful claim could massively push up the insurance premiums, as well as damaging the reputation of the clinic and decimating its future client base.

'Not that sort. Just a bit of personnel wrangling.'

It was an intentional red herring but he regretted having said it. Firstly, he regretted lying to his wife on principle. Secondly, he could imagine her now having visions of a cat fight between the nurses.

He went back to the kitchen to finish his *coq au vin*, warming it up in the microwave. But he ate quickly, not savoring it as he had before. And as soon as he had finished, he went to the living room – a quasi space-age environment of white leather, glass and chrome. Flopping down on the couch, he switched on the 50-inch LCD TV using the remote and flipped through several news channels. At first he clicked on CNN, but then remembered that Susan White had named another channel.

His wife wasn't a great one for TV and was quite happy to read a book while he surfed the digital channels. But his odd behavior could hardly be expected to pass without comment.

'Why the sudden interest in American news?' she asked.

Stuart kept his eyes glued to the screen.

'I just need to check up on something.'

Then he sat there watching a report about basketball. This was rolling news. If what Nurse White had said was correct, it would come round again.

He had to see for himself.

11:55 PDT

'No, Mr Governor, I swear I didn't leak anything to the press . . . I don't know . . . No, sir, I'm sure it wasn't anyone in my office . . . There was a guard outside the cell, but he couldn't have heard anyth . . . Well yes, I suppose he might have told the guard . . . Okay, I'll check it out . . . Yes, sir, I will.'

After hearing of Martine's report, Alex had expected the governor to give him hell. But even he hadn't realized just how forceful Dusenbury could be. Crucially, though, the governor had not withdrawn the clemency offer.

Alex wondered who the source of the leak was. It could have been anyone. The governor was right. A careless word from Burrow to the cell guard. A bit of gossip through the prison grapevine . . . and then someone decided to put in a call to the TV station.

Alex tried to put it aside. He had to focus. Nat was in his office going through the school yearbooks and checking up online to see if he could find out any more about the conflict between Dorothy and Clayton Burrow. Alex had remained with Juanita to discuss the DNA evidence further. All the while, a thought had been nagging away at him.

'Juanita, there was something you said earlier . . .'

'Yes?'

'About the freezer where they found the breast tissue.'

'What about it?'

'You said "technically it was his mother's freezer."'

'Well he still lived with his mother.'

'Were his parents divorced?'

'No, they were never married. I don't think they even lived together.'

'So it couldn't have been his father who killed Dorothy?'

'Not unless he suddenly came back into their lives, just long enough to murder a girl that his son clashed with at school.'

She was smiling to soften the blow. But he could see how silly she thought his idea and realized himself that it was *he*, rather than his client, who was clutching at straws.

'What about his mother?'

'What you mean – like, "how dare you be nasty to my son!" kind of thing?'

'Okay, you've made your point,' Alex replied, embarrassed.

'No, I'm not saying you should drop it altogether. It might be worth checking her out. Just let's not put too much hope in a long shot.'

Before Alex could reply, the intercom buzzer sounded.

'Yes?' Juanita answered.

'UPS. We have a special delivery from Sunnyvale.'

Juanita looked up.

'Dorothy's laptop,' she said. Alex nodded. 'Bring it up,' she said into the intercom, pressing the buzzer to open the door.

Five minutes later Juanita was looking through the folders and files on the laptop, while Alex was in the other room with Nat.

'Listen, I was talking to Juanita about Clayton's mother. I think we should check her out. Clayton lived in the apartment with her and she had access to everything that he had access to.'

'Like what?' asked Nat.

'The knife he kept under his pillow, the floorboards, the freezer.'

'Yes, but she wouldn't have had access to Dorothy. She'd've had to find her and either kill her and dispose of the body, or force her to some location and then kill her.'

'Well maybe she did. I mean, we don't know when or where Dorothy was killed. Or how.'

'Not to mention the small matter of motive.'

Alex felt like he was facing a wall of resistance on all fronts.

'The point is, we don't know enough to rule his mother out a hundred percent! And right now it's all we've got!'

Nat backed off from Alex's display of frustration.

'Okay, so how do you want to play it?'

'I want you to go over there and talk to her.'

'Where does she live?'

'San Pablo. The Circle S Mobile Home Park.'

'The one they're closing down?'

'Right.'

'You sure she hasn't moved on already?'

'There's only one way to find out.'

'I'll get right on it.'

Nat grabbed his keys and jacket and was out the door within five seconds. Alex returned to the reception area to find Juanita pounding at the laptop with an unusual amount of aggression, while peering at the screen with a look of intensity that he didn't often see in her.

'Has that computer disrespected your family?' he asked, putting on his croakiest Brando/Don Corleone accent.

She looked round, her expression a mixture of confusion and anger, to see a puerile grin on his face.

'Ha fuckin' ha.'

Alex walked up to see what was going on.

'There's something strange about this computer.'

'Strange?' he echoed.

'The hard disk has been wiped.'

Alex looked at the screen. Juanita was using Norton Utilities to inspect the disk content at a raw-data and deleted-file level.

'So how come it's still working?'

'I don't mean they reformatted it. I mean that all the deleted files have been overwritten. Normally the deleted files remain on the hard drive until the space is needed. It just deletes the directory entry and tells the directory that the space is available. But there are programs that overwrite the deleted files completely – sometimes making several passes with the erase head just to make sure.'

'And why would anyone do that?'

'What kind of a chicken-shit question is that?' She sounded cute when she was angry. 'To delete any trace of the files and stop them from being recovered!'

'That implies there was something in them worth deleting.'

'No shit, Sherlock.'

Alex leaned forward, peering at the screen with growing excitement.

'Making it all the more important that we recover their contents.'

'Which would be very nice, except there's no way we can do that.'

'Maybe there is.' The phone was already in his hand by the time he said it. 'Let's call David.'

'David?'

'My son.'

'The one at Berkeley?'

'I only have one son.'

'How do you know?' she asked with a cheeky grin. Alex sensed that there was more to Juanita's displays of impertinence than mere mockery. Melody had been just like that. It was her way of flirting with him. He wondered if it was the same with Juanita. She had certainly given him a few hints. He wondered how much of it was real and how much was just his imagination.

The lawyer in him knew that office romance was a dangerous game at the best of times – especially with a subordinate. If he did decide to go down that road, he'd have to tread carefully. But in any case it was a bit too early: the pain of losing Melody was still too raw . . . and today was hardly a day to be thinking about that sort of thing.

Juanita pressed the speed dial button and then handed Alex the phone.

'Hi, Dave . . . Yes, I am, but I need your help . . . We have a computer with a hard disk that's been wiped . . . No, I don't mean reformatted, just the deleted files have been overwritten . . . How many passes?'

Alex looked inquiringly at Juanita. She shook her head.

'We don't know. But what I want to know is . . . *it is*? Scanning tunneling . . .'

Juanita mouthed the word 'microscope' to show that she understood.

'You mean only if she just wiped it once? Oh I see. Okay, I'm sure you know what you're doing. I'll courier it over.'

And with that he put the phone down.

'He can recover the data,' said Juanita.

'How d'you know?'

'When I hear one side of a phone conversation, I can usually figure out the other. Read Godel, Escher, Bach.' She started walking away.

'I tried. I couldn't get beyond the dialogue between Achilles and the Turtle.'

'Besides – you're smiling.'

12:20 PDT

'Mrs Burrow?' Nat called out nervously through the closed door of the mobile home. No answer. 'Anyone home?' Still no answer.

Nat opened the door, tentatively, and gingerly stepped inside. Technically it was trespassing, but the door was unlocked and time was of the essence. He looked round nervously. The living room was a mess. Surveying the ashtrays and half-empty plates with three-day-old, dried-out food encrusted on them, the words 'trailer trash' came to mind.

He was about to start looking round when he was shocked to hear the sound of a flushing cistern – and he realized that he was not alone after all. For a few seconds, he waited with some degree of trepidation, looking in the direction of the bathroom and wondering if he was going to be confronted by a Stanley Kowalski type in a wifebeater.

To his relief, the figure that emerged was female, albeit the female equivalent of Stanley Kowalski. Sour-faced and borderline angry, she was closer to her mid-century than her youth. Under her eyes, the bags were noticeable, and although she wasn't currently smoking, she looked as if she ought to have a cheap cigarette dangling from her lips.

'Who are *you*?' she sneered.

'My name is Nathaniel Anderson.'

He held out his business card. Her eyes dropped to his outstretched hand, but she made no effort to take the proffered card, or even gave any indication that she was interested in looking at it. He put it away in his breast pocket.

'Are you Sally Burrow?'

'Who wants to know?'

He realized that she was just being melodramatic, but a little clarification was called for.

'I work for a lawyer called Alex Sedaka.'

'I don't like lawyers,' she snarled.

'Neither do I,' he replied, trying to sound chummy. 'But a man's got to earn a living.'

Her face remained as sour as ever. He debated making a second attempt to break the ice but rejected the idea on the grounds that the humor would probably go over her head.

'So, *are* you Sally Burrow?'

'Last time I checked,' she said.

'Mr Sedaka – the man I work for – is representing your son.'

'Who?'

'Mr Sedaka . . . Alex Sedaka.'

'No, I mean, who d'you say he's representing?'

'Your son.'

'I don't have no son.'

'Clayton. Your son Clayton.'

'He ain't no son of mine!' she shouted, flopping into a chair. 'Not anymore.'

Nat looked at her, trying to assess the situation, unsure of how to proceed. He decided to sit down too, taking the fact that she was seated as tacit permission to do likewise.

'I presume you disowned him after he murd— after he *killed* Dorothy Olsen.'

'You can call it murder if you like,' she said, finally taking out and lighting the cigarette that ought to have been in her mouth all along. 'I believe in calling a spade a spade.'

Nat realized that Sally Burrow was a lot more astute than he had given her credit for. The fact that she had picked up on his reluctance to use the word 'murder' proved that. He realized that he would have to tread carefully and not underestimate her intelligence, or at least her cunning.

'And that was when you disowned him?'

'Not immediately.'

'But that was *why* you disowned him.'

'Right.'

'When did you decide he was guilty?'

'I don't really remember. I guess it happened . . . kind of gradually.'

'Well what did you think when he was arrested?'

'I didn't know what to think.'

'Did you stand by him during the trial?'

'I didn't *go* to the trial.'

'So you *already* thought he was guilty by then.'

'What else was I supposed to think? With her panties under the floorboards in his bedroom and her blood on them? And his jizz!'

'You don't think it could've been planted?'

'Gimme a break!'

'Okay, so let's say he's guilty. That *still* doesn't explain why you didn't stand by him.'

'Why the fuck should I?'

'I mean . . . he *is* your son.'

'I already told you. I ain't got no son.'

'Did you have one *before* the murder?'

Sally Burrow's eyes narrowed suspiciously.

'What's that supposed to mean?'

'I was wondering if maybe you saw the signs of the way your son was going *before* he killed Dorothy Olsen.'

'Are you tryin' to make out that I . . . *knew* what he was gonna do? Like I'm some kind of a . . . accessory to what he done?'

'No, I'm not suggesting that you knew he was going to kill Dorothy. I was just wondering if there were any early signs of Clayton turning into the sort of person that he eventually turned into . . . if you see what I mean.'

'We didn't talk much. He had *his* life and I had *mine*.'

Nat seemed to be having trouble digesting this.

'Didn't talk?' he echoed.

'Didn't talk,' she confirmed, drawing on her cigarette.

What he said next surprised even him.

'Has it occurred to you that if you'd given him more attention and affection he might not have become the violent person that he became?'

He didn't know afterward what had *possessed* him to

say it. But in some strange, indefinable way, he was glad that he had.

Sally Burrow looked as if she'd just been poleaxed. Her lower jaw dropped open and the cigarette fell to the floor.

'*You've got a fuckin' nerve comin' into my home and talking to me like that!*'

'All I meant was—'

'I don't need you preachin' to me! *Get the fuck out of here!*'

She was on her feet now, lurching toward him, and he noticed that she was not a small woman by any stretch of the imagination. He twisted sideways like a corkscrew as he rose from the seat to avoid her menacing onslaught and sprinted the few steps to the doorway.

She was still chasing him out in the yard when he had opened up a distance of twenty yards between them. Puffing through her smoker's lungs, to be sure, but still chasing.

He was just glad she didn't have a gun.

12:31 PDT

The young man sat cross-legged on the floor before the shrine in his apartment in Daly City, his eyes closed. He was trying to remember Dorothy, remembering her kindness toward him even when he was at his lowest ebb. He remembered one time when she had faced particular brutality. He had watched from a safe distance but had been too frightened to say a word. Afterward he had run into her arms crying and it had been *she* who had comforted *him*. There were tears in his eyes now as he opened them.

He looked at the clock on the wall. It wouldn't be long now. Soon he would have closure. In his pocket he had a piece of paper that was most precious to him. It was a spectator's pass that allowed him to go to San Quentin and witness the execution.

The TV was on in the background. But the sound was turned down. He wanted to be left alone with his thoughts until it was time to go to the penitentiary. But at the same time, he wanted to stay in touch, to hear about further developments on the case.

Clayton Burrow had a very savvy and tenacious lawyer,

he had heard. And a smart and savvy lawyer wasn't going to give in until the fat lady sang.

He wondered how Burrow was feeling as he awaited execution. What was going through his mind? Was he afraid? Terrified? Or maybe he was just resigned to it. Maybe he just didn't care. Just like he didn't care about others or how much pain he had caused them.

Stop it! he ordered himself.

But he couldn't stop it. It had been in the news so much these last few days that it was hard to think about anything else.

On the rolling TV news, Dorothy's face appeared for the umpteenth time. It gave way a few seconds later to that of Martine Yin, with the governor's San Francisco office as her backdrop. Jonathan would have ignored it, but the words 'breaking news follow-up' flashed up, causing him to grab for the remote control. In haste he pressed the button to turn the sound up.

'So far the governor's office refuses to confirm even that there is an offer on the table. But we *can* confirm that Burrow's lawyer Alex Sedaka visited Burrow in prison right after his meeting with the governor and left the prison less than half an hour later. At this time we have no information on whether Burrow has accepted the offer.'

The young man's face was dissolving into confusion as he struggled to understand what Martine Yin was saying.

Offer? What offer?

'Similarly, we have been waiting outside the governor's office for any word of the outcome from this quarter.

One thing we *do* know is that even if Clayton Burrow were to reveal where he buried the body, they would still have to dig it up and confirm that it was the body of Dorothy Olsen before granting him clemency, but—'

'*No!*' the sound echoed from the young man's mouth, partly the plaintive whine of a frustrated child, partly the angry roar of a wounded lion. Blinded by rage, he picked up the nearest object and hurled it across the room. The telephone landed against the wall with a smashing sound, and bits of plastic flew off in all directions.

The picture changed to that of the steps of the Federal Supreme Court with a legion of reporters milling about trying to interview a man who looked like he didn't really want to talk.

'These latest developments follow on from the valiant efforts of Burrow's lawyer Alex Sedaka to secure a stay of execution and a re-trial for his client.'

It was recent footage of Alex emerging from the Supreme Court, despondent after his failed attempt to get the original trial verdict overturned.

'Only a few days ago, Mr Sedaka was in Washington DC, arguing before the Supreme Court that his client didn't have a fair trial because of differences in two obscure court rulings.'

The lawyer was flanked on one side by his assistant who was holding Alex's briefcase and looking down in a somewhat bashful, self-effacing manner. Alex was speaking silently, answering the questions as they were thrown at him. But the sound of his voice was absent. Only Martine Yin's voiceover could be heard.

'Once these arguments were rejected, Sedaka had no

choice but to throw himself upon the mercy of Governor Dusenbury. And Dusenbury's mercy appears to be carrying a price tag. The question remains: is Clayton Burrow – who has always maintained his innocence – able and willing to meet that price?'

The young man smiled now as an idea flashed into his head.

He walked across the room to the phone and picked it up. No dial tone. The impact with the wall had damaged it. He would just have to find another handset.

12:40 PDT

David Sedaka had to pull strings to leapfrog the queue for the scanning tunneling microscope at the Berkeley lab. But he was an old hand at university politics and he knew which strings to pull. There had been a bit of grumbling about this. One aggrieved PhD student pointed out that Sedaka was a theoretical physicist not an experimental one. Theoretical and experimental physicists regarded each other with mutual disdain: the thinkers and the stinkers was the way the former group liked to describe it.

David was a member of the Joint Particle Theory Group at Berkeley, where he was developing exotic theories on anti-matter and gravity. He had recently published a paper called 'Unilateral anti-matter decay in an accelerated expansion universe,' in which he had advanced the revolutionary prediction that anti-matter possessed neither gravity nor anti-gravity but was subject to the gravity of matter and could decay into photons on its own without needing to collide with matter.

In appearance, he was the epitome of a nerd: slightly short, wearing glasses – even though he could afford laser surgery – and with dark hair so curly that it was rumored that he used hot rollers and foil to keep it that way.

He had removed the hard disk from the computer and had carefully separated the platters, removing them from the spindle. Then he had placed the first platter in the chamber under the head of the scanning tunneling microscope.

There was an old and ongoing debate in the computer industry as to whether it was possible to recover over-written data from a computer hard disk with a scanning tunneling microscope. One of the more common scare-mongering rumors was that the data was never deleted completely because the magnetization that overwrote it 'was not in exactly the same place on the disk as the original bit' or because the 'magnetization levels varied.'

There were even rumors that the National Security Agency was routinely recovering erased data in this way. In fact, a number of computer companies had made an awful lot of money, at the expense of gullible and para-noid computer users, by selling them products that promised to overwrite their deleted data with 'multiple passes' and offering them 'military level' security.

The reality was that it was practically impossible to recover overwritten data from the newer computers, or data that had been overwritten with more than one pass. With older computers, where each 'bit' was spread out more than on modern computers, you might be able to recover data that was overwritten with a single pass. But that was about it.

The good news for David Sedaka was that this

computer was about ten years old and the hard disk was only five gigabytes and so the bits were spread out over a larger area. The other piece of good news was that the data had been wiped with only one pass, as far as David could determine. That meant that he could recover it – in theory.

The trouble was, there was so much of it. Where to begin? The reality was that data recovery was as much an art as a science. You could start off by looking at the directory and the tables that allocate file space, but they too may have been changed or overwritten. And also, a file that was created and then changed a few times, might be 'fragmented.' In other words, different parts of it might be stored on different parts of the disk.

In practice, what this meant was that even if part of the task of recovering data could be automated, a lot of it was a hunt-and-find exercise. And that had to be done painstakingly, using subjective judgement.

David knew that it was going to be a long day.

But as he looked at some of the data he had recovered, he felt as if he might have found something interesting already. He decided to tell his father. The trouble was, he'd had to leave his cell phone outside the lab in case it interfered with the sensitive electronic apparatus. Now he went to get it – and he was walking briskly.

12:46 PDT

While Alex and Juanita waited for Nat to return and David to report back, they sat on opposite sides of her desk looking through the old high school yearbooks. Juanita had already been online, looking at legal records of name changes. And Alex, in desperation, had taken it a stage further by looking at a website describing the *meanings* of names, in a futile effort to try and work out what Dorothy might have changed her name to. He hadn't come up with anything plausible – and he knew it was an outlandish idea to begin with – but he was desperate for anything that might help.

Right now, they were looking for anyone who could tell them anything about what was going on when Dorothy disappeared. The trouble was, most of the phone numbers were old and out of date. Of course Alex and Juanita could look up the numbers elsewhere, but some of the numbers were unlisted. In other cases, they were able to find a landline number, but it was daytime, so most of the people were out at work. All they could do was leave messages and hope that the people would call them back while there was still time.

As Alex pored over one of the yearbooks, he realized that he had spent an inordinate amount of time looking at the class photographs, as if hoping to find some clue in the faces of Dorothy or Clayton. Dorothy looked sad, her doleful eyes staring out at the camera, as if her sad life were written into them. In some ways she reminded him of his daughter Debbie. They would have been practically the same age in fact.

Not that *Debbie's* life had been sad. Perhaps that was why the eyes stood out as a point of difference. But Alex tried not to think about Debbie's eyes. They were Melody's eyes too, and to look into them was to see his late wife resurrected before him. That was why it was so much easier with Debbie living across the other side of the country. The memory of his late wife twisted like a knife inside his gut. But he had to put it out of his mind for now. Today was not the day to dwell on his own misery.

It was then that he noticed something strange.

'Juanita?'

'Yes, boss?' She spoke irritably.

'Will you stop calling me that?'

'What do you want me to call you? "Master"?'

'You don't have to call me anything.'

'Are you *ever* going to tell me what you wanted to say a second ago or are we going to spend the rest of our lives discussing what I should call you?'

He sighed with irritation. The truth of the matter was that they were both in over their heads and feeling the pressure.

'Take a look at these pictures.'

He slid the two yearbooks across the desk to her. They were both open on the double page spreads of the relevant class photographs, one Dorothy's junior year, the other her senior.

'What am I supposed to be looking at?'

'First, take a look at the junior year in the 1997 yearbook.'

'Okay.'

'Right, now what do you see?'

'A bunch of teenagers looking pleased with themselves.'

'Do you see Dorothy Olsen?'

'Yes.'

'And Clayton Burrow?'

'Sure.'

'Okay, now look at the senior year pictures in the 1998 yearbook.'

'Okay,' she said, by now sounding really bored.

'Do you see Dorothy?'

'And Toto,' she said, snorting through her nose.

Alex ignored her.

'Do you see Clayton Burrow?'

'Ye—' She broke off and surveyed the spread of pictures more carefully. 'Er, no, actually I don't. Unless he had a temporary face transplant.'

'So what does that tell you?'

'That he was away on yearbook day?'

'He'd've had a second chance on "make-up" day.'

'Maybe he was away then too.'

'Then they'd've listed him and put "No photo available," wouldn't they?'

'I guess.'

'So what does that tell us?'

She looked at him puzzled.

'I don't know.'

'It tells us that he wasn't there.'

'But like you said, they would have listed him and put "no photo av—"'

'Wasn't there *at the school*!'

'But you *just said*—'

'Wasn't there *at all*. Not just on those days.'

Juanita turned to face Alex, as the mist began to clear.

'You mean like . . . he dropped out of school before that?'

'It's a possibility.'

She was still trying to take it in.

'And what does *that* mean?'

'It means . . . did he fall . . . or was he pushed?'

Before Juanita could reply, or even think of anything suitably smart to say, the phone rang. She reached for the receiver. But Alex was so keyed up, his hand got there first.

'Alex Sedaka.'

'Hi Mr Sedaka?' said an unfamiliar male voice.

'Yes.'

'I'd like to talk to you about the Dorothy Olsen case.'

'Okay.' Alex was disappointed. He had been hoping that it was the prison calling to tell him that Burrow had changed his mind.

'I mean, I need to see you.'

A second phone line rang. Juanita went to another room to get it.

'Can you tell me what this is about?' asked Alex.

'I'd prefer to tell you in person.'

Alex was wary of such offers. Ordinarily he would be inclined to play ball, if only out of curiosity. But right now his time was at a premium.

'Can you at least tell me who this is?'

Ten miles away, in Daly City, the young man on the other end of the line was looking at a photograph on a mantelpiece.

'My name is Jonathan Olsen.'

12:49 PDT

'Alex Sedaka's office,' said Juanita, answering the phone in Nat's office.

'Oh hi, it's David here.'

'Hi, David. What can I do for you?'

'I was wondering if I could speak to my father.'

'He's on the other line at the moment. Can I take a message?'

'Yes, tell him I've found something.'

'Can you tell me what it is? I can pass it on to him.'

'I'd rather tell him direct.'

'Trust me, David, it is probably better if I explain it to him.'

She could almost see him smiling at the picture of the computer-savvy secretary explaining it to the boss. 'Okay, well basically I've recovered the most recent virtual memory file.'

'Do you want to send that to us to take a look at?'

'Well actually I've already taken a look at it.'

'And?'

'I understand that Dorothy Olsen went missing right after her high school prom in May 1998.'

'That's right.'

'Well I've found a fragment of an EasySabre receipt dated just four days before she disappeared.'

'EasySabre?'

'An online subsidiary of American Airlines Sabre booking system. They offered it through Compuserve.'

This took Juanita by surprise.

'But I thought they checked all the airlines when she vanished. And they certainly must have checked them after they arrested Burrow.'

'Yes, but EasySabre wasn't only used by American Airlines. It wasn't even only used for flights to and from the US. Pretty much all the airlines used it – including this one.'

'Which one?'

'Quetzalcoatl Airways.'

'Wait a minute, weren't they that Mexican outfit that went bust a few years ago?'

'That's the one.'

'But surely they would have checked it out at the time? I mean, didn't they check all the airlines that flew from the US?'

'Yes but Quetzalcoatl *didn't* fly from the US. And I think they went bust before Burrow was arrested. Remember that when Dorothy vanished initially there was no evidence of a crime? It was just a missing persons case and she *wasn't* a juvenile. They filed a report and pretty much left it at that. It was her mother who checked the airlines initially and she only had civil powers of inquiry. By the time Burrow was arrested, that airline didn't even exist.'

'But you said this EasySabre wasn't only used for flights to and from US airports. So there would still have been a record of it.'

'Yes, but the cops probably only *checked* for flights from the US. Don't forget, by the time Burrow was arrested, they had so much *physical* evidence, they thought it was an open and shut case. They probably didn't think it was worth checking flights that originated from outside the US. And you know the old rule: if you don't look, you don't find.'

'But wouldn't the defense have pressed for discovery?'

Juanita waited in silence. But the truth of the matter was they both knew the answer.

'An overworked public defender? A crap defense? You know the story, Juanita. They do regular re-runs at the Hall of Justice every day of the week. He got a bum deal.'

Strangely, this didn't upset or bother Juanita. The fact of the matter was that whatever the reason for this monumental oversight, the current news was heartening. At least it meant that there was a way forward. Juanita could barely contain her excitement.

'So where did she fly *to*?'

David hesitated again.

'Unfortunately I don't have that information. I don't even know where the flight was *from*.'

'I don't understand. How can you know that she bought a ticket but not where it was to?'

'It's to do with the way the computer stores information. It was on the disk swap area.'

'What's that?'

'You know how computers use disk swapping if they

haven't got enough RAM for what they're trying to do? They use part of the disk as virtual RAM. Well in this case, part of the receipt got copied onto the virtual disk area.'

'But why only *part* of the receipt?'

'The receipt as a whole probably spanned a cluster or sector boundary. So the part of the receipt it didn't have room for got written onto the disk swap area. The other part probably only ever existed in RAM. If it wasn't for the cluster spanning and the remnant in the swap area, I wouldn't have been able to recover it at all.'

'So you've got the date and the airline, but no idea where the ticket was from or to?'

'It was probably from Mexico. It couldn't have been from the US because they'd've caught it when they checked EasySabre for outgoing flights.'

Juanita thought for a moment.

'She could have driven down to Mexico and then caught the flight.'

'Easily. But I guess that doesn't help us unless we can find out where she went to from there.'

'And can you?'

Juanita was praying that David would come back with an affirmative reply.

'I don't expect to find the other half of the receipt. I've pretty much covered the disk swap area. It was the first thing I checked, after the file allocation table and directories.'

'Wouldn't she have downloaded the receipt?'

'Maybe yes, maybe no. But if she reformatted the whole disk that suggests that she was being secretive. So the answer is *probably* no.'

'And there's nothing you can do?'

Again there was a brief hesitation in David's response.

'Nothing on the computer itself.'

Juanita smiled to herself.

'Why do I hear that sound in your voice?' she asked.

'What sound?'

'Like the vocal equivalent of a gleam in your eye?'

'Well . . . let's just say that I have an idea of one way I might be able to get it.'

'How "might" is "might"?'

In the time it took him to take a breath, her heart skipped a beat.

'I won't bullshit you. It's a long shot.'

12:53 PDT

'How long are we going to hang round here?' asked the driver.

Martine looked at her watch. He was right: they'd been here a long time and nothing was happening. It wasn't just that nothing was happening, it was also that there was no sign that anything was *going* to happen. Worse still, some of the other news crews were starting to appear. They were parked further up the street and trying to make it look like they weren't interested. But it was obvious that they were.

They were actually parked more strategically than Martine's crew. If anyone left the governor's office building, they'd have to follow the one-way system toward Larkin Street. That meant that CNN just up the road had a better chance of staying on their tail.

'So what do you think we should do?' asked Martine. 'Go back to San Quentin?'

They'd have a full crew there later on in the day as the execution time loomed nearer. But the question was, should they sit it out there now or stay here in the hope that something broke from the governor's office?

Martine knew that she could call in another team to cover the governor's office and get back to the penitentiary. But this was *her* story and she wanted to be in the right place at the right time when the story broke. Her gut told her that she was closer to the story here outside the governor's office than treading water back in Marin County.

But nagging away at Martine was the thought that the real story was with Burrow's lawyer Alex Sedaka.

He was the one who had to carry the message of the governor's conditional offer of clemency to Burrow. If Burrow was reluctant, *he* was the one who would have to persuade him. If Burrow accepted the offer then *he* would be the one who had to convey that acceptance to the governor, along with any details of where the body was buried. Before the day was done, many people would know one way or the other. But Alex Sedaka would be the *first* to know.

And Martine intended to be the second.

'Change of plan. We're going to pay Alex Sedaka a little visit.'

13:11 PDT

Nat was driving back to the office from the mobile home park in San Pablo, wondering how he was going to summarize his meeting with Sally Burrow. He decided not to tell Alex about the leading question that had led to the premature termination of the interview. But the question was, what *would* he tell him?

Sally Burrow's attitude – if it was sincere – suggested that she would *not* have done anything to help her son, least of all kill for him. She sounded convincing when she said that they had led separate lives and she hadn't noticed what her son was turning into.

This strengthened, all the more, Nat's conviction that it was Sally Burrow's hands-off approach to both love and discipline that had led Burrow down that slippery road to become the bully that he was.

But a bully was one thing – a murderer was another thing entirely.

Nat knew that he had to concentrate on how he summed this up for Alex. The boss was in a very tense mood at the moment, and Nat felt that he was likely to snap at any moment. He had shouted at Juanita over something that wasn't her fault. How would he react to Nat coming home empty handed from his visit to Clayton's mother at the trailer park?

But then again, it had always been a long shot. Alex knew that. All Nat could do was report back on what Sally Burrow had said.

He was getting near the building when he noticed activity. It looked like some news people staked out by the building, one with a shoulder-mounted camera. The annoying thing was their van was parked in his reserved parking space! He drove past, glaring at them angrily. Then he noticed someone entering the building – and he recognized the face.

He decided not to go in just yet.

13:19 PDT

'So why exactly did you want to see me?' asked Alex.

He had led Jonathan into the meeting room and got Juanita to make coffee for both of them. But Jonathan Olsen didn't seem too anxious to talk. He seemed more concerned with looking round, almost as if he was admiring the décor.

'I saw on the TV about the governor's offer to Clayton Burrow.'

'Yes,' said Alex matter-of-factly, 'I think everyone in the state has heard about that offer by now.'

'The thing that surprised me is that it was my mother who persuaded him.'

'She didn't tell you beforehand?'

'I'm not in contact with my mother.'

Alex remembered that Esther Olsen had told him that she was estranged from her daughter. He didn't know that this estrangement extended to her son.

'Is that by . . . ?'

'By my choice, yes. We kind of fell out with Mom – both Dorothy and myself.'

Alex felt a pang of sympathy for Esther Olsen. It seemed as if the world was collapsing on top of her head.

'For the same reason?'

'More or less.'

Alex knew he had to tread delicately here. But then again, Jonathan had come to him.

'Is it something you'd like to share?'

'Let's just say that Dorothy got a raw deal.'

The words 'raw deal' suggested something financial. But this was unlikely – if it was purely financial it could have been easily remedied.

'From your mother?'

Jonathan shrugged.

'Let's just say that there are sins of commission and sins of *omission*.'

Alex nodded. He knew that he wasn't going to make any more headway if he cross-examined. But he sensed that Jonathan wanted to talk.

'Why did you want to see me, Jonathan?'

'I was wondering if Burrow has accepted Dusenbury's offer.'

'You know that anything a client says to his lawyer is privileged.'

Jonathan squirmed uncomfortably.

'But I'd've thought that they'd have to make it public at some point. I mean, at least if he accepted the offer.'

'At some point maybe. But at this stage I can't even confirm or deny that there *was* an offer.'

Jonathan seemed uncomfortable, as if he wasn't sure himself why he was even there. He appeared to be looking round nervously, almost as if he was expecting something to happen.

'Can I ask you a question, Mr Sedaka?'

'Of course.'

'Why did you take this case?'

'Well that's kind of an open-ended question, isn't it? Why did I take on this case?' Alex was buying time as he thought about it. 'I guess, because I'm a lawyer. Because Burrow asked me to. Because one of my staff persuaded me that it was a noble cause.'

Jonathan looked like he was trying to hide the fact that he was smiling when he heard these words. But he said nothing.

'You think I'm a total cynic, don't you?' Alex continued, trying to break the ice with a confessional tone and an amicable smile on his face.

'You said it yourself, you're a lawyer.'

'Look, I don't mean to be rude, Jonathan, especially in light of what you've been through. But is that the only thing you came here to ask?'

He wasn't trying to hasten Jonathan on his way; he was trying to break down the barrier of reticence that was holding him back.

'When I asked why you took on this case, what I meant was: do you think he's innocent?'

'I can't say what I know or what he told me because that's privileged communication. But I guess I can tell you, in a general sort of way, that a lawyer doesn't have to believe in his client's innocence to take on a case.'

'No, but I also know that lawyers are human – *some* lawyers.'

He smiled when he added the last bit. Alex returned the smile.

'And you want to know if I was motivated by idealism or if I'm just another slave to the almighty dollar.'

'Exactly.'

'Well, you know, when it comes to representing a penniless defendant, there *are* no almighty dollars on the table. We call it pro bono work.'

'I know all about pro bono work, Mr Sedaka. But there's more than one road to Rome, isn't there?'

'I don't know what you mean.'

'Really?' asked Jonathan, with raised eyebrows. 'There's professional kudos and prestige. There's book deals and Hollywood, there's—'

'*Now hold on a minute!* I'm *not* planning on turning your sister's death into a book deal or a Hollywood movie if that's what you're thinking . . . Or should I say, your half sister?'

He was monitoring Jonathan for a reaction. There was no sign of panic or anger or any other emotion on Jonathan's face. He held his head back, but it was more like he was trying to remember something or just to concentrate.

'You know about that?'

'We have the DNA report. I was wondering if it affected your relationship with her . . . one way or the other.'

'I don't think it really did. I mean, we were loyal to each other. We couldn't have been any more loyal if we were full siblings. So I guess you could say it didn't affect us.'

'But you *did* know about it?'

'It came out in the heat of a domestic argument. But after that it was never talked about – at least not by me or Dorothy.'

'You didn't want to know more?'

'We knew all we needed to know.'

'So which of you . . . was . . . ?'

Jonathan was shaking his head.

'I don't want to talk about it.'

A tense silence settled between them for a few seconds. Alex knew that he would make no more progress on this point. Not with Jonathan at any rate.

'You know,' Jonathan said, 'he used to bully her in high school.'

Alex surveyed Jonathan's face for signs of emotion. There was none.

'Verbally or physically?'

'Mostly verbally. Like, he used to make fun of her name.'

'Dorothy?'

'*Our* name. He used to call her "Al Jolson" – like that was funny.'

'I knew there was some animosity between them,' Alex acknowledged. 'I kind of figured that bullying might have something to do with it. Either that or unrequited love.'

'Unrequited love?' Jonathan scowled and his tone was a sneer. 'On whose part?'

'Either. It was just speculation.'

'Well you can take my word for it, there wasn't.'

'I take your word for it. But tell me this. If he bullied her, that wouldn't necessarily lead to him killing her, would it? I mean, making fun of someone's name isn't exactly heavy-duty bullying. And murder is quite extreme for a high school bully.'

'True.'

'On the other hand, all that bullying might have given her a motive to want to see *him* suffer.'

Jonathan scowled again.

'What are you saying? That she faked her own death and framed him?'

Alex hesitated. He chose his next words carefully.

'You're the second person who's raised that possibility today.'

Jonathan got up and reached for his jacket.

'Well before you get carried away with the idea, let me tell you that he had a motive to hate her too.'

'And what's that?'

Jonathan was putting on his jacket as he replied.

'She got him canned over the bullying.'

'That doesn't sound like much of a motive for a jock who was probably just coasting in class in the first place.'

'Oh it was enough of a motive for a sleazeball like Burrow. He liked to win, don't forget. And getting kicked out of the school made him a loser. It gave Dorothy the last laugh. You can imagine how someone like Clayton Burrow would have taken that.'

And with these words, Jonathan angrily left Sedaka's office.

Alex wasn't surprised by what Jonathan had told him just now. But it had huge implications for the case. One of the things that had given Alex doubt over Burrow's guilt was the absence of specific motive. Not that you needed motive to find a man guilty. But a weak motive or no motive is a point in favor of the defense. And it was the weakness of the motive that had given Alex a sense of hope until now.

But now Clayton Burrow had motive.

'I have to go back to the pen,' he told Juanita through the open doors of the office as he grabbed his own jacket.

'Why? Something's come up?'

'Could be. I need to get some straight answers from my client.'

'Good luck.'

She sounded mocking. But he was too busy to think about it. As he was walking toward the entrance, she remembered something.

'Oh, boss, there's something I forgot to tell you. We had a call from David.'

'I haven't got time right now. Call me on my cell phone.'

He slipped out and closed the door behind him.

13:33 PDT

Nat had gone once round the block and parked down the road, waiting in his car and watching the entrance to the office building. He had seen the boy leave, and was about to get out and walk into the building, when he noticed a flurry of activity. A camera was suddenly hoisted onto the shoulder of the cameraman and Martine patted down her hair quickly and sprang into action.

A second later, Alex came into view. He had just emerged from the building and they were poised to ambush him. Martine walked up smartly with a microphone and appeared to ask him a question. She thrust the microphone toward his mouth and tried to intercept him when he moved to the side, but he kept walking as if she wasn't there, and she moved aside when they collided. He offered no apology as he walked over to his car, got in and drove off.

Martine was about to speak into the microphone – presumably to comment on Alex's rudeness – when she appeared to change her mind and instead barked an instruction at her crew. Within seconds they were back in the van driving off in pursuit of Alex, or at least in the same direction.

Nat got back into his car and drove it to the parking space vacated by the van. Then he got out and entered the building. As he did so, he had that prickly feeling on the back of his neck.

13:42 PDT

Juanita had gone back to her internet search. It was a frustrating process, as she didn't really know what she was looking for. At the back of her mind she wondered about the relationship between Dorothy and Jonathan, the fact that they were only half siblings.

Did Jonathan know? Had Alex asked him?

Alex! She had forgotten that she still hadn't told him what David had told her. Alex had told her to phone him. She put him on speaker.

'Hi, Juanita.'

She quickly filled him in on what David had explained about the EasySabre booking and his fear that he wouldn't be able to find any more details, at least not within the tight timeframe they had available.

'But did he say he'd try?' asked Alex.

'Oh yes, he'll give it his best shot. But I was just wondering, boss, maybe we should ask Mrs Olsen.'

'I'm sure if she'd known anything about Dorothy booking a trip at that time she'd've told us already.'

'We may as well ask her. We've got nothing to lose.'

'Okay, go ahead.'

'By the way, I was just wondering, why this sudden rush to see Burrow? Did Jonathan say anything important?'

He told her what Jonathan had said about Dorothy getting Burrow canned.

'So now, all of a sudden, he's got a *real* motive.'

'Yes,' Alex acknowledged bitterly, almost like it was a personal betrayal. By holding out on him, Burrow had actually made it harder for Alex. Yes, on the one hand the information strengthened the possible motive, And maybe Burrow – in his naïvety – was afraid that just knowing it would weaken Alex's sense of resolve and commitment. But the prosecution probably had that information anyway. The important thing was that the same information gave Alex room to maneuver. It meant that Dorothy had a motive to do the very thing that Burrow claimed.

'I wonder why it never came out at the trial.'

'I think it may have been touched upon briefly – at least the fact that they hated each other's guts. But the prosecution wanted to emphasize the *physical* evidence. The motive was presumably just the icing on the cake. The DA had no reason to emphasize it and the defense didn't dare argue that there wasn't a motive because then it would open the door on the prosecution coming back with evidence of motive on rebuttal and then it would look even stronger in the eyes of the jury.'

'But wait a minute, boss. That reminds me of something you said.'

'About what?'

'About his mother having a motive.'

'If I remember rightly, Juanita, you rained on my parade when I came up with that one.'

'Yes, but now it's a whole different ball game. If he actually got Burrow expelled, doesn't that also mean that his mom had a motive? Now it's no longer a case of revenge on the girl who didn't like her son. It's a case of revenge on the girl who got her son canned! That kind of ups the ante, don't you think?'

'It might . . . I guess. It depends what Clayton's mother was like. We'll have to ask Nat when he gets back.'

'I'm surprised he's not back already. Oh, wait a minute. I think that's him.'

'Look, find out what he learned and we'll talk later. I need to step on it and I want to make sure I get to San Q in one piece.'

'Okay. Talk to you later.'

Nat came through the door just as Juanita hung up.

'Is Alex in?'

'No, I was just talking to him. He's on his way back to San Quentin.'

'Anything new?'

'Not really. Jonathan Olsen was here and the boss decided to go and see Burrow right after that.'

Nat was taking off his jacket.

'Any particular reason?'

'I think maybe he wanted to check out some of the things Jonathan told him.'

'Like what?'

'Apparently, Dorothy got Clayton Burrow kicked out of high school.'

'*Really?*'

'You sound surprised.'

'I'm just surprised it's never come up before.'

'We've never had time to go over the facts in such fine detail. When you've got a client on death row it's more of a legal issue than a factual one.'

'Not really. The only way to get the judges to budge is with new facts.'

'Exactly,' said Juanita with a victorious smile. 'So there's not much practical use in going over the *old* ones.'

'Then why's Alex off on a wild goose chase to San Quentin now?'

'Maybe 'cause he's got nothing else.'

Nat went into the kitchen and re-filled the coffee maker. 'Coffee?'

'Yes, please,' Juanita replied. The sound of the grinder and the smell of coffee beans filled the air. Juanita raised her voice above the background noise. 'So what's your take on Mrs Burrow?'

'She gives body and soul to the phrase "trailer trash."'

'Do you think the latest info about Burrow getting canned elevates her as a suspect?'

'Why should it?'

'It kind of strengthens her motive, doesn't it?'

'Only if you buy it.'

'And you don't?'

'Clayton Burrow was the kind of kid who would probably have got canned from high school sooner or later, regardless of anything that Dorothy Olsen or her brother might've done.'

'That doesn't mean he didn't blame her . . . or that his mother didn't blame her.'

'No, but I've just met the woman and I can tell you that, unless she's Oscar-winning material, she hates her son's guts. There's no way she would have killed for him. She is a selfish woman. What's that word Alex likes using? Narcissistic. She didn't even notice what Clayton was turning into, when it was happening in front of her nose. When she finally did wake up and smell the coffee it was only for long enough to resent the monster that she'd unleashed upon the world – almost like a latter-day Frankenstein.'

'Will you quit with your literary comparisons?'

Nat, she recalled, had a bachelor's degree in English Literature.

'What I mean is, everyone misunderstands Frankenstein. He wanted to create life, but he created something that he couldn't love. The monster didn't start out a monster. It started out as a creature with feelings that his creator couldn't bring himself to love. And love was all the creature wanted. So the creature became a monster because he was starved of the love that he craved. I think it was the same with Burrow. It's like that saying that Alex misquoted over the phone to you.'

Juanita raised her eyebrows, quizzically.

'Hell hath no fury,' Nat explained.

'Oh, yeah. *Everyone* misquotes Shakespeare.'

'Congreve actually. William Congreve. The full saying is "Heaven hath no rage like love to hatred turned. Nor hell a fury like a woman scorned." But it isn't just a woman. A man needs love too. And sometimes it's harder for a man because he's culturally indoctrinated not to show it.'

'Are we still in English Lit class? Or have we moved on to Sociology 101?'

'I'm just saying that monsters are created, not born. And it was Sally Burrow who created Clayton, both the boy and the monster. And all because she couldn't love him.'

'You feel sorry for him, don't you?'

'I don't really know. It's the old free will debate. At what point do we stop feeling sorry for the wrongdoer and start blaming him?'

'And when *do* we?' asked Juanita as Nat brought in the coffee.

Nat opened his mouth, but nothing came out. The issue wasn't quite as straightforward as it sounded. After a second or two, he found his voice.

'In the immortal words of that guy from *Kung Fu*: "I seek not to know all the answers . . ."'

Juanita held up her right hand and put on a mock Chinese accent.

'". . . but rather to understand the questions."'

They burst into childish laughter.

'You may know your books,' said Juanita. 'But I know my TV.'

'In that case, you should remember that Kwai Chang Caine didn't have a Chinese accent!'

And with that, Nat scooped up his coffee and went to his small office. Juanita took a sip of her coffee and then put in a call to Esther Olsen. She introduced herself and quickly came to the point.

'Look, one of the things we've found on the hard disk of Dorothy's computer is a booking with an online travel agent. But some of the data is missing and we don't know where it was to. I was wondering if you could help us out.'

There was silence on the other end of the phone.

'Mrs Olsen?'

'I'm sorry. I don't know.'

Juanita thought quickly. There had to be a way to get some more information.

'In order to make an online booking one normally needs a credit or debit card. Do you know if your daughter had one?'

'She had a debit card. She got it with her new bank account when she gained control of her trust fund from her grandfather. Jonathan did too.'

'Do you, by any chance, have any of her old bank statements?'

Again there was hesitation.

'Er, no . . . she used to shred everything.'

'You're sure she didn't leave anything or maybe forget to shred something?'

'Positive.'

'Okay, thank you.'

Juanita put the handset down with the uneasy feeling that Esther Olsen was holding something back.

13:51 PDT

David opened the second button of his short-sleeved shirt against the sweltering heat. The air conditioning had broken down again and the early afternoon sun was getting to him. He wished he had worn a loose-fitting T-shirt. Hot weather didn't agree with him – something Debbie used to tease him about when they were children. But right now he needed his concentration more than ever.

He had already established that Dorothy had bought a ticket from a now defunct Mexican airline company, Quetzalcoatl Airlines. The receipt was from the EasySabre electronic booking system. And as he had told Juanita, the first company to offer self-service online booking through EasySabre was Compuserve Information Services.

If Dorothy had a Compuserve account, then it might still have a record of the booking or a copy of the receipt. He also knew that CIS had been taken over by AOL in February, 1998, in a complex three-way deal. Because the Compuserve brand was still popular in its own right, it continued to function under AOL and so David knew that there was a chance that Dorothy's account might still exist in some passive form even now.

So after telling Juanita what he had discovered, he logged on to the Compuserve website and spent the better part of the next hour trying to track down and get into her account.

The difficulty was how to find it. When Compuserve started out, they used ten digit numbers: six digits, then a comma, then four more digits. But then they had changed and allowed their customers to use a name followed by '@compuserve.com.' The trouble was that many customers had the same name, so they had to resort to letters and numbers. Thus one John Smith might become johnsmith@compuserve.com, but another might have to become johnsmith275@compuserve.com.

He tried 'dorothyOlsen' as the user ID, reasoning that she'd be more likely to use her full name. But it didn't offer him a password reminder. It simply flashed up a message that said 'Invalid User ID.' He followed up with 'dolsen,' but again drew a blank. Various others along those same lines followed, including both names backward and various name and number combinations like 'dolsen1,' 'dolsen01,' 'DOlsen,' etc. But every time he was greeted by the same message: 'Invalid User ID.'

After a while he was cut off because of 'too many attempts' and he had to log on from another computer. But the screen reply remained stubbornly the same.

He took the opportunity to go out and get some sandwiches. But when he came back, all he could do was try more permutations of her name and random numbers, constantly having to break off when he found himself greeted by the 'too many attempts' message.

He knew that this was no way to go about it. His approach was about as unscientific as it could be. The trouble was, there was no mathematical solution. But there might just be a psychological one. He knew that if he was to make any progress, he was going to have to get inside Dorothy's mind.

14:08 PDT

Juanita took a deep breath of fresh air as she left the building. She felt a bit guilty taking an outside lunch. There was still so much work to be done. But there was someone else covering the office, and they had reached an impasse. There was no point sitting round waiting for the phone to ring. Plus she was going stir-crazy. She needed a break from the confinement.

So she made her way to the deli, grabbed a tray and stood in line. She looked round, wondering what she was even doing there. It wasn't hunger that had drawn her out of the office; it wasn't even boredom. It was tension. But even tension wasn't the right word. It was frustration – the frustration of trying to do a job and knowing that it was an uphill struggle. Fighting the good fight was all very well. But some battles are over before they've even begun.

She took a Caesar salad and mineral water from the refrigerated unit and moved along the line to pay.

As she carried her tray to her favorite table in the corner, she told herself that she wouldn't be long.

Favorite, she thought wryly. Normally she wouldn't

be eating here at all. She'd buy a take-out and eat it at her desk. But on this occasion the strain was too much and she'd needed a break.

She played round with her salad, but hardly ate a bite.

What she didn't realize, in her self-absorbed state, was that through the plate glass window of the deli, she was being watched.

14:13 PDT

'I had a visit from Dorothy's brother back at the office.'

'Well whoop-de-do!' Burrow mocked. 'And how is the wimp?'

The look on Alex's face was as neutral as a seasoned poker player. But Burrow sensed the disapproval in the tone.

'I'm sorry. I guess I shouldn't make fun of him.'

Had the sarcasm been a glimpse of the 'old' Burrow coming through the camouflage, Alex wondered. Or was it just the tension and fear taking its toll on the condemned man?

The guards had gone through the preliminaries even more quickly this time, or at least it had seemed that way to Alex. Just as well because Alex was working against the clock.

'I was wondering why you singled out Dorothy. Was there any particular reason for it or was she just an easy target?'

'Is there ever an easy target?'

Burrow was looking down at his hands, clearly despondent.

'I've seen pictures of her, you know. She wasn't an ugly duckling.'

'What's that got to do with it?'

'Well it's usually the ugly kids that get bullied.'

'Yeah . . . usually.'

'So why'd you pick on her? 'Cause she was Jewish maybe?'

Now Clayton looked up, smiling painfully, almost resentfully.

'Come on, Alex, don't give me that crock of shit. You've known me long enough.'

'I've known you for *six weeks*! And that's six weeks as you are *now*. God knows what you were like *then*.'

'So what do you think? I'm some fuckin' redneck?'

'We haven't got time to bullshit each other, Clayton, so I'll spell it out to you. *Yes, you are a fuckin' redneck!* Or at least *were!*'

'Okay, you're right! But I ain't an anti-Semite . . . It was 'cause she was a dyke.'

Alex looked at him, surprised.

Clayton shrugged guiltily. 'These days I'd probably get a buzz out of it.'

'So you're a normal, red-blooded male,' replied Alex, going with the flow of the irony.

'So now you know.'

'So now I know,' the lawyer echoed. He paused for dramatic effect. 'Well almost, but not quite.'

'What's that supposed to mean?'

'Well actually I do know. That is, I *know* that she got you kicked out of the school.'

Clayton looked at him surprised.

'I suppose Jonathan told you that?'

'Exactly. But the important thing is that I know. And the even *more* important thing is that you didn't tell me. How the *fuck* am I supposed to defend you if you hold out on me?'

'Is it so important? I mean, you know that me and Dorothy hated each other's guts. Do the details really matter?'

'Goddamn right they matter! I've been fighting this case on the premise that you didn't really have a motive.'

'Since when do you need motive to find a man guilty? And since when does having a motive make a man guilty?'

'The point is I've been fighting your corner on the premise that the prosecution exaggerated the motive. Now it turns out that they didn't.'

'Whatever premise you've been fighting on, it hasn't done us any good,' Burrow spat out bitterly. 'So what fuckin' difference does it make?'

'Maybe if I'd known, I would have used a different strategy.'

'Or maybe you wouldn't have tried so hard. It's easier to write me off now that I've got a strong motive.'

Alex was shaking his head wearily.

'I haven't given up on you, Clayton. When Dusenbury made his offer I came running here to tell you. You're the one who shot me down in flames.'

'You wanted to know where Dorothy Olsen is. I can't tell you what I don't know.'

'I don't like being lied to, Clayton.'

'I'm not lying.'

'Lying, holding out. It's all the same! If you're not straight with your lawyer, you can kiss your ass goodbye.'

'Well it looks like I'm not the only person who's been lying to you.'

'And just what's that supposed to mean?'

'It means Dorothy Olsen didn't get me canned. Her brother did.'

14:19 PDT

He had made sure not to catch the woman's eye as he entered the deli. He lined up with his tray and ordered his hot pastrami on rye, realizing he'd have to be quick. Even though she had found a newspaper and was casually browsing it, she would soon finish her Caesar salad and leave. Then the opportunity would be lost.

It seemed to take an eternity and he regretted asking for mustard, which drew the process out even longer. He added a bottle of mango juice to the tray while he was waiting in line and then took the tray to the checkout. He paid with a twenty and let them give him change, realizing that it was quicker than fiddling round in his own pockets for coins. Then, when they gave him the change, he just dumped it on the tray and swept off in the direction of the table in the corner.

He wondered when she would notice him. She seemed so absorbed in her thoughts that maybe she wouldn't. She had effectively screened out the background noise of the deli, so why should she look up now? Even when he reached the table, she seemed more absorbed in the newspaper than she was in the movement round her.

'Is this place taken, Miss Cortez?'

Juanita looked up.

'Oh hi, Jonathan.'

14:22 PDT

David was frustrated by his lack of progress. Ordinarily, he would just take this sort of thing in his stride. Finding the right user ID was as much an art as a science. It called for both diligence and patience.

But patience was a virtue only when the luxury of time was available. In this case, David knew, they were operating under a sparse chronological budget. They had less than ten hours before Burrow was scheduled to die.

The worst part was that there was no guarantee that there was anything worth finding. At least now he had something *specific* to look for. That was better than groping in complete darkness. But even if he could get the user ID, there was no guarantee that he would get the password. In the meantime, it was painstaking work. All he could do was keep trying.

Fortunately, his father's enthusiasm and tenacity were contagious. That was why David had skipped lunch to carry on working on this. This was, after all, an emergency. Only in this type of emergency there was no 911 number they could call to bail them out.

Suddenly David was struck by an off-the-wall idea.

He didn't really place much hope in it, but he typed in 'dorothyolsen911' and hit the enter key. Only this time, he didn't get an 'Incorrect User ID' message. Instead he was greeted by the words 'Incorrect Password.'

He selected the password reminder online option and found himself confronting a series of questions: 'Date of Birth,' 'Mother's maiden name,' and 'Name of High School.' He had already made sure that he had all this information. Once it was typed in, he found himself in Dorothy Olsen's Compuserve account.

14:28 PDT

Nat was holding down the fort at the office.

'Alex Sedaka's office.'

'Oh hi, this is David Sedaka. Could I speak to my father?'

'He's not in the office right now. Can I take a message?'

'Is Juanita there?'

'No, she isn't. But I can take a message for her too.'

'Is that Nat?'

'Yes.'

In the short time that Nat had been there, he had never actually spoken to David. He knew that David was a few years younger than himself – twenty-four to his twenty-seven – but there was no time for pleasantries.

'Okay, well, look,' said David, 'do you know when he's getting back? This could be important.'

'Well he should be back within the hour, but you can call him on his cell.'

'Maybe you could do that. I want to get back to the computer and see what else I can find. I have to leave the lab every time I need to make a call. Basically, just tell him that I've managed to log in to Dorothy Olsen's old email account and I've found the EasySabre receipt.'

'Holy shit!'

'My sentiments exactly,' said David. 'It shows that she booked a one-way flight from Mexico to Luton Airport in the UK. The booking was made on May 19, 1998 and the flight date was May 24 of that year – the day after she disappeared.'

14:34 PDT

'So how do you manage when there's only three of you?'

The crowd in the deli was thinning out, but Juanita and the young man were still engaged in earnest conversation.

'We're a small office. Sometimes even *three's* a crowd.'

'Yes, but I mean . . . in a case like this? One minute, you're running up to DC to argue a motion before the Supreme Court, next minute you're meeting the governor here in Frisco.'

'That's the way Alex likes to operate. At one time he didn't have anyone, it was a one-man band. He did everything, research, interviews, drafting briefs, litigation.'

'Why?'

'He's an individualist. He likes to run his own show.'

'But isn't it risky? I mean, what if something comes up and he needs to go back to the Capitol to get a ruling?'

'We can go to the Federal District Court. But we've also got a partner firm on standby up in DC.'

'But I thought Mr Sedaka went there in person to argue the motion? He was on the TV outside the court afterward.'

'Yes, he went there for that because that was the last-chance saloon as far as the court proceedings were concerned. But if anything new comes up that the District Court can't or won't handle, we've got another firm on standby to file a motion and even argue it if it's called for.'

The young man shook his head.

'That seems like kind of a strange way to operate – for a big case like this.'

'You have to remember that until recently we didn't have any cases as big as this.'

'What about that case with the girlfriend of the drug baron?'

'Estella Sanchez? That wasn't really a *big* case in terms of workload. An *important* case, maybe, but hardly a *big* one.'

'*People* magazine called it "a landmark case."'

'The media like to exaggerate. I suppose it did set a precedent, but the same could be said of any case that goes before the Supreme Court – or at least every successful case.'

'Still . . . it must have taken some serious work to win it.'

'All we really had to do was file the certiorari motion and one well-written brief. That hardly puts it in the same league as murder with special circumstances. We've never dealt with a capital case before.'

Juanita knew that time was ticking by. This was originally supposed to be a short lunch break. But she sensed that she was making some progress here, even if the flow of information so far was going from her to him. It was almost as if *he* was pumping *her* for something. But she knew that she was getting somewhere, and she had to hang in there. She had to find out *what* he was looking for.

'So why *did* you take on a capital case this time?'

'We didn't so much take it on as inherit it. The white-shoe firm that had it before us saw it as a sure-fire loser and were looking to unload it.'

'You didn't have to take it on.'

'Oh there's kudos even in losing – if you put up a brave enough fight along the way.'

'Brave enough and *public* enough.'

Juanita smiled.

'Touché.'

'So why did the big league firm want out?'

'I guess they got cold feet. But we weren't alone. Plenty of others were ready to pick up the Burrow case.'

'Then how come you got it? Surely some of the other law firms were in a better position? I mean in terms of their size, not location.'

'It was partly Burrow's decision himself. I think he may have heard about our success in the Sanchez case and decided we were hot.'

'So your boss didn't do anything special to get the case?'

'Not Alex, no. But I think Nat was kind of enthusiastic about it.'

'Nat?'

'Nathaniel Anderson, our legal intern.'

'Why did *he* want it?'

'Nat is an idealist. To him, it was a matter of principle.'

'He thinks Burrow is innocent?'

'I wouldn't say that. Heck, I'll spell it out to you: he thinks Burrow is probably guilty. But he also realizes that there are issues at stake that go beyond one miserable lowlife like Clayton Burrow.'

'So how come he isn't in the office?'

'Who says he isn't?'

'Well I didn't see anyone else back there in the office.'

Juanita felt a tingling sensation, as she remembered how Jonathan had looked round in the office. *Was he spying on them?*

14:41 PDT

Getting stuck in traffic is a pain in the ass at the best of times. But when you've got a client on death row, with the execution scheduled for just over nine hours' time, it was a nightmare. That was the position in which Alex found himself now. He was still in Marin County and the bridge wasn't even in sight.

Plus – and this was the kicker – he felt as if he wasn't making any progress with Burrow either. The logjam that his car was stuck in seemed in some way like a paradigm for the case. His client was as stubborn as ever and seemed determined to die. He was putting on a brave face. But Alex could sense that he was scared. The only question was, if he was scared, why didn't he take the bait? Why didn't he grab the lifeline that the governor had thrown him?

Was he protecting someone? And if so, who? The only person he might be protecting was his mother. Alex had asked him that, point blank, but Burrow had denied it. And he seemed quite sincere. It was neither a half-hearted denial nor one of those over-emphatic denials that rings loud and hollow. But still, a man like Burrow might have learned to lie over the years – and convincingly.

What Alex needed was a second opinion. He was about to call the office when his cell phone rang. It was his daughter.

'Hi, Debbie,' he said.

'Hi, Dad,' she replied through clenched teeth. He was the only person in the world who could get away with calling her Debbie – and live. To everyone else, she was Deborah. It was nothing personal, more of a professional requirement. When you're a hotshot corporate lawyer with a leading Wall Street firm, you can't afford to be taken anything other than seriously.

'Are you calling from work?'

He knew that two thousand seven hundred miles away she was smiling.

'Dad, I've been at my desk since quarter past seven.'

'Sorry.'

He knew that she'd probably been there since half past six. She was ambitious and she worked hard. Like father like daughter.

'Listen, I . . .' She trailed off. There was always an awkwardness between them. It had been there since long before his wife died, but the killing had been a blow from which their fragile relationship still hadn't recovered. Melody had been the bridge between them.

'I just wanted to wish you . . . good luck. With the Burrow case.'

He wondered if she had heard about the clemency offer and if he should tell her about Burrow's unexpected rejection of it. He decided not to. He could consult her about it as a lawyer – if she had any expertise to contribute – but he couldn't tell her as his daughter.

'Thanks.'

He didn't know what else to say. He often thought about things he wanted to talk about when they next talked, but somehow he always seemed to dry up and forget what had been on his mind when one of them picked up the phone and the conversation actually took place.

'Look, I know you're busy today. But if you need to – if you *want* to talk to anyone – I'm here for you.'

A soft center inside a hard shell – the exact opposite of her mother.

'Bye, Dad.'

'Bye, Debbie.'

He felt a desolate loneliness as he pressed the red button on the cell phone. But it wasn't just Debbie he was missing; it was her mother. He wondered if Melody had felt fear when she looked down the barrel of the gun.

She had been working the graveyard shift at A&E in the hospital nine months ago when the two gang members were brought in. Normally they try to separate gang members from rival gangs and don't bring them in to the same hospital. But when a gang shootout left two victims – one from each side – knocking on death's door, time was of the essence. So fate would have it that Hector Ramirez and Esteban Delgado were brought in to the A&E Department of St Mary's Hospital, without any one of the overworked doctors so much as knowing that it had been Delgado who shot Ramirez, before getting shot himself.

All Melody Sedaka knew was that Esteban Delgado was a seriously injured man and it was her professional duty to save him. But while Melody succeeded in her duty with Delgado, Hector Ramirez was pronounced dead on arrival.

She had been warned that with Delgado behind bars and thus inaccessible to the rival gang, she might be targeted instead for revenge – for saving the man who had killed their friend. But she had refused to let it interfere with her work. Even the normal security escort to her car had been given short shrift by Melody. So – one week after Thanksgiving – it had been relatively easy for one of Ramirez's homeys to sneak into the parking lot and gun her down as she was about to get into her car.

Shortly after that, sixteen-year-old Eduardo Rivera was stopped in a Cherokee jeep because of a busted tail light. When the cops radioed in to check the license plate, they found that the jeep had been seen driving away fast from a shooting. A search of the jeep revealed a Glock, and Rivera was arrested on the spot. Then the evidence technicians went in. Ballistics matched the gun to the bullets and cartridges from the Melody Sedaka killing, while fingerprints – albeit on the barrel, not the stock – linked the gun to Rivera. He also had gunshot residue on his left hand, but not on his right. The fingerprints on the barrel were also from his left hand.

The Public Defender – who was representing Rivera – pointed out that his client was right-handed and that the lack of right-handed prints on the stock or gun residue on Rivera's right hand suggested that the boy was merely driving the getaway car and dumping the gun.

151

This was what his *lawyer* was saying. Rivera himself was saying nothing. He had invoked his right to silence and stayed schtum ever since. In the absence of any denial or explanation from Rivera, the cops and DA had concluded that this was Rivera's initiation for gang membership: 'Kill the bitch who saved the man who killed our brother and you're a member.' They pointed out that negative results from the gun residue test to the right hand did not prove conclusively that he had *not* fired a gun from that hand and he might have wiped the prints from the stock while holding the gun by the barrel.

There were, however, some in the DA's office who had their doubts.

Alex knew all of this, but had been in too much shock to process the information. He had no idea whether Rivera was guilty or not, and frankly he didn't care. That was perhaps why the DA had thought it an ideal time to try and persuade Alex to abandon his law firm and join the DA's staff. So far Alex had refused. But the DA wasn't yet ready to stop trying.

Ironically, while Rivera was still trying to prove himself a man, Delgado was now busily re-branding himself as a returning Catholic and campaigner against gang violence. Alex had wondered if this was a ploy to reduce his prison sentence. But he was due out shortly anyway. Maybe his brush with death had really changed him into a better man. The jury was still out on that one.

Strangely, one of the factors that had given Alex pause was a visit from a young Hispanic woman who introduced herself to him as Eduardo Rivera's cousin. She had never been part of the gang culture, but she came to him to personally apologize for what her cousin had done. She offered no excuses and when he was initially rude to her, she had taken it all in her stride.

By then it was his turn to apologize to her and – over lunch at a nearby deli – it emerged that she was attending night school for a law degree and was a fast typist with good shorthand skills. One week later, the young woman – Juanita Cortez – started work for him as his secretary.

He remembered now that he had been about to call Juanita when Debbie had phoned. He reached out to the cell phone in its hands-free cradle.

'Alex Sedaka's office,' Nat's voice answered.

Alex was surprised.

'Oh hi, Nat. Where's Juanita?'

'She's out for lunch.'

'Out?'

Now that really was a surprise.

'I sent her. I think it was all getting to her.'

'Do you know when she'll be back?'

'Any minute I'd guess. Shall I get her to call you?'

'No, it's actually you I wanted to talk to. I was wondering how it went with Burrow's mother.'

'Well I didn't get much. I think I kind of offended her by some of my questions.'

'That's hardly surprising. What was it, like: "How dare you accuse my poor boy of doing anything bad? That bitch had it coming"?'

'Oh, no, if anything it was quite the opposite. She's written him off – disowned him completely. It was more like, "I'm not to blame for the way my son turned out. He's just a bad apple."'

'Yes, but did the apple fall far from the tree?'

'It's hard to say. I mean, she's a tough, heartless bitch. But I wouldn't say she was bad. Her sin was the sin of indifference. She said herself that she had her life and he had his.'

'Maybe if she'd given him a bit more attention, he would've turned out different.'

'That's exactly what I said.'

'Not to her face, I hope?' The moment of hesitation lasted too long. 'Oh you *didn't*?'

''Fraid so,' said Nat, sheepishly.

Alex was forced to smile at Nat's shoot-from-the-hip approach.

'And how did she take it?'

'She chased me out of the trailer park with a 12 gauge pump action – figuratively speaking.'

'Well thank the Lord she didn't have a real one.'

'Ay-men!'

'Okay, is anything else going on? Any more crap with those reporters outside?'

'No, they left after you brushed them off.'

'Well when Juanita gets back, get her to call me.'

'Will do.'

Alex pressed the red button, suddenly wondering how Nat knew about him brushing off the reporters.

14:46 PDT

'I tried to put up a fight, but he just beat the crap out of me.'

'I guess that makes it kind of hard for you to accept what we're doing.'

'Not really. I mean you're just doing your jobs. The law says a man's entitled to a lawyer when he's accused of a crime. And you're just giving him his legal rights.'

They were walking back to the office now. Juanita felt that she had made as much progress with Jonathan at the deli as she could. And it was quite obvious that he wanted to go back to the office with her. Whatever it was he was interested in, it was something at the office.

Maybe he thinks we leave some files lying round, Juanita thought. If so, he was liable to be very disappointed.

In the meantime, Juanita was determined to turn the tables and get some information out of Jonathan.

'So how old were you at the time?'

'Well Clayton and Dorothy were seventeen and I was five years younger than Dorothy, so I guess I would have been twelve.'

'You must have hated Clayton Burrow a lot.'

'Not half as much as he must have hated me.'

'Why? I mean, if Burrow beat you up, wouldn't he have been satisfied after that? Why would he bear a grudge?'

'Because he got kicked out of school on account of it.'

'How did that happen?'

'He beat me up in front of a dozen other kids. I wasn't one to snitch, but it got back to the principal and he got canned.'

'So you think that Burrow blamed your sister for telling the principal about him beating you up and killed her to get revenge?'

'It's a possibility.'

'But why wait so long? I mean, why wait until the senior prom?'

'I guess he'd seen *Carrie*. He probably did it for dramatic effect.'

'But it's not like he humiliated her in public like in *Carrie*. Your sister just *vanished* on the night of the prom. No one saw her again.'

'Clayton Burrow wasn't the brightest button. He'd've probably done something more dramatic if he could. He wouldn't have had the brains to pull it off. He probably just bundled her into a car, drove her off to a quiet location and killed her.'

'So what did he do with the body?'

'I guess he buried her.'

'Well enough that the body was never found?'

'I guess so.'

'Can you think of any reason why he'd refuse to reveal where the body was buried?'

'Why should he? He's still claiming he's innocent.'

'But if his life depended on it. He could save himself by—'

'So it's true?'

Could this have been all he was after?

'Let's say it is true. Does it make sense that he'd keep quiet even when he could save his life by spilling his guts?'

'I guess not.'

They had arrived back at the office building. Jonathan held the door open for Juanita. She smiled a polite thank you and walked through.

'There was something else that had us puzzled.'

'What?' he asked as she pressed the elevator button.

'Well we have evidence that Dorothy bought an airline ticket a week before she disappeared.'

He seemed startled by this. She was watching him carefully and although he had tried to hide it, she had noticed.

'Where to? The ticket, I mean.'

She debated telling him that they didn't know. But this would give him the advantage. If he thought they already knew, he might be less inclined to hold out with whatever *he* knew. But he had caught her with a solid counter punch and she couldn't bluff it.

'We were hoping you could tell us.'

This was good cross-examination technique, she realized. Now he couldn't be sure whether they knew where the ticket was to or not. Alex would have been impressed, just as she had been impressed by him: you can study law at night school but cross-examination technique can

157

only be learned by studying a master at work. The important thing was that now Jonathan would be wondering if she was just trying to test him. The elevator arrived and the doors opened. Jonathan waited politely for Juanita to enter first.

'I don't know anything about it,' said Jonathan, stepping in behind her. 'Did she *get* the flight?'

The doors closed behind them.

'Can you think of any reason why she wouldn't?'

They heard the familiar hum and felt that heavy sensation of being inside a rising elevator.

'Apart from the obvious one,' said Jonathan, 'no.'

'It's just that if she *did* fly,' said Juanita, 'then that would explain her disappearance. Maybe she left and never came back.'

Jonathan shrugged.

'Or maybe she came back and was killed *after* that,' he said.

Juanita wondered if this statement was just a theory or a reflection of personal knowledge. But she didn't want to show how desperately she needed to know the answer. That would put Jonathan squarely in the driver's seat. She was saved by the whirring halt of the elevator and the opening of the doors.

'Is that what you think?' asked Juanita. Without waiting for an answer, she started walking down the corridor, forcing Jonathan to hasten to keep up with her. When they had reached the door to the law firm's office, Jonathan still seemed to be considering Juanita's question.

'I don't think anything,' he replied cautiously. 'I'm just doing what you're doing: speculating.'

He opened the door for her. Nat was sitting at the reception desk, manning the phones. He looked up.

'Oh, Nat, this is Jonathan, Dorothy Olsen's brother.'

They nodded politely and mouthed 'hallo.' Then Nat turned away to the computer screen that had been the object of his attention when they entered. Jonathan, for his part, appeared to be in a dream.

'Well, thank you, Jonathan. It was a pleasure talking to you.'

Juanita's words seemed to snap Jonathan out of his reverie.

'Oh yes, thank you.'

He turned abruptly and left.

Juanita was puzzled by his sudden urgency.

Monday, October 18, 1999

The open window had made it easier, but he would have got in one way or the other. He hadn't waited this long just to do nothing. The first thing to do was find the large hunting knife. That was the easy part. Everyone knew that Burrow kept it either under his pillow or under the bed. He had bragged about it in school.

The intruder found it quickly under the pillow and slumped into a sitting position on the floor to do the next bit. The blood was in a vial, but he didn't just want to pour it on the knife. That would get it all over the place.

Instead he poured some onto a Kleenex and wiped it onto the knife. He held it like that for a few minutes, letting it partially dry. Then he used the knife to prise up one of the floorboards under the bed. It didn't matter that this left some blood prints by the edges of the floorboards. The knife probably would have still had some wet blood on it. And the fact that it was under the bed meant that Clayton probably wouldn't see the blood, even if he looked under the bed when he found the knife missing.

He put the knife into the cavity beneath the floorboards. The blood on it would continue to dry in situ. That was what the investigators would expect. They would assume that Burrow had hidden the blood-stained knife under the floorboards while the blood was still wet and that the blood dried later.

Next came the panties. He had kept them refrigerated in a sealed plastic bag. He wasn't sure if the semen or the blood would still be identifiable. He knew that DNA from sperm was hard to detect after three days, when the sperm dies. But there were new DNA technologies more powerful than Short Tandem Repeat, like Low Copy Number. With these new technologies they could probably link the sperm to Burrow. And even if not, the fact that they would find them here under the floorboards in his bedroom would be more than enough to clinch it. And the blood would certainly be identifiable, because they could match it to Esther Olsen using a mitochondrial DNA comparison.

However, the panties would only suggest rape, not murder. The knife might suggest murder but even that in conjunction with the disappearance would not necessarily clinch it. There had to be one final piece of evidence that would close the case and make up for the lack of a body.

That killer piece of evidence was the breast tissue. It had been removed with surgical precision and now it was going to be used with similar exactitude to make sure that Clayton Burrow was found guilty of the murder of Dorothy Olsen.

He opened the freezer and carefully removed the items

in the front and then moved the items already at the back forward to create some room at the back. Standing on tiptoes and stretching to reach in, he placed the breast tissue – wrapped in foil and plastic – at the back of the freezer. Then he moved the front items to the back and put the removed items to the front.

Before closing the freezer, he studied the results of his work. The freezer looked exactly as it had before. He reckoned that neither Clayton nor his mother would check the back of the freezer. Most people have things at the back of their freezer that they have forgotten about completely and this was especially true of slovenly people like the Burrows.

He closed the freezer and used another Kleenex to wipe his fingerprints.

Then he went across town and found a pay phone to place the call that would nail Clayton Burrow.

14:54 PDT (August 14, 2007)

'So how'd you hook up with Jonathan Olsen then?'

Juanita was back at the front desk and Nat was sitting there with a cup of coffee.

'He came here while you were out.'

'Yes, but I mean, didn't he leave before I came back?'

'Yes, but he saw me at the deli and invited himself to join me.'

'Kind of a coincidence, don't you think?'

'He was probably hanging round outside aimlessly and decided to go for something to eat and got lucky.'

'Or maybe he followed you.'

Juanita smiled.

'You're getting paranoid. But, maybe you're right. So what? His sister's gone and we're trying to save the neck of the man who he thinks did it. He wants to talk. He wants to understand.'

'And that's it?'

She looked up and met his eyes.

'You're very suspicious today, Nat.'

'It just seems kind of strange that he comes round, talks to Alex, and then just happens to bump into you outside.'

'Okay, maybe he *did* follow me. He wants to talk. He *needs* to talk.'

'To us?'

'To someone – *anyone.*'

'Just talk?'

Juanita thought about this for a moment.

'Okay, maybe more than just talk.'

'Like what?'

'I think he was trying to pump me for information. That's why I stretched the break for so long.'

'I'd've thought it would've been the opposite way round.'

'You have to understand that I wasn't just sitting on my tush spilling my guts. I was pumping *him* for information too.'

'What did he want to know?'

'Well at first he was asking about how many people we have working here – shit like that.'

'That's it? Nothing more specific?'

'Then he started asking about why we took the case and did we think that Burrow was innocent.'

'It seems funny to wait till today and then come round in person asking dumb-ass questions like that.'

'I think he was using that as a stalking horse for what he was really after.'

'And what was that?'

'He wanted to know about the deal Dusenbury offered.'

'I hope you didn't tell him anything.'

'I didn't have a choice.'

'Oh Juanita!'

'I told you! I had to, I was pumping *him* for information too.'

'Like what?'

'Like the airline ticket Dorothy bought just before she disappeared.'

'You know about that?'

'Yes, David Sedaka told me.'

'So how did Jonathan react?'

'He was jumpy.'

'Did he admit to knowing about it?'

'No. He said he didn't know where the ticket was to, acted all innocent and asked *me* where it was to.'

'Did you tell him?'

'How could I? I don't know.'

'But I thought you said David Sedaka told you.'

'Yes, but *he* doesn't know. He was only able to recover partial information.'

'Oh, but he told me—'

'*What?*'

Nat looked embarrassed.

'He called again. He managed to hack into Dorothy's old Compuserve account and he found the EasySabre receipt. It was for a flight from Mexico to London.'

Juanita's heart skipped a beat.

'*London?* We'd better tell Alex! We need to check if she made that flight!'

15:06 PDT

While Nat was telling Juanita about David Sedaka's last success, David's tenacity was beginning to pay off in yet bigger dividends as he made yet another discovery on the hard drive. Again, he had to leave the lab to go to the phone. The office they had let him use had a computer on the desk. He switched it on as he called Alex Sedaka.

'Alex Sedaka's office,' Juanita answered.

'Oh hi, Juanita. I've found something else that could be of interest.'

'What?'

'Well after I found the receipt, I decided to check the hard disk on the computer doing a word search for London and one of the things I found was a deleted PDF of a brochure from something called the Finchley Road Medical Centre.'

'What's that?'

'It's a private medical center in London, catering to wealthy clients – mostly women.'

'What do they do?'

'Anything from cosmetic surgery, liposuction, gastric bands for weight loss. You name it; they do it.'

166

15:14 PDT

'Okay, we've got less than nine hours left and the name of the game is saving our client from death by lethal injection, even if he's less than enthusiastic about saving himself.'

They were sitting round the conference table. Alex had finally made it back to the office and things had taken on a new urgency.

'Surely with the flight to London and the medical center, we've got all we need?' Juanita ventured.

Alex was shaking his head.

'I wish we could be sure. But the fact is, the way things are, we don't even know if she made that flight.'

'But the medical center,' Juanita reminded him.

'That shows that she had some *information* on a medical center in London. We don't know what her interest was, whether it was for herself or someone else. Even if it was for herself, the most that shows is an interest or possibly an *intention*. It doesn't prove that it went anything *beyond* intention.'

Nat nodded reluctantly.

'The prosecution will probably concede that she may

have had the *intention*, but that the intention was *thwarted* by Burrow's action in murdering her.'

Juanita felt like she was in a minority of one.

'So are we just going to sit here and do nothing until more evidence drops from the sky?'

Alex looked at her sympathetically.

'We're not going to sit here doing nothing. But we're not going to get our hopes up either. We need to keep looking. In the meantime, I'm going over to the District Court to file for an ex parte temporary restraining order based on the proof of ticket purchase and downloaded brochure on her computer.'

Nat nodded.

'You could also try and make something from the fact that it was deleted.'

'Technically she reformatted the entire hard disk, Nat. But I take your point.'

'And what am I going to do?' asked the intern.

'Actually, we're going together, Nat. I need you there, 'cause if we get the TRO one of us is going to have to serve it while the other waits for the State to show up. They'll try and get it overturned asap, so we'll need to be there for a full hearing.'

'What do you want me to prepare?' asked Juanita.

'I'll need copies of the airline receipt and a statement from David. If he can get it notarized by someone at Berkeley that'll help, but it isn't vital. Also get him to email over the brochure.'

Juanita looked edgy.

'Do you think they'll grant it – the TRO?'

Last minute temporary restraining orders on executions

were common in capital cases. Sometimes lawyers even waited till the eleventh hour to apply so as to give the court no choice. Of course strictly speaking the court always had a choice. But judges were reluctant to refuse such a request when they didn't know what might come out of it. And to rule against a defense petition ex parte – when the State wasn't even present – meant they couldn't even share the blame with anyone else if hindsight proved the decision wrong.

'I reckon they'll grant the TRO. But the State won't wait till tomorrow to argue the matter. They want to fry Burrow tonight.'

'Then maybe we should wait till the last minute,' said Nat. 'That way we might get more evidence.'

'We're going to try and get more evidence anyway. But I'd rather file now. I don't want to start playing games. If we cut it too fine, the District Court will *assume* we're empty handed and that'll make them *more* likely to brush us off. If we get the ex parte TRO now and then hit 'em with even stronger evidence when the State argues res judicata, we'll have the best of both worlds.'

Res judicata meant 'already judged' – a standard prosecution response to last-minute defense petitions based on alleged new evidence. Of course the prosecution would say that new evidence petitions were themselves a standard defense ploy to buy time.

'Apart from what we've already got,' asked Juanita, 'what more evidence do you think we'll find?'

'There's the question of whether or not she made the flight. While we're at the District Court we'll file a discovery motion to get the information from Sabre, the parent company of EasySabre. They should still have the information. They save everything – even if it's only on a back-up tape.'

Nat looked dubious.

'If we file for discovery before the same court, won't it alert the judge to the possibility that maybe she *didn't* make the flight? Shouldn't we treat it as axiomatic that if she booked the ticket, she made the flight? The State won't be there to argue otherwise.'

'That's a risky strategy, Nat. We haven't got the time to go shopping between courts. If we file for discovery before the District Court, at least it'll also show the judge that we're taking it seriously and not just sitting on our backsides.'

Nat nodded. Juanita spoke up again.

'Do you think we should try and get a British law firm to file a request to UK immigration and border control to see if she entered?'

Alex looked at his watch.

'There's no time. London's eight hours ahead of us. And in any case they probably won't appreciate that time is of the essence in a capital case.'

'A *judge* over there surely would.'

'They don't have the death penalty in England. If it gets to a minor clerk in the first instance, they might not appreciate the urgency of the situation. And even if they do, they'll probably pass the buck from one to another to avoid getting landed with it. All they'll try and do is get it off their desk as quickly as possible – even if they can't get it to the right person or to someone who has the authority to decide. Aside from that, it's unlikely that UK immigration would *be able* to respond fast enough to our request.'

'Okay. I just thought it was worth a try,' replied Juanita, pouting.

'I'll tell you what we'll do. We'll ask for a stay of execution and make the TRO our fallback position. If we get a full stay, we'll call a British law firm and get them to chase it up with UK immigration. But in the meantime there's something more important I need you to do.'

Juanita felt another jolt of adrenaline.

'Shoot.'

'I want you to contact the Finchley Road Medical Centre by phone and ask them if Dorothy Olsen had treatment there and if so for what.'

'Isn't that privileged information?'

'Not in England. Only lawyers have privilege there, not doctors.'

'But it's still *confidential*. I mean, we'd need a court order from a British court to force them to disclose it, no?'

'Okay, but let's ask at least. Explain the situation here. Make it clear to them that an innocent man's life is on the line. At minimum we need confirmation that she was there, also when she arrived and when she left. We don't *have* to know about the treatment. Maybe start off by asking for everything and then use a fallback position that even just written confirmation of her arrival could save a man's life. That way they'll feel a bit of sympathy and see it as a fair compromise.'

Juanita was looking at her watch.

'I'm thinking, it might be kind of difficult.'

171

'Why?'

'Well it's twenty past eleven at night over there in England. The people who have the power to make decisions will all have gone home.'

'That's why I want *you* to do it. You can talk to the nursing staff. If they come up with anything, we'll get them to wake up the administrators.'

'I'll do what I can. You're probably right about the nurses. If they're on the graveyard shift they might not be so busy. Maybe it'll be easier to get them to talk than the day staff.'

'Any other business?'

Alex looked round. They all exchanged glances and shrugged. It was like a football huddle, complete with the adrenaline rush, but sans the testosterone. Juanita suddenly remembered something.

'There was one thing. This business about Jonathan and Dorothy only being half siblings.'

'Yes, I tried to get Jonathan to open up about that, but he clammed up like a shell.'

'I was wondering if it might be worth checking out.'

'It's not as important as the medical center. Anyway, how can we check at short notice?'

'You could ask Mrs Olsen.'

'I'd rather not. Not unless we have to. She's a frail old woman and she doesn't need that kind of heavy-duty problem.'

'Maybe we can just Google "Edgar Olsen" and see what comes up.'

'Okay. But first talk to the medical center asap.'

'Okay, boss.'

'Okay, let's kick some judicial butt!' said Alex, forcing an artificially enthusiastic smile.

Minutes later, Alex and Nat were gone and Juanita was on her own. She was calling the Finchley Road Medical Centre on the speakerphone with one hand, and, being adept at multi-tasking, she was Googling 'Edgar Olsen' with the other.

Why delay? she thought. *I'm a woman. I can do two things at once.*

It might even be a complete red herring. But it was still hanging over them. They were whistling in the dark and had to grab hold of any lifeline that came their way.

Several items came up that referred to a 'car crash.' Most of these were from local newspapers and they dated back thirty years. Juanita was amazed that newspaper editions from long before the existence of the world wide web had been digitized and made available online. However, in order to access them one almost invariably had to register with the newspaper or organization.

Juanita had a dummy email account just for this sort of thing, to avoid getting spam in her main mailbox, but she still had to go through the whole process of registering and confirming her membership before eventually being able to log on and find what she was looking for.

February 17, 1977 – Pomona, CA – A three-year-old boy was killed when the car his father was driving collided with a pick-up truck on Route 66. Jimmy Olsen was in the back seat of the car travelling east when a driver headed west swerved across the

173

median line. Edgar Olsen, the boy's father, tried to avoid the pick-up truck but was hit from the side. The boy was taken to Pomona Valley Hospital a short time later but pronounced dead on arrival. The driver of the pick-up truck was arrested for driving under the influence of alcohol.

So Edgar Olsen had two dead children.

15:23 PDT (23:23 BST)

Susan White was at the nursing station when the call came. But it was another nurse who took the call.

'Yes, it comes through to here when the switchboard is closed . . . I'm afraid the Administrator isn't here now. It's almost midnight – well twenty past eleven . . . I don't think that would be practical . . . What do you mean a matter of life and . . . ?'

The nurse noticed Susan White looking at her, like a puma coiled to spring into action, almost as if Susan could hear the other side of the conversation.

'Look, wait a minute, there's someone else here who may be able to help you.'

The nurse covered the mouthpiece of the receiver with her hand.

'It's some woman with a foreign accent. She says she needs to speak to someone in a position of authority and it's a matter of life and death. She sounds a bit . . .'

'Okay, I'll deal with it.' Susan virtually snatched the phone away.

'Hallo, my name is Susan White. To whom am I speaking?'

'I'm Juanita Cortez. Are you in the administration?'

'No, I'm a staff nurse here. All the admin staff have gone home. May I ask what this is about?'

'I work for Alex Sedaka. He's a lawyer and he's representing a client on death row for the murder of a girl called—'

'Dorothy Olsen!'

'You *know* about it?'

Susan struggled to keep her breathing under control. This was not what she had been expecting. Before she had been paralyzed by fear. Now she was almost relieved.

'I saw a report about it on the news.'

'Then you must know that time is of the essence.'

'I know.'

'So can you give me some more information?'

Susan White was about to blurt something out, but she held back. There were data protection issues involved. She couldn't just discuss a patient's details over the phone with a complete stranger, not without some sort of formal authorization.

Who was this person? Was she who she said she was? Did she have standing to receive any information at all? Maybe she was a member of one of those religious 'pro-life' organizations in the American Bible Belt. Could a nurse give out the information? Did the disclosure need some kind of authorization from the Data Protection Registrar? Or the courts? Or the patient – if indeed the patient was still alive?

Susan White had never wanted to think of herself as a 'jobsworth' – but to disclose information about a patient over the phone was truly more than her job was worth –

especially this particular patient . . . in the light of what had been done.

She took a deep breath and spoke.

'Look, I can't give out information over the phone – I mean, I'll need to speak to the Administrator—'

'But you said—'

'I'll call him at home!' She decided not to mention that she had *already* spoken to him at home – and about precisely this case. 'But in the meantime, can you tell me what information you need?'

'As much as you can give us. When she arrived. When she was discharged. What treatment she had.'

'That last bit might be the hardest.'

'If you can tell us when she arrived and left,' Juanita persisted. 'We have the date she flew to England. The medical records aren't as important as the timings and placings. And if you have her current or most recent contact details that would help massively. But it's the dates that matter most.'

'Okay, I'll speak to the Administrator and see if I can get them. What's your number?'

Juanita gave the number.

'Okay, I'll call him and get back to you.'

'Thank you. Please hurry. It really *is* a race against time.'

15:27 PDT

'Okay, if she doesn't call back in the next fifteen minutes, call her again.'

'Yes, boss.'

Juanita had called Alex while he was on his way to the Northern California Federal District Court, to brief him on what the nurse at the medical center had said. She also filled him in on what she'd found out about Edgar Olsen's son by his first marriage and the tragic accident. Alex's reaction to Jimmy Olsen's death had been that it was interesting but almost certainly irrelevant.

The District Court was in fact right next door to the governor's San Francisco office. Alex and Nat were going in separate cars this time, so that afterward one could serve the restraining order while the other would be able to return to the office or remain at the court, depending on subsequent developments.

Alex debated with himself whether to call the governor. There was a doctrine – favored by most DAs and not a few judges – that last-minute evidence of this kind should be addressed by gubernatorial clemency rather than tying up valuable court time. But the governor had made an offer contingent upon Burrow revealing the whereabouts of the body.

Alex thought that he wouldn't have much luck if he went back to the governor with a new appeal for clemency based on such radically different grounds as a claim of innocence based on new evidence. It would call for quite a mental adjustment from the governor. When they had met in the morning, the tacitly agreed premise was that Burrow was guilty. Now Alex was moving to the view that he might very well be innocent. It still wasn't a strong conviction, but it was growing inside him.

The response from the clinic seemed to confirm their suspicion that Dorothy had got there. But even if she had, she might still have been killed afterward. The fact was that she had vanished off the face of the earth and there was still strong circumstantial evidence that she had been murdered.

At this stage all they could prove was that she was *planning* to go to London. Until they got something in *writing* from the clinic, there was nothing to prove – in court – that she *had* got there. The statement over the phone to Juanita would not be admissible. And even if Alex assured the governor that he would have the proof shortly, what good would it do him when – as far as he could say – Dorothy had still fallen off the edge of the earth after that?

Besides, Dusenbury was probably still pissed off about the leak. Even if it had been just a careless word from Burrow to a prison guard, it was still Alex's responsibility. He was not exactly in the governor's good books. Dusenbury may have been willing to spare Burrow in return for the location of the body. But if it was a case of 'Burrow is innocent – and we've got new evidence to prove it' then the governor would probably say that that was the business of the courts.

It was frustrating, but Alex realized that he'd have to wait it out.

Dvorak's *New World Symphony* rang out on Alex's iPhone.

'Hi, David. What's up?'

'I've found something else on the hard disk.'

'Tell me.'

'It's a poem.'

'A *poem*?'

'Or at least part of one.'

Alex felt a trace of irritation.

'I'm looking for evidence to prove that Dorothy Olsen went to England and you're giving me *poems*?'

'This isn't just a poem. It's something very personal and I think it might be relevant to her disappearance.'

'Why? What does it say?'

'I think it'll be better if you see it. I'll email it over.'

'Okay.'

Alex put the phone down, feeling guilty that he had snapped at his son.

15:29 PDT (23:29 BST)

Susan White had hesitated before calling the Chief Administrator. Stuart Lloyd had said he would call her back hours ago, but he hadn't. She had tried to put it out of her mind, but that call from Juanita Cortez had brought it all to the forefront again.

The phone in her hand felt cold and the clock on wall looked forbidding.

How would he react to being called at this time?

But then again he had promised to call her back and hadn't. If she disturbed him now it would surely be his own fault.

There was no alternative. A man's life was on the line and, as Juanita had told her, it was now a race against time.

Taking a deep breath, she dialed the number.

'Yes!' a female voice snapped.

'Hallo, Mrs Lloyd. It's Nurse White here. Could I speak to Mr Lloyd?'

'Do you know what time it is!'

She was about to apologize when she heard a man's voice in the background.

'I'll take it.'

There was a brief, muffled exchange and then Lloyd came on the line.

'Hallo.'

'Hallo, Stuart. It's Susan here.'

'I know. Look, I'm sorry I didn't get back to you. But the truth of the matter is we really can't tell them anything.'

'But they *called*!'

'What? Who?'

'The lawyers . . . of the man on death row. They called and asked us about Dorothy.'

'They *know*?'

'They know that she came to the medical center. They know that she had a ticket to England and that she paid money to the center.'

'How do they know?'

'They must've found records of *some* sort.'

'So what do they need *us* for?'

'They just need some sort of confirmation or proof.'

'We can't give it to them.'

'So what are we going to do?'

'All the files are on the computer so we can tell them that it's covered by the Data Protection Act.'

'But there's a human life at stake, Stuart!'

'That may be. But we have to be careful about what we give out. Aside from the data protection issue, this could open a whole can of worms about—'

'I *know* about that! So what are we going to do? Just let an innocent man die?'

'I took a look at some of the coverage on one of the American news channels. He's not so innocent.'

'It's not for us to judge. We're sitting on evidence that his lawyers need! We don't have the right to play God!'

She was breathing so heavily that only now when she held her breath did she realize that Stuart was short of breath too.

'Okay, look, what I think we should do is tell them to submit their request in writing. Then we'll try and get a lawyer to give us some advice.'

'At this time?'

'We'll wake someone up if necessary. But get them to fax us in writing *exactly* what information they need.'

'Okay. I'll call them now.'

As soon as she had broken the connection, she started dialing again: 00 1 415 . . .

'Alex Sedaka's office.'

'Hallo, is that Juanita?'

'Yes.' The voice was excited.

'It's Susan White here. Nurse White. I've just spoken to our Chief Administrator and he told me to ask you to put in a request in writing stating exactly what you want.'

'Are you . . . ?'

The voice sounded embarrassed and had trailed off.

'What?'

'Look, I'm sorry for asking it this way. But are you stonewalling us?'

Susan White didn't know what to say. This woman at the other end of the line had twigged it perfectly and it would be futile to deny it. But she wanted to help.

'I . . . I know it might seem as if we're being a bit . . .

It's just we have certain laws here to do with confidential data. You can get court orders, but it takes time.'

'Just tell me this: will we get this information in time?'

Susan White hesitated for a moment.

'I'll do my best.'

15:36 PDT

'Your Honor, the airline booking receipt clearly shows that on May 19, 1998 – less than one week before Dorothy Olsen vanished – she booked an airline ticket for London.'

Alex was speaking, while Nat sat there quietly with the documents, ready to hand them over when Alex introduced them.

'The date of the flight was the 24th of May, *just one day* after she vanished. And remember that she vanished in the evening. So she could have hidden the night before or gone to the airport.'

The District Court judge – a man in his sixties who had pretty much seen it all – looked skeptical.

'Did she take a suitcase or any baggage with her?'

'Not as far as we know, Your Honor. But she had received an inheritance from her grandfather and she had just turned eighteen less than two months before that. That would have given her enough money to buy new clothes wherever she ended up.'

The judge sighed wearily.

'Is there any evidence that she took the money? Where was this trust fund?'

'It was at a bank, Your Honor. She liquidated the trust fund a few days before she vanished and bought some expensive jewelry with the money.'

'Expensive jewelry?' the judge repeated, surprised.

'Yes, Your Honor.'

'And was any of this known at the time of the trial?'

Alex hesitated. He would have loved to answer this question in the negative. But as an officer of the court, he couldn't lie.

'It was known about the trust fund and the jewelry – including the fact that it disappeared.'

'So it doesn't qualify as new evidence.'

The judge sounded almost disappointed.

'Not the trust fund or the jewelry. But the airline booking is new. We've only just discovered that – and that was through sheer luck. There was no way we could have known it. The police or FBI should have discovered it when they quizzed the airlines. They apparently limited the search to flights from the US. It appears that she drove to Mexico and then caught the flight.'

'And what about this medical center?'

'Well there again, it was a matter of luck. We only obtained Miss Olsen's old laptop computer today. We didn't even know of its existence until today.'

'But none of this actually shows that she was on the flight. All it shows is her intentions. Maybe someone stopped her. Maybe she was trying to get away with someone.'

'My paralegal phoned the medical center. It's late at night in England, but she spoke to one of the nurses. The nurse confirmed that Dorothy Olsen was there, but for legal reasons couldn't tell us the dates or what treatment she received. We'd need a court order from a British court for that. And that'll take time, Your Honor. Probably a few days. That's why we're asking for a stay of execution.'

'What about the airline booking? How soon can you get that information?'

'If you can issue an order against them now, Your Honor, we could probably serve it on their CEO or COO tomorrow morning. But it would still take time to access the records. This was nine years ago, don't forget, and although the information would almost certainly have been saved, it might be on a back-up tape.'

'How long?'

'Well if we could give them say forty-eight hours to comply and then schedule the hearing for twenty-four hours after that . . .'

The judge was shaking his head.

'I'm not prepared to go that far. At least not at an ex parte hearing.'

'Well there's no chance of getting it today. Even if you issued the order now and we managed to serve it, they'd argue that it was too short notice to comply.'

'All right,' said the judge, returning his attention to the documents. 'I know this is your first capital case, so I assume you wouldn't try any cynical shenanigans like some old hands at this get up to. I'm going to take this at face value. I'll issue a temporary restraining order now just to be on the safe side, but I'll also schedule a hearing for both parties at quarter past four, when I'll listen to arguments from the other side. If you fail to attend the hearing for any reason, I'll rescind the TRO.'

'And the airline booking?' asked Alex, tensely.

'I'll issue two orders. One to be served on the local office, giving them three hours to comply. The other to the COO or CEO at the head office, which you'll have to fax or courier over to New York or Delaware or wherever their corporate HQ is located. I'll give them till the end of business tomorrow, say five pm.'

Nat was looking at the judge as if to ask 'why do we need both?'

'The order to the local office of the airline will almost certainly be overturned on appeal. They'll say the notice period is too short and they'll probably prevail. There's a tiny but finite possibility that they might actually comply. But I wouldn't count on it.'

Minutes later Alex and Nat were outside the court building on Golden Gate Avenue, looking pleased with themselves.

'I can't believe how easily we got it!' said Nat.

'It's too early to start celebrating. There's still that full hearing in less than an hour.'

'So who's going to serve what?'

'I'm going to serve the TRO on the warden at San Quentin. I want you to serve the order on the local airline office, then fax the other to the New York branch of Baker & Segal. Tell them to serve it on the COO or CEO, basically whoever they can get to quickest.'

'Do you want me for the full hearing?'

'Be available just in case. I might even need you to cover for me. It depends how fast I get back from San Quentin.'

'Okay.'

They split up and went to their respective cars. After Alex drove off, he put in a call to Juanita and she briefed him on her conversation with the nurse at the medical center, including her probing question to Susan White about the medical center's true intentions. Alex weighed it up in his mind.

'Do *you* think they're stonewalling us?'

There was a few seconds of silence on the other end of the line before Juanita replied.

'I wouldn't say that. I've checked up on the British Data Protection Act and it is a legal minefield.'

'My question is, do they *want* to cooperate?'

'I don't know about the Administrator; I've never spoken to him. But I think the nurse genuinely wanted to help. She sounded sincere and I think she'll try.'

'Okay, well get drafting then. Let's keep it simple. We want the date Dorothy arrived and the date she left. Ask what treatment she received, but state that this is less important than the dates. State explicitly that if the treatment details are a problem, they shouldn't delay, just ignore the question and send us the dates. We don't want to give them any excuse for delaying.'

When the call ended, Alex remembered that David had said he was going to send him the poem that he had found on Dorothy's computer. He logged on to his email account from his iPhone and found the message with the attachment already there. He clicked on the attachment and it opened:

You dragged me before the mirror
And ripped the clothes off of me
Forcing me to face the fact
That I am not, that I am not
The thing that you want me to be

Alex felt uneasy as he read the lines. To whom were these words addressed? To her tormentor? To the boy who had bullied her at school? Was this her final message to Clayton Burrow?

. . . ripped the clothes off of me

What did it mean? And who did it? Alex knew that he had to find out. And there was one person who could tell him.

15:42 PDT (23:42 BST)

By the time the fax from America started coming through, Susan White was already standing by the machine. The wording was pretty much what she had expected. She knew that she would probably get more attitude from Mrs Lloyd if she called again, but she didn't have a choice. Aside from that, Stuart had indicated that it would be all right to call him once the request came through. If she didn't call him, he wouldn't do anything: not consult lawyers, not ask for advice and not authorize her to transmit the information to Alex Sedaka's office.

This time, much to Susan's relief, Stuart answered the phone himself.

'Hi, Stuart. They've faxed over the request.'

'What does it say?'

She read it out to him.

'Okay, can you fax it over?'

'Sure. What are you going to do?'

'I'm going to have to get some legal advice.'

'Do you think you can get it quickly?'

'Look, Susan, I'll do what I can!'

She hadn't expected him to snap like that. *But was it*

191

because he was under pressure or because he didn't have
any intention of doing anything?

'Okay. I'll fax it over.'

She put the phone down and faxed it to his home.
While it was going through, the phone rang again.
Another nurse answered.

'What . . . look, I'm sorry, I don't know anything about
that . . .'

She was looking helplessly at Susan, who could hear
shouting at the other end of the line. Susan mouthed
'I'll take it,' and the other nurse handed the phone
to her.

'Hallo, who is this?'

A man's voice introduced himself, a cold, impersonal
voice with an American accent. A chill went up Susan
White's spine.

'What do you want?'

'I understand,' said the man, 'that you've received a
request to send over some information about Dorothy
Olsen to the law offices of Alex Sedaka.'

'What of it?' asked Susan defensively.

'Well I'm just calling to tell you that that would be a
breach of doctor–patient confidentiality as well as of the
Data Protection Act.'

'But there's a man on death row who's going to—'

'I know that.'

'But you can't just let him—'

'It's not for you to decide. You are not authorized to
tell them *anything*. Is that understood?'

'So . . . you're just going to let an innocent man die?'

'That's none of your concern!'

'Look . . . I know that you have the law on your side. But there's a human life at stake.'

There was silence on the other end of the line. Susan wondered what was going through the man's mind right now, what sort of inner turmoil.

'Okay, you can tell them about the abortion.'

15:48 PDT

David was feeling bothered by his father's reaction to the verse that he had discovered. It might not have been particularly relevant to their investigation, but they had to work with what they had and David had felt that having found it, it was his duty to pass it on.

However, David wasn't one to take it personally. It was just that the reaction showed what enormous stress his father was under. He had just over eight hours to save a man's life and they had found very little. In any case, his father was right. Poems were not going to help them. They needed cold, hard, solid facts – like the fact that she had bought a ticket to England, or the fact that she had downloaded a PDF brochure of a private health center in London.

What they didn't have was any proof that she had actually got there. And this kind of proof would be very hard to get from the United States. Or would it?

If Dorothy had gone to England, she would have had to use money when she got there. Unless she went to some cloistered nunnery she would have had to function in the real world. Of course she had the jewelry, but she could hardly have used that as a negotiable instrument in day-to-day transactions. The fact that she had liquidated her trust fund and bought the jewelry was moderately compelling evidence of her intention to flee. But would she have traded the jewelry for money and risked having a lot of bulky cash on her in London? Or would she have opened a new bank account where her money would be safe and readily accessible when she needed it?

The answer was probably the latter. And, given sufficient time, they could probably get court orders and search through banking records to find her. But time was of the essence. They had only discovered late in the day that she had even been *contemplating* going to England. Would the courts give them the time they needed now to prove that she actually did? Or would they take a more stubborn and intractable line, on the grounds that the defense should have done this before?

Clayton Burrow had become a pariah and the courts had shown no particular desire to give him the benefit of the doubt. Even David had little regard for Burrow. But they were now seeing faint signs that he might be innocent after all, at least of murder. He couldn't ignore that even if the courts could.

The only question was, how to make progress. Assuming that Dorothy *had* opened a bank account in London, how could they find out about it and prove it quickly? Well the first thing to do was to work out where she might have banked. The Finchley Road Medical Centre provided a useful starting point. She probably didn't know London and would likely open a bank account somewhere near where she was staying or where she had some interest.

Using Google as his first source of reference, he searched for British banks. Then, armed with a list of names, he searched for 'Finchley Road' in conjunction with various bank names.

It was the first stage of what he suspected would be a long and arduous process.

15:53 PDT

Alex was crossing the Golden Gate Bridge when the call came through.

'Hi, Juanita.'

'Hi, boss. I've got some good news and some bad news.'

'Give me the good news.'

'They told me what treatment Dorothy had at the medical center.'

'What?'

'She had an abortion.'

'An abortion?'

'That's what they told me.'

'Why would she go all the way to London for an abortion?'

'I don't know.'

'Okay, so what was the bad news?'

'They refuse to tell me anything else. They said they can't send us any written confirmation of the date she arrived or tell us the date she left.'

'So they're giving us the opposite of what we asked for.'

'I'm afraid so.'

'And they refuse to give it in writing?'

'That's what she said.'

'It doesn't make sense.'

'Maybe so, but I don't think she was lying.'

'No, I accept that, Juanita. It just seems rather strange.'

'Something's occurred to me, boss. Maybe it was Clayton who got her pregnant, maybe she tried to blackmail him.'

Alex remembered that he hadn't told Juanita about the poem.

'You think he killed her to silence her?'

'Maybe someone else killed her to protect him.'

'Like who?'

'Like his mother.'

'When I suggested that, Juanita, you ridiculed me.'

His tone was chiding.

'Okay, I'm sorry, boss. But now I'm not so sure.'

15:58 PDT

Nat felt the warm, humid air as soon as he stepped out into the open. After the air conditioned airline office, it was like stepping into a steam room.

He had just served the court order on the local office of the airline and he had to walk half a block to get to his car. He waited for almost a minute in the car while the air conditioning kicked in. Only then did he take out his cell phone and put in a call to Alex's number.

'Hi, Nat,' Alex answered.

'I served the order on the local office. They looked kind of . . . shocked.'

'Do you think they'll comply?'

'Probably not. They seemed a bit afraid, but I don't think they can. I think they couldn't get the information that quick even if they wanted to.'

'What about the other one?'

'I've got time to get it back to the office and still make it to the hearing.'

'Are you sure?' Alex asked.

'Positive. I'm only five minutes away.'

Alex knew that five minutes could mean anything

from two minutes to twenty. But he didn't want to micro-manage – especially not someone as dedicated and motivated as Nat.

'Okay, just drop it off there and let Juanita deal with it. Just make sure you're at the District Court when the ADA gets there.'

'Okay.'

Nat pressed the red button and put the cell phone in the glove compartment. As he did so, a picture fell out. Nat reached down and picked it up. He always carried the picture round with him, ever since he'd found it . . . a reminder. It was a picture of a young man, one of those spontaneous, frat party pictures where the alcohol-fueled revelry is interrupted when someone pulls out a camera and starts taking pictures. In this case, it was just a snapshot of a young man raising his glass and smiling. The previous picture in the sequence had been a reverse angle shot of the young woman who had taken this picture, evidently taken by the man. She too was smiling with delight. But that picture wasn't here now. He kept it at home.

Whether the two people loved each other or were just posing was anyone's guess. It took a bit of supplementary information to answer that one.

16:09 PDT

'A restraining order?' said the warden incredulously.

'It's only temporary. They've scheduled a full hearing at four thirty that my assistant is going to handle.'

'Then why did he issue it? The execution isn't scheduled until a minute past midnight.'

The warden didn't sound angry, just puzzled.

'I think the reasoning was that if the DA convinces him to let it go ahead then a TRO is easier to rescind than a fixed stay but, on the other hand, if *we* convince him to *halt* the execution, then the order's already in place.'

'Okay, well I'm at the mercy of the system as much as your client,' said the warden, amiably. 'I guess what happens now is in the hands of the court.'

'Yes. Look, I need to see Burrow to let him know where things stand.'

'Of course.'

A few minutes later, Alex was face to face with his client. He told him about the verse of the poem that David had found.

'A poem? You came here to ask me about a fucking *poem*?'

Burrow was incredulous.

'No, I came to see you to tell you about the temporary restraining order.'

'Which may get torn up in the next ten minutes.'

Alex just stared at him. It was like a Mexican standoff. Except that the threat and counter-threat weren't physical. In fact there was no counter-threat. Alex owed Burrow nothing but his best professional services. And it was up to his client to be honest with him.

'Did you rape her, Clayton? Is that what she's talking about?'

'You know nothing, Alex! You don't know what it was like as a kid, surrounded by friends, cheering you on every time you found an easy target.'

'I know about bullying, Clayton.'

'You don't know how easy it is, when everyone's telling you what a great guy you are!'

Clayton was visibly distressed. But he kept it at bay by shouting. He was hiding his regret behind a wall of anger. It was all he had left.

'Is that why you did it? For the plaudits?'

'What?'

'For the *approval* of your peers. You bullied her because everyone else was egging you on and giving you their approval when you did it?'

'Take a hike! Look, you're not going to save me. We both know that. So why bother? Why not just get the hell out of here and forget about me?'

'You know I can't do that.'

'Why? 'Cause I'm your client?'

'Partly.'

'I can always fire you! Then I won't be your problem any longer.'

'Yeah, you can sack me. But that doesn't mean I'm going to forget you.'

'You might as well. There'll be nothing in it for you.'

'If you're talking money, there's not a cent in it for me now. I'm doing this pro bono.'

'Well *stop*!'

'That's not the way I work.'

'You've done your best. I'll write you out a satisfied customer statement before they strap me down.'

'What are you trying to hide, Clayton?'

'To hide?' He wasn't even trying to conceal the tears anymore. 'They're going to kill me in less than eight hours – whatever that restraining order says. You think I've got something to hide?'

'No, I think you've got *nothing* to hide! . . . But I think you're trying to hide something anyway.'

'What are you talking about?'

'I think you're trying to hide something from yourself. I think you're trying to avoid facing up to what you did.'

'You think I'm a murderer? So why did you put in all this effort for me?'

'Did you rape her, Clayton?'

'*Yes I raped her!* I raped the goddamn motherfuckin' dyke bitch! And I've regretted it ever since!'

16:14 PDT (00:14 BST)

The voice changer program worked better than he'd expected. That was just as well because he didn't have the time to go out and buy one. The hardware types were probably not as good anyway. Technologically, they were never up to date. This one was dead easy to use, was free and he'd been able to obtain it without getting up from the desk in the office that they had let him use. All he'd had to do was log on to a software download site, read a few customer reviews and download the one he wanted. He didn't have to buy the full version, because he wasn't going to save any files, just change his voice as it came out the other end.

The banks in England were all closed at this time. But the major high street banks all had helplines. Some of these closed down at 20:00 or 22:00. Others worked till midnight, while a few even operated 24/7.

David was steadily working his way through these, logging on to various banking websites, phoning up using Skype, pretending – through the voice-changing software – to be Dorothy, explaining that 'she' hadn't used the account for a long time and had forgotten her log in details. If he had known at least some of the account details – like the account number or card number – he would have been able to do this online. But as he didn't have any of these details, he had to do it by phone, where the security checks were supposed to be more rigorous. Of course the reality was that they were not. And that was what he was trying to take advantage of in this exercise in social engineering.

In case after case he was being told that they couldn't find any trace of that name or account, and, once he was satisfied that that bank or branch could be eliminated, he told them that the account was over fifteen years old. The reason for this was that he had already established that if it had been left untouched for that period, the account would have become classified as a dormant account. That enabled him to end the conversation without arousing too much suspicion.

The trouble was, there was no way he could be sure of his assumption that she would have opened an account at a branch near the medical center. His reasoning was that she would probably have found a place to stay near the center and opened a bank account nearby. But what if he were wrong? What if she had found a place further out, which would have been cheaper? She could have been living anywhere in Greater London.

But he still hadn't exhausted all the banks and branches on his list of the Finchley Road area, so he wasn't on the verge of giving up. It was actually a *huge* list. Finchley Road was a long road and there were other major streets round it.

Finally, his luck started to change. He got hold of a

bank and branch, explained about 'her' old account that he thought 'she' had just used 'six years ago' – and was told by a young woman with an Indian accent that they had to go through some security checks before they could reactivate her account and give her the details.

'No problem,' said David, confident in all the information that he had assembled from Juanita for this part of the exercise.

'First of all, I need your date of birth.'

'April 1, 1980,' said David, the software disguising his voice and giving it that soft, feminine touch, enhanced by the deliberate nervousness that he was injecting into it.

'Next, I need to know your mother's maiden name.'

'Segal.'

'Finally, the answer to the security question you set yourself. The question was, "Dog's name."'

A queasy feeling gripped David's stomach and a column of heat rose up inside him. His cheeks flushed bright red. This was one question that he hadn't prepared for. He couldn't just end the conversation and then come back. That would just set off alarms. Even if he got through to a different operator at the call center, which he probably would, they might well have flagged the account by them.

He had to answer now and he had to answer correctly. But how? He didn't have a clue what her dog's name was. In fact he couldn't even imagine her owning a dog. A dog could be a friend to someone who is otherwise friendless. But David's father had told him that, according to Esther Olsen, it was Dorothy's *computer* that was her friend. She never said anything about a dog, or at least his father hadn't mentioned anything.

He had to play for time, or at least give himself an excuse for failure that would not arouse suspicions.

'I've actually had several dogs in the past ten years. I can't remember which one it was when I opened the account.'

'Well I have to have an answer before I can give you the account details and password.'

David was frantically running dogs' names through his head: Rex? Rambo? Toto?

Toto!

The dog from *The Wizard of Oz*! Dorothy's dog! It had to be.

'I think the dog I had at the time was called Toto,' he said.

'I'm afraid that's not the one I've got here.'

Damn!

Now he had blown it for sure.

'If you don't remember, we may have to do some sort of written verification. That'll only take seven working days.'

They hadn't closed the door! He still had another chance!

'I really do need it sooner if possible.'

'Can you not remember the name?' asked the girl at the call center sympathetically, as if she were almost willing 'Dorothy' on to get it right.

Why would she choose this question for a security question if she didn't have a dog? thought David. It made no sense. And then he remembered something.

The girl hadn't said 'Your dog's name' – she had simply said 'dog's name.' In other words, the name of *a* dog.

'I'm afraid I'm going to have to hurry you,' said the girl.

What name would Dorothy Olsen associate with a dog?

'*Clayton!*' David blurted out.

'That's the one,' said the girl triumphantly.

16:17 PDT

The guard outside peered in, as if concerned that Clayton's flare of anger was going to erupt into physical violence. Alex signaled him to back off. The guard sat down and returned to his newspaper.

Clayton was now avoiding the lawyer's eyes and there was a break in his voice, as if he couldn't trust his throat to hold it together.

'Do you want to tell me about it?'

He didn't *want* to talk about it, but Burrow had finally broken and they both knew that he *had* to.

'It was on April the first . . . her birthday . . . her *eighteenth* birthday. I told her it was a birthday present . . . a coming-of-age present. It was my idea of a joke.'

'I presume she didn't see the humor.'

Alex silently cursed himself for saying it. It sounded judgemental – which it was. But it was the wrong time to say it. Judgement was the one thing that Clayton was running away from.

'She didn't show any emotion at all. She begged and pleaded at first . . . and then she just stopped. Silence.

Like she didn't feel anything . . . or didn't want me to know what she was feeling.'

'That's it?'

'I think she may have been crying . . . but you know . . . like . . . crying silently.'

'And how did you feel?'

'At the time . . . or now?'

'Stop jerking my leash, Clayton.'

'I'm not—'

'You *are*!'

'At the time I didn't feel a thing. No, I *did* feel a thing: I felt *satisfaction*! I was angry. She'd got me canned, remember. I was kicked out of high school because of her. I wanted revenge.'

'So how did you do it?'

'I lured her to a construction site that night and raped her.'

'How did you lure her?'

'I told her I'd kidnapped Jonathan.'

'And she *believed* you?'

'I'd stolen his cell phone. She called the number and I answered. *Then* she believed me.'

'So you lured her to this construction site and raped her there?'

'That's right.'

'And then?'

'Then I let her go.'

'Weren't you worried that she'd go running to the cops?'

'I told her that if she did I really *would* go after Jonathan.'

'And would you have done?'

'Of course not!'

'There's no "of course" about it. You were already a rapist. Why stop there?'

'I'm not a murderer.'

'Who said anything about murder?'

'You did—'

'No, I didn't.'

'I mean, I did!' He looked embarrassed, confused. 'I mean, I threatened to kill Jonathan if she told anyone. But I wouldn't have done it.'

'Do you think she believed you?'

'I . . . I don't know.'

Clayton was trapped. To say 'yes' meant that he was a plausible murderer, to say 'no' would beg the question as to why she didn't tell anyone.

Alex stepped in to help him.

'She might have been afraid that even if you didn't kill Jonathan, you might still beat him up. You'd already done so once.'

'Yes,' Clayton rasped, his voice almost gone.

'And also, like many rape victims, she might have felt that she wouldn't be believed. You could have said that she consented.'

'I don't think so,' Clayton replied with a wry smile. 'She was a lesbian, don't forget.'

'Did other people know that?'

'It was a more or less open secret.'

'So at the time you raped her, you knew that you were raping her against her sexual preference?'

'I guess.'

'And how do you feel about it now?'

'Now . . . now . . .'

He trailed off and broke down sobbing into his hands.

Alex felt a strange mixture of pity and disgust. After a while, the sobbing subsided, but Clayton didn't look up.

'Did you know she was pregnant?'

Clayton's head rose slowly. He looked shell-shocked, but held it together well.

'Pregnant? At the time . . . when I raped her?'

'Probably not.'

'You mean I . . .'

'Yes.'

Clayton was struggling for breath, like the news had knocked the wind out of him.

'How do you know?'

'Because she had an abortion.'

'When?'

Alex had to think about this. She was raped on April 1, 1998 and she had bought the ticket to England on the 19th of May, just over six weeks later. Alex thought about the timings. If he had got her pregnant with one shot then it was probably during the most fertile time in her cycle. That would be the midpoint between periods. When she missed her next period, did she realize what had happened? Or did she try to rationalize it away? Did she have irregular periods? Or did she just *tell herself* that she did?

And then, when she missed her next period, did panic set in? Did she wait a few days to be sure? And when she finally could evade the issue no longer, what did she do? She couldn't talk to her mother. She certainly couldn't talk to her father. And she didn't have a sister.

Who else was there to talk to? Her thirteen-year-old brother? Too young. A high school friend? Did she *have* any friends? Probably not. That was the problem of the bullied child: no friends to turn to. No one to seek support or advice from. She would have had to face it alone. It must have been terrifying: the decision to have an abortion. So she booked a ticket on the 19th and flew to England the day after the prom.

But why England? There were abortion clinics all over California.

'You said this morning that you thought Dorothy was still alive and that she set you up.'

'Yes.'

'Do you really believe that?'

'I don't know. I guess I was just clutching at straws. But I didn't kill her.'

'Do you think the rape was her motive? For setting you up, I mean?'

'Why? You starting to believe me?'

'What if I were to tell you that we have evidence that Dorothy was alive the day after she vanished? That she went to London on Sunday the 24th of May, the day after the prom.'

Clayton looked at Alex, hesitantly.

'"What if?" Is that one of those mind games, like the cops play?'

'No, it's not a mind game – and it's not a hypothetical. We *have* such evidence. She went to London and had an abortion.'

Alex was watching carefully to see how Clayton reacted. As things stood now, they knew that she had made it to London, because the nurse had told Juanita that Dorothy had had an abortion. But they knew nothing of what had happened to her after that.

'Well if you know that, can't you take it to the courts? To the governor?'

All of a sudden, Clayton seemed full of hope, as if he had not only a second chance at life but also a purpose to live. It pained Alex to know that he had to shoot down those hopes, or at least temper them with a dose of realism.

'We *are* going to the courts. But it's not quite as simple as that. We can show that she went to England and had an abortion. But we don't know what happened next. She might have come back to America and tried to blackmail you.'

'That's garbage!'

'It's what the DA will suggest. And the next thing he'll say is that you might have killed her to silence her.'

He met Clayton's eyes, monitoring them for a reaction.

16:21 PDT

The DA's office had felt that they owed Martine Yin a favor for blowing the lid on Dusenbury's clemency offer. So they decided to return the favor and let her know about the TRO.

It didn't really help their cause. Those who wanted Burrow dead wanted him dead regardless of any District Court decisions and those who opposed the death penalty weren't going to change either.

But it made strategic sense to keep Martine Yin onside – especially after Sedaka had alienated her with his boorish reaction to her attempt to get a quote from him as he left his office.

So the clerk who had taken the call from his counterpart at the District Court – acting on his own initiative and hoping that it would win him a few brownie points from his masters – put in a quick call to Martine. He had got the cell phone number from the TV station after introducing himself, and he got through to Martine herself within seconds.

'Martine Yin,' said the woman on the other end.

'Oh, er,' he stuttered nervously. 'Is that Martine Yin?'

'Yes,' she said impatiently.

'I'm calling from the DA's office. I was wondering if you got the news about the temporary restraining order.'

Martine was an old pro who was used to people trying to excite her with the promise of big news.

'What temporary restraining order?' she asked, her tone level.

'The Federal District Court granted it just over half an hour ago.'

Martine listened to the details with growing excitement.

16:24 PDT

The girl at the call center had told David that the details would be sent to 'her' last stored email address. That was no problem for David as he already had the account details and the password. When he had hacked into the Compuserve account with the security questions, the first thing he had been required to do was reset the password to something memorable. He had set it to '1eibbeD' which was 'Debbie1' backward. It was his idea of a little joke at his big sister's expense.

So now it was with excitement that he logged on and typed in the password. But a second after hitting the 'Enter' key he got the shock of his life when he was greeted by the words 'Incorrect password or User ID.'

How the hell could that be?

16:27 PDT

'Silence her?' Burrow echoed. 'That's ridiculous.'

'Is it? The legal issue isn't whether it did happen, but whether it *could* have happened. We can show that she was still alive for a short period after she vanished. We can even show that she went to another country of her own accord. But that still doesn't prove that you didn't kill her. And it *certainly* doesn't prove that she framed you.'

Clayton was still struggling to make sense of it all.

'But the whole basis of the prosecution's case was that I killed her *on the night she vanished* and buried the body that same night! They implied that I was jealous on the night of the prom while she went to celebrate and I was out in the cold.'

'That may have been the *implied* motive. And given sufficient time we could argue that this new evidence undermines the entire basis of the prosecution's case. But time is the one thing we haven't got. And the courts don't usually like last-minute appeals like this.'

'But it's like a basic flaw in the prosecution! I mean, it just blows a hole in their case.'

'It would if we had it in writing.'

'What do you mean?'

'We've got evidence on a computer that she booked a ticket and paid a London clinic for the abortion. And we've got an *oral statement* from a nurse confirming that she *had* the abortion. But we haven't yet got the passenger manifest to show that she actually *boarded* the flight. And the nurse can't give us anything in writing to confirm that Dorothy had the abortion. It's just an oral statement over the phone at this stage.'

'*Why* can't the nurse give us it in writing? I mean, surely they must have some records of the abortion in England.'

'They do, but they also have certain bureaucratic obstacles. We may be able to get the records in time, but there are no guarantees.'

Clayton's breath was slowing down.

'So why did you come here?' The tears were about to start again. 'To raise my hopes and then smash them against the rocks?'

Alex had to think about this. Why *had* he come here? Was it just to ask about the rape that he'd suspected from the poem? Or was there more to it than that? Some nagging doubt in his own mind?

'I need your help, Clayton. I need to understand some things.'

'Like what?'

'Like, why me?'

'I don't understand.'

'How did I get to be running the final stages of your appeal? A one-man band with no track record in capital cases.'

219

Burrow shrugged his shoulders helplessly.

'What do you mean? I thought you wanted the case.'

'I *did* want the case. It was an important matter of principle and I was ready to give it my all – using other firms in DC and elsewhere to fill the gaps. But why did you *choose* me? Why did *you* want me? There were other law firms lined up to take it – *big* law firms, *prestigious* law firms. You could've had your pick. Yet you chose me. I mean, I'm flattered, but I still don't understand why.'

Burrow appeared to be struggling to remember, like it was some distant, faded memory that no longer mattered to him.

'Well . . . I didn't know much about you. But I think some other prisoner recommended you. I only have limited association with other prisoners, but I'm not completely isolated. Some other prisoner recommended you . . . and what did *I* know about law firms? I needed advice and someone offered it.'

'Do you remember his name? The prisoner?'

Alex was wondering which of his clients was currently in San Quentin.

'Not really.'

'Did he say he was my client?'

'No. But he said he'd seen you on TV. You'd just won some big case, remember. Some drug dealer's girlfriend had got a long stretch because of her boyfriend. And you took the case to appeal and blew the prosecution apart.'

'Estella Sanchez.'

It was a statement not a question.

'But you didn't hear about the case directly . . . someone told you, someone recommended me?'

'That's right.'

'But you don't remember who?'

'I don't think he ever told me his name. In this place you don't always use names. He was just the guy in the cell next to mine.'

Alex nodded. There was nothing sinister in it. Just one prisoner trying to help another with a bit of advice. And Alex happened to be the man of the moment, because of his success in the Sanchez case.

But there was still another question nagging away at Alex.

'In the poem, Dorothy said: "You dragged me before the mirror / And ripped the clothes off of me." Do you know what she meant by that?'

'I guess I ripped her clothes off.'

'You "guess"?'

Alex was beginning to get a bit irritated with Clayton's 'guessing.' But then again, he realized that Clayton wasn't trying to run away from morality as such, merely from moral judgement. It was too late to take back what he had already done. All he could do was run away from moral condemnation. But the worst condemnation – the most damning judgement – came from his own conscience. Thus it was from his own conscience that he was fleeing.

'I mean, I did.'

'But what about the mirror?'

'I don't know.'

'Was there a mirror where you raped her?'

'No . . . it was in a shed.'

'So, when you raped her, you didn't drag her in front of any mirror?'

221

'No.'

Alex looked into Clayton's eyes and knew that he was telling the truth. So what the hell was Dorothy talking about in the poem?

16:31 PDT

David was frantically trying to regain access to Dorothy's Compuserve account, checking and double checking that the Caps Lock key was off and that he was typing carefully.

Could I have mistyped the password? he wondered. *Quite possibly. I was terribly excited after all.*

He realized that there was only one thing to do. He had to go through the same rigmarole again: gain access through the security questions and reminders.

The date of birth and mother's maiden name questions came up and he answered them. But when the third security question came up it was no longer asking for the name of the high school, it wanted 'Dog's name.'

She set up several security questions here, David thought. *The system cycles through them at random.*

Smiling, he typed in 'Clayton' and found the email containing the user ID and password reminders for the bank. He made a note of them and then logged out.

Next stop, the bank.

He logged on with the user ID and password and started poking round. There weren't too many transactions.

She had started the account with fifty-five thousand pounds sterling. But then he scrolled down to see what she had spent it on.

Sure enough, the Finchley Road Medical Centre was listed. But it wasn't their name that surprised him. It was something else entirely.

16:34 PDT

'None of this proves that Dorothy Olsen is alive or even that she survived the night of her disappearance.'

The ADA who was addressing the judge was a woman in her late twenties; dark-haired and smartly dressed, she could have been Martine Yin's older sister, except that she went a little bit lighter on the makeup to underplay rather than exaggerate her femininity. In her line of work, emphasizing her femininity might seem too blatant a ploy, whereas playing it down enabled her to cash in on her appearance, even while appearing not to.

'We concede that she reserved the flight. But that doesn't prove that she boarded it. We concede that money was paid out of her account to a medical center. But that doesn't prove that she was the one who paid it.'

Dawn Henderson was one of several ADAs in the sex crimes unit of the DA's office. Although her tone was quiet, her manner and tenacity were as intense as that of any man and she fought her corner like a seasoned pro.

Nat rose to speak.

'Your Honor, most people who book or reserve airline

flights subsequently board those flights. Not to do so would be the exception. In that sense it is more probable than not that she boarded.'

He was there alone, because Alex was on his way back from the prison. It was ironic that, having served the restraining order on the warden of the prison, Alex was not there to argue the case in person when the restraining order was in danger of being overturned.

'That might be the case if viewed in isolation,' Henderson responded. 'But the fact that Miss Olsen was never seen again suggests that it is more probable that she did *not* board the flight.'

'Your Honor, while that may be true of the airline reservation and the payment from Miss Olsen's bank account, the same cannot be said of the information we obtained from the Finchley Road Medical Centre itself. They confirmed that Miss Olsen was indeed a patient at the center and that she had an abortion there.'

He sat down and again Dawn Henderson rose.

'But this is entirely hearsay. Counsel hasn't even brought along the secretary who allegedly spoke to the medical center—'

'She's covering the phones! We're a small law firm.'

'Or brought along a notarized statement from her.'

'She's a paralegal and I would have thought that on this point at least Counsel would trust the ethics of a professional colleague, whatever her personal views.'

'Even if we accept that this Miss . . .'

'Cortez.'

'. . . Cortez was telling the truth, what does that prove? She spoke to a person on the phone who *claimed* to be a member of staff at the medical center. This person claimed to be a nurse, not a member of the administrative staff or someone who was likely to have access to the records – and remember this case occurred some nine years ago. How do we know Miss Cortez really got through to the medical center? How do we know that the person she was talking to was telling the truth? And if she was telling the truth, so what? The airline reservation showed that Miss Olsen went there in May 1998. Even if she had the abortion a month later that still only pushes her death back a month.'

The judge – the same man who had granted the temporary restraining order – turned to Nat.

'She does have a point there.'

'That's why we're trying to get the records from the medical center. But they're eight hours ahead of us. It's the middle of the night there. It's impossible to get this sort of information out of hours – especially in England where they have very strict privacy and data protection laws.'

'Then why was it left so late in the day?' asked Henderson. Her manner was truculent, her tone accusatory. Alex had warned him that she would give no quarter.

'As we explained at the earlier hearing, we only found out about it because we have a computer expert who was able to recover deleted files from Dorothy Olsen's computer. And the only reason we have that computer is because Mrs Olsen gave it to us.'

'Why didn't they ask her to give it to them earlier, Your Honor?' asked the ADA contemptuously.

'We didn't even know of its *existence*. And the first time we ever met Mrs Olsen was today at the governor's office. Look, let me stress again that the important thing here is that not only do we have written evidence that Dorothy Olsen was *intending* to go to England, but we have oral evidence that she went there and had an abortion. Yes, I admit that at this stage – at such short notice – we haven't got it in writing. But even with this time difference between London and California, we were able at least to obtain oral confirmation. And given a little more time we're confident that we can get it in writing.'

The judge turned to the ADA.

'That does seem reasonable, doesn't it, Miss Henderson?'

'Again we're moving away from the big picture here. All this evidence proves is that Dorothy Olsen was alive for a short period after she vanished. With the operative words being: "a short period." No way does that prove that she's still alive and no way does that prove that Clayton Burrow didn't kill her.'

Nat took a deep breath.

'Your Honor, the People's case was based on certain implicit assumptions. Chief among them was the assumption that Dorothy Olsen had no plans to leave or vanish or run away and that she was either killed round about the time that she vanished or that she was kidnapped at that time and then killed a short while later. If we can show that she not only was not killed or kidnapped at that time but that she went to a foreign country and had an abortion, that suggests that the key presumptions of the prosecution case were wrong. Yet it was on a basis of those key presumptions that my client was convicted.'

Dawn Henderson was shaking her head.

'None of these assumptions formed any part of the prosecution case, Your Honor. The prosecution case was based on rock solid *physical* evidence found in Burrow's home. There was the blood-stained knife and the victim's underwear. The knife had the victim's blood, the underwear had the accused's semen. And to top it all off they found the victim's breast tissue in the freezer at Burrow's home. It was an open and shut case based on the physical evidence found in the residential premises where Burrow lived.'

'With his mother,' Nat interjected.

Dawn Henderson turned to him.

'Oh come on. You're not going to suggest that his mother did it?'

'I'm suggesting that the case against my client was a lot less clear-cut than the prosecution implies. And the fact that we've now discovered new evidence that throws the whole prosecution timeline out of whack should at least be investigated further. All we're asking for is *three days*.'

'All right,' said the judge. 'I've heard enough.'

Both Nat and Dawn looked at him anxiously.

16:38 PDT

Juanita was sitting in the office feeling inadequate and wondering what else she could do. Nat must by now be in court, arguing the case against the DA. Alex had gone off to San Quentin to talk to Burrow and David was working on recovering more data from Dorothy's hard drive.

She had faxed the District Court order over to Baker & Segal in New York to serve on the airline, ordering them to produce the passenger manifest. But for Juanita, there was very little now to do.

She had spent the last half hour turning over theories in her mind. Currently she was moving increasingly toward the theory that Clayton's mother did it. When Alex had first proposed the idea, it had seemed unlikely. But now it seemed a lot more plausible. Dorothy's pregnancy already added a new dimension to it and, when Alex had told her about the rape, things really started to fall into place.

The house was shared and the space under the floorboards where most of the evidence was found was already there. So it was natural that Sally Burrow would hide the evidence there. According to Nat she wasn't the brightest button and she probably thought that it was easier to dump the evidence there than to dispose of it. Dorothy had probably tried to blackmail Clayton with the evidence that she'd preserved and Sally Burrow had probably found out and murdered Dorothy to protect her son. Her claim now that she had disowned her son was probably just a pretence. And Clayton Burrow for his part was probably protecting his mother.

But there were some things that didn't make sense. Why the mutilation of the body? It might have been to give the police the impression that it was a sex crime by a maniac and not an attempt to silence a potential accuser. But why then was the body never found? The disappearance of the body would imply deliberate concealment. But then why retain the body parts? Why not dispose of them?

Suddenly Juanita found herself gripped by a thought that was even more sinister.

Maybe her relationship with her son was even more complicated. Maybe she retained the evidence in order to give her a hold over her son. Maybe there was some incestuous attraction. That might explain the bad blood between them now. I mean, what if it finally dawned on Sally Burrow that Clayton didn't reciprocate her perverted love? It would be a case of . . . what was that phrase Nat had used? . . . 'heaven hath no rage like love to hatred turned.'

But there was something else that didn't make sense: why would Dorothy use the evidence for blackmail rather than just to bring Clayton to trial? Could the semen-stained panties be used to support a successful prosecution? If so, then why not do so? Why try to blackmail him? Indeed, what would be the point of blackmailing him? He was the only son of a deadbeat, trailer-trash mother, whereas Dorothy came from a family with money. She'd inherited eighty-six thousand dollars from her grandfather. What could she possibly hope to get out of Burrow through blackmail?

So maybe it wasn't blackmail for money. Maybe Dorothy was trying to make him squirm . . . to make him suffer as he had made *her* suffer. But then Sally Burrow found out and killed Dorothy to protect her son and tried to make it look like a sex killer – hence the mutilation. Then Sally Burrow told Clayton what she had done, thinking that this, at last, would drive him into her arms and satisfy her sick lust for her son.

But he didn't want that . . . didn't want her in that perverted way and hadn't wanted her to kill Dorothy. Maybe he was already feeling guilty . . . guilty that he had made Dorothy suffer and guilty that he had inadvertently brought about her death. Or maybe he just feared that he would become a suspect. So he went back to where his mother had told him she had killed Dorothy and moved the body and buried it so it wouldn't be found. And he thought he was safe.

But he didn't know that his mother had retained the other evidence. And in her anger at what she saw as her son's betrayal, she phoned the police, disguised her voice and tipped them off about the evidence. She couldn't reveal where the body was buried because she didn't know. But she could tip them off about the evidence that she had retained. The rest was history: the police raid, the discovery of the evidence, the arrest, trial and conviction.

There wasn't any hard evidence for it – other than as an alternative interpretation of the evidence against Clayton. But as a theory, it was complete and consistent! It even explained Sally Burrow's volatile reaction to Nat's tough questions. It wasn't that she felt insulted at the suggestion that she had turned her son into a murderer: it was the fear of a guilty person at the prospect of being found out. She knew that close questioning might lead Nat to the answer and she feared saying something that might give her away. So, after she couldn't drive him away with her initial hostility, she seized upon the first excuse for an argument to chase him out of her home and up the street.

To Nat, Sally Burrow was just an ignorant redneck, no better than her son. But Nat was a man. He didn't always see things clearly. Juanita understood the Sally Burrows of this world. Clayton's mother was a devious woman who used her cunning to protect her son in the hope that it would bring him to her bed and when that failed she punished him for that rejection by framing him for the murder that *she* had committed.

But Clayton, for his part, still felt guilty that he had brought about the whole calamity and in this final, desperate, last-minute effort to salve his conscience, he resolved to take the rap and become the sacrificial lamb.

That was the theory. The question was, could they prove it? The answer was . . . that the answer was out of their hands. Now all they could do was hope that one of their lines of inquiry would yield some results.

Just then, the phone rang. Nat's name flashed up on the display.

'Hi, Nat.'

'Bad news.'

'Oh shit!'

'I'm sorry. I fought like a tiger, but so did the DA.'

'Did the judge say why?'

'He babbled for two minutes, but ultimately it boiled down to res judicata.'

'Did you tell Alex?'

'Not yet. I haven't been able to reach him. Anyway, I'm on my way back. Look, Juanita . . . I'm sorry.'

'It's not your fault. You did your best.'

'Then why don't I feel I did?'

'Don't blame yourself, Nat.'

'I'd better tell Alex.'

'Okay, bye.'

They ended the call and Juanita sat there for a long time, not moving. The phone rang again.

'Alex Sedaka's office.'

'Hi this is the Idylwood Care Center. Is it possible to speak to Alex Sedaka?'

Juanita tensed up.

'He's not in the office at the moment. I'm his paralegal. May I take a message?'

'I'm calling on behalf of Esther Olsen. I'm afraid I have some bad news.'

16:41 PDT

If Clayton Burrow can't tell me about this 'mirror' business, then maybe Jonathan Olsen can.

Alex had just passed the Paradise Drive exit for Corte Madera on his right and was painfully aware of the passage of time. The phone rang.

'Hi, Nat.'

'I'm afraid it's bad news.'

'Fuck!'

'My thoughts exactly,' said Nat.

'Look, I'll be back at the office asap, but there's something I've got to do first.'

They left it at that. Alex wasn't normally one to swear. But he felt the shock and pain and anxiety about the deadline now looming before him. And there was only so much he could do in so short a time.

It wasn't that he didn't have enough hands to do the work, it was just that he was no longer sure what else he should be doing. He had never handled a capital case before and he couldn't escape the feeling that there were other things that he ought to be doing that he had not yet done.

Of course, he knew that one isn't supposed to leave anything till the last minute so the fact that he had little more to do was a good sign. It meant that all the important and proper things had been done already. It wasn't really a case of him forgetting something: it was a case of him having done all that could be done and there being nothing else left to do.

But the thought of spending Burrow's last day doing nothing troubled him.

However, there was still one lead to follow and that was the one his son had provided with that brief extract of poetry from Dorothy's computer. This new line of inquiry was quite promising. Dorothy couldn't confide in her mother and didn't have any friends, so she confided in her computer in much the same way as Anne Frank had confided in her diary.

But the trouble was that David's progress in getting information off the hard disk was painstakingly slow. And some of the things he found were quite cryptic. So Alex needed an interpreter. But what interpreter could there be when the whole point of talking to the diary was to make up for her inability to talk to anyone else?

Alex reasoned that even if she didn't confide in other people, there was one person who might be able to provide some insight into the way her mind was working at the time; and that was her brother Jonathan.

It was for this reason that Alex was driving to Daly City now. Of course there was no guarantee that Jonathan would cooperate. But it was worth a try.

It was then that the phone in the hands-free cradle started flashing and blaring out Dvorak's *New World*

Symphony. The name in the display said 'David.' Alex felt a stab of hope as he answered.

'Hey, Dad, listen! I've found her bank account in England!'

'What?' he asked.

'She opened a bank account in London!'

'Great! We've got to get a court order for it before—'

'There's no need! I've hacked into it!'

'What do you mean? I mean, *why*?'

Alex hadn't asked him to do that. He would never ask *anyone* to do anything illegal, let alone his son.

'So that we can get proof that she got there. Opening a bank account and conducting bank transactions proves that.'

'I didn't ask you to do that! It's blatantly illeg—'

'Yes, I know! It's illegal. And you didn't ask me and I didn't tell you I was going to do it beforehand. So you're in the clear and I'm ready to put it in writing.'

Alex was angry.

'It's not as simple as that. I'm an officer of the court. I'm not allowed to sanction an illegal act, even *after* the fact. I'll probably have to report what you told me – even though you're my son. I may even be compromising my position by continuing this conversation. I shouldn't be allowed to derive benefit from the information.'

'Look, let's not pussyfoot round, Dad! You've got a client on death row and time is of the essence. So let's save the recriminations for later!'

Alex felt the force of his son's reciprocal anger. In any case, David was right. Saving the client *was* the highest priority. And the dilemma wasn't quite as bad as Alex had implied. Ethically he *was* allowed to derive benefit for his client once he had heard what David had said, but he was *also* obliged to report his son's illegal act at the first reasonable opportunity thereafter. The only admissions of illegal acts that he could keep to himself – and indeed *had to* keep to himself – were those made by his client referring to acts that had taken place in the past.

'Okay, you hacked in. I won't ask you how. But did you find anything – anything useful, I mean?'

'I sure did. I basically phoned the bank helpline using voice-changing software and pretended to be—'

'I said I didn't want to know *how*!'

'Okay, I'm sorry. But I found something that I think may be relevant.'

'Spill it!'

'After the date when she was supposed to have gone to England, she made a *whole series* of payments to the Finchley Road Medical Centre at various intervals over the next year or so.'

'What sort of amounts are we talking about?'

'Well it was a few thousand at a time – the two biggest of which were ten thousand British pounds each.'

'*Ten thousand?*'

Alex was in shock.

'Yes.'

'So how much was the total?'

'I added it up and it came to about forty thousand British pounds.'

'Holy shit!'

'I hope it helps,' said David, after a brief pause.

'It does and it doesn't.'

'What do you mean?'

'Well first of all, if I use it then it'll mean you'll have to admit to what amounts to committing a criminal offense.'

'If it'll save an innocent life, I'm ready to take my chances, Dad. Maybe I can get away with it because it was in England. They're not likely to extradite me.'

Alex smiled. David was so much like his mother, emotional but fully committed to helping others. Ironically, Debbie was like her father, only more so: professionally ambitious and ego-driven. The truth of the matter was David could be tried for the offense in the US, because he had logged on from the US. But Alex didn't want to worry him by telling him that now.

'I'll need you to print it out and fax it over to my office asap. I'll call Juanita and tell her to expect it.'

'Okay, I'll do it right away. There's just one thing, Dad.'

'Yes?'

'You said it does help and it doesn't. What did you mean by that?'

Trust a scientist to pick up on the minutiae!

'It means that it doesn't make sense. The nurse at the clinic told us that Dorothy had an abortion. Since when does it cost forty thousand pounds sterling for an abortion!'

'I can think of a few theories,' said David.

'Like what?'

'Maybe she paid them to let her take the identity of a dead patient. Or, maybe it was to disguise her appearance with plastic surgery so the new identity would work. Then again, maybe they were blackmailing her over something.'

'We're getting a little paranoid here, aren't we, David?'

'I can think of something even more paranoid. How do we know that she was transferring the money at all? Maybe she was dead? Maybe they brought in a ringer to milk her account.'

16:45 PDT

'Alex Sedaka's office.'

'Hi, Juanita.'

'Oh hi, boss.'

'Listen, you remember that quip you made about Clayton having a face transplant for the school yearbook?'

'What about it?'

'I'm beginning to think you may have been on the right track.'

'Are you bullshitting me?' she asked, not troubling to hide the irritation in her voice.

'I don't mean Clayton: I mean Dorothy.'

He quickly filled her in on what David had told him about the payments to the medical center and the various theories that went with it.

'So what, now you think she had some sort of plastic surgery to disguise herself so that she could resume life under a new identity?'

'It's possible.'

'Only in Hollywood,' she said skeptically.

He wondered if she meant action movies, or real-life aging actors trying to extend their careers. However, now wasn't the time to discuss the movie industry. What mattered was the evidence that Dorothy was alive at least a year after her disappearance.

'Look, David is going to fax over the paperwork to you.'

'It's coming through even as we speak, boss. I can see it on the machine.'

'Okay, what I want you to do is get Nat to sprint over to the District Court with it for another TRO petition – and I want you to phone the clerk to let them know he's on his way.'

'But would it make any difference after the last time?'

'*Yes*, because these are transactions *after* she vanished and was presumed dead! Also, the payments are to a business in England – the very place that she bought that airline ticket to. That means she went there and spent money there – long after she was supposedly dead.'

'Shall I tell them to put your "face off" theory into the petition?'

Alex was amused by the mockery. He realized that she was just trying to relieve her own tension.

'Just the facts, ma'am – just the facts.'

'Okay.'

'Then, when you've done that, put in another call to the clinic in London. Try and talk to the same nurse you've been talking to and tell her that we know about the large payments. Try to take her by surprise and ask her what it was for.'

'Okay, but can I ask you a serious question, boss? Do you think this is kosher?'

'Frankly I don't. Unless she had some rare form of cancer or something, I can't think of any reason for her to pay that kind of money. That's why we need to ask them.'

'I think David's other theory about someone milking the account is plausible.'

'You think a medical clinic would *do* that?'

'Let me put it this way, boss, your assumption that respectable professionals would never do anything dishonest is touchingly naïve.'

'Well thank you for that vote of confidence, Juanita. Anyway, let's not make any assumptions. Let's take 'em by surprise and see if they're ready to talk.'

'Okay.'

'Meanwhile I'm gonna step on it to Daly City.'

He had already told her, when he called from outside San Quentin, that he was on his way to see Jonathan.

'Oh boss, there was something else.'

'Be quick.'

He was approaching the Silva Island overpass and wanted to concentrate on driving.

'Esther Olsen has had a relapse. She was taken to the Idylwood Care Center and she's been asking for you.'

16:49 PDT (00:49 BST, August 15, 2007)

Susan White was sitting by the phone, desperately hoping against hope for a call from Stuart Lloyd. She didn't know whether he was actively dealing with the problem and trying to get legal advice or had simply forgotten about it and gone to bed.

It was quiet on the ward, on this graveyard shift, so she and the other nurses were not rushed off their feet. But they still had to remain alert. But the only thing that she could concentrate on was the telephone. She wanted to phone Stuart to find out how things were progressing, but she didn't dare. If he was working on it, he would feel insulted and, if he had gone to bed, he wouldn't take kindly to being woken up at ten to one in the morning.

But a man's life was at stake. And she was reduced to sitting here on the sidelines waiting for permission from others to do the right thing.

She was tempted to jump the gun and just fax them the information. But it wasn't as easy as that. The information was on a password regulated computer. She couldn't just access the files even if she wanted to. There was a hard copy – some of the original notes were even handwritten – but this too was secured under lock and key. She would have to break into a filing cabinet to gain access to it.

And breaking locks wasn't exactly her specialty.

She told herself that she would do it if she could be sure that it would help. But she couldn't even be sure of that. She didn't know anything about the legal procedures in America and she could end up ruining her career, getting a criminal record and still not managing to save the innocent man whose life hung in the balance.

She nearly jumped out of her skin when the phone finally rang. She answered, hoping to hear Stuart's voice on the other end.

'Hallo, is that Nurse White?'

It was the woman from the law firm in America. Susan felt a stab of disappointment.

'Yes.'

'First of all I was wondering about your efforts to get the legal go-ahead to send us the paperwork about Dorothy Olsen's stay there.'

The hesitation was palpable.

'I'm afraid not. We're still waiting for clearance. But you have to understand it's very difficult at the moment. It's after midnight here.'

'Okay, but you are still trying?'

'Oh yes.'

This time there was no hesitation. Susan felt guilty about lying. But she didn't know what else to do.

'Thank you. And if you fax us the paperwork for the *whole* year – not just the abortion – we'd be grateful.'

Susan broke out in a sweat.

'What do you mean the whole year?'

'Well she was there for a whole year, wasn't she?'

'Who told you that?'

'She paid over forty thousand British pounds . . . over the course of a year.'

'That doesn't mean she was . . .'

Susan knew that she had already said too much. But she realized how desperate these people were, and understandably so. She wanted to help, but her hands were tied. Finally, she decided to spill her guts. If she couldn't tell them the whole truth, the least she could do was stop wrong-footing them with vain hope.

'Look . . . I'm sorry if I've messed you around. But I don't think my boss is doing anything about it. I think he's decided that there's nothing he can do. I mean . . . I think he's probably just gone to bed.'

'To *bed*?'

'I'm sorry.'

'So you're just gonna let our client die?'

'Look, it's not my decision!'

'I'm sorry. I didn't mean to attack you.' Juanita's voice was conciliatory. 'Could you at least tell us . . . even if you can't send anything in writing?'

'I've already told you: she had an abortion.'

'Yes, but we have conclusive evidence that she paid you forty thousand pounds sterling – I mean, she paid the medical center.'

'I can't confirm or deny that,' the nurse replied timidly.

Juanita was gentle in her response.

'You don't have to. We already know it. What we need to know is, what was that money for?'

'I can't tell you.'

Susan felt for Juanita. She could understand her help-lessness. She couldn't even blame her for trying emotional blackmail. But it was clear that the sympathy game had gone as far as it could go.

Juanita spoke again.

'Look . . . what if we could obtain the consent of Dorothy Olsen's mother . . . or her brother . . . or even both?'

The seconds ticked by.

'It wouldn't make any difference. There's nothing I can do.'

'I don't understand. Surely if we can obtain the consent of Dorothy Olsen's surviving relatives—?'

'There's *nothing* I can do!'

There was silence on both ends of the line.

'Okay. Well thank you anyway.'

Juanita knew that there was no point flogging a dead horse. But she wondered why Nurse White had suddenly turned so hostile . . . and then so . . . guilty.

16:53 PDT

'First of all, thank you for agreeing to see me.'

Alex was in Jonathan's living room, the room that looked like a shrine in honor of Dorothy. As he looked round, he felt the full measure of Jonathan's obsession. But he wondered if such an obsession could have gone sour. Could love have turned to hate?

'Well I reckon if I could drop in on you at short notice, you have the right to do the same with me. And I assume it's something important.'

To Alex this was a conversation filler: obviously it was important when a man was just seven hours away from execution for the murder of Jonathan's sister.

'Look, I'll come right to the point. Did you know about the rape . . . at the time, I mean?'

Jonathan looked only marginally stunned by the question.

'Yes,' he said reluctantly. 'She told me.'

'You would have been . . . what? Fourteen?'

'Thirteen, nearly fourteen, I guess.'

'And she told you? Or you found out some other way?'

'She told me. She came to the house in tears. She was crying quietly because she didn't want Mom to hear.'

'Why? Was she sleeping?'

'No, nothing like that. She just didn't want to tell Mom. She didn't want to talk to Mom. She'd got to the stage that she hardly talked to Mom at all. They were like strangers in the same house.'

'Did your mom try and talk to her? To break the ice?'

'She made a few half-hearted attempts. But I guess things had already gone too far by then.'

'*What* had gone too far?'

'What do you mean?'

'What was the cause of the problem? What was it that had driven them apart?'

Alex remembered that Jonathan had avoided this subject when they had talked in his office.

'It's something I don't talk about.'

'Any particular reason?'

Jonathan looked at him with anger and then broke into a smile.

'If I tell you *why* I don't want to talk about it, then I'd be talking about it. You never stop being a lawyer, do you?'

'I'm a lawyer 24/7.'

He waited for Jonathan to say more. But the look on Jonathan's face showed that he had said all he was going to say.

'It must have been hard for you.'

'What?'

'The rape of your sister.'

'Hard for *me*?'

249

'Well I mean, thirteen years old . . . the only person in the world your sister could turn to.'

'I don't think I was old enough to realize how serious it was. I mean, I knew what rape meant, but there's a difference between factual knowledge and emotional knowledge.'

Alex nodded approvingly at Jonathan's insight.

'You were very close to her, weren't you?'

'Like you said . . . I was the only person in the world she could confide in.'

Alex was wondering if the rape had undermined this bond between them. She was no longer pure. Someone else had 'had' her. Did that matter to Jonathan? Could he have killed her to stop anyone else having her?

'Your mother gave me Dorothy's computer. We've been looking at the contents.' Jonathan looked surprised. 'It had been wiped, but my son has been able to recover deleted files using a scanning tunneling microscope at Berkeley.'

He was monitoring Jonathan's face for a reaction.

'Interesting.'

The tone was as non-committal as the words, but Alex sensed that Jonathan was afraid.

'And one of the things we've found is a poem.'

'A *poem*?'

Jonathan was smiling with apparent curiosity. Alex sensed that he was toying with him.

'Yes. It read: "You dragged me before the mirror / And ripped the clothes off of me." We thought that the words "ripped the clothes off of me" had something to do with the rape. But we didn't understand the words:

"You dragged me before the mirror." I was wondering if you might know what that meant?'

Alex noticed that Jonathan was avoiding his eyes.

'I haven't a clue,' he replied. But there was a break in his voice. Alex sensed that he was getting somewhere.

'We also have evidence that she went to England.'

'To *England*?'

'Yes.'

Jonathan turned away.

'I didn't know it was to England. Your secretary – Juanita – told me she'd bought an airline ticket to somewhere, but she didn't know where to.'

'Well it was to England, to London in fact . . . to have an abortion.'

Jonathan whirled round.

'*Really?*'

'Yes.'

'Any other information you want to drop on me?'

'Yes . . . she paid the clinic forty thousand pounds sterling.'

He had been watching Jonathan's face carefully, monitoring it for the slightest of reactions and for a fraction of a second he thought he saw a fleeting smile. But it was gone in an instant.

16:57 PDT

'We're back outside San Quentin prison,' said Martine Yin into the microphone, 'where crowds are beginning to gather ahead of the impending execution of Clayton Burrow. As you can see behind me, two groups have formed: one to show their support for the murder victim and voice their approval of the forthcoming execution; the other to protest against not only this execution, but the death penalty in general.'

The camera zoomed out and panned to show one group of demonstrators and then returned to Martine.

'Show us yer tits, babe!' yelled one of the prison inmates in the association room where they were watching the news report on the large TV.

'Earlier today, *Eyewitness News* exclusively revealed that the governor had offered clemency to Burrow on the condition that he reveal where he buried the body of the victim. However, there is no information to suggest that Burrow has agreed to this deal. Furthermore, a spokesman for the warden of the prison has confirmed that he has received no instructions and that plans for the execution are continuing until he is informed otherwise.'

The image of Martine talking to the camera was replaced by the shots of her unsuccessful attempt to get a statement from Alex.

'Earlier today, this reporter tried to obtain a comment from Burrow's lawyer Alex Sedaka. But Sedaka preferred to stay mute at this time.'

'Typical of a lawyer,' yelled one inmate as he watched the communal screen. 'They never talk when you want 'em to and they never shut up when you don't!'

Several of the other inmates laughed at that.

'You know, I recommended him,' said Charlie, another inmate.

A couple of the others looked at him.

'When?' shot back one.

'When I was in the cell next to him. Burrow needed a new lawyer 'cause the other firm had given up and were trying to ditch the case. So I told him to try this Sedaka guy.'

'Did Sedaka represent you?'

'No, I was represented by some wet-behind-the-ears kid from the Public Defender's office. But he told me about Sedaka. Sedaka had just won some big case with a drug dealer's broad and everyone was calling him the next big thing in criminal law.'

'And who was the kid?' asked another inmate with a cheeky grin.

'Why?'

''Cause I just want to be sure not to hire him!'

'Why?' asked Charlie irritably.

''Cause if he was any good, you wouldn't *be* here!'

The other inmates laughed. Charlie merely scowled.

'For your information he must be pretty good, 'cause he told me that he was working off his notice at the Public Defender's office and Sedaka had just hired him.'

17:06 PDT

'As my rabbi used to say to the congregation every Yom Kippur: it's nice to see you again.'

Nat couldn't fail but smile at the District Court judge's attempt at levity. He wasn't sure if most rabbis were failed comedians, or most comedians were failed rabbis.

'Yes, I know, I'm sorry but—'

'Oh don't apologize. You've got a client who's due for execution in a few hours. You've got the right to do whatever is necessary within the law.'

'Thank you, Your Honor. Basically what we've now been able to obtain are bank statements showing that Dorothy Olsen opened a bank account in London a few days after she vanished. More important, however, these statements show that she made a series of payments to the Finchley Road Medical Centre in London. This went on for more than a year *after* she vanished.'

'May I see these bank statements?'

Nat handed them over to the judge. The judge looked at them and noted the transactions highlighted with a green highlighter pen. But there was something about these statements that troubled him.

'These look like computer printouts.'

'Oh they are.'

'So these are not originals – and they're not bank-certified copies?'

'No, they're new printouts. You see, Dorothy Olsen used internet banking—'

'Did they have that in those days?'

'It's been around since the eighties but it took off in the mid-nineties.'

'How did you get these?'

'From Dorothy's online account.'

'The bank gave them to you?'

'No, Your Honor. My boss's son – David Sedaka – is a computer expert and he was able to—'

'*He hacked into the bank?*'

'Not exactly, Your Honor. Hacking directly into a bank's computer system is quite hard. But when the bank provides online banking to its customers, the weak spot is the customer themselves. You can't just hack into a bank's computer, but the bank offers online banking to customers and David Sedaka was able to obtain her user ID and password and, armed with this information, he was able to log on to Miss Olsen's bank account in England.'

'That was highly illegal and could result in federal charges.'

The judge sounded like a teacher lecturing a student who had just been caught cheating in an exam.

'We know that, Your Honor, and David Sedaka has indicated that he accepts responsibility and is ready to face the consequences. But in the meantime, the evidence exists and it does present the case in a whole new light.'

'If the State was here, they'd no doubt be arguing the fruit of the poison tree.'

'With a man's *life* hanging in the balance?'

'They can be ruthless at times,' said the judge with a smile.

'The question is, are you?' asked Nat.

'How do we know that this actually was Miss Olsen making the payments? Maybe this was some form of post-mortem embezzlement. She could have already been dead.'

'The payment went out to an established and respectable medical center. They've already confirmed that she went there for an abortion and—'

'Hold on a minute! This wasn't for an abortion!'

'We know that. And it could even be that the account *was* being milked by someone else. But that in turn could mean that she died during the procedure and they covered it and then milked her account.'

The judge looked irritated at this.

'Now we're back in the realms of speculation, aren't we?'

'Okay, I take your point, Your Honor. But the one thing we can be sure of is that money was leaving her account – *which she opened in England* – for more than *a year* after she was supposedly dead. And that suggests that she was alive during that period at least – while at the same time *choosing* not to get into contact with those she would normally have been in contact with.'

'*Suggests* it, Mr Anderson, but doesn't *prove* it.'

'True. But it does present the case in a radically new light, Your Honor.'

17:19 PDT

After his father's unexpectedly harsh reaction to his hacking into Dorothy's bank account, David decided to return his attention to the computer and the deleted data from the hard disk.

From the feedback he had received, it was clear that the poem he unveiled had caused quite a stir, notwithstanding his father's initial skepticism. The consensus now was that this was Dorothy's expression of rage toward Clayton Burrow. It had even enabled Alex to get a confession out of Burrow for the rape of Dorothy Olsen, although he still denied murder.

So it made sense for David to try and unearth the rest of the poem. It was obvious that the verse was just a *fragment* of a poem, because it had no title. Normally a writer, even an amateur, would give their literary work a title and, even if it was on their own computer, would add their name as the author.

The fact that there was nothing before or after the verse relating to it, suggested that it was a fragment from an earlier save, not the final version. But where was the rest? It was probably there, it was just a question of finding it. He thought about the words for a minute.

> You dragged me before the mirror
> And ripped the clothes off of me
> Forcing me to face the fact
> That I am not, that I am not
> The thing that you want me to be

Presumably the whole poem was written in that style. But he was a scientist not a linguist or a poetry expert. How could he search for a particular style? How could he describe the style in a computer program?

Then it hit him. The verse was addressed to someone referred to only as 'you.' The rest of the poem was probably written in the same style. So the trick was to write a program that would look for two or more instances of 'you' in close proximity! He could create a search application in C++, the very powerful, high-level language used to create fast-running programs.

In a matter of minutes the search program was running and the master program was feeding it text from the sectors of the disk platter considered to be the most likely candidates for the rest of the poem.

It wasn't long before he found another verse.

> You crushed the hope out of me
> Not in cold blood but angrily
> And only when you died

> Did I resolve the mystery
> Of your vicious assault on my dignity

More words of reproach aimed at her tormentor.

David could see that this was not just the work of the same hand but probably the same *poem* as the other verse. This was Dorothy's expression of anger and bitterness toward an enemy who had made her life a misery.

He had to tell his father. Again, he made his way to the office just outside the lab where he had left his cell phone. He had keyed in the number and was about to press the green button when something struck him. He put the phone down and went back to the computer. For a few seconds, he just stood there in front of the terminal, staring at the words on the screen.

'*Only when you died . . .*'

His father's speculation was wrong.

'Only when you *died*.'

Clayton Burrow wasn't dead.

Whoever this poem was addressed to, it was *not* Clayton Burrow.

17:27 PDT

'Alex Sedaka's office . . . hallo?'

Juanita put the phone down angrily just as Nat entered the office.

'Do you want the good news or the bad news?' he asked.

'Just spit it out, jackass!'

'They refused to grant another ex parte TRO, but they've scheduled a full hearing for eight thirty. If we're successful, they'll grant a stay of execution. The DA's been notified. We've given them copies of the bank statements, so hopefully they'll see reason and agree to reopen the case.'

Juanita smiled but then frowned.

'I'm not sure with this DA. He seems to be using the case as a résumé builder.'

Nat went into the kitchen to make some coffee.

'Do you want a cup?' he called out to her.

'Yes . . . and make it strong.'

He started making the coffee for her while she carried on typing.

'So who was it?' he asked.

'What?'

'On the phone just now.'

'What?'

'When I came in. You were talking to someone.'

'Some idiot. They keep calling and hanging up.'

'Maybe there's a problem with the line. Maybe they can't hear you.'

'No, they keep hanging up after I speak. If they couldn't hear me, *they'd* speak.'

'Maybe it's the other way round. Maybe *you* can't hear *them.*'

'*They're* not staying on the line long enough to be talking.'

'So call them back.'

He was bringing in the coffee.

'I can't. They're withholding the number.'

'Oh really?' Nat was surprised now.

'That's why I think it's deliberate. I keep seeing "number withheld" on the display when it rings and then, when I answer, they give me the silent treatment.'

'Okay, if they call again, let me answer.'

'Why?' she asked with a grin. 'You think the caller's a misogynist?'

'Or maybe just a gynophobe,' he replied, smiling back at her.

'Have you been taking one of those correspondence courses again?'

'Ha fuckin' ha.'

When the phone rang again, she instinctively reached for it. As she scooped it up she noticed from the caller display that it was again from a withheld number.

She quickly waved her other hand to alert Nat. He leaned over and took the receiver from her.

'Alex Sedaka's office,' said Nat.

'We need to talk,' said a familiar voice.

17:34 PDT

Alex hadn't made any further headway with Jonathan. He knew that Jonathan was lying, or at least holding back something. But he couldn't force it out of him. He had to remember that Jonathan Olsen was the brother of the girl that his client had been convicted of murdering. Whatever new evidence there was to show that Dorothy was alive a year later, it didn't prove that she was alive *now*. And whatever Jonathan knew, there was no reason to assume that he was wrong in blaming Clayton Burrow for his sister's death.

But what Alex wondered was how much *Esther* Olsen knew. True, she and Dorothy were estranged at the time of Dorothy's disappearance and hardly talked to each other. But they had still been living under the same roof. Could Esther Olsen have been so oblivious to what was going on in Dorothy's life?

And the issue had now taken on a new urgency because of the deterioration in Esther's condition. Juanita had told Alex that she was now in hospital and that she had been asking for him. So now he was driving to the Idylwood Care Center in Sunnyvale to visit her.

Dvorak's *New World Symphony* blared out and David's name flashed up on the display.

'Hi, David.'

'Hi, Dad. Quick newsflash.'

'What's up?'

'More poetry.'

Alex smiled.

'Anything significant?'

'I think so.'

'I can't read anything right now. I'm on the road.'

'Want me to read it out to you?'

'If you think it's significant.'

'You tell me. First of all I found one verse earlier. It went like this: "You crushed the hope out of me / Not in cold blood but angrily / And only when you died / Did I resolve the mystery / Of your vicious assault on my dignity." Note the five-line pattern and note also how it rhymes round the sound "ee" in four of the five lines.'

'Okay, you said that was earlier.'

'That's right and I was going to call you right away. But *then* I noticed the line "And only when you died." That's the bit that doesn't make sense. Clayton Burrow is still alive.'

'Not for much longer unless we get a move on.'

'Okay, but at the time she wrote this, assuming it was before she went to England, it was never in question that he wasn't. And that means that it's addressed to someone other than Burrow. But at the same time, it's clear from the language and the tone that she has a grievance against this person. She blames this person for making her suffer.'

'I see what you mean. In fact, when I asked Jonathan

265

about why he said that Dorothy got a raw deal from her mother, he came back with a rather cryptic reply. He said "there are sins of omission as well as commission."'

'Yes,' David persisted, 'but this isn't about a sin of omission. You can tell from the language that this isn't just someone who *let* her suffer. This is addressed to someone who actively *made* her suffer. But that's not all. I found another two verses. Just listen to this: "Because I was too young to understand / You were only trying to set me free / You didn't really want to change me / You wanted an alternative reality / You wanted to turn back the clock." That's *one* verse. And then the next. "And resurrect a child of three / But I saw things differently / My needs were shaped more selfishly / I had to escape my cell / I had to escape my shell / And find my own path to liberty." That's it.'

'Good work, David.'

'So *is* it significant?'

There was something about that line 'and resurrect a child of three' that rang a bell in Alex's mind.

'Edgar Olsen lost a child of three in a traffic accident,' Alex said, thinking out loud.

'Edgar Olsen being?'

'Dorothy's father. He had a child by his first marriage and the boy was killed in a car accident.'

'That's interesting because there *was* one other thing.'

'What?'

'Well note the variations in the rhyming pattern. It always rhymes round the sound "ee" but in different places depending on which verse – something that a poetry critic would probably analyze to death.'

'I thought you weren't into all that "liberal arts crap" – as you used to call it.'

'I'm not. I am, however, a scientist with a methodical approach and I did some checking on the internet.'

'Let's hear the punchline.'

'I found a poem by Sylvia Plath with a similar five-line structure and irregular rhyming pattern built round a single vowel phoneme. It's called "Daddy."'

17:42 PDT (01:42 BST, August 15, 2007)

Susan White was going through a crisis of conscience. Stuart had promised her that he would try to get some sort of legal clearance or assurance that they could disclose the information and then call her back. But since then she had heard nothing . . . and the silence was deafening.

Was it because the answer he got from his advisers was negative? Or hadn't he even bothered to seek advice?

He probably went back to sleep!

She wondered if she dared call him back. If he was awake and still working on it, he could hardly blame her for asking for an update. If he was asleep and got angry with her she could take him to task for breaking his promise – especially with a life on the line.

She could, perhaps, justify it by telling him that she had additional information. Since they last spoke, the woman from the law firm had revealed the fact that they knew about how much money Dorothy had handed over to them.

That's it! He can't blame me for that!

She pressed the quick-dial key for Stuart's home number. It rang seven times before being picked up.

During every one of those rings, Susan came perilously close to hanging up.

How would he react to being called at this time?

But she held her nerve. She kept telling herself that she had justice on her side.

'Hallo!' said an angry, female voice. Stuart's wife had answered. This was what Susan had been afraid of – *one* of the things at any rate.

'Hallo, could I speak to Stuart – Mr Lloyd?'

'Who *is* this?'

'It's Susan White . . . from the medical center.'

'Have you gone mad?'

'I'm sorry. Mr Lloyd said he'd call me back. It's urgent.'

'Do you know what time it is?'

'It's a matter of life and death.'

She didn't know how much Stuart had told his wife, but she figured she owed this woman at least *some* explanation.

'He's gone to sleep.'

'To *sleep?*'

'Yes, to sleep! It's . . . nearly two in the morning.'

'But it's eight hours before that in California.'

'What's California got to do with it?'

She realized that Stuart hadn't told his wife anything.

'Who is it?' said a tired, disoriented man's voice in the background.

'It's no one. Go back to sleep.'

When Susan heard these words, she was furious. She realized what was going on. But she wasn't sure how to handle it. Mrs Lloyd evidently didn't know about the man on death row. She didn't realize that Susan had meant it literally when she had said it was a matter of life and death.

She must think I'm just a hysterical nurse.

The truth of the matter, she realized, was that it was with Stuart that she should really be angry. *He* was the one who had broken a promise. *He* was the one who knew the score yet had chosen to do nothing about it. *He* was the one who was turning a blind eye while a man's life hung in the balance.

Susan realized that if she could explain the latest developments to Stuart he might change his mind. The call from America telling them not to pass on the information . . . then the call from the law firm revealing that they knew about the forty thousand pounds. But she couldn't tell him unless she could speak to him and she couldn't speak to him unless she could get past the gatekeeper.

She considered telling Mrs Lloyd about the man on death row, the phone calls, everything. Stuart would be furious and it would be a flagrant breach of confidence. If Stuart hadn't told his wife about the case, then it was hardly Susan's place to do so. But if she didn't tell her then she would never get to him.

Any way she looked at it, her choice was simple: let an innocent man die or make her boss extremely angry – and she wasn't ready to let an innocent man die. But if she was going to make him angry, why do it with a half-baked gesture? Why not make sure that her action at least yielded the right result?

In that moment she decided what to do.

'Okay, I'm sorry for disturbing you, Mrs Lloyd.'

'Good*night*!'

Susan put the phone down. The time for talking was over. She went to the office and sat down at one of the computers. She was never much of a typist, but the computer had a word processing program and it was easy to correct errors. The letter she typed stated the dates when Dorothy had been at the medical center, both her arrival and discharge. She decided not to mention anything about the money or medical details. The woman had said they only needed the dates.

But the letter needed the authority of the medical center to ensure that it would be taken seriously by the courts in America. That meant it had to be on the medical center's letterhead. But it also needed one other thing: the imprimatur of someone in a *position* of authority. And a nurse, even a senior nurse, hardly carried the gravitas to convince a US court to cancel an execution at the eleventh hour.

No, it needed the signature of a senior figure at the medical center. And who could be more senior than the Chief Administrator? Using her anger at the thought of injustice to overcome her trepidation, Susan typed the name 'Stuart Lloyd' at the foot of the letter. And, just to make sure that she didn't give them an excuse to say it arrived too late, she put the date of the 14th instead of the 15th, this being the date in the United States. Then she hit 'print'.

As soon as it came out, she grabbed it and put it on the desk to sign.

'Is everything all right?'

Susan practically jumped out of her skin in shock.

It was Danielle, the young nurse who had only started on the ward two months ago. She was standing by the door, looking at Susan with a puzzled expression.

'Oh yes . . . everything's fine.'

Danielle still looked concerned, but at least she showed no sign of suspicion.

'Oh . . . okay. Well, look, if you need anything, just let me know.'

Susan watched, her heart pounding, as Danielle stepped back and closed the door. She waited to give Danielle time to walk away and then returned her attention to the letter. She held the pen poised over the space for the signature, racked with last-minute indecision. It was a crime. Regardless of motive, forgery was forgery. At minimum it would get her sacked and at maximum it could land her in prison. They would ask her why she didn't simply give her own signature. They would make it look as if she signed his name in order to hide her own identity and cover up her breach of ethics, rather than to impart more authority to the letter. She would be vilified and her motives questioned.

No matter . . . at least an innocent life would be spared. It was the right thing to do.

Fighting to control her shaking hand, she signed 'Stuart Lloyd' at the bottom of the letter. This was no illegible scribble – she didn't want to give them any excuse to doubt the authenticity of the signature or the letter – it was clearly signed in a neat, legible script.

She took it over to the fax machine and inserted it in the input feed. Then she keyed in the number from the fax that the lawyers had sent requesting information. She hesitated again just before pressing the green button. She closed her eyes and stabbed the button. Her lungs remained full while the tones of the number and the almost musical tone of the two fax machines 'hand-shaking' rang out. The paper slid slowly into the machine and the light scanned across it, emitting a green glow from the edges of the scanner plate.

Only when the final bleep indicated that the connection had ended and the words 'transmission complete' appeared on the liquid crystal display, did she resume normal breathing.

She looked at her watch. In ten minutes her work shift would be over and she could go home with a clear conscience.

18:01 PDT

'I got here as quickly as I could, Mrs Olsen.'

'I know.' The voice was weak. 'You are a good man, Mr Sedaka. Even though it might seem to you that we are enemies, I know you are a good man.'

Alex was embarrassed. Everything about this woman made him feel uncomfortable . . . no, not really uncomfortable . . . just self-conscious.

'Mrs Olsen, I'm afraid I haven't really made any progress with Clayton Burrow.'

'I know,' she said gently and gave Alex a weak but reassuring smile to make it clear to him that she was not chiding him for his failure.

'Clayton Burrow says he doesn't know where your daughter is.'

'Does he still claim to be innocent?'

Alex was hesitant.

'Well I'm not really sure if . . .'

He trailed off when he saw Esther Olsen shaking her head. She looked awfully frail, much more frail than she had in Dusenbury's office, much more frail indeed than he had expected. At first the doctors hadn't even wanted to let him in to see her. But he pointed out that it was *she* who had asked for *him* and when they had advised her against it, she had insisted.

'He's *still* denying the murder,' said Alex with a sigh.

Esther Olsen nodded in reluctant acceptance.

'But he has admitted something.'

A hint of a smile crept onto her face and she tried to sit up. But she dropped back onto the pillow, fatigued. Alex leaned forward.

'You're too weak,' he said comfortingly. 'Don't try.'

'What did he say? What did he admit?'

'I don't really know how to say this . . .'

'*Tell* me.'

'He admitted to raping your daughter.'

Esther Olsen nodded slowly, as if accepting the solace of at least a partial admission.

'This is good,' she said, more to herself than to Alex. 'This is good.'

'Mrs Olsen . . . did you know about it? At the time, I mean?'

For the first time since they had met, Esther Olsen couldn't hold Alex's gaze. She looked away, almost guiltily.

'Mrs Olsen?'

'We hardly spoke to each other.'

'I know that, Mrs Olsen. But you were still living under the same roof as your daughter. Did you know?'

She nodded slowly.

'Yes, I knew. I overheard her talking to Jonathan.'

'About the rape?'

'Yes.'

'When was that?'

'A week before she vanished.'

'Exactly a week?'

'Yes. I mean she vanished on a Saturday and this was the Saturday before.'

Alex was quickly doing the arithmetic in his mind. Dorothy had vanished on the 23rd of May. But she was raped on her birthday, April the first. Why would she be telling Jonathan about the rape seven weeks after it happened? He remembered that Jonathan had said 'she came to the house in tears.' That must have been on the day it happened.

But on May 19 she had booked a ticket to England and then she vanished a few days later. So when Mrs Olsen overheard Dorothy talking to Jonathan a week before she vanished, was it the rape she was talking about or the . . .

'Mrs Olsen . . . did you know that Dorothy was pregnant?'

Esther looked at him, surprised. But even before she spoke Alex knew that it was not surprise about the pregnancy: it was surprise that Alex knew about it. Her face betrayed more than she intended. They both knew that the secret was out.

'Yes, I knew.'

'And did you also know that she had an abortion?'

Esther Olsen looked surprised.

'Are you sure?'

'Pretty sure.'

'This I did not know.'

She sounded sincere. But this didn't make sense.

Dorothy must have decided on the abortion before she bought the ticket.

'You didn't hear her talking about it to Jonathan?'

'I heard whispering.'

'And she didn't mention having an abortion?'

'Yes, she mentioned it.'

'But I thought you said—'

'I said I didn't know she *had* one. But I knew that she was considering it. She talked about it to Jonathan. Of course he couldn't really advise her. He was just a child. But I think she was using him as a sounding board for her own thoughts. I wished she could have talked to me about it. She was the loneliest child in the world and she couldn't come to her mother for advice.'

'Why didn't *you* talk to *her*?'

'I couldn't approach her about it. I couldn't so much as mention it without running the risk that she would accuse me of eavesdropping. We would have had a shouting match and she would have ended up hating me even more. I had to wait for her to come to me. She never did. And that is the biggest regret of my life.'

'What would you have told her?'

'Just being there for her would have been enough. But I don't know if I could have advised her. We belonged to different generations. My decision was different to hers.'

The words landed on Alex like a punch from a hard-hitting heavyweight.

'*Was* different?'

'When I had to make such a choice, I chose to *have* the baby.'

Alex was stunned by this.

'When you had to . . .' He trailed off and composed himself. 'Wait a minute, you were *raped*?'

18:04 PDT

'Okay, look, I can't come round now.' The voice was muted. 'I'm expected to keep working as long as there's a chance of saving him. I'll try and get away as soon as I can. Love you.'

Nat put the phone down.

The reception area had been empty when the fax arrived. Juanita had gone out to buy sandwiches and he had heard the fax machine from the other room, but hadn't thought anything of it. He wouldn't even have bothered to check it if it wasn't for the fact that he was restless. It was now the end of what would normally have been the working day and, although he often worked overtime when they had a big case coming up in the morning, this was normally the time that he would head home.

But he was wandering aimlessly into the reception area with his umpteenth cup of coffee of the day when he noticed that the paper tray of the fax machine was empty. Juanita must have been so busy that she had forgotten to refill it. He took some new paper out of a half-open packet, fanned it and put it into the tray.

When he slid the tray into place the fax machine came to life and started printing. He realized that there must have been a fax stacked up in the memory. It turned out to be just one page. He picked it up, glancing at it as he walked back across the reception area.

When he saw the letterhead he practically spilt his coffee. And when he started reading it he had to sit down and put the cup on the desk.

This was something that he had not expected – and he was not pleased. He quickly went over to the shredder.

18:05 PDT

Alex had initially been cool to David's attempts to analyze the poem. But his interest perked up when David told him about the stylistic resemblance between Dorothy's poem and the Sylvia Plath poem. In the absence of any other directions, David took this as a green light to continue searching for more verses. If possible, he wanted to find the whole thing.

It might not be of any further help, but there was nothing better to look for. They had found out about the flight to England and the medical center. Further hacking of the bank account was taboo. This was the only thing left.

By now he had the routine down pat. He set the computer to do another search for sequences with several instances of the word 'you' in close proximity. In seconds the scanning tunneling microscope and computer combination had thrown up another result.

> I knew his name was Jimmy
> And he died when he was three

In a car accident, with you at the wheel
No wonder you felt guilty
You never spoke about him

18:06 PDT

'No, Mr Sedaka, I wasn't raped. But it *was* an unwanted pregnancy. I made the mistake of having a one-night stand with a virtual stranger three days before I was married.'

This came as a shock to Alex. Esther Olsen didn't seem the type. Then again, was there such a thing as 'the type'?

Besides, who was he to judge? His own youth had been equally reckless. He had got Melody pregnant while she was in the middle of her medical studies. They married in haste four months later. And like Esther Olsen, Melody had carried the pregnancy to term and had the baby. It had almost derailed Melody's career. Only Melody's tenacity and determination – together with a supportive mother of her own – had kept it on track.

'How did it happen?'

'It was at one of those drunken frat parties. You know the type.'

'I know the type,' Alex confirmed. 'So what was it, you had unprotected sex with a stranger and you got pregnant by him?'

'That's right.'

'And then when you got married you took precautions?'

It didn't make sense.

'I don't understand.'

'I mean, what makes you so sure that it was him? This stranger? How do you know it wasn't your husband?'

'Trust me, I know.'

'What, you did a DNA test? Or just a blood group test?'

Esther Olsen's voice rose for a moment.

'It's . . . not important. The fact is, I know.'

'And you don't know who the father was? His name, I mean.'

'No. Like I said, it was at a party. I didn't know many of the people there. We'd both had too much to drink and he was one of the few people who didn't become obnoxious when he drank. Most men do.'

A thought entered Alex's head.

'You said you didn't have an abortion when you had to make the choice?'

She was looking at him, silently.

Alex pressed on.

'So the child was . . .'

'Dorothy,' she confirmed.

'Did she know?'

'It's not important.'

'Did *your husband* know?'

'It's *not* important.'

'Help me here . . . I need to understand.'

'Why does it matter? She was my daughter even if she wasn't Edgar's. And I loved her even if he didn't.'

'Where is he now? Edgar, I mean.'

'Dead.'

Alex's mind was reeling. Could this have something to do with the estrangement from her daughter?

'What did he die of?'

'It was suicide.'

'At home?'

That would explain why Esther Olsen didn't want to talk about it. Alex wondered how many secrets had come out in the Olsen household before he died.

'Not at my house. He'd moved out already.'

'Do you know why?'

'We'd broken up by then. He moved out so he could enjoy his independence.'

'No, I mean, why did he kill himself?'

'He was a troubled man – even before the marriage. He'd lost a son from a previous marriage. He blamed himself and he never really recovered from it. It had always haunted him. I think it's what led to the break-up of his first marriage. Finally the burden got too much.'

'How did he do it?'

Alex wondered if it was something violent, like slashing his wrists, or something more prosaic, like tranquilizers or a hosepipe through the exhaust.

'With a revolver. He blew his brains out.'

18:19 PDT

David looked at his watch. Time was moving on and he realized that he wasn't making progress. He'd passed on all the information he'd got, but his father had indicated that it wasn't enough. They needed some form of documentary evidence that Dorothy was alive – or that someone else had killed her. He could hardly expect to find that on a computer that she had left behind before she went to England. But it might give some indication of where to look for her.

They had used the bank statement evidence, but the judge had declined to grant another restraining order. Apparently they'd have to argue it out at a full hearing, scheduled for half past eight. And even the evidence they had, only showed that Dorothy had been alive a year or so after her disappearance. While this clashed with the original theory that Clayton Burrow had killed her on the night of her disappearance, it didn't undermine the technical basis of the charge.

The charge was that on some date between Dorothy's disappearance on Saturday May 23, 1998 and the discovery of the physical evidence on Tuesday October 19, 1999,

Burrow had murdered her, dismembered her and buried the body. The latest date when they could prove that she was alive was about the middle of June 1999. That still left a four-month window of opportunity for Burrow to have committed the crime.

Of course, it was possible – notwithstanding the physical evidence – that Burrow was innocent. But the evidence was strong. What mattered was not *when* he killed her, but *if* he killed her. And the evidence still said that he did.

But the one thing that was becoming increasingly apparent was that Dorothy Olsen was a deeply tormented soul and the torment came from more than one quarter. The evidence at the trial suggested that Dorothy was dead. But was Clayton Burrow the murderer or merely the fall guy?

If he had raped her *before* her disappearance, then he would have been the *perfect* fall guy for the murder. And who might have framed him? Obviously the real murderer. But who was the real murderer? David didn't know. But what he did know was that Dorothy appeared to have had another tormentor in her father. The extracts from the poem that he had found added credence to this theory.

David decided to phone his father now. Maybe it was nothing. But it was for his father to decide what to do with the evidence.

'Yes, David?' Alex answered. David could tell by the background sound, and by the tone of voice, that his father was driving.

'I've found another verse.'

'Surprise me,' said Alex.

David read back the last stanza, placing particular emphasis on the line: 'No wonder you felt guilty.'

'Yes, I was just talking to Esther Olsen about that.'

'What did she say?'

'She said he blamed himself for his son's death. That's why he committed suicide.'

'*What?*'

'Apparently he killed himself.'

'Good God. What a family.'

'My thoughts exactly.'

'But was it definitely over his son's death?'

'What do you mean?'

'Well the death of his son by his first marriage would have been years before. Why kill himself after all that time?'

'It's not so unusual. Guilt and torment often mounts up. Besides, what else could it be?'

'Maybe something to do with Dorothy?'

18:26 PDT (02:26 BST, August 15, 2007)

'Where are you going?' asked Juanita.

Nat realized that she was probably surprised to see him on his way out. On a normal day this wouldn't have been so unusual. But today was hardly a normal day.

'I need some fresh air. I'll be back in a few minutes.'

He would have said a cigarette break. But she knew that he didn't smoke.

As soon as he got outside, he whipped out his cell phone and put in a call to the Finchley Road Medical Centre. A nurse answered.

'I'd like to talk to Stuart Lloyd please,' said Nat, remembering the name on the letter from the center.

'Who is this?'

'My name is Nathaniel Anderson. I'm calling from the United States.'

He regretted using his real name now. He didn't know who this woman was or what her status was.

'I'm afraid Mr Lloyd isn't here. He's gone home.'

'Home?'

'Yes, it's half past two in the morning.'

Nat realized that she was right. He hadn't thought about that.

'So . . . I mean . . . like when did he leave?'

'I don't know. He usually leaves round five thirty or six o'clock.'

'That's impossible! He sent a fax to my— He sent a fax less than half an hour ago.'

'Well not from here. I started my shift half an hour ago and he wasn't here. At least I don't think he was. It would have been most unusual for him to be here at this time.'

'Well it might have been a bit longer than half an hour ago. It was stuck in the memory of our fax. The machine had run out of paper, so it might have been sent before that.'

'Like I said, I've been on a double shift since ten last night and I got here a bit before that and I didn't see him. I also didn't see any lights on in the offices or other departments. There's only one small ward here, the rest is out-patients. I suppose he could have been here though.'

Nat's mind was reeling.

What the hell is going on?

'Look, I need to speak to him.'

'He'll be here tomorrow morning. He usually arrives by eight thirty.'

'No, you don't understand: I need to speak to him *now*.'

'Like I said, that's not possible.'

'I need his home phone number then.'

'I'm afraid that's impossible, we're not allowed to give out the home phone numbers of staff.'

Nat was growing increasingly irritated.

'Okay, well what about his cell phone number?'

'His cell phone?'

'Yeah. His . . . *mobile*.'

'Yes, I do know what a cell phone is,' she replied testily. 'But we're not allowed to give that out either.'

'Look, dammit, I need to talk to him!'

'Why now? What's so urgent?'

'He sent a fax revealing confidential information about one of your patients!'

'I'm sure Mr Lloyd wouldn't do such a thing—'

'Well he did!'

Nat was about to shout again, when he realized that it didn't really matter. By tomorrow morning, London time, Clayton Burrow would be dead. If Stuart Lloyd had sent the fax in the belief that he was doing his duty and then gone home, there was no point rousing him from his slumber.

'Okay, thank you, Miss . . .'

'Michaels. Nurse Michaels. Could I ask your name again? I can leave a note for Mr Lloyd to let him know you called.'

'Oh there's really no need.'

'Are you sure? I mean, if there's any problem about that fax—'

'I represent Miss Dorothy Olsen.'

'Dorothy Olsen?'

'The patient. The one the fax was about. I'm her legal representative. And she objects most strongly to having her confidential information disclosed to unauthorized persons.'

18:39 PDT

'He blamed himself because he was guilty,' the woman said firmly.

Alex was in the home of the first Mrs Olsen. Anita Olsen – or Anita Morgan as she now called herself – was a fifty-five-year-old woman with blonde hair, slim and elegant in her appearance. She had agreed to see him at short notice, more out of curiosity than anything else. He had told her who he was and what he was doing and she agreed to meet him at her house.

She was neutral on the issue of Clayton Burrow's guilt, not having followed the case all that closely. But she was in no doubt as to her husband's responsibility for the death of their son.

'How do you mean "guilty"? In the criminal sense?'

'Oh no, in the criminal sense it was that drunken lout who swerved across the divider line.'

'Then . . . ?'

'It was the way he responded to it.'

'How do you mean?'

'Instead of swerving toward the emergency lane, he swerved left. The other car slammed straight into the passenger side, killing Jimmy instantly. Edgar was more concerned with saving himself than protecting little Jimmy.'

Anita Olsen sniffled into her handkerchief. He understood her emotions, but the gesture seemed somewhat contrived, a trifle false.

'Jimmy was in the front?'

He couldn't believe that anyone could have put a three-year-old kid in the front passenger seat, even in those days.

'No, he was in the back, but he was on the right side. I mean, he wasn't sitting, he was moving round, the way three-year-olds do.'

'He wasn't in a safety seat?'

'In 1977? Children's safety seats were an optional extra back then. He wasn't even wearing a safety belt.'

For a second the neutral look on her face gave way to a grimace, as if she were about to break down in tears. But she fought them away and regained her composure.

'Did he have time to think about it? Edgar, I mean. When he swerved?'

Anita Olsen looked at him coldly.

'Oh I know what you're thinking: that it was instinctive . . . the natural human urge toward self-preservation.'

'I'm sorry. I wasn't trying to make excuses for him.'

'No, you're right. It *was* instinctive. And he probably didn't even know which side of the car Jimmy was on. When the back seat was empty, Jimmy was all over the place. You couldn't keep him still. It's just the fact that he wasn't wearing a seat belt. That was Edgar's responsibility and he should have made sure he was wearing one.'

Alex looked round the room. In some ways it reminded him of Jonathan's place. Not that it was a shrine or anything quite as extreme as that. Just that over the mantelpiece there was an ever changing reminder of little Jimmy. It was one of those digital picture frames – a fifteen-inch one – and it was showing a rotating selection of pictures of Jimmy from baby, through toddler, to the cute dark-haired three-year-old he was shortly before he died. One could tell from their grainy look that they had been scanned. Some of them showed little Jimmy together with his father or mother. Sometimes both. There were even a few short video snippets, obviously converted from 8mm movie footage.

Alex wondered if Anita Olsen had put them there for his benefit or if she always had them running through the cycle like that.

Whatever the reason, it was a moving treatment in every sense of the word. But then the pictures changed and various pictures of girls appeared. Again they were toddlers and young children, but then at last some of them were teenagers. Then a woman in her twenties appeared. For a minute, Alex thought this was one of the daughters. But then he realized that it was in fact Anita herself.

'May I ask you a personal question?'

'You can ask. I don't guarantee an answer.'

She was smiling. He sensed the nervous tension. As a lawyer he was trained to put people at ease, but he realized that in this case he had succeeded in doing the opposite.

'Did you have any more children?'

'Not with Edgar. I had two girls by my next husband.'

'Ah,' he said, grateful for the clarification.

'When did you break up with Edgar?'

'About a year after Jimmy died: early 1978.'

As it cycled back to Jimmy, Alex noticed some footage of the boy playing soccer with a man who was every bit as blond as Anita. He stood up and took a step forward toward the frame.

'Is that him?' asked Alex. His tone was more puzzled than curious.

'Who? Edgar?' said Anita. 'Yes. Why?'

'I was just wondering why he dyed his hair blond.'

'He didn't. That's his natural color.'

'You don't see many blond Jewish men,' said Alex with a wry smile.

'Oh Edgar wasn't Jewish.'

Alex shot Anita a surprised look.

'His second wife was, but he wasn't. I remember he had a kind of fascination with all things Jewish though.'

'What, you mean like . . . he believed in those silly Jewish conspiracy theories?'

Anita smiled.

'Oh no, nothing quite so dramatic. No, it was more of a fascination that he developed when he was living in New York. He picked up a lot of Jewish expressions and he liked the food. He always used to complain that you can't find any good kosher delis on the West Coast – at least nothing to beat Richie's in the Big Apple, he used to say. I think that explains why he became so fascinated by Esther. Apparently she was quite a good cook. But he was of Norwegian origin – like me. That was how we met. There was this club called the "Scandinavian Club." It was used by rich men to meet beautiful women. But Edgar *really was* of Norwegian extraction. I think he always thought of himself as a bit of a Viking – at least in business.'

Alex walked toward the frame and stared at the images.

'A Viking who was fascinated by Jews,' said Alex with a wry smile as he continued to stare at the frame. 'Fascinating.'

'Why, what's the matter?'

'I was just thinking about something in biology – something called . . . Mendel's Law.'

18:44 PDT

Juanita was irritated by the fact that Nat was taking such a long break. She knew that she had been a long time too, but that was different. She had gone out to get sandwiches for both of them. He had gone just because he felt like a break.

Admittedly, at the moment she was just marking time, waiting for some of these lawyers or the medical center to get back to them. But it was as if he wasn't pulling his weight.

But she knew that this was unfair. He had done a lot so far. It was just that it was lonely with Alex out of the office. It was silly, she knew. But the thought of a man's life hanging in the balance and his fate in their hands was a strain that she would have preferred to share than to shoulder alone. It was an awesome responsibility and it frightened her. Juanita had always viewed the law as standing alongside science as the central pillar of support for human civilization: man's social contract with his brethren to create and maintain a just society. But, for the profession's practitioners – lawyers, judges, their staff and even *jurors* – it was an onerous burden to carry.

As if to emphasize the point, a ringing tone followed by several bleeps and high pitched tones told her that a fax was about to come through. It reminded her of the theme from the original *Star Trek* series.

She went over to the machine as the fax was coming through and tried to read it. But it was upside down and she had to wait for it to emerge fully and turn it round to read it, while a second page came through. It was a covering letter for an affidavit of service from the law firm in New York, confirming that the District Court order had been served on the airline company. The covering letter explained that they had served the order on the Chief Operating Officer of the airline; apparently he hadn't been very happy about it.

She looked at the next page, the affidavit of service itself. It was a simple one-page affair stating that the order had been duly served at such and such a time on such and such a date. She took it out of the machine and was about to walk back to her desk to staple the pages together when another sheet started coming through. She waited for a second and saw that it was the journal: the automatic printout of the last twenty faxes that they had sent or received. She always filed the journals too, so she waited for it to print out. Then she took it and walked back to her desk, glancing at the journal. She noticed that the last item was the fax from the law firm that had just come through, but it was the one just above it that caught her attention. It showed the time as 01:45 and the date as 15-08-2007. That didn't make any sense. How could it have come in the morning and what on earth was the *fifteenth month*?

Then, as she looked at the number – beginning with +44 20 – she realized that this was from England.

In England they put the day before the month! It's from August 15!

But that's tomorrow . . .

She looked at the time. It had been sent at 01:45 am London time. Now it all made sense. England was eight hours ahead. She did a quick mental calculation and worked out that this was 5:45 pm Pacific Daylight Time.

But that didn't make sense either. She was in the office at that time and she would have heard if a fax had come through. Then she remembered that she *had* heard a fax come through. But she had been too busy to look at it . . . *the machine must have run out of paper!*

A fax had been sent over from England! But where was it?

Before she could gather her wits, the front door swung open and Nat walked in, looking pleased with himself.

'Any news?' he asked.

18:46 PDT

'I don't understand,' said Anita Morgan.

'It's a biological law to do with the inheritance of physical characteristics. Things like eye color and hair color are all controlled by dominant and recessive genes. I don't remember much of my high school biology, but I do remember that blond parents can't have a dark-haired child. You must have faced a lot of comments over that.'

He was being deliberately offensive in the way he chose to phrase it. With a client on death row and the clock ticking away, he needed answers – *fast*. Ordinarily, offending a woman was the last thing he would do. But in the present circumstances it was a small price to pay for the answers that he so urgently needed.

'We didn't actually. The people we associate with are too well-bred to make such comments. But you're right in your insinuation. Little Jimmy was *not* Edgar's son.'

Although he had already figured it out for himself, Alex's mind was reeling.

'So the son for whom he yearned . . . the son whose death he mourned and felt guilty over . . . wasn't even his son?'

'That's right. Rather ironic really.'

'And he never guessed?'

'Oh he knew.'

'How did he feel about it?'

'I . . . I'm not sure. I think he understood . . . in a way. I did it for *him*.'

'I don't understand.'

'You see . . . As you said, Edgar always wanted a son. But he was sterile – or at least sub-fertile. We both had ourselves tested at a clinic and I—'

'Clinic?'

Alex held his breath.

'Yes, a fertility clinic. Why?'

'Where was this clinic?'

'I don't know. Los Angeles, I think.'

He exhaled again.

'So it was definitely in the United States?'

'Yes, in California. I *think* it was LA.'

'Sorry, I didn't mean to interrupt. Please continue.'

'Well anyway. I got my results and it said I was okay. No problems of any kind. I never got to see his results and he brushed me off when I raised the issue. Basically, he was in denial.'

'So what exactly was it that you did for him? Artificial insemination with a donor?'

'Er no, it was rather more direct than that. You see Edgar was too stubborn to admit his . . . er . . . little problem. But I wanted children and I knew that he did too. So I had an affair with a mutual friend.'

18:49 PDT

Juanita was sitting at her desk, trying to remain calm while Nat hovered round.

Had Nat taken the fax? Destroyed it? What did it contain?

She debated whether to ask him about it, but she knew that she couldn't. If he was up to something, anything she asked would merely alert him to the fact that she was on to him. With Alex out of the office, she didn't like that idea.

She had never really felt comfortable with Nat. There was something about him that put her in a continuous state of unease. She had tried to mask her own feelings with humor, sometimes even flirting with him. That was just a defense mechanism that she had adopted precisely because she *did* feel so uncomfortable in his presence.

The phone rang.

'Alex Sedaka's office.'

'Hi, it's Lee Kelly here.'

Lee was a fifty-five-year-old career burglar and by all accounts a good one. Considering how prolific he was, he got arrested surprisingly little.

'What can I do for you, Mr Kelly?'

'I'm calling from the Park Police Station on Waller Street. I've been busted and I need Alex to rep me at the arraignment.'

'Mr Sedaka isn't here at the moment, I'm afraid, and he won't be available all day.'

'But I *need* him.'

'Mr Kelly, I don't mean to be rude but there's no way Mr Sedaka can see you today. I don't know if you've been following the news but we have a client on death row and unless we can get a stay of execution he's going to be fried at one minute past midnight. So I think you can understand that right now you're very low on our list of priorities.'

'Maybe he can fit me in? I mean, it's only a few minutes in court.'

'I'll pass it on to him, Mr Kelly. But I strongly advise you to use one of those local attorneys at the arraignment court to get you bail and then Alex can take over as attorney of record when he's not under so much pressure.'

'You want me to put my ass in a sling for one of those courthouse scavengers? No way, José.'

'Well all I can do is pass on your message—'

'There's no need to pass it on. I've got his cell phone number, so I can—'

'No, Mr Kelly, please don't call him now, he won't—'

The line went dead.

18:51 PDT

'I don't suppose you'd like to tell me the name of this friend?'

'It's not important.'

'I don't mean to pry. It's just that I have a client . . .'

He shook his head, realizing the futility of it. Anita already knew about that. Just then Alex's cell phone rang. He looked at the display. The Park Police Station. That meant it was probably a client. He couldn't handle it right now and in any case they should call the office.

He pressed the red button, sending the call through to voicemail.

Anita Morgan was staring at him.

'May I ask *you* a question, Mr Sedaka?'

'Sure.'

'What exactly are you trying to find out? I mean, what does all this have to do with the death of Dorothy Olsen?'

'I don't really know. It's just that Clayton Burrow may be innocent. And that implies that someone else is guilty.'

He didn't see any reason to share the information about Dorothy's trip to London or the abortion. She was still most likely dead. But it was now clear that Clayton wasn't her only tormentor.

'And who do you think that someone might be?'

'Well we've discovered evidence that she had a troubled relationship with her father.'

'And you think Edgar might have killed her?'

'I haven't ruled it out.'

'Well I wouldn't know about their relationship. We divorced in 1979 and never saw each other after that.'

'Never?'

'There was no need to. We didn't have any other children and there was a lot of bitterness. I blamed him for Jimmy too, remember.'

'Yes, but was Edgar capable of murder?'

'To tell you the truth, Mr Sedaka, I don't know. He was a deeply troubled man. He could be moody at the best of times – and especially so after Jimmy's death.'

'Well if he knew that Jimmy wasn't his son, that must have played on his mind too.'

'Oh absolutely.'

A thought entered Alex's head.

'There's just one thing I don't understand. If Edgar was sterile, how come he had another son with Esther?'

Anita was about to say something when she stopped dead. He noticed her swallowing and suppressing a smile, as if a new thought had entered *her* head.

'I notice that you said a *son*.'

'I meant Jonathan.'

'I know who you mean. But you didn't express any surprise over Dorothy.'

Alex blushed and squirmed with embarrassment, remembering what Esther had told him about the one-night stand at the frat party. He realized that he had inadvertently breached a confidence. But he had more important things on his mind right now.

'I can't talk about it.'

'Oh it's all right!' said Anita with a teasing smile that rolled back the years. 'I know that neither of them was his biological child.'

Alex responded with a smile of his own, out of sheer relief.

'I guess I'll have to ask Esther about it.'

Anita became enthusiastic.

'Well actually I may be able to help.'

'About the fathers of Dorothy and Jonathan?'

'I don't know about Dorothy, but I can tell you about Jonathan.'

'Yes?'

Anita sat down on the armchair, prompting Alex to sit back down on the sofa.

'About three years after Dorothy was born Esther came to me in despair. She told me how bitter and angry Edgar was, how he alternated between rage and self-pity, sarcasm and depression. She thought he suffered from bi-polar disorder – I think they called it manic-depression in those days. She told me that he wanted a son and seemed to blame both her and Dorothy for the fact that he didn't have one. She said she'd tried everything to get pregnant again but it just wasn't happening. But by that stage the family had become completely dysfunctional. She'd even resorted to getting Dorothy to dress up as a boy in the hope that it would placate his anger. But that only made him worse.'

She paused. Alex sat forward.

'Go on.'

'Well at that point I told her that it wasn't her fault. I mean, I didn't pry and ask her who Dorothy's father was, but I told her about Edgar firing blanks. That surprised her, but it also frightened her because she realized that her secret was out with me – part of it at least. I think she may have suspected that Edgar wasn't Dorothy's father before, but I confirmed it. She spent the next two or three minutes crying in my arms and then she disengaged and realized that Jimmy couldn't have been his son either.'

'*And he would have known that too.* He would also have known from the moment Esther told him she was pregnant with Dorothy that she had cheated on him.'

'Exactly. First I have a son that he knows isn't his and, although he wants a son, it makes him feel inadequate. But at least he loves his son. Then the boy dies in a car accident, with Edgar driving, and he feels guilty. And I don't spare his feelings, because he's deprived me of *my* son too. We have violent arguments amid all the anger and guilt and recriminations. Then he marries again and before you know it, his wife is pregnant – and once again he knows *he's* not the father. That must have tormented his masculine pride. But at least he hopes it'll be a boy. And then it's a girl – so he's even more resentful.'

'That would certainly mess up a man's mind.'

'Exactly. And all Esther's efforts to try and put it right only backfired and made it worse.'

307

'But what about Jonathan? You said you knew who his father was?'

'More than that – I introduced them.'

'You *what*?'

'Esther thought that the only thing that would placate Edgar's constant fits of rage wasn't just to have another son, but to have one who reminded him of Jimmy. But he still wouldn't admit that he had a problem and so he wouldn't sign the consent forms for artificial insemination with a donor. So I decided to help her out by fixing her up with the same family friend who . . . er . . . sired little Jimmy.'

19:06 PDT

Juanita remembered that Alex had called her when he arrived at Anita Morgan's house and asked her not to call him unless it was urgent. The truth of the matter was that she wasn't really sure how urgent it was.

The missing fax bothered her and she felt she ought to tell him. But that would be rather hard to do with Nat hovering round. She wondered again whether she should simply ask him. But if a fax had come through from the London clinic he should have told her about it. And there was something else that she remembered too.

Suddenly the phone rang. It was Alex.

'I've finished with Anita Morgan.'

'Did you find anything out?'

'Quite a lot. Anything at your end?'

She told him about the message from the New York law firm.

'Anything else?'

Now was the time to voice her suspicions about Nat. But the light pattern on the wall opposite Juanita showed that his door was open. Nat could hear every word that she was saying.

'I'll check with Nat. Nat! Anything to tell the boss?'

'No, nothing!' Nat called back.

'I heard,' Alex replied before Juanita could say another word. 'Okay, I'm on my way back.'

After she had put the phone down, she noticed Nat's shadow. She looked up.

'Are you all right?'

'Sure,' she replied, trying to sound as nonchalant as possible. 'Why?'

'You sounded like you wanted to say more . . . like you're holding something back.'

19:24 PDT

Lee Kelly had been trying to call Alex for over thirty minutes. At first it had rung a few times. After that it kept going straight to voicemail, almost like the lawyer was brushing him off.

Lee knew that Alex wasn't like that. Alex was a good man and Lee was a good client. Yes, he was a career criminal but he was never violent. And because he was all too aware of the three strikes and you're out rule, he now confined himself to burglarizing business premises with no residential premises attached. That meant he could afford to break into a branch of Wal-Mart or Sears, but he wouldn't touch one of those Korean shops where the owner lived above the premises.

Alex knew this and he knew also that Lee was money in his pocket, at least on those rare occasions when he failed to stay one step ahead of the law. He was a pretty good burglar and he seldom got caught. But when he did, it was Alex who had the honor of getting him out and fixing him up with a bail bondsman. To Lee, the risk of getting caught and sent to jail was an occupational hazard.

But it was good business for Alex. What Lee liked about Alex was that he never prejudged or tried to moralize with him. He did at times try to persuade Lee to consider going straight, but his arguments were always practical, on the lines of 'aren't you getting kinda old for this sort of thing?' The trouble was that at fifty-five, Lee considered himself too old to do anything else. He didn't have any real social security and he knew that his mind was too stultified to acquire new skills. Changing his ways was not really an option.

'Hell, I'll be coming up to retirement pretty soon,' he once told Alex. 'This is for my pension.'

Indeed, the last time Alex had suggested that Lee reconsider his chosen occupation, Lee had put on his best Fagin accent and launched into a surprisingly convincing rendition of 'I'm Reviewing the Situation.'

They had both smiled at the time. But the truth of the matter was that the reference to saving for the future was all too ironic. The reality was that Lee had let most of his ill-gotten gains slip through his fingers.

The phone was ringing again. Finally Lee got through to Alex.

'Hi, Mr Sedaka. I've got a job for you.'

19:27 PDT

Juanita was sitting tensely at her desk waiting for Alex to get back, when the phone rang. It was Alex.

'Hi, Juanita. Listen, I'm going to be delayed slightly.'

He told her about the calls from Lee Kelly. She told him that he had called the office and that she had tried to get him to use one of the two-bit shysters who hang round the courthouse.

'I figure I owe it to him. He's one of my oldest clients – in both senses of the word. Anyway, it's not like we can do anything. We're still waiting for the full hearing at eight thirty.'

After they hung up, Juanita sat thinking. They were rapidly running out of options – and she still hadn't told Alex her suspicions about Nat. Now it was going to be even longer before she could tell him.

No! I have to tell him now!

She had an idea. Quietly and surreptitiously, she took her cell phone and slipped it into her pocket. Then she asked Nat to listen out for the phone and went to the bathroom. She lowered the toilet cover and sat there, texting Alex.

Fax journal showed fax from England when I out
getting sandwiches but wasn't there when I got
back. Think Nat took but not sure. Nat also didn't
tell initially what David told him re travel
booking receipt till slipped out. Think Nat up to
something.

After sending it, she flushed the toilet and returned
to her desk. Alex called back within a minute on the
office line.

'Alex Sedaka's office.'

'Hi, it's me. Am I on speaker?'

'No, b—' She had to force herself not to say boss.

'I got your text.'

'Okay,' she replied in a neutral tone.

'You know, it's funny, but he said something earlier
that made me suspicious.'

'What?'

'Something about me brushing off the reporters
outside, but it wasn't clear how he knew.'

'Uh-huh,' Juanita mumbled, to make it clear that she
still couldn't speak.

'So he knew about the travel receipt to London and
didn't tell us at first?'

'Yes.'

'And then it slipped out.'

'Yes.'

'And you think a fax arrived from England?'

'Yes.'

'Because it was listed in the journal printout?'

'Yes.'

'How many pages?'

'One.'

'Okay, listen, I promised Lee I'd rep him at the arraignment and I don't want to bail out on him. But this is too important to mess round with. So what I want you to do is go outside on some pretext and call the clinic on your cell phone. Tell them to re-fax the papers or whatever it was they sent. Then stand by the fax machine and make sure you're there when they come through.'

'Okay.'

19:32 PDT

David Sedaka was feeling the frustration. He was making progress, but it was painfully slow. Ordinarily that wouldn't be a problem. Any sort of data recovery is a painstaking process. Just as debugging a computer program is naturally slow. But normally that doesn't matter because the time is available. And when the job is done, the achievement is all the more satisfying.

But when time is in short supply, every minute is a minute of torture. And for David, the pain was growing.

If it wasn't for the fact that a human life was at stake, David would have called it a day and gone home for some rest. Sometimes the best way to make progress on a problem is to put it aside for a while and sleep on it. But that was not an option. He had to solve it today. And looking at his watch he knew that meant less than four and a half hours.

But once again, his search macro looking for combinations of the word 'you' had come to his aid. He had modified the macro slightly and found another verse of the poem. He was moved by the words he read. It was as if Dorothy had poured her heart out into this poem, talking to her computer and saying to it all the things that she longed to say to a friend – if only she had had one.

But the words also shocked him. Three words in particular.

'I killed you.'

19:36 PDT (03:36 BST, August 15, 2007)

'*More* sandwiches?' Nat asked, looking Juanita up and down.

'You don't have a monopoly on fresh air.'

She hoped she hadn't sounded too aggressive when she said it. She was feeling the tension, knowing – or at least strongly suspecting – that this man was up to something.

As soon as she left the building she walked up the street and turned a corner. She wanted to make sure she wasn't visible from Nat's office, as well as make sure that he wasn't following her. She didn't think he was likely to, but she had to be sure. If Nat was up to something, what was his game and what was his motive?

She remembered that Martine Yin had blown the story about Dusenbury's offer of clemency. They still didn't know the source of the leak. Could it have been Nat? Certainly he was one of the few people who knew. The governor was sure that it was no one on his tight-knit staff and Juanita knew that it wasn't her or Alex.

Maybe *that* was it. Nat was the source of the leak and

now he had intercepted the fax from London with the intention of leaking it to the press.

But why? Nat wasn't a journalist. They had seen his résumé and, apart from the Grand Tour, all it showed was academic studies and an impressive legal internship with the Public Defender's office. Why would a budding lawyer risk his career to pass on a few juicy titbits to the press?

The obvious answer was money. But then you'd expect him to be dealing with magazines like the *National Enquirer*, not respectable news networks.

Maybe the fax from London was nothing. Maybe it was just a formal statement that they couldn't supply the requested information.

There was no time to think about it. She keyed in their number.

'Finchley Road Medical Centre,' a woman's voice answered.

'Hallo, could I speak to Nurse White please?'

'Susan? I'm afraid she's off duty.'

'When did she finish?'

'At two.'

'What?'

'Two am. She worked the ten pm till two am shift.'

'I don't understand. She sent us a fax a couple of hours ago.'

'Wait a minute, are you calling from America?'

'Yes. I'm sorry, I should have said. I'm calling from the law firm of Alex Sedaka.'

'Oh yes. Look, I don't know any more than I told the man.'

319

'What man?'

'The man who called earlier . . . from the law firm.'

'From the law firm?'

'Yes. He called not long ago.'

'*Our* law firm?'

'I . . . I think so.'

'And what *did* you tell him?'

'I told him that I didn't think Mr Lloyd could have sent the fax because he wasn't here at that time as far as I know. Also, I'm sure he would never disclose confidential information about a patient without permission.'

'And did the man you spoke to give his name?'

'I think he did, but I can't remember. He just said that he represented the patient.'

Juanita felt her mouth going dry.

'Represented the . . . you mean Dorothy?'

'I think so . . . yes.'

'I want you to think carefully. Could the man's name have been Nathaniel – or Nat – Anderson?'

'I think it was – yes!'

So that was it! He had phoned them pretending to be Dorothy's representative to get them to send her details! He wasn't leaking information to the press or trying to *sabotage* their efforts. *He was bending the rules in order to help them!* He knew that the clinic wouldn't release the information without some sort of authorization. So he phoned them and pretended to be Dorothy's representative and asked them to fax over the information! She smiled with relief.

But why had he intercepted their fax? If it contained the information they needed then why not produce it?

She realized why. Because they hadn't sent the information! They presumably sent a letter asking for signed papers from Dorothy herself. Or maybe they'd sent something else referring to Nat's request. But whatever it was, it showed what Nat had done, without actually getting a result and he was afraid that he would get into trouble if she or Alex saw it. So instead he intercepted it to cover his tracks.

He probably hadn't given up yet. If they had asked for a signed power of attorney from Dorothy, he would probably forge one. It was a risky strategy – too risky for Juanita to consider herself, let alone Alex – but she could understand a zealot like Nat doing it. She knew that she ought to stop him, for his sake as much as for high principle. But with Clayton's execution less than five hours away, she couldn't bring herself to do so. Maybe, just maybe, it would work.

She decided to call Alex right away to tell him that her original suspicions were unfounded. But she wouldn't tell him her suspicion that Nat was going to forge a power of attorney. Prior knowledge might compromise Alex's ethical position.

19:41 PDT

Nat had waited nervously in case Juanita came back suddenly. There was something edgy about her that worried him; he feared that she might be on to him. He wanted to make a phone call, but he knew he had to be careful. She said she was going out for some fresh air, but how long would she be gone for? Five minutes? Ten? He couldn't be sure and things had come so far now, it was too late to take a risk on things going wrong.

The phone rang. He answered it.

'Oh, hi, Nat. It's David here.'

He heard a note of excitement in the voice.

'Hi, David. Before you ask, they're both out.'

He said it with a nervous laugh. David picked up on it.

'That's what I was afraid of. I don't suppose you know where they are?'

'Well Juanita just went out for some fresh air and I think your father's taken a detour to an arraignment.'

'Arraignment? Who? Why?'

'He got a call from a client. Lee Kelly. A burglary charge, I think.'

'*Now?* Couldn't he have got you— I'm sorry, I didn't

mean it like that. But couldn't he have unloaded it on another lawyer?'

'I don't know.'

'Well how are things going with Clayton Burrow?'

'We're treading water right now . . . waiting for Baker & Segal to get back to us. We've served the local court order to the airline and I have to chase it up but I don't think we'll get anywhere.'

'Well look, I've got something else that may be of use.'

'Yes?'

'More of that poem.'

'Er . . . right.'

'Yes, I know it sounds silly. But apart from the travel information and the payment to that health center this is the best I can do. And it *does* seem to be saying something about her state of mind which may be relevant to what happened to her.'

'Just tell me what you've found.'

'I found a verse of the poem that really does remind me of Sylvia Plath's poem "Daddy."'

'Are you sure she wasn't just plagiarizing?'

'I don't think so. There are similarities, but differences too. The verse reads: "Daddy, I know I am guilty / Though someone killed you first / I killed you as surely as if / I had pulled the trigger myself / Bang Bang! All over."'

'And that's it?'

'That's it. And I Googled the Plath poem. There's a verse in it that starts with a remarkably similar line.'

'I can see the similarity of the poems. But what's this got to do with Dorothy's death?'

'Well I read in Wikipedia that Sylvia Plath committed

suicide. I was wondering if this poem was Dorothy's suicide note.'

'We already considered that. But if she committed suicide, why was no body found?'

'Maybe she did it somewhere remote.'

'Look, David. I know you're trying to be helpful, but we've considered all these possibilities. But it's not just a question of coming up with theories. We've got less than four and a half hours to come up with *evidence*!'

'Okay, well maybe this poem isn't evidence per se. But I was just wondering . . . how did Dorothy's father die?'

There was silence at the other end.

'Nat?'

'I'm sorry. I was just trying to think.'

'You see what I mean. Is it possible that there was some sort of confrontation between them?'

'Yes, I see what you mean. I'll pass it on to your father.'

'Okay, thank you.'

David rang off. Nat held the receiver in his hand. He wanted to make another call. He had to do it. His hand trembling, he started to key in the number.

20:02 PDT

Juanita had returned to the office and Nat had now left for the District Court. She knew that the TRO hearing would be starting very soon. Had Alex been able to make it? Or was he still tied up with that asshole Lee Kelly – leaving Nat to handle the stay hearing alone? She couldn't understand why Alex made such a doormat of himself for such undeserving people. Then again, was Clayton Burrow any more deserving?

The phone rang again.

'Alex Sedaka's office.'

'Hi, Juanita,' Alex said. 'I'm waiting for Lee Kelly's arraignment. But I have a feeling I'm going to be here for a while.'

'Can't you unload it on one of those courthouse scavengers – as Lee called them?'

'I wish I could.'

'But you filed the form with the clerk, so you're the attorney of record.'

'Yeah.'

'Does that asshole Kelly understand we've got a life hanging in the balance?'

'I haven't had a chance to talk to him. He's penned up with about forty others and they won't let him out till it's his turn.'

'What a crock of shit,' she mumbled under her breath.

'Listen, Juanita, I wanted to ask you something. Do you really think Nat was just playing fast and loose to get the medical center to 'fess up with the info?'

'I think so.'

'And when you called them back, the nurse you spoke to before wasn't there?'

'That's right. She's off duty.'

'Okay, well I guess that's pretty much a dead end then.'

'Not exactly the best choice of words, but I'd say so.'

'Listen, there's something else you can do for me. I need to know the date of Edgar Olsen's suicide.'

'Why?'

'Well I've been thinking about some of the things Anita Morgan told me – as well as David's theory about Edgar Olsen feeling guilty about Dorothy. I'm wondering if Dorothy came back and confronted him about the way he treated her. Maybe *he* killed her to silence her.'

'We still don't really know *how* he treated her.'

'Maybe not, but I'm beginning to get some idea.'

20:24 PDT

Alex was heading toward panic. He couldn't wait here much longer. He was going to have to unload Lee Kelly's case onto another lawyer whether he wanted to or not. It was just that, for reasons of his own, he didn't want to.

He wondered if Juanita's original suspicions about Nat were well-founded or just a sign of stress. She had never been one who was prone to imaginings. Then again, until today he had always trusted Nat. But with hindsight there were certain peculiarities in Nat's behavior. Even the tenacity with which he had badgered his way into a two-bit law firm was curious in retrospect.

And even when Juanita retracted her suspicions, it was like she was holding something back. Was Nat still trying to get the information from the medical center by pretending to be the patient's lawyer? Was Juanita now helping him? They were both determined to save Burrow if they could. They were both dedicated enough to commit such a desperate act.

'*People* v. *Lee Kelly*. Code 459, burglary. One count.'

Alex was shaken out of his musings as Lee Kelly was led out of the cage. Alex stepped forward and stood next to his client. They had literally ten seconds to communicate with each other before the judge – a fifty-something, African-American woman – addressed them.

'Is the defendant represented by counsel?'

'Yes, Your Honor. Alex Sedaka. I appear on behalf of the defendant.'

'Does the defendant wish to enter a plea at this time?'

'The defendant pleads not guilty and requests Release on Recognizance.'

The judge turned to the ADA, a woman in her early thirties.

'The defendant has eighteen priors and is a career criminal, Your Honor.'

'That's over the course of thirty-seven years, Your Honor,' said Alex. 'That's less than one every two years.'

'You sound like you're boasting on behalf of your client, Mr Sedaka.' The judge turned to the prosecutor. 'Is he a flight risk?'

The ADA looked down at her notes.

'He's never jumped bail, Your Honor. But he is a career criminal and a recidivist offender. For this reason we oppose RoR. However, we're ready to consider bail.'

'In what amount?'

'A hundred and fifty thousand dollars.'

'Oh gimme a break!' Lee blurted out.

'You're out of order, Mr Kelly. You'll address your remarks through your counsel. Keep your client in line, Mr Sedaka.'

'I apologize, Your Honor.'

Lee nodded and mouthed his own apology to Alex.

'Does the defendant wish to propose a counter-figure?'

328

'Yes, Your Honor. While we maintain that RoR is indicated in the present circumstances, our fallback position is that if bail *must* be set then, in the absence of a felony specification, it should be treated as misdemeanor burglary and bail set at five thousand dollars.'

'Your Honor,' the ADA chipped in, 'there's no way the People will consider misdemeanor burglary.'

'Okay, but that still leaves a choice between felony first and second.'

'We're inclined to go for first, Your Honor – subject to discussions with defense counsel.'

This was just a bargaining tactic, to secure a plea. Setting bail high and threatening first degree burglary was just for added leverage. The ADA was inviting the judge to collude in the enterprise.

'Was it a domestic burglary?'

'That has yet to be determined, Your Honor.'

'Your Honor, my client has no priors for domestic burglary,' said Alex as the judge turned to him. Alex hadn't even seen the case file, so he was whistling in the dark. 'If it *was* domestic, it would be a first.'

The judge turned back to the ADA. She shook her head as if she had seen it all before. The judge quickly flipped through the bail schedule for the San Francisco district.

'In the absence of a charge specification, bail is set in the amount of forty thousand dollars. Does the defense agree to waive the right to a speedy—?'

'Yes, Your Honor.'

'Okay, we'll set the preliminary hearing at . . . October 10. Next case.'

They went to settle the paperwork with the payments clerk and Alex was in such a hurry to get to the Federal District Court for the hearing on the new evidence, that he paid the money on one of his own credit cards, rather than haggling with one of the bail bondsmen. Then he turned to a grateful looking Lee Kelly.

'Now *I've* got a little job for *you*.'

20:43 PDT

Juanita was Googling 'Edgar Olsen' and 'suicide' in an effort to get the date of death.

'Gotcha!'

May 17, 1998.

The phone rang.

'Alex Sedaka's office.'

'It's me,' said Alex, sounding glum. 'I just had a call from Nat.'

She felt the hope drain out of her.

'What happened?'

'They turned us down.'

'Did they give any reasons?'

'Res judicata, not enough evidence, evidence too weak, should have been introduced before.'

She was about to say something, but she couldn't trust her voice to speak. Throughout the day she had kept her emotion at bay. She was a professional after all and this was just another case. But this was different. It was a capital case. A man's life was in their hands . . . and they were failing him.

Yes, he may be guilty. But he was still a human being and whatever his faults he still had virtues too.

And there were increasing signs that he was innocent . . .

She was about to speak, but again she felt the lump in her throat stopping her. For a second she thought that she could hold up. Then she broke down, sobbing into her arms.

20:45 PDT

'How'd she take it?' asked Nat.

'As expected.'

Alex and Nat were driving back to the office separately, talking to each other on their cell phones.

'Was she crying?'

'It sounded like it.'

'Maybe *I* should have told her directly.'

'Look, we haven't given up . . .'

'No, but let's face it, Alex, we're running out of options.'

'I'm going to have to call the governor and try and convince him with what I've got.'

'What do you think he'll say?'

'I haven't a clue.'

'Will you call him now or from the office?'

'I'll call him now. One last thing . . . I asked Juanita to get me the date of Edgar Olsen's suicide.'

'And?' replied Nat, keenly.

'She told me it was May 17, 1998.'

'Any particular reason for your interest?'

'Well I was just considering the possibility that Dorothy's father might have killed her.'

Nat hesitated and then spoke again.

'But May 17 was before she left, wasn't it? And she was alive at least six days after his death. So he couldn't have killed her.'

'I said it was just a theory. And you're right. The date of the flight was the 24th May. But what's interesting is that she bought the ticket on May 19 – *two days* after Edgar's suicide.'

'That still rules out any possibility of him killing her.'

'Yes, but it doesn't rule out the possibility of *her* killing *him*. We know from the poem that she had some sort of grudge against him. Maybe she killed him and staged it to look like suicide. Maybe that's why she went to England for the abortion.'

'What's going to England for an abortion have to do with making it look like suicide?'

'I mean, that's why she went to *England* for the abortion instead of having it over here – *because she had to get out of the country fast!* She was afraid that if she stayed in America she'd be arrested.'

'But if she staged it to look like suicide, she wouldn't need to run away.'

'Maybe she couldn't be *sure*. And then there's all that money she paid to the medical center. That could've been a payoff for their silence. They might have found out that she was wanted for murder and blackmailed her.'

'But she *wasn't* wanted for murder.'

'But she might have *thought* she was.'

'Yes, but she would hardly have told *them* that.'

'What about if she was under anesthetic? Or when the anesthetic wore off? Don't people sometimes say things at that stage that they wouldn't say otherwise? I heard it's like sodium pentothal.'

He was expecting Nat to shoot him down in flames and tell him that he was on a flight of fancy. But Nat's response surprised him.

'Of course! Now it makes perfect sense!'

'What does?'

'What David said.'

'David?'

'Yes. He called again . . . while you were out.'

'And what did he say?' asked Alex, excitedly.

'He found another verse of that poem.'

'And he thought it was significant?'

'Well it pretty much backs up your theory about Dorothy killing her father. He kept going on about the similarities to a Sylvia Plath poem.'

'"Daddy"?'

'Yes. But it wasn't just that. It was the actual words that he found.'

'Well don't tease me. How did it go?'

'It went: "Daddy, I know I am guilty / Though someone killed you first / I killed you as surely as if / I had pulled the trigger myself / Bang Bang! All over."'

20:53 PDT

Chuck Dusenbury was now at his home in Sacramento. He had given Alex a special number at the office and he was now having all calls to that number diverted to his home. He was eagerly awaiting developments. He had told Alex Sedaka that he could rescind the death warrant at any time until the execution took place, but he preferred to hear from him before nine.

The phone call came just minutes before nine. It was taken by an aide and put through to Dusenbury.

'Governor Dusenbury,' said Alex.

'Yes.'

'Alex Sedaka.'

'I've been waiting for you to call.'

'Yes, I know, sir. And I'm sorry it's taken so long.'

'So what's the news?'

'Well, as you know, Clayton told me that he didn't kill Dorothy and doesn't know where her body is.'

'Yes.'

'You may also know that initially I was skeptical of his innocence. But now I have found certain exculpatory evidence that puts matters in a different light.'

'Go on,' Dusenbury prompted.

Over the next few minutes, Alex told the governor about the airline ticket, the PDF brochure from the medical center, the oral confirmation from the medical center about Dorothy arriving there, David's hacking into Dorothy's bank account and the subsequent payments she had made to the medical center over the course of the next year. He explained that he only had documentary evidence of the purchase of the airline ticket and the bank transfers and he had to admit that the evidence of most of the bank transfers had probably been obtained illegally, although he had not personally sanctioned it or known in advance that it was going to take place. He admitted that the medical center had not sent over any written confirmation that Dorothy was ever at the center and that the person who had provided the oral confirmation was now off duty and currently not contactable. Nevertheless he could vouch for the fact that she had given such oral confirmation and was prepared to stake his own reputation on the authenticity of the information.

After Alex had finished, the governor remained silent for a few seconds. When he finally spoke, his tone was almost apologetic.

'Listen, son, I know you've been working your butt off on this case – and I have to confess I always had doubts about Clayton's guilt, and I still do. I mean, I even accept the oral evidence – which is hearsay. Unlike the courts, I can do that.'

'I know, sir. That's why I'm appealing to you at least to stay the execution.'

'But you just haven't given me enough. The only way I can grant a stay would be to rescind the warrant without issuing a pardon or clemency.'

'But you could do that. And if we don't come up trumps you can re-issue the warrant.'

'I know, and if you gave me enough evidence that's what I'd do. If we had enough oral evidence I'd rescind the warrant right now and wait to see the written confirmation. But the way things stand now, you haven't proved Burrow's innocence, much less that Dorothy's *alive*. You've just shifted the time of her death a year and a bit.'

'I know, sir. But that undermines the entire basis of the original prosecution case. Their case was that he grabbed her on the night of the prom and killed her then and there.'

'That was the theory. But that wasn't the evidence. It's important that we distinguish between what the prosecution speculated on and what they actually *proved*. The main evidence against Burrow was the physical evidence. That was pretty much what nailed him. The disappearance gave them a plausible timeframe, but there was nothing sacrosanct about that timeframe. It could've been a different time: he'd still be just as guilty.'

'Yes, but the fact that she disappeared on the night of the prom and yet was still alive over a year later suggests *deliberate concealment* on her part. The fact that she vanished and stayed in hiding, suggested that she *wanted* people to think she was dead. That suggests that she was planning to have someone blamed for her death.'

'Or that she was afraid of someone who was already trying to kill her.'

'But why would she play possum? Why not just go to the cops?'

'Maybe because she couldn't prove it, Alex. Maybe because she didn't trust anyone. Maybe because she didn't think they'd believe her – or wouldn't care.'

'But that's ridiculous!'

'Is it? Try and think about it from her point of view. A frightened girl, no friends, completely alienated, her father dead, estranged from her mother. Who could she tell? Who could she trust? Who did she feel comfortable talking to? She had no one to turn to. Not her mother. Not her teachers or school friends – she didn't *have* any friends. She was a loner. Maybe her brother, but he was too young. All she could do was run and hide. And because she had financial resources in the form of her inheritance, she had the means to run away and hide. She had just turned eighteen and had access to the trust fund.'

'Did you – pardon me for putting it like this, sir.' Alex's voice was now rising. 'But did you *know* about this before?'

There was silence again for a few seconds.

'I knew about the trust fund. I knew about her alienation and the fact that she was estranged from her parents.'

'How could you . . . ?'

'Look, don't forget, son, Est— Mrs Olsen sat with me for over an hour before you came and she poured her heart out to me. I know all about it because she told me . . . and because I listened. But if you mean did I know about Dorothy going to London or about those financial payouts, then the answer is no.'

'Is there anything I can say to change your mind?'

'Say? Nothing. But there is something you can *do*.'

'What?'

'Bring me proof that someone other than Clayton Burrow killed Dorothy Olsen – or better yet, bring me proof that she's still alive.'

21:04 PDT

'We've done our best,' said Alex solemnly. 'There's nothing more we can do.'

For a long while, no one said a word. They could have been Buddhist monks in a state of meditation. As they stood in the reception area, they formed a triangle. Juanita looking at Alex and Alex at Nat. Nat, though, was looking at the ground.

It was Juanita who broke the silence.

'Are we just going to give up?'

There was a hint of defiance in her tone. But what good was defiance when they had run out of ammunition?

Alex spoke softly.

'We've tried everything. There's nothing more we *can* do.'

'What about the medical center in England?' snapped Juanita.

Alex studied Nat for even the slightest reaction. There was none.

'Is the nurse you spoke to still on duty?'

'No.'

'Are any of the administrative staff there now?'

'I doubt it. It's the wee small hours of the morning in London.'

'Then there's nothing we can do. Unless David comes up with something.'

'Do you think he will?'

'I don't know. But he's still looking. And if he managed to hack into Dorothy's bank account who knows what else he might find.'

Juanita sniffled, but held back the tears this time. She forced herself to speak.

'Don't you think someone should be with Clayton now? He must be desperately lonely.'

Alex was touched by Juanita's compassion. The fact of the matter was they all knew that Clayton Burrow was a rapist as well as a bully who had made Dorothy's life a misery and who had beaten up her younger brother when he tried to defend his sister. In his youth he had been a truly repulsive character and, whatever suffering he was going through now, it was hard to escape the view that he had brought it on himself one way or another.

And yet . . . he was still a human being and they couldn't abandon him. Not because it was their job, not because there was kudos and prestige in saving a man from the death penalty, but because he was a human being and in his years under the threat of death he had changed in some way to become some semblance of a decent person.

'Look, I don't expect you guys to hang round here,' said Alex slowly. 'You can go home.'

Juanita gave Alex a pained look.

'But what if they send a fax through from London?'

Alex shook his head.

'I don't think that's going to happen.'

'But what if it does?' Juanita persisted.

'Okay, look, I'm not *telling* you to go home. I'm simply saying that you don't have to stay . . . either of you.'

'I'm staying!' said Juanita, flatly.

'Nat?'

Nat looked up and met Alex's eyes.

'I'll stay too. But I need to do something first. I'll be back in an hour.'

Alex smiled. Juanita had been right – not with her original suspicions but with the explanation she gave afterward. Nat was trying to get the information from the medical center by pretending to be Dorothy's legal representative. He couldn't do it in front of them because it was unethical and could get Alex disbarred. So instead, he was going to stick his neck out and put his own career on the line. He was the same fiery idealist that he had been when he first badgered Alex into giving him a job. He still had that youthful passion that had so impressed Alex.

The trouble was that Alex was not sure if he should allow him to do it. True, they had a client on death row who was just three hours away from execution yet probably innocent. And for an innocent client facing death, a decent lawyer should be ready to go the extra mile. But breaking the law by misrepresentation was a serious matter. What good would it do him to save one innocent man if he lost the capacity to save anyone else thereafter? That was why as a lawyer he could go so far but no further. He could bend the rules but not break them.

And letting Nat go off on his own so that he could contact the medical center and misrepresent himself as Dorothy's lawyer was bending the rules right the way round.

But what of Nat himself? What if he was caught? Should he lose it all for Clayton Burrow? Did Clayton Burrow deserve *that* much help? Hadn't Clayton Burrow done enough damage?

The most he could hope for was that Nat would not get caught.

'Okay,' said Alex. 'You do what you have to do.'

21:09 PDT

Jonathan was eating a microwave dinner. He knew that he had plenty of time, but he wanted to get to San Quentin early. The place would be crawling with reporters and it might take a long time to get in and he didn't want to get held up.

It had been a roller-coaster day for him, first hearing the news about the governor's offer, then seeing the news, before visiting Alex Sedaka and talking to Juanita.

In some ways he felt that he could no longer hate Clayton Burrow. Yes, Burrow was a bastard. Yes, he had deserved to suffer. But it was almost as if he had suffered enough – as if his execution would be an anti-climax. Jonathan still felt the anger that he had felt toward him nine years ago. But somehow he couldn't experience it with quite the same intensity.

Time heals every wound, so they say.

The phone rang.

'Hallo.'

'Hi, Jonathan.'

Jonathan froze.

'Where are you?'

'I'm in my car.'

'You're calling me on a cell phone.'

'It's okay, I'll keep it brief. Look, everything's going okay, but from what I've been told, someone is getting too close.'

'Who?'

'Alex Sedaka's son, David.'

'What's his son got to do with it?'

'He's a computer geek at Berkeley. He's got hold of the computer and he's been reading the wiped files using a scanning tunneling microscope.'

'Oh I know that.'

'You do?'

'Yes, Sedaka told me. But what can he find?'

'I don't know. I'm probably worrying over nothing. It's been such a long time. But he's found quite a lot already.'

'Is there any way we can stop him?'

'Only by getting the computer.'

21:15 PDT

'You know, I don't understand you, boss.'

Alex and Juanita were sitting in the reception area with mugs of coffee. It was still light outside, but all the office lights were on.

'How do you mean?'

'Well you don't want to pretend to the London clinic that we represent Dorothy, to get them to send the paperwork from when she was there, but you're ready to get a burglar to break into someone's house to check him out – even though you trust Nat now.'

'Christ, I forgot all about that!'

Alex went for the phone and started keying in a number.

'What do you mean?'

'I want to call it off!'

'But I thought you wanted to be sure?'

'I *am* sure! It's obvious that Nat's going to call the medical center again. He just doesn't want *us* to know. Or rather he doesn't want *me* to know. He doesn't want to compromise my position . . . Dammit, straight to voicemail. Kelly's probably switched it off.'

'Why would he do that?'

'I guess he doesn't want his phone going off when he's doing a burglary.'

'I notice you dodged my question – about the irony of the situation.'

'I guess it's a case of the exposure risk.'

'I thought you said the exposure risk was low in the case of what Nat's doing.'

'It is. But it would be like a timebomb ticking away – or like the sword of Damocles. That's an old Greek legend about—'

'I *know* what the sword of Damocles was!'

'Sorry,' said Alex, blushing.

'You'd better try again,' said Juanita. 'Calling Lee, I mean.'

Her tone was muted by guilt . . . or was it fear?

21:20 PDT

The light was ebbing and the area round the lab was deserted. The front entrance was locked. Jonathan could press the button and ask to be admitted, but then he would be challenged for ID. He could try forcing an entry. But that would only set off an alarm and alert others long before he had the chance to do what he had come there for.

There was, however, one other way he could gain access. He knew that the fire exits were sometimes left open. In theory they were locked from the inside and could be opened with a handle mechanism inside the door. They were also supposed to close automatically behind people when they left that way. But in practice, the mechanism to close them didn't always work properly. The doors closed, but they didn't always click shut. And they had such exits on every floor by the fire stairs.

The area by the fire stairs at the back was used as a small parking lot. The dumpsters were also there. But people didn't really hang round there and people who were leaving for the day would hardly waste time if they happened to look up and chance upon the sight of a man walking up – rather than down – the fire escape.

So he knew it would be perfectly safe to enter the building that way.

He tried the fire door on the ground floor, but it was locked. The same was true on the first floor and the second. But it was open on the third. That was all he needed.

21:26 PDT

Miles away, another, somewhat more professional, burglar was breaking into the small rundown house rented by Nathaniel Anderson.

But, unlike the man who had entered the lab at Berkeley, Lee Kelly didn't have any clear idea what he was looking for. His brief was broader than that. He was here to look for anything that might have a bearing on Nat's origins or past. And anything that might explain his interest in Clayton Burrow or the Finchley Road Medical Centre.

Normally when he did a burglary he was looking for valuables and he knew exactly where to look. Prior to the introduction of the 'three strikes' statute he *had*, in fact, done some domestic burglaries, but never been caught in the act. He knew that jewelry was stored either in a dresser or the bottom of a wardrobe, sometimes in a box under the bed and occasionally – rarely – in a safe. The procedure for searching drawers was to start with the bottom one and work your way up, not closing them. That way time was kept to a minimum.

When he came for electronic goods, it was even more

straightforward. But on those jobs he brought a pick-up truck for easy loading, not a motorbike for a fast getaway.

In this case he had to look and make decisions fast. Alex had told him a bit but not much: an employee who was acting suspiciously, the need to check up on his background and whether he had any contact with the press or any prior involvement with the case. Did he grow up in the same town as Dorothy Olsen – the victim of the crime in the case that Alex was working on? Did he know Dorothy or anyone else in her family? Did he know Clayton Burrow?

But how do you check these things out? Photographs, documents, a diary . . . It was hard to know where to begin.

Lee started with the obvious hiding places: shoe boxes, whether in the wardrobe or under the bed. They were the classic hiding places for documents. But that was only if the person was actually trying to *hide* the documents. If he was not, then they could be in other more practical places, like a desk drawer or writing bureau or a bedside cabinet.

There were a couple of shoe boxes, but all they contained were an old pair of sandals and a hardly-worn pair of sneakers.

In the living room, there was a writing bureau – he had passed it on the way in. He flicked through several piles of papers quickly. There were bills, credit card statements and such like. Another contained legal briefs, case notes and things obviously to do with his work.

Then he felt something hard against his palm, something rigid. He pulled it out from amid the papers.

A passport. He opened it to look at the name and when he did he got a jolt of surprise.

The passport didn't belong to Nat. It belonged to the dead girl: Dorothy Olsen.

21:31 PDT

Gaining access to the building on the third floor had been straightforward enough. But Jonathan still had to get to wherever the computer and the scanning tunneling microscope were located.

He thought that at this time it would be easy, that there wouldn't be many people about. But the trouble was there were a few – and that made it even harder. During the day, when lots of people were about, an unfamiliar face wouldn't attract any attention. But when there were fewer people, it was the exact opposite. And some of the people who were about were security people. They didn't just guard the entrances: they patrolled the corridors.

He had to get to the staircase and down to the ground floor where the microscope was situated.

And the question was what he did when he got there. How would he get what he had come for without David noticing?

He started walking down the central staircase. This was relatively safe as any suspicions that anyone might have would be allayed by the fact that he was walking *down* the stairs and was therefore apparently leaving.

However, once he got to the foot of the stairs on the ground floor, he turned not toward the exit but toward the lab housing the microscope. On the way he saw two people walking the other way to him in a corridor: a middle-aged woman and a security guard. He was worried that his eyes would give him away so he mumbled something toward the woman and nodded in her direction as he walked past her. He hoped that this would allay the security guard's suspicions. But, just to make sure, he glanced down at his watch as he got close to the passing point with the security guard.

When he got to the end of the corridor, he turned left and walked up to the doors of the lab. There were two glass port holes that enabled him to look inside. He saw a man with curly hair working alone there – a man whom he assumed to be David Sedaka.

But the problem was what to do now.

Should he go in and challenge him? That would lead to a physical confrontation. Or should he try to lure him out? Or wait for him to leave? He couldn't just stand here outside watching. He had to act now.

21:33 PDT

Lee Kelly was staring at the passport trying to figure out its implications.

He realized that if Nathaniel had the passport, he had quite likely taken it off Dorothy Olsen. The question was, how . . . and *when*? He flicked through the pages and looked for the visa stamps. There was only one. It showed that she arrived at London's Heathrow Airport on May 25, 1998. Alex had said something about her booking a plane ticket for the 24th – one day earlier. The difference in date was presumably due to the time difference or the length of the flight.

But the interesting thing was that there was no exit stamp to indicate that she had *left* England.

He knew that some countries don't stamp the passport on exit, only on entry. Was that the policy in England at the time?

It was before 9/11, so it might have been that they didn't stamp the passport on exit. The United States didn't, even now. Did that mean that she had come back to the USA? Either way, the question was when and how did Nat get her passport? Had he stolen it from her? Had he killed her? Had he gone to England and killed her there and then stolen her passport so that she would not be identified? Could that be why they never found a body? Because she had been killed in England and it had been classified as a death of an unknown person? Could he have killed her, taken her passport and then also planted *false* documents on her so that she had been wrongly identified in England? That would further reduce the likelihood of the body being identified as that of Dorothy Olsen.

But then again, why assume that she was dead? If her passport was here was there not a more obvious answer?

He was hiding her! She was staying here at his place in hiding, unable to go out.

But then why wasn't she here now? Had she heard him breaking in and run away, thinking he was the police? There was no sign of any open windows, other than the one he had prised open in order to get in. Was she hiding in the house? It was hard to imagine where. He had looked round in all the places large enough.

Or had she been in hiding here until recently until it got too hot for her to hang round? And had she now run away altogether or merely found somewhere else to hide?

Whatever the explanation, one thing was sure: the visa stamp in her passport offered documentary proof that Dorothy Olsen had arrived in London on or about the time she had disappeared. And that was what Alex Sedaka wanted. Lee closed the passport and was about to put it in his pocket when he noticed that something had fallen out.

It was a piece of thin white cardboard.

21:35 PDT

Jonathan made his way to the basement and sought out the closet where the electricity supply was controlled. It was locked, but with nothing more than a cheap padlock. He didn't know much about picking locks, but he'd brought a large screwdriver with him. Instead of going for the lock itself, he looked at the flimsy plate on the closet door. Without much difficulty – and with surprisingly little noise – he prised it open.

He found himself presented with a dazzling and somewhat confusing array of circuit breakers. Eventually he found one marked 'main lab.' He was about to throw the switch when he realized that this wasn't enough. Throwing the switch might cause David Sedaka to leave the lab in consternation, but he would still be hovering about outside, leaving Jonathan no way to get in undetected.

He looked at the top and bottom of the cupboard, eventually finding three large switches at the top. These evidently controlled the main flow. The lab presumably had three-phase wiring and each of these master circuit breakers controlled one phase. To black out the lab entirely he would have to throw all three switches.

But then he realized that even that wouldn't work. The emergency battery would kick in and the temporary lighting would come on. This wouldn't be enough to operate the lab equipment, but it would be enough to supply lighting which, again, would render untenable any effort to sneak into the lab.

He struggled to come up with an idea. What could he do that would get David out of the lab and give him free access to the lab? A phone call telling him that something untoward had happened to his father? Forget it! David would simply call his father's office to verify it.

A fire? That would be a very serious thing to—

Of course! That was it!

Not a real fire, of course, just a fire alarm. The button was there staring him in the face by the basement exit to the parking lot. It couldn't be simpler.

In a flash he pushed the button. The klaxon rang out.

He heard voices, questions, puzzlement and heard scurrying footsteps. The footsteps were retreating. No one was coming down to the basement. At some point, they could probably check where the alarm had been set off. But they hadn't done so yet. He still had time.

He waited a few seconds longer and then started running up the stairs. But he felt self-conscious about the lights being on and so he ran back down and threw the three circuit breakers, plunging the building into darkness. It felt surprisingly long before the emergency lighting came on – although he realized in retrospect that it was barely more than a second.

Again he ran up the stairs to the ground floor, but this time he did not stop. He raced straight into the lab where he had seen David Sedaka working. He saw the computer, but he realized that he didn't need it. David Sedaka had opened it and taken out the hard disk and dismantled it. It was the platters from the hard disk that he needed and they were right there by the computer that David had been using. But that wasn't Dorothy's computer. It was a laptop and it was connected up to the scanning tunneling microscope, presumably to control the operations.

Jonathan scooped up the platters in one hand and ran. As he ran out, he felt a hand push against his chest. He felt himself being hurled back and when he had regained his bearings he looked up to see a curly-haired man standing there.

'What are you doing here?' asked the man.

'Nothing.'

'What have you got in your hand?'

Jonathan looked down. The platters seemed so small and fragile, it was hard to believe that anyone could even notice them, especially in this light. But when he looked up he noticed that David Sedaka's eyes were still on the platters. And he knew what he had to do.

Quick as a flash, his free hand formed a fist and shot out, flooring David Sedaka with a single punch.

21:37 PDT

Lee Kelly picked up the small rectangular piece of white cardboard that had fallen from the passport and flipped it over. It was a photograph of a young woman in her twenties looking at the camera with a bright, sunny smile on her face.

He couldn't tell when or where the picture was taken. There were people in the background, but the woman filled the foreground and the people in the background were too small to glean any information from. It looked like it was taken at a party. It had that sort of look and feel to it. But it was impossible to be sure.

For a second or two he thought that it was a picture of Dorothy. But looking back at the passport picture he had second thoughts. The eyes were similar, but the bone structure was different.

But the question was, why was it inside Dorothy's passport? Just having the passport was suspicious enough, but why the picture? Putting it inside the passport suggested that it was there for safe-keeping – an important picture inside an important document.

But why? Why was it so important?

And who was the woman?

21:41 PDT

Alex was driving to Jonathan's place. Juanita had convinced him that he couldn't just give up on Burrow, but the problem was where to go from here. Jonathan seemed like a potential weak link. Esther had told him that she had heard them talking just a few days before Dorothy vanished – indeed, a few days before Edgar Olsen had committed suicide.

That couldn't have just been about the rape. The rape was six weeks earlier. So they must have been talking about the pregnancy, rather than the rape itself. But if it was about the pregnancy, then it would probably also have been about the abortion, or at least the question of whether or not to have one.

Jonathan could therefore *not* have been ignorant of Dorothy's plans to go to England.

And if he knew, then Alex had to find a way to break him and get him to admit the truth. Clayton Burrow's life depended on it.

The cell phone rang in the hands-free kit. Alex looked at the display.

'Hi, David.'

'Hi, Dad, listen, you're not going to believe what's happened!'

'What?' asked Alex, excitedly.

'Someone broke into the lab and stole the platters from the hard disk!'

'*What?*'

'We had a little bit of a confrontation.'

'Who?'

'Me and the guy who did it. The fire alarm went off and as I was leaving the building I noticed something out of the corner of my eye. I looked round and saw this guy running toward the lab instead of toward the exit.'

'What did he look like?'

'By the time I looked round he was walking away from me so I only saw his back.'

'Did you tell anyone?'

'Not exactly. I went back myself to see what he was up to.'

'Wasn't that a bit risky?'

'Well he went in and I couldn't see what he did, but he came out of the lab like three seconds later holding something in his hand. So I challenged him.'

'That was dangerous.'

'Not really. I mean, he wasn't so big.'

Alex was surprised that his son was being so blasé about it. He wasn't exactly noted for being the world's best action hero. Debbie had always been the athletic one. David was the nerd with his nose in a book half the time.

'So what did he say?'

'He said he wasn't doing anything, but I could see

he was holding something in his hand. I wasn't too sure what it was, but it was clear that it was something he wanted to hold on to.'

'So why did you let him go?'

'I didn't exactly *let* him. While I was looking down at whatever it was he had in his hand he caught me with a sucker punch.'

'Holy shit!'

'Don't worry, I'm okay. I think he just broke my nose.'

'Good God, hadn't you better get to a doctor?'

'It's not the first time I've broken my nose, Dad. Remember the baseball game?'

'Now you're not still going on about that, David! You know she didn't mean it.'

'I'm not blaming her, Dad. All I'm saying is if I could take a broken nose as a child from Debbie's Little League baseball bat, then I can take one as an adult from some punk who manages to catch me with a sucker punch.'

'Okay. Well just take care of yourself.'

'I will, don't worry.'

A motorbike sped past Alex's car, just as he was about to pull out to overtake.

'Asshole!' he muttered.

'What?'

'Just some guy on a Suzuki.'

'You okay?'

'Sure I'm okay. It's *you* I'm worried about.'

'Don't be.'

'All right. Just one thing, David. Do you think there was anything more to be gleaned from those hard disk platters?'

'I don't know, but there's still one left.'
Alex was surprised.
'I don't understand.'
'There was one left in the microscope.'

21:44 PDT

Nat was worried. Things were getting out of hand. He had made several calls but wasn't getting an answer. Every time he called the landline, it rang for several moments and then went to voicemail. With the cell phone it went straight to voicemail. That meant that the cell phone was switched off. And that troubled Nat.

He was glad that he had been vague with Alex and Juanita about where he was going. Because that gave him a window of opportunity to stay out of the office for longer than just a few minutes. He wasn't sure that his trip was worthwhile. But he wanted to make sure.

However, he felt hot and sweaty in his clothes. It had been a long day. So he decided to take a small detour and drive to his own home first for a change of clothes.

He pulled up in the street, not bothering to pull onto the driveway. He would only be a few minutes. Also he was tired. So tired that he didn't notice the faint glow of the flashlight inside the living room.

It was only when he had unlocked the door and pushed it open that he sensed something was wrong. He noticed a faint light go out just as he opened the door. A trick of the light, he thought as he stepped inside and switched on the living room light before closing the door behind him.

It was then that he heard a sound. He raced into the bedroom just in time to see a man on the bed clambering out the window. Instinctively he leapt forward and grabbed the leg that was still inside the room. He yanked hard and the man let out a cry of pain. It was then that he noticed for the first time that the man was rather old – well in his fifties at any rate.

The man pulled away and tried to kick his leg free. But Nat had locked the man's leg in a tight overarm grip. The man tried to use one of his hands to push Nat away. But youth and strength triumphed over age and the man – who was not of particularly large build – found himself being dragged back.

He still had the other leg over the window ledge, locked round it and creating a grip that made it hard to dislodge him from there. But when Nat shifted his attention from the man's leg to his torso, using both his arms and hands to grab the man, all the fight went out of the intruder and he allowed himself to be dragged back in.

He looked at Nat's panting mouth and his intense eyes and – obviously fearful of Nat's intentions – he pleaded with him not to hurt him.

'I'm not resisting. Just tell the cops I didn't resist, okay?'

Nat well understood what was going through this man's mind. He was a burglar, caught in the act of breaking into domestic premises. Under the three strikes rule that was a very serious offense.

'Okay, I'll put in a good word for you,' said Nat with a smile, whipping out his cell phone. 'I might even be able to get you a lawyer.'

'I've already got—'

He broke off abruptly. Nat, though, wasn't listening and had keyed in 911 and reported the break-in to the police, adding that he had caught the burglar, but that the 'perp' was cooperating. The police told him to wait there with the suspect. After the call ended, Nat closed the window and allowed the burglar to assume a sitting position on the bed.

'What's your name?' asked Nat.

'I'm in custody. You're not supposed to question me until you've read my Mirandas.'

'I see you know the ropes,' said Nat with a smile.

'I've been round the block a few times.'

'Now why doesn't that surprise me?' The burglar said nothing. 'But I'm not a cop. Anyway, whatever you say to me now will *not* be used against you.'

The burglar nodded, still showing signs of fear.

'So what *is* your name then?' Nat persisted.

'Kelly.'

'Kelly what?'

'No, Kelly's my last name. Lee . . . Lee Kelly.'

Nat froze. That name sounded familiar. He remembered his conversation with David Sedaka two hours ago.

Lee Kelly was the burglar that Alex had taken a detour to represent at the arraignment.

What a coincidence that he should break into my place now.

21:57 PDT

'Yes, he's all right, apart from a broken nose. I just wanted you to know. It looks like someone is trying to sabotage us.'

Alex was on the phone to Juanita as he pulled up outside the building that housed Jonathan's apartment.

'Be careful, boss. Whoever it was must be pretty desperate.'

'My thoughts exactly. That means we're on to something. You be careful too. If anyone comes to the office when Nat and I aren't round—'

'Oh do me a favor! I grew up on the streets where they eat suits like you for breakfast!'

'Sorry, you're right. I'm sure you can handle yourself. But stay alert.'

Alex ended the call and parked the car. As he walked up to the entrance he noticed a Suzuki motorbike parked just outside. It reminded him of the one that had overtaken him earlier.

He walked up the stairs of the building and knocked on Jonathan's door.

'Who is it?' a tense, nervous voice called out from inside.

'It's Alex Sedaka!' Alex called out.

'What do you want?'

This was strange. Jonathan hadn't been so cagey last time Alex was here. Then again, last time Alex had phoned first. But still . . .

'I just want to talk!'

'Just a minute!'

Alex heard a faint thumping and thudding, like doors or drawers were being opened and closed. He assumed that Jonathan had locked the door and taken the key out and was now trying to find it.

After almost a minute, the door opened and Jonathan stood there looking sweaty and agitated.

'I have to talk to you,' said Alex. 'This has gone on long enough.'

'Come in,' said Jonathan swallowing nervously.

He moved aside to let Alex across the threshold. As soon as Alex was in Jonathan shut the door behind him. Something in Jonathan's face drew Alex's eyes, to the hand at his side.

The next thing Alex *saw* was the hand lurching toward his torso and a sparkle of pocket-sized lightning, matched by a crackle of miniaturized thunder.

And the next thing he *felt* was a jolt of pain as his muscles stopped functioning, his vision became blurred and his legs gave out.

22:04 PDT

'The police are taking a long time,' said Nat, trying to pass the time and conceal his own fear as to why Lee Kelly was here.

'You know what they say: you can never find a cop when you need one.'

'So how come you didn't take anything?'

Lee felt a stab of fear, but recovered quickly. He was a pro after all.

'I didn't have time. You caught me, remember.'

Nat wasn't sure whether to face up his hole card. It might shock Lee into admitting something. But it would also tip his own hand – probably to Alex. And he wasn't ready for that just yet.

He regretted calling the police. If he had a little longer with Lee he might be able to get some answers out of him. But the police could arrive at any moment. Besides, he was kidding himself. He wouldn't harm or kill this man, even if he had the opportunity. There were limits to how far he would go.

He wouldn't hurt the innocent . . . and this man was innocent – relatively.

He heard a car screech to a halt and seconds later there was a knock on the door. The police had arrived. The next few minutes were spent on formalities as Nat showed his tenancy agreement to prove that he was the legal tenant of the house and signed the complaint. They wanted him to come to the police station to make a full statement, but he had already prepared his excuse.

'I work for Alex Sedaka, the lawyer representing Clayton Burrow. I'm still working and my boss is going to be wondering where I am.'

'Okay, can you come to the station in the morning?' asked the patrolman.

'Sure,' said Nat. 'No problem.'

The patrolman closed his notebook while his partner, who had already cuffed Lee Kelly, led his man away.

'Listen, maybe I shouldn't say this, but off the record I hope they fry your client.'

Nat looked shocked, but only for a second.

'I'm not in the business of judging,' said Nat. 'I just want to make sure that the system works – that includes defending a man in a capital case.'

'I'm sorry. I guess I was out of line with that wisecrack.'

But Nat wasn't thinking of that. He was still thinking about why Lee Kelly should have picked *his* place to break into – and right after Alex had got him bail.

When Alex came to, he found himself handcuffed to a radiator in a bedroom. Jonathan was sitting on the bed looking at him. He did not look happy. He was holding something in his hands, looking at it almost with fascination. It was a cell phone. As Alex's eyes regained their focus, he realized that it was his own iPhone.

But what was he planning to do?

'Jonathan?'

'You awake?' The voice was nervous. Alex had expected a trace of aggression, given the circumstances in which he had got here. But there was none. He could tell that Jonathan was more afraid than he was.

'Yes. What's going on?'

'I didn't mean to do it. I mean, I didn't want a confrontation.'

'Then why did you attack me?'

'I mean with . . . He just grabbed me.'

Alex was confused.

'What are you talking about? Who grabbed you? Clayton?'

'I mean at the lab! David.'

'The lab?' Realization dawned on Alex. 'It was *you*?'

'I just wanted the hard disk. I didn't want him snooping round anymore. I didn't mean to attack him. I just wanted to grab the disk platters and run out. But he caught me and shoved me back against a wall. Look . . . is he all right?'

Alex remembered that Jonathan had never been a bully. He was the kid who *stood up* to the bully even when he knew he was going to get beaten. He was not the sort of person to take pleasure in hurting an innocent man.

'He's fine. His nose may be a bit crooked unless he gets it set, but aside from that he's fine.'

Jonathan permitted himself a smile.

'Okay . . .'

'Okay,' Alex echoed. 'So now . . . can you let me go?'

'Let you . . . ?' Jonathan seemed to snap out of a trance. 'Oh yes! Of course.'

Jonathan leaned forward and was about to insert the key into the lock of the handcuff on Alex's wrist when he paused.

'If you didn't come here about David, what *did* you come here for?'

'I came here to ask about Dorothy and why she went to England.'

'I don't know anything about that. I didn't even know she went to England. I don't even know if it's true. I've only got *your* word for it – and you're trying to save that scumbag Burrow.'

'It's true I'm trying to save him. But a lawyer's not allowed to falsify evidence: he could get disbarred.'

'Some lawyers are ready to risk disbarment.'

'Not me . . . and not for someone like Burrow.'

'Well even if it's true, I don't know anything about it.'

'Oh, I think you do. You see, your mother told me that she heard you and Dorothy talking about the rape a few days before she vanished.'

'Heard us?'

'It was just whispering through the walls. But she heard Dorothy crying and she heard the word rape.'

'So? I knew about the rape. I never denied that.'

'Yes, but the rape took place on Dorothy's eighteenth birthday: that would be April the first. Your mother heard you and Dorothy talking about it a week before she vanished. That was on the 16th May.'

'So what?'

'Well I was wondering why she would be talking about it then?'

'Why shouldn't she?'

'Surely if she wanted to talk to you about the rape, she'd've talked about it before?'

'Maybe she did.'

'So what brought it up again six weeks later?'

'Maybe she couldn't bring herself to talk about it sooner.'

'Maybe,' Alex agreed. 'But I think that she decided to talk to you then because she had just found out that she was pregnant. When she realized she was pregnant, that was the trigger. She had to talk to someone.'

'Why would it take her six weeks?'

'Oh she would've suspected before, Jonathan. But she was probably in denial. May 16 is round about the time she would have finally realized.'

'And what if it was?' asked Jonathan slowly.

'And we know that she had an abortion. So maybe she was talking to you about her *intention* to have an abortion.'

'Again,' said Jonathan irritably, 'so what?'

'Well she had the abortion in England. So if she talked to you about the pregnancy and having an abortion – and if she had the abortion in England – then don't you think that would suggest that she probably *talked* to you about going to England for the abortion?'

Jonathan opened his mouth to speak. But no words came out. He looked away, unwilling to meet Alex's eye.

'You see, Jonathan, I'm not trying to corner you into an admission that you knew what Dorothy was planning – although I think you did. But the thing that has me puzzled is *why* she went to England for an abortion. Why not have it done right here?'

Jonathan finally turned to look at Alex.

'And is that just a question? Or do you have some sort of an answer in mind?'

'Well she booked the ticket right after her father blew his brains out. And then there's the whole question of who she blamed for her pregnancy.'

'Well I think that, at least, should be obvious,' Jonathan sneered.

'Oh I'm not doubting for a minute that Clayton Burrow got her pregnant. But the question isn't who made her pregnant, but rather who she *thought* was responsible at the time. And remember, Clayton Burrow raped her *once*. What are the chances of getting her pregnant with one shot?'

Alex studied Jonathan for a reaction. But there was none. He pressed on.

'And then there's another thing: we've found some files on Dorothy's computer that suggests some resentment toward her father. I told you about that reference to him "ripping the clothes" off of her, didn't I? So could it be that Clayton wasn't the only one who forced himself physically on Dorothy? Could it be that her father routinely forced himself on her?'

There was a ghost of a smile on Jonathan's face. But it vanished just as quickly as it had appeared. Alex continued.

'Dorothy was estranged from both her mother and her . . . and Edgar Olsen. You told me at our first meeting that Dorothy got a raw deal. When I asked you to elaborate on this all you said was that there are sins of commission and sins of *omission*. Could one of those sins of omission be a mother turning a blind eye to a husband's sexual abuse of her daughter?'

'You got any more theories?'

Alex knew that he was playing a dangerous game. Jonathan may not have been violent in the past, but he had zapped him with a taser just now and he had him handcuffed to the radiator.

'Well all of this leads to the question of whether Dorothy believed that it was her father who got her pregnant. And that in turn leads to the question of how she might have reacted to that belief.'

'You think, after years of abuse, she suddenly took it into her head to get revenge?'

'This wasn't just abuse. Now she was pregnant,

remember. A whole different ball game. And it certainly must have thrown her hormones out of whack.'

'Let's say it's true. So what? What are you here for? And what does it have to do with Clayton Burrow? You can't say that my father killed Dorothy, because he died before she did. So it's a nice theory, but it doesn't really add up to a hill of beans as they say.'

'No, not in itself. But it would explain a number of things. For example, why did Dorothy go to London to have an abortion? Possibly to get away from the US before she got arrested for murder. Even if they eventually decided that Edgar's death was suicide, she wasn't to know that at the time. Those evidence technicians are very good at recognizing when a crime scene has been staged. Maybe she panicked and fled.'

'You said it explains a number of things,' said Jonathan. 'That's only one.'

'Well, then there's the money. She paid the London clinic forty thousand pounds. That's a sizeable chunk of her inheritance. Why would she do that? Could it be that they found out what she had done and started blackmailing her?'

'A clinic? Blackmailing someone?'

'Maybe not the clinic itself. Maybe someone on the staff using the clinic as a conduit for the money.'

Alex was staring at Jonathan, still waiting for a reaction. Finally Jonathan smiled.

'It's a very interesting theory, but there's just one problem: you've got it backward.'

22:11 PDT

Lee Kelly had stayed silent throughout the drive to the police station. It was not like him to get caught doing a job, but to get caught twice in one day was particularly embarrassing. However, it wasn't professional pride he was worried about. It was prison.

This was a domestic burglary – and they were taken much more seriously. The fact that he did it while out on bail made it all the more grave.

But there was more to it than that. The person whose house he was breaking into was that of his own lawyer's legal intern. Would that fact come up in the case? And the reason he was doing it was because Alex had asked him to. He was not supposed to breathe a word of this to anyone. It could get Alex disbarred. But was he to think about himself first, or his lawyer? If he kept quiet, could Alex save him? Could Alex keep him out of prison? Would the truth come out in spite of his silence? Did Nat realize the connection?

As they searched him they found the passport – Dorothy's passport. But the overworked cop at the desk didn't even bother to look inside it. He just logged it as 'US passport' and bagged it along with everything else in Lee's possession and marked the evidence bag. The only job of the custody officer was to secure the prisoner and inventory the items in his possession at the time of arrest and bag them up and store them until he was released. It was up to the assigned case officers to investigate.

Of course, Lee knew that they might look at it later. But the risk was small. Would Nat tell the police about it? Would he even know it was gone? Nat had seen Lee trying to flee empty handed. Would he even realize what Lee was there for?

The custody officer had also found the picture of the young woman. He was about to bag it up with the rest of Lee's possessions when Lee spoke.

'Can I keep that? It's my mother.'

The custody officer looked at the picture and then back at Lee skeptically. This man was born in the fifties. The picture was in color and looked like it was more recent than that – and it was of a young woman. If it had been this man's mother when she was young, he would have expected it to be an old black and white picture. But still . . .

'You're not supposed to have anything on you other than the clothes on your back when you're in the lock-up – just in case you try and harm someone, or yourself.'

Lee mouthed the word 'please,' and gave the custody officer his most pitiful look.

'Well . . . okay then.'

The custody officer gave it back and Lee quickly put it away.

'Thank you. Look, would it be all right if I called my lawyer now?'

22:14 PDT

'What do you mean I've got it backward?'

They were sitting there eyeball to eyeball. Jonathan had the height advantage sitting on the bed whereas Alex was on the floor. But Alex did not feel as if he were at a disadvantage. It was Jonathan who was angry. It was Jonathan who was afraid.

'Dorothy never thought Edgar got her pregnant. He wasn't even her father.'

'She *knew* that?'

'Of course she knew it!'

'And what else did she know?'

'She knew that it was Clayton Burrow who got her pregnant.'

'How could she have been so sure?'

He was wondering if Jonathan was going to say that she knew Edgar Olsen was sterile.

'Because my father didn't touch her! I mean, not sexually.'

This caught Alex by surprise.

'According to that poem we found, he ripped the clothes off of her.'

'There's more than one way to abuse a person. He didn't abuse her physically. He abused her psychologically.'

'Ripping her clothes off doesn't exactly sound like purely *psychological* abuse.'

'He only did that once, in a moment of rage. Basically he just snapped because she was flaunting her sexuality in front of him.'

'Okay, so he didn't sexually assault her. So what *did* happen? She found out that she was pregnant and you say she blamed Clayton Burrow. But Burrow didn't die the very next day. Edgar Olsen did!'

'How do you know?' asked Jonathan, fear now in his voice.

'Because your mother heard you talking about it on the 16th May. Edgar Olsen died on the 17th.'

Jonathan lowered his head. He appeared to be going through some inner turmoil. Finally he raised his head, dry eyed, but with a hardened expression on his face.

'Okay, I'll tell you. It's true, Dorothy came to me on the 16th when she finally realized she was pregnant. I'd known something was up before then because of the way she was acting. But that was when she finally told me – about the rape and about the pregnancy. She'd only just found out for sure that she was pregnant, although she'd suspected it for some time. I tried to comfort her, but she was inconsolable. There was nothing I could say. She was both afraid and angry – afraid because she wasn't sure what she was going to do about the baby and angry with Burrow at what he had done. She must have brooded about it all night, because the following day she decided to kill him.'

'To kill him?'

'Yes.'

'To kill Burrow?'

'Yes.'

'How?'

'With my father's gun.'

'And what? She went to Edgar's place to get his gun and he caught her?'

'No, not exactly. You see, my father bought the gun way back in the eighties when there were all those crime scares. But by the late nineties crime was going down and he more or less forgot about the gun. So it just sat there at the back of the closet at our house.'

'Wait a minute. I thought he was no longer living at the house?'

'That's right, he wasn't. He'd moved out into a condo. But he didn't take all his stuff with him. I mean, he took the important stuff, but he didn't go through everything.'

'And one of the things he left behind was the gun?'

'Like I said, things had changed. I guess he wasn't so paranoid by then. Or maybe he just forgot it 'cause it was at the back of a closet. At any rate, for whatever reason, he didn't take it.'

'And Dorothy found it?'

'Found it. Looked for it. Knew it was there. Whatever. The following day she came to my room with the gun and told me she was going to kill Burrow.'

'So what made her kill your father instead?'

'Did I say she did?'

'Well he died, didn't he? And the cause of death was

gunshot wounds from his own gun. Or are you going to tell me that it really was suicide?'

'I wanted to stop her.'

'What?'

'I didn't want her to do it.'

'Why not? You hated Burrow. He beat the crap out of you. And now he'd raped your sister.'

'I didn't give a shit about Burrow! But I didn't want Dorothy to get into trouble for it. I may have only been a kid but I knew that people who commit crimes like that usually get caught. Rape you can get away with because rapists can always say the girl consented. But amateur murderers usually get caught. And she was an amateur. I knew that if she killed him she'd get caught.'

'And what? You thought you could do it and get away with it?'

'Hell, no! I knew that with my luck I'd've botched it big time. I may have been a bit hot-headed but I knew my limitations.'

'So what did you do?'

'I persuaded her to give me the gun. I told her that we should think about it and plan it properly. I was going to put it back.'

'But you didn't put it back, did you?'

'Not back in *our* house, no. You see, I knew that if I put it back in the closet or wherever – the way she was feeling – she might take it again and kill him and get caught. So I decided to take it to my dad's place.'

'And what? Just give it to him without an explanation?'

'I didn't exactly have a clear plan. I just knew I had to get the gun out of the way – to stop Dorothy using it.

When I got to his place, I told him I missed him and wanted to see him. He invited me in. He was usually happy to see me. He never treated me badly the way he did with Dorothy. Then, when he went to the bathroom, I crept into his bedroom and tried to hide the gun in a closet there. But he caught me and demanded to know what I was doing. He accused me of snooping. He could do that, you know, go from being friendly one minute to being angry the next. He didn't usually do that with me, but he did with Dorothy and he knew that Dorothy and I were close. Then he saw the gun.'

'And what happened? Did he grab it?'

Jonathan hesitated for a second and his lips twitched upward. It was nearly a smile – but not quite.

'I wish I could latch on to that excuse. But he didn't. Instead he just demanded to know what I was doing with it.'

'And what did you tell him?'

Jonathan took a deep breath.

'I told him the truth.'

'The truth?'

'Yes. Everything. I told him I was putting the gun there so it would be out of Dorothy's reach. And I told him why.'

'You told him about the rape?'

'*Yes, I told him about the rape!*' Tears were now welling up in Jonathan's eyes. 'And you know what he did? He laughed.'

Jonathan choked back his tears.

'Laughed?'

'And he said . . .' He swallowed the lump in his throat.

Even after these years, the memory evidently still pained him. 'He said: "With any luck it'll cure that bull-dyke bitch."'

He broke down in tears. Alex hated to press him, but he had to know the rest.

'And then what happened?'

'I just snapped at that point. I swung the gun round to his head and he turned away in fear. It all happened too quickly: I just didn't think.' Alex said nothing. As a lawyer, he knew that this was not the time to put words into someone else's mouth. 'I . . . I pulled the trigger. The next thing I knew, his brains were splattered all over the wall.'

22:20 PDT (06:20 BST)

Alone in the office, Juanita was getting worried. Nat still hadn't come back and she couldn't reach Alex on the phone. If Nat was really trying to get the clinic to send the papers, then wouldn't he have done it by now? What was taking him so long?

And where was Alex?

Time was running out and so were their options. One by one the doors had been slammed in their faces and it felt like they were boxed in on all sides. Unless they could come up with something fast, Clayton Burrow would be dead in two hours.

Juanita wanted to have another try with the medical center herself. They had evidently faxed over something, according to the journal, so someone at the center must have been cooperating with them. The problem was that she didn't know what Nat had been doing in the meantime and she didn't want to step on his toes. If she phoned them up and contradicted something that he said, it would be disastrous.

But the problem was she couldn't call Nat either. If she asked him about his progress with the medical center then she would have to admit that she knew what he was doing. This would be all right if she was correct. But what if she was wrong? She still couldn't be sure. And, if she was wrong, then she was just wasting time by holding off.

She knew what she had to do. She couldn't wait any longer. If he had called them in the guise of Dorothy Olsen's legal representative, it would be to tell them to give the information to Alex Sedaka's law firm. And if that was the case, then there was no reason why she shouldn't call them as Alex Sedaka's secretary and ask them for the information again.

She dialed and tapped her fingers nervously while she waited for an answer.

'Finchley Road Medical Centre.'

'Hallo, my name is Juanita Cortez. I'm calling from the law offices of Alex Sedaka in San Francisco.'

'Oh hi, I spoke to you earlier.'

'Yes, you're not Nurse White, are you?'

'No, like I told you, she's off duty.'

'Listen, it's not actually Nurse White I need to speak to. It's the administration. As I explained to Nurse White, we desperately need that information about Dorothy Olsen.'

'And, as I explained to that man who called earlier, we cannot release that information without authorization.'

Juanita got angry.

'You do understand that this is a matter of life and death, don't you? You do understand that we have a client who's scheduled to be executed in less than two hours for the murder of Dorothy Olsen unless we can prove that she was alive after the date he's supposed to have killed her!'

'I can't give out that information without permission. It would be more than my job's worth.'

'Well in that case, can you let me speak to someone in authority – someone who *can* make a decision?'

'The best person to talk to would be Stuart Lloyd. He's the Chief Administrator.'

'So can I talk to him?'

'Well he isn't here yet. I mean, it's only six twenty. But he should be here by eight o'clock.'

'But that'll be too late! Our client is scheduled to die at one minute past midnight.'

'Well that's plenty of—'

'I mean *our* time! That's eight o'clock *your* time!'

'Look, there's nothing I can do. If you like, you can give me your number and if he comes in early then he can call you.'

Juanita was about to give it, when a call came through on another line. She looked at the display and saw that it was from Nat.

'I'll have to call you back.' She pressed another button on the switchboard. 'Hi, Nat.'

'Hi, Juanita. You sound harassed.'

'I'm holding the fort alone here. Where are you?'

'I'm sorry. I went home for a change of clothes.'

'*A change of clothes?*'

She was incredulous.

'Yes, I was feeling uncomfortable. I'm sorry.'

'Well are you coming back now?'

'Not yet. I have something else to do.'

'I don't suppose you can tell me what this "something else" is?'

'Not right now. Look, Juanita, there was an incident at my house.'

'What sort of an incident?'

'There was a burglar.'

'A burglar? What is this, an epidemic?'

'What's that?' he asked, apparently oblivious to Juanita's use of humor to relieve the tension.

'Nothing. So what did this burglar get away with?'

'He didn't get away at all. I caught him.'

'Oh my God! Are you all right?'

Juanita realized now who the burglar was – and she was worried.

'Yes, I'm fine.'

'When you say you caught him . . . ?'

'He was kind of old and he didn't put up much of a fight.'

'So what happened? Did you call the police?'

'Yes. They arrested him. And I'm supposed to go to the station to make a statement.'

'Can't it wait?'

There was a brief hesitation. Then Nat spoke again.

'Is there anything that I can do at this stage anyway? I mean . . . look, I don't mean to say this, but we seem to have run out of options.'

Juanita was silent. She was trying to read his words . . . and his tone. Had he really given up? Had he tried to get the medical center to give the information? Had he run up against the same obstacles as she had? And what about the burglar? It must have been Lee Kelly.

Alex hadn't been able to contact him to call it off and now he had been caught red handed. Would he snitch on Alex? And would Nat figure it all out? He may not be as experienced as Alex but he'd been round the block a few times.

'Okay, look, you do what you have to,' said Juanita. 'I'll see you when I see you.'

'Okay. Wait, listen, did you say you were holding the fort alone?'

'Yes, why?'

'So did Alex go back to San Quentin?'

Juanita wasn't sure whether to answer this. If Nat had figured out that Alex had sent Lee to spy on him, then it might be better to hold back, or even lie. But on the other hand, if their suspicions were unfounded, then wouldn't it be better to rebuild the bond of trust by telling him the truth?

'No, he went to see Jonathan.'

'*What for?*'

Juanita noticed the unusual intensity in his voice.

'He thinks Jonathan knows about Dorothy's flight to England.'

'When did he go there?'

'About forty minutes ago.'

'Has he called in yet?'

'No. And I can't call him either. It's like his phone's switched off.'

'Okay. I'll be back as soon as I can.'

When Nat rang off, the feeling of desolation returned to Juanita. She wanted to do something. But they had already tried everything. She had hoped that she might get somewhere with the medical center, but had run up against the same brick wall as before.

The thing that was nagging away at her was that they had sent *something*. That meant that *someone* at the medical center was trying to help – or had at least seen fit to send them something in writing.

But the fax wasn't there now.

So where was it? Had Nat taken it? Thrown it away? Shredded it?

Of course!

She raced over to the shredder, lifted off the grinding mechanism and began fishing out papers. She remembered reading how the Iranian students at the American embassy had spent hours sticking shredded documents together at the time of the embassy siege in 1979 after Khomeini seized power in Iran. They had hoped to find things that they could use to embarrass the United States. But most of what they found was mundane material like requisition orders for stationery.

The point was that they kept at it, laboriously re-assembling every page.

It can be done.

And if Nat *had* shredded it, then it would be among the strips at the top of the pile.

22:24 PDT

Jonathan was sitting on the bed, looking down at his hands. He was no longer crying. Whatever mixture of emotions had coursed through him – guilt, regret, fear – had all passed now. All that was left was a kind of exhausted passivity, as if he could now accept anything else that life threw at him.

'Jonathan, I can't condemn you for what you did. I think I understand the pain and torment your father put Dorothy through. And it must have pained you no end to witness it. And to see it at such a young age yourself, must have made it all the more painful. But there are some things that I need to understand. Like, how did you shooting your father lead to Dorothy running away to England?'

Jonathan looked up.

'After I shot him, I went into a complete panic. But some kind of self-preservation instinct kicked in. I wiped the gun and dropped it near the body. I wasn't trying to stage the crime scene or anything like that. I mean, I didn't think to make it seem like suicide. I just didn't want to leave any evidence pointing to me. So I just wiped the gun, dropped it and ran.'

Something in these words didn't quite make sense to Alex.

'Wait a minute. You *didn't* stage it to look like suicide?'

'No. I didn't think of that at the time. I didn't think of anything other than saving my skin. I just wanted to get out of there.'

Ordinarily, Alex would have known better than to interrupt a man when he was in the full flow of a confession. But he needed clarity.

'Okay, so what happened then?'

'I ran home, terrified. And I told Dorothy what had happened. She got me to wash my hands to make sure there was no gunshot residue and throw my clothes in the washing machine to make extra sure. She also made me take a shower.

'By the time I got out of the shower I'd already calmed down and I began to think I'd got away with it. Even though the gunshot was loud, no one had come out of their apartments to see what it was. No one had seen me leaving and no cops had come knocking on the door. I'd remembered to wipe the prints off the gun and washed away any evidence that might have been on me or my clothes. I mean, I was naïve enough to think I had. If I'd come under suspicion, they'd probably have found some evidence.

'I know now that there's a limit to what you can wash away. There were probably traces of my father's brains on the T-shirt. The trouble was, while

I was over the hysteria, Dorothy had just hit panic mode.'

'Why?'

'Because she'd remembered that she'd loaded the gun. *Her* prints were on the shells.'

22:28 PDT

Nat was driving frantically, trying to put it all together. Alex had decided on the spur of the moment to go to Jonathan's place. Why? Something was going on . . . but what? Was Juanita holding something back? Why was she being cagey?

By this stage, Nat was panicking himself. He had to find out.

With a press of a button on his cell phone, he called Juanita again.

'I was just wondering if we'd heard any more news from David.'

A pause.

'Why do you ask?'

She sounded suspicious.

'Well the way I see it we've run out of options unless David can come up with something that we can take to the governor.'

'David was attacked in the lab. Or just outside it.'

'Holy shit!'

She told him the details as Alex had described them to her.

'So now we've got nothing,' Nat said, sounding sorrowful.

'Not unless Jonathan gives us something. Oh . . . and the other platter.'

'What other platter?'

'Well whoever attacked David didn't know that one of the platters from the hard disk was still inside the microscope.'

22:32 PDT

'I wanted to go back and retrieve the gun – or go there with gloves and wipe her prints off the shells,' Jonathan said. 'It was a revolver so we'd have had to take each of them out and wipe them – and possibly also the one from the shot I fired. That would have been on the floor somewhere.'

'That would have been risky. They might have found the body already.'

'I know. I mean, Dorothy realized that at the time. That's why she wouldn't let me do it.'

'And that's why she had to flee.'

'Exactly. She knew that they'd dust the shells for prints and it would only be a matter of time before they matched the dabs to hers.'

'Did she have a rap sheet?' asked Alex, surprised.

'No, but we figured they'd check with the CDMV.'

Alex nodded approvingly at Jonathan's sharp logic – or possibly Dorothy's. The California Department of Motor Vehicles kept thumbprint records of drivers licensed by the State.

'You think they'd check?'

'Sooner or later. And with murders, they always consider other members of the family and check their prints. They'd know it wasn't a robbery because nothing was taken.'

'But I don't understand one thing. Edgar Olsen's death *was* accepted as suicide. How could that have happened if neither of you went back to stage the crime scene and make it look like suicide?'

'I don't know. That's something that I've never been able to figure out. All I know is that, up until the time Dorothy left, the police and the coroner were staying tight-lipped. After she fled, I found out that they were treating it as suicide. But by then it was too late to tell her. I'd lost all contact with her.'

'And did they say *why* they accepted it as suicide?'

'Well the entry wound was in his right temple. I mean, that makes perfect sense 'cause he turned away just before I fired. But there was something else . . . something that didn't make any sense at all.'

'What?'

'They said the gun was in his right hand.'

'But you said you dropped the gun on the floor after wiping it?'

'I did!'

'Then someone else must have put the gun in his hand.'

22:36 PDT

Juanita had isolated the strips that she felt were most likely to form part of the fax from London and was now making the first strides in sticking them together. Because she had been so careful about skimming the strips off the top of the pile, she was actually finding it surprisingly easy. The hardest part was sticking the strips together.

So far she had managed to align fourteen strips. They appeared to be from the left of the page; they included the signature. The signature itself was illegible. But the name typed underneath it was unmistakeable: Stuart Lloyd. And underneath that was the title 'Chief Administrator.'

So that nurse was wrong. He hadn't gone home early. He had sent them this letter.

22:41 PDT

'Look, Jonathan,' said Alex quietly. 'I meant what I said before: I can't condemn you for what you did. It's not my place to judge you. But what you did then was on the spur of the moment. And it was against a man who had wronged your sister. But I haven't wronged Dorothy . . . or you.'

Jonathan looked at him, confused.

'I never said you did.'

'Then would you . . . ?'

He raised his restrained hand as high as the handcuff would allow. There was a tinkling sound as the other cuff rattled against the radiator pipe.

'Oh! Yes . . . sorry!'

Jonathan crouched down with the key and unlocked the handcuff round Alex's wrist. Alex rubbed it.

'Look, Jonathan. I can't represent you, there would be a conflict of interest. But I have friends in the legal profession and I can get you a good lawyer.'

'Thanks,' said Jonathan absently. He seemed to be in a trance.

'I don't suppose I could have my phone back?'

'Sure,' said Jonathan, handing the iPhone back to him. Alex switched it on and noticed that there were several messages. He called his voicemail to hear them. Several of the messages were from Juanita. She didn't say what she wanted, just asked him to call her whenever he could. There was no particular urgency in her tone.

But then there was one from another familiar voice.

'Hi, Alex, listen it's Lee – Lee Kelly. I'm at the police station again. Look . . . I'm sorry . . . I got caught. I mean, Nat caught me.'

Alex froze.

'I don't know if he was suspicious of me. I mean, he called the police and held me until they came for me, but I don't know how much he figured out. I just wanted to let you know, because he might be on to you. I mean, he might have realized that *you're* on to *him*.

'But the point is, I found something and it's something quite incredible. I don't want to say over the phone, but I just want you to know that I've found something that'll just about knock your socks off! So please get here asap!'

22:46 PDT

When Alex got into his car, a pair of eyes was watching him. Even if the man who watched him hadn't seen Alex's car outside the apartment building, he'd known that Alex was going to be there because Juanita had told him.

It didn't take long. Within a few minutes of his arrival, he saw Alex leave the building, get in his car and drive off. Nat waited a few moments longer and then entered the building. He walked up to the third storey and rang the doorbell.

'Who is it?' asked Jonathan.

'It's me,' Nat replied.

The door opened in a flash and they stood there face to face. There was a moment of tension when neither of them spoke, then Jonathan smiled.

'Come in.'

He stepped aside and Nat entered. Jonathan closed the door.

They looked at each other awkwardly, as if neither wanted to be the first to break the ice.

'So . . .' said Nat hesitantly. 'We finally get to meet.'

'Yes,' said Jonathan with a smile. 'Finally.'

Again the awkward silence. Again it was up to Nat to break it.

'So . . . er . . . What did Alex want?'

'He wanted to know about my father's death.'

'Does he suspect something?'

'More than just *suspect*. He was *sure* it was murder even before he came here.'

'And what did you tell him?'

'I told him the truth.'

'*What?*'

'Why not?' There was no life in Jonathan's voice. 'I'm tired of lying. I'm tired of all the secrets.'

'But you've put yourself in jeopardy.'

'You don't understand. I don't *care* anymore. I just want all this to end.'

'It *is* going to end.' Nat looked at his watch. 'In just over an hour.'

'Will it?'

'How do you mean?'

'Will it end?'

'Of course it'll end. No one's going to campaign for a dead man. No one cares about the dead. That's why you should have blamed Dorothy for your father's death.'

'Why?'

'Because, Jonathan, it's always a good idea to blame the dead. They can't answer back.'

There was an impish smile on Nat's face when he said this and, after looking at him for a moment in mild surprise, Jonathan's face melted into a smile.

A fraction of a second later, they rushed into each other's arms.

23:02 PDT

'I didn't tell them anything. I'm not going to snitch on you! I wouldn't do that! But you've got to help me. I don't want to go to jail again – not at my age.'

Lee Kelly was in a state of panic when Alex got to the police station. He hadn't sounded this agitated when he left his message. Then he was more concerned about letting Alex know what he had found. But now he had had time to think about it and the alarm bells were ringing in his head about the fate that awaited him.

He hadn't yet fallen afoul of the three strikes rule, because this was the first time in his life that he had been caught breaking into domestic premises – indeed the first time in his life that he had done it since the three strikes law was introduced. But the fact that they *were* domestic premises made it likely that he would get at least *some* kind of custodial sentence. And the fact that he went out and did the job right after being released on bail would also count heavily against him.

One thing was for certain: he wouldn't make bail this

time. He knew it and Alex wasn't even going to ask for it. In the meantime, Alex wanted to know what Lee had found that had got him so excited.

'First of all I found Dorothy's passport.'

'Her *passport*?'

'Yes. From way back when.'

'Well let's see it!'

'They took it away from me.'

'Shit! Did they say anything?'

'No, they didn't take it away as evidence. They just listed it as one of my possessions and bagged it up with the rest.'

Alex was relieved. He knew that he could get it. If it was evidence then he'd have to file a discovery motion and it would take an eternity – far too long to help Burrow. But if it was simply one of Lee's possessions, then he could get Lee to sign a property release in his favor and they would hand it straight over to him.

'I don't suppose you took a peek inside, did you?'

Lee smiled a mischievous smile that belied his age.

'Sure did.'

'And?'

'It showed a stamp for when she entered England. But I couldn't see any sign that she ever left.'

'Then how did Nat get it?' Alex wondered out loud.

'Could he have followed her there?'

'That's what I'm wondering.'

'There was something else I found. I don't know if it's significant. It's just strange the way I found it.'

'What do you mean?'

'Well as I was putting the passport in my pocket,

something fell out. I looked down and it was a picture – a photo.'

'The passport photo? What, like, it was loose?'

'No, it wasn't the passport photo. It was another photo. It must have been tucked inside one of the pages of the passport.'

'Well what was it a picture of?'

'Just some broad. She looked a bit like the girl in the passport, but maybe a bit older.'

'*Older?*'

Alex was getting excited.

'I don't know if it was the same woman. It probably wasn't. I just thought it was interesting that it was tucked inside the passport. I mean, if the passport is significant then maybe the picture tucked inside it was too. Otherwise why put it there?'

'Well did you make sure they didn't lose the picture when they bagged it up?'

'I did better than that. I got to keep the picture. I told them it was my mom and they let me keep it.'

For a moment Alex was a bit skeptical about this. But then he remembered how convincing a talker Lee could be. It was the most effective item in his burglar's tool kit.

'So you've still got it?'

'Sure.'

Lee reached into his pocket and took out the small picture. He handed it over to Alex. The lawyer took one look at it and froze.

In an instant, Alex had recognized the woman in the picture: it was a young Esther Olsen.

23:05 PDT

Nat closed the door behind him, trying not to make a noise.

It was sad really. It had taken them so long to finally meet and yet he couldn't stick around. There was somewhere he had to be by midnight, indeed *before* midnight.

He felt guilty about many things. Guilty about hurting people he loved. Guilty about lying to people who trusted him. Guilty about not having made the right choices in life.

In many ways, he realized, he and Clayton Burrow were kindred spirits. But in other crucial respects they were different. Nat had ideals. Even now – doing what he was doing – he still had ideals.

Maybe he was making up his own rules, instead of following those of society. Maybe the world would not approve of what he was doing. Jonathan had been right when he said there were sins of omission as well as commission.

But the one thing Nathaniel Anderson knew was that he had to stick to his path. He had chosen it and now he was going to follow it to the end of the road, regardless of the temptations to stop or go astray.

The only thing he regretted was that he couldn't share the end with Jonathan. Jonathan was entitled to witness the crowning moment. But Jonathan couldn't be there with him.

As he got in his car and drove off, Nat felt an almost physical twinge of pain in the pit of his stomach at leaving Jonathan in that state.

23:07 PDT

Alex was still thinking about the picture as he waited for the case officer.

To judge by the all-too-familiar Budweiser can in the hand of a toga-clad youth in the background, it looked like it was taken at a frat party. The thought brought back a flood of memories from his own student days – those wild nights of carousing and getting laid – not always with protection. He was never as wild as the worst of the frat boys, but not quite the nerdy scholar that Juanita had imagined him to be.

Even Melody had been less than an angel, as he discovered when she gave in to his urging in the back of his blue Pontiac Firebird. The resulting pregnancy hadn't exactly forced them into marriage – that was on the cards anyway – but it had certainly hastened it.

No, there was nothing unusual in a pretty girl smiling for the birdie at a drunken frat party. The question was why should Nat have such a picture? Where did he get it and why had he kept it? The same of course applied – in spades – to Dorothy's passport.

He was still struggling to think of a reason when the

case officer entered. Alex was surprised that it was an African-American woman, in her mid-thirties – a tall, striking woman of exquisite complexion with an athletic build.

'Hallo, Mr Sedaka, my name is Grace Nightingale. Sergeant Grace Nightingale. I'm the case officer in the Lee Kelly case. I understand you asked to see me.'

'Yes. Thank you for agreeing to see me at such short notice.'

Despite his professionalism, he felt a wave of attraction for her.

'What can I do for you?'

Alex quickly outlined the background to the Clayton Burrow case, the fact there was circumstantial evidence that Dorothy had gone to England, the fact that the passport confirmed this and the fact that Nat was actually his legal intern. In his effort to summarize these facts in the shortest possible time, he effectively gabbled and he realized that it probably sounded to Sergeant Nightingale that he was on the verge of hysteria.

'Look, Mr Sedaka, this is all very interesting, but I'm not involved in the Clayton Burrow case in any way. And I don't really see what this has to do with the burglary at Nathaniel Anderson's house – apart from the coincidence of one of your clients taking it into his head to burglarize the home of one of your employees.'

Alex shifted uncomfortably. He wasn't sure how much she had surmised or how far her speculations had carried her.

'Okay, I'll cut to the chase. We can use this passport to prove that Dorothy Olsen went to England. So in that sense, the passport is evidence in a capital case and could save a man who is due to be executed in less than an hour.'

'And you want me to release the passport as evidence in this other case? But why didn't you just get your client to sign a release for it? Until you told me this, it was listed as one of his possessions, not as an exhibit in the case against him. Now that you've told me this it's a whole different ball game. I have to contact Mr Anderson and ask him if he wishes to include the passport in the complaint. You can probably file a discovery motion, but I don't see how we can get anything done in the next fifty minutes.'

'No, you don't understand. I'm not asking you to release the passport. If I'd wanted that, I wouldn't have told you all this. I'd have just got Kelly to sign a release and got the passport that way.'

'Now you're really lost me.'

'Look, I've had several District Court hearings today, as well as conversations with the governor. And they're all playing hardball. The consensus seems to be it's not enough just to prove that Dorothy Olsen left the country alive. I have to establish what happened to her afterward. This passport – *Dorothy Olsen's* passport – doesn't just show that she was alive and went to England. The fact that it was in *Nat's possession* suggests that he *knew* this and that he had some sort of contact with her. The fact that the passport shows no exit stamp suggests that he may have killed her in England and then brought her passport back with him.'

'Why would he do that?'

'Maybe he was planning on giving it to someone else to help him gain access to her money. We know that money was taken out of her account for over a year after she vanished. He might have killed her and got someone to pose as her and used this other girl to milk Dorothy's bank account.'

'Well I don't know if I buy this theory. I mean, it's plausible, but no more than that. And what do you want *me* to do? This is something you're surely going to have to take to the governor and argue it out with him – or the courts if that's quicker.'

She sounded sympathetic, like she really wanted to help. But she also sounded firm, as if to underscore the fact that she couldn't.

'If I take this to the governor now, the first question he's going to ask me is if I have any proof that this passport was ever in Nat's possession in the first place.'

'But I thought you said that Lee Kelly found it there.'

'Yes, he *did* find it there. He wouldn't lie to me and there's no other way he could have got it. But how do I convince the governor of that? The word of a career burglar that he found the passport at the house of a law-abiding citizen isn't going to cut any ice with a no-nonsense hard-head like Dusenbury. I need to be able to *prove* that this passport was in Nat's possession.'

'And how do you propose to do that?'

'I can't, Sergeant Nightingale, but *you* can!' She looked at him blankly. 'With fingerprints.'

She swallowed nervously before speaking.

'Do you know how long it'll take to get fingerprints off that passport?'

'It isn't hard: you just put it in a sealed chamber, fill the chamber with cyanoacrylic vapor and voilà! It's done all the time. They've lifted prints off forty-year-old Nazi war documents.'

'Yes, Mr Sedaka, I know all about fingerprint science. It's part of the police exam – at detective level, let alone sergeant. But it's not quite as simple as that. First of all, not all paper retains fingerprints equally well.'

'I know, but passports are made of pretty good quality paper.'

'Yes, but that's the problem. The great paradox is that the worse the quality of the paper, the easier it is to get fingerprints off it. Good quality paper is bad for retaining dabs.'

'Yes, but we're not talking forty years here. The passport is nine years old, but it's quite likely that he handled it more recently. We're still in with a chance.'

'Okay, maybe he did handle it recently, but there are other problems. Just switching on the machine costs money and, like every other department, we're on a budget. That's why we usually do batch jobs with several pieces of paper, whether from one case or several. You don't just put one document in the machine and switch it on. You wait until you've got enough pages to run the machine.'

'But a man's life is at stake here!'

'I *know* that! And I'm not just brushing you off here but there's another complicating factor. A passport isn't like a flat page. It's a document with pages. We have some machines where you can put in a book – or in this case, a passport – and then turn the pages with robot arms so that every page gets exposed to the cyano-acrylic vapor. But I don't think we have such a machine available locally. We may have to send it to a lab in SoCal or maybe the one in Sacramento. But they're not open 24/7 like we are.'

'Well why can't you just cut the pages out and space them throughout the machine? That'll also solve the problem of running the machine when it isn't full.'

'There's another problem there. The passport is a legal document. Technically it's the property of the United States government. We can't just cut it up without authorization from Homeland Security – or at least a District Court order.'

'But it's a man's *life*!'

'I know that, but we're cops! We have to go by the book.'

'And for that you're ready to let a man die?'

'Look, we don't even know that we'll find what you're looking for. For all we know we might not even find this man's dabs on the passport. For all we know he might not have handled it. How do I know you're telling the truth? You might just be an over-zealous attorney who's ready to go over the top to save his client's neck.'

Alex was about to deliver an angry retort, but he cut himself short. He realized that Sergeant Nightingale was right. He *was* an over-zealous attorney and he *had* gone over the top to help his client. But he had come too far to drop the matter now.

'Okay, does it have to be a court or Homeland Security?'

'Who else could it be?'

'To get a court order we have to go there and come back. I was thinking about the governor. I know he's not federal, but the courts'll take too long and Homeland Security won't be open till tomorrow morning – and even then it'll take days to cut through the red tape.'

'How quickly can you contact the governor?'

'I can get him on the phone right now. The question is, if he authorizes it, will you do it?'

Grace Nightingale took a deep breath and thought about it for a couple of seconds.

'If Governor Dusenbury authorizes it, we'll cut the pages out of the passport and run the fingerprint test now. But how quickly can we get the governor on the line at this time? Is he even awake?'

'Oh he's awake now. In fact, he's waiting for my call. Like I said, he gave me his direct line. If you call it and tell him you've got me beside you, he'll speak to me.'

'Do you know if Mr Anderson's fingerprints are on file in this state?'

'He has no priors as far as I know, but there should be a thumbprint on file at the CDMV.'

'Good enough,' said Grace, nodding. 'We can access their database from the secure terminals here.'

Alex gave her the number and she put in the call. It was the governor who answered, but she spent half a minute verifying it was him. Then she put Alex on the line. He outlined the problem in record time and then held his breath.

'All right, I'll sign an order for them to run the tests right away and fax it over, but I don't know how quickly they can do it.'

'That's exactly what I was thinking, sir. Is there any possibility that you'd consider granting a stay? We've found quite a lot even though it's inconclusive. The airline ticket, the payments to the medical center, the passport, the stamp in the passport, where it was found. I know it's not enough for clemency, sir. But isn't it enough to grant a stay . . . just to make sure?'

'It's all too uncertain. The only thing we have in writing is the ticket and the money. They show an intention to go to England and someone taking money out of her account. The rest is all hearsay.'

'But if it's true,' said Alex, looking at his watch, 'then an innocent man is going to die in forty-five minutes' time.'

'I know. But you've come to me late in the day. If you'd come to me with answers it would be a whole different story. But all you've got are unanswered questions.'

'Yet you were prepared to spare Burrow even when you were sure he was guilty, if he revealed the whereabouts of the body.'

'That was because Esther asked me to. She's dying, as you know, and I was ready to do it for her – as a humanitarian gesture.'

Alex realized that he faced a choice. He could run with what he had already and have another try with the Federal District Court for a TRO. That might buy him time until tomorrow morning. But after two applications today already – both shot down in flames – it was clear which way the Court was leaning. They had given him the benefit of the doubt the first time. They were not likely to this time, no matter how strong the alleged evidence.

But the governor was different. On the one hand he was playing hardball. But on the other hand, he appeared to have a soft spot. And Alex thought he knew what it was.

The only trouble was . . . was there enough time?

'Sir, may I ask you a question? If *Mrs Olsen* were to request a stay of execution now?'

He heard the governor breathing heavily.

'Then I'd grant it.'

23:16 PDT

Nat was driving north through San Francisco. He realized that he had cut it fine, time-wise. The execution was scheduled for a minute past midnight but he had to get there before that. That was why, when he found himself stuck behind an eighteen-wheel rig, he made a risky overtaking maneuver.

Seconds later Nat found himself in front of a police car with flashing lights and a siren. Not wanting any trouble, he pulled over. The police car stopped in front of him and a police officer stepped out and approached him.

'Are you aware that you were driving erratically back there?'

'It was a judgement call. I thought it was safe.'

'I'll need to see your driver's license and vehicle registration.'

Nat handed them over. The patrolman looked at them and put in a call, to check that the vehicle wasn't stolen and that Nat didn't have any outstanding warrants.

Nat wasn't afraid. They weren't going to find any warrants or theft reports or even unpaid parking tickets.

The thing that bothered him was that all this checking was going to take time – and time was the one thing that he didn't have.

Sometimes highway patrolmen like to check these things because they're being thorough. They would look pretty stupid if they let a driver go only to discover that he was a wanted man in half a dozen states. And if a driver drives erratically, it can mean that he's under the influence of drink or drugs, or that he's on the run from the law.

But in many cases, traffic cops stop drivers for no other reason than to make up the numbers or because they're bored or because they don't particularly like the look of the person they've stopped.

Nat didn't know which of these was the case in this case, but he sensed hostility from the cop.

'I'm going to have to ask you to take a breathalyzer.'

Nat could have hit him – and *would* have, if he thought he'd get away with it.

23:20 PDT

'I'm sorry, I can't let you in here, sir. You can come back in the morning.'

'In the morning it'll be too late! I've got to see her now!'

Alex was standing eyeball to eyeball with a hospital security guard.

'There's no visiting after hours – except for terminal patients. That's the rule.'

'She *is* a terminal patient.'

'Well unless she's listed you as next of kin and she's in the terminal ward, you can't come in.'

Alex looked round helplessly. At this time there were very few people about in the corridors, even staff. But he knew that it was only a matter of time before other security staff arrived. He *had* to see Esther and he knew that he was never going to convince this rent-a-cop or any of his colleagues. Alex could see that this man was clearly bigger than he. But, then again, David was bigger than Jonathan Olsen. That hadn't stopped Jonathan putting David flat on his back with a single punch. And it wouldn't stop Alex now.

His left fist shot out and caught the security guard square on the nose. The guard yelled with pain, but stayed on his feet. But he was just a little too slow to react. A right sunk deep into his midriff and a savage left uppercut settled the issue.

Not looking down at the results of his work for long enough to feel guilty about hurting a man who was only doing his job, Alex raced up the stairs to the ward where Esther had a private room. He opened the door and went into the dimly lit room, not quite knowing what to expect. He didn't even know if she would be awake.

He looked at her in the bed while his eyes became accustomed to the dark. Eventually he got to the point that he could make out her open eyes squinting at him.

'Hallo, Mr Sedaka,' she said quietly. She showed no sign of fear, and it was obvious that she had seen him before he saw her.

'I'm sorry I disturbed you, Mrs Olsen. But it's important.'

'You didn't disturb me. I knew you'd come.'

The voice was weak, but it held a quiet confidence – the confidence of a woman who wanted something and knew what she wanted.

He walked closer and sat by the bed, so he could speak without his voice carrying to the corridor.

'I wouldn't have come if I didn't have to. But I spoke to the governor. He said he'd only grant a stay of execution if you asked him to. I know I have no right to ask you. But I have found out a few things that I need to tell you. I know that Dorothy went to England for the abortion. We have the airline receipt, we have proof that she paid money to the medical center. We know that she never left England. We know that Edgar didn't commit suicide. It was murder. And there's no gentle way to tell you this, Mrs Olsen, but we have evidence that Edgar abused Dorothy. I'm sorry to have to tell you that, but I need you to help me. I need you to tell me what I *don't* know, so it behooves me to be honest with you.'

'It's been weighing on my conscience for a long time now – half a lifetime, in fact.'

'What has?'

'The abuse . . . Edgar's abuse of Dorothy.'

'You knew about it?'

'Yes, I knew. And I did nothing to stop it.'

There are sins of commission and sins of omission.

'But it wasn't sexual abuse, was it?'

'It depends what you mean by sexual abuse.'

23:22 PDT (07:22 BST)

Susan White lived in a box-sized room in a nearby flat, just a minute's walk away from the clinic. But she could never sleep comfortably there. It was too close to work. There was too much of a sense of being 'on call.'

But that wasn't the only thing that was disturbing her sleep. There was the thought of that innocent man on death row. She had sent the letter to his lawyers – with Stuart Lloyd's forged signature. But she hadn't been able to follow up on it. There were too many people about. She had wanted to phone them and ask what was happening. But she was afraid of someone overhearing. Even now she was afraid of being discovered. She could lose her job over the forgery. She could even be prosecuted for it.

And then there were the original shenanigans with the Dorothy Olsen case. It had been Stuart's decision to fiddle the dates. But Susan had been a party to it. At minimum, it was gross professional misconduct. And it might well have been a crime in its own right. Even if Stuart was the principal guilty party, she was clearly complicit as she had countersigned the forms. And she had been there when Dorothy was admitted.

Susan looked at her watch. She couldn't have had more than five hours' sleep. She was still desperately tired. Her next shift didn't start until ten. But she knew what would probably happen. She would toss and turn desperately trying to get back to sleep and then would nod off just before her alarm clock was set to go off.

But she was determined to at least *try* and get some sleep.

She felt her eyelids drooping and felt a wave of tiredness wafting over her. But, as she sank back into the realms of sleep, the face that appeared before her was that of Dorothy Olsen – the tearful face of a vulnerable young girl begging them not to make her wait any longer, pleading with them to put her out of her misery.

23:23 PDT

'I . . . I don't understand,' said Alex.

'Edgar always wanted a son and when I gave him a daughter he was bitterly disappointed.'

'Was this because of the son from his first marriage that he lost?'

Her eyes widened.

'You *know* about that?'

'I spoke to Anita Morgan. She told me the whole thing: the car accident, the decline in their marriage, Edgar's sterility or sub-fertility, your desperation to give him a son.'

'Yes, but do you know *why* I was so desperate to give him a son?'

'I don't know . . . to make him happy I guess.'

'No, Mr Sedaka, it was not to make him happy. It was to stop him being *un*happy. Because when Edgar was unhappy he took it out on other people. And the person he took it out on most was Dorothy. Even when she was a baby.'

'What did he do to her?'

'Oh he didn't hit her or anything like that. He just

shunned her. He would hardly talk to her. He used to walk out of the room when she crawled in. He never picked her up, never held her in his arms.'

'Was that because he knew that she wasn't his daughter?'

'It was that plus the fact that she was a girl. I think he would have forgiven me if it had been a boy. I mean, Jimmy wasn't his son either. And he never took out his frustration on Jonathan. But Dorothy bore the brunt of it.'

'Did you try to talk to him about it?'

'You couldn't talk to him. He would cut you off with a sarcastic comment or if you stood up to him he'd just walk out of the room.'

'Mrs Olsen, you said before that it wasn't sexual abuse. But we know that Edgar once held Dorothy in front of a mirror and ripped her clothes off. Jonathan said that it was something to do with her "flaunting her sexuality in front of him." Do you know what he meant by that?'

'Yes. And it was partly my fault. You see, I think I made her what she became.'

Alex wasn't sure if he was in the mood for a Freudian analysis, but he had to let her tell it in her own words.

'How?'

'When she was about four and Edgar was being cold toward her, I sat her down and explained to her that he wanted a boy. It was a stupid thing to do but I did it. I couldn't talk to him about it, so I was reduced to talking to her. I told her that he wanted a boy so that they could do boy things together. And she asked me what are boy things . . .'

There were tears welling up in Esther Olsen's eyes. She brushed them aside and carried on.

'And I told her that it's the way they dress and the things that interest them like cars and electrical things. So she started acting like the way she thought a boy acted. She even got hold of a pair of scissors and cut her hair short so she'd *look* more like a boy. But the more she did it the angrier it made him.'

'And this was before Jonathan was born?'

'Yes, but it carried on after that. You see, after Jonathan was born, he treated Jonathan well and he was a bit less cold toward me – even though he knew that he wasn't Jonathan's father – but he was just as cold and unkind to Dorothy. And the more he rejected her, the more she tried to act like a boy. When she reached puberty she started dressing like a boy – and of course by then she had her own allowance so she could buy clothes for herself.'

'I'd've thought that that sort of thing would have made her a target for ridicule from her peers. And that would surely have been a deterrent.'

'You'd've thought so but Dorothy had been so toughened up by the harsh treatment Edgar meted out that she was oblivious to anything her classmates could have thrown at her.'

'Oblivious?'

'Well maybe not completely oblivious, but certainly indifferent.'

'So was it just cross-dressing? I mean, Jonathan didn't say cross-dresser, he just said "her sexuality." And Clayton Burrow called her a lesbian.'

'It started with cross-dressing, but it pretty soon

430

developed into other things. She started getting pictures of pretty girls and putting them on her walls. Edgar tore them down a couple of times, but she just put them back up. And she kept a scrapbook of pictures of girls in swimsuits. He didn't know that because she kept it under her bed.'

'Was it just an act or did she really like girls – sexually, I mean?'

'It probably started as an act, but developed into something more than that. I mean, she did experiment with girls. She found girls who were interested online and she used to date them.'

'Did you try to stop her – or did Edgar?'

'He didn't pay enough attention to her to know what was going on. It was only what she flaunted in his presence that angered him.'

'But didn't you think of telling her that she was only making it worse by the way she was behaving?'

'Yes, but you see, at least this way, she was getting *some* reaction from him. When she kept a low profile he just ignored her altogether, shunned her. So for her, the choice wasn't a good reaction from him or a bad re- action: it was a bad reaction or none at all. She chose a bad reaction as the lesser of two evils.'

'But it must have hurt her. I mean, she wrote a poem that betrays her feelings and shows how much he hurt her.'

'Oh I'm sure it did. She didn't show it to anyone round her but the only way I could sense it was by the constant hurt look in her eyes.'

'But what about him ripping the clothes off of her?

Jonathan knew about it, so it must have been when he was old enough to understand. And what was that about the mirror?'

'Well, as I said, she used to dress up in boy's clothes. When she got older she was able to buy her own clothes. But sometimes she used to try on Edgar's clothes and admire herself in the mirror and practice picking up girls. I knew she was doing it, but I didn't stop her. By that stage she'd already decided what she was. There was no point fighting it. At least *I* knew that. But Edgar didn't. He just wouldn't accept it. He thought that *she* was in denial, but in reality *he* was. Then one day – when she was about fourteen – he caught her dressing up in his clothes talking to an imaginary girlfriend and he just flipped his lid. I mean, he just blew a fuse and exploded.'

'What did he do?'

Alex already knew, but he had to hear it from Esther Olsen – he had to be sure.

'He just ripped the clothes off of her, just like you said.'

'In front of the mirror.'

'Not exactly. He threw her on the bed and more or less wrestled with her to rip the clothes off her. And he was deliberately hurting her, 'cause he carried on even when she screamed "okay" and said she'd take off the clothes. But he wanted more than that. After he finished ripping the clothes off of her – and I mean *all* the clothes, including her underwear – he didn't just let her go. He dragged her back to the mirror and held her in front of it. He kept shouting at her: "You've got to accept reality! You've got to accept reality."'

Alex asked: 'What was *she* doing? I mean, how did she take it?'

Esther was struggling to speak, as if the memory was still too painful.

'She was screaming and crying . . . struggling not to look at herself . . . or at him. And even when she opened her eyes – and by this stage she was squinting because her eyes were filled with tears – she just crossed her legs and tried to avoid looking at herself. But Edgar wasn't having it. He was determined to make her see the truth – or rather *his* truth. So he forced her legs apart and screamed at her: "You're a girl! Not a boy! You're a fucking girl!"'

Esther broke down in tears again. But there was something troubling Alex, and troubling him deeply.

'But you said that you had problems communicating with Dorothy and that she didn't talk to you about these things.'

'Yes,' murmured Esther Olsen, faintly.

'Then how do you know about it?'

'*Because I was there!*' she screamed, sobbing.

'There? What, there in the room?'

'No . . . not in the room. At least not at first. But in the house. When it started, I was downstairs in the kitchen. But I heard what was going on. I heard the shouting. And so I crept up the stairs and . . . saw . . . what he was doing.'

'And you did nothing to stop him?'

'No,' Esther sobbed into her hands. 'But it was worse than that.'

'How could it get any worse?'

'Because she saw me. She *saw* me . . . and she knew that I did nothing . . . nothing to stop him . . . and she never spoke to me again . . . never one word. If she wanted to say anything to me after that . . . she said it through Jonathan.'

At this point, Esther broke down completely and could talk no more.

So that was it, Alex realized. The great sin of omission. That was how Dorothy became estranged from her mother.

Alex patted Esther's arm gently. He wanted to comfort her. Even though he had only met her that morning, he felt as if in some way there was a bond between them.

'Mrs Olsen, there was something else I wanted to ask you. It's to do with Edgar's death.'

'I could probably have done it myself. If she hadn't done it. *He* was the one who was responsible for Dorothy hating me. He *deserved* to die! I accept my share of the blame. But if he hadn't treated her like that . . . it would never have happened.'

'But why do you think *Dorothy* did it?'

'I heard them talking about it afterward. I mean, it was all in whispers and I only heard fragments. But I heard them talking about the body and his brains being splattered and then Dorothy said something about her fingerprints being on the bullets.'

'Mrs Olsen, it wasn't Dorothy. It was Jonathan.'

She was shaking her head.

'I . . . I don't understand.'

'He went there to put the gun there, to get it out of Dorothy's reach. Dorothy was going to kill Burrow

434

because of the rape – because he'd got her pregnant. But Jonathan talked her out of it. Only he was afraid that she'd try again, so he decided to take the gun to Edgar's place and hide it there. But Edgar caught him and there was a confrontation. Some harsh words were said and it ended up with Edgar being shot.'

'But why did Dorothy . . . ?' Esther trailed off.

'Because her fingerprints were at the crime scene. She'd loaded the revolver. In preparation for killing Burrow.'

'My God! And all this time I thought it was Dorothy who . . .'

'But the thing I don't understand is why the police thought it was suicide. And why was the gun found in Edgar's hand? Jonathan said that he dropped it on the floor.'

Esther raised her head, now suddenly stronger than before, as if this latest revelation had breathed new life into her.

'That was me. I got him to help her. I just didn't know that was the way he'd go about it.'

23:27 PDT

'Okay, you're clean,' said the patrolman, looking at the breathalyzer.

Of course I'm clean, thought Nat. He knew perfectly well that this was harassment. Nat hadn't touched a drop and there was no smell on his breath that could have been mistaken for liquor. This was a complete farce and he had half a mind to make an official complaint about it. But right now he had more important things to think about.

The thing that had made it annoying was that it had taken the patrolman several attempts to activate the breathalyzer device. And in every one of those minutes, Nat was squirming and fidgeting resentfully, which had probably made him look even more guilty.

'Is that it, patrolman? Can I go now?'

'Not quite, there's just one more thing.'

'What is it *now*?'

'I'm still going to have to write you up a citation for the reckless driving.'

For the next two minutes Nat stood there while this pain-in-the-ass patrolman wrote out the citation.

'Just sign here.'

Nat signed, gritting his teeth against the anger. The signature entailed no admission of guilt or liability. It simply confirmed that he had received the citation and knew what it meant.

'Thank you very much, sir. Have a nice day. And drive carefully now.'

Nat got back into his car and drove off, fuming. He looked at the dashboard clock and saw how little time he had to get there. He wanted to floor the gas pedal but he knew that if he did, he was quite likely to be stopped again for speeding. He put his foot down as far as he dared, but his eyes kept darting down to the dashboard to make sure that the needle didn't cross the wrong line.

23:33 PDT

'Who, Mrs Olsen? The way *who* went about it?'

Alex was still reeling from what Esther had told him. But then again, she was reeling from what he had told her. And Alex suspected that the surprise was bigger for her. She had carried round – for nine years – the belief that it had been Dorothy who had killed Edgar. Now she knew that it was her son.

'I thought that she needed a lawyer. So I called an old friend. I mean, he was originally a personal friend of Anita's and a professional friend of Edgar's. I'd first met him at the wedding. Edgar invited him. But by the time I called him for his help over the killing I had something of a relationship with him myself.'

'Wait a minute, would this be the old friend that you and Anita Morgan called in when you wanted to have a son?'

'Yes. But you have to understand that it wasn't as coldly clinical as you make it sound. We'd met a few times over the years at social and business events. Anita was often there too. And I think she may have picked up on the fact that there was some sort of chemistry between us.'

438

'You loved him?'

'I think I did. But we never really let it get to that stage . . . the stage of acknowledging our feelings to ourselves or to each other.'

'Why not?'

'He was a young ambitious lawyer with political aspirations, and he had a young pregnant wife at the time. It wouldn't do for him to play the role of home-wrecker – especially as I wasn't just married by then but also had a daughter. So we carried on in secret for a while, kidding ourselves that it was just wild, physical passion with no strings attached . . . until we decided that it would only end up hurting both of us.'

'And what happened? With Edgar's death and the cover-up, I mean.'

'Well like I said he was a lawyer. I thought he could represent Dorothy in court. Remember, I thought it was Dorothy who killed Edgar. But he just asked me for the address and various other details. He said he was going to check with the local police to see what they knew already. It turned out that at that time they hadn't had any report about shots being fired in that area. They didn't know about the shooting. They didn't know that Edgar was dead. And then he called me back afterward and said it was all sorted out and I didn't need to worry. I asked him what he meant, but he just repeated: "Don't worry. It's all taken care of." When the body was found, I was informed that my husband had committed suicide. And then I realized.'

Alex was incredulous.

'You think a lawyer staged the crime scene to look like suicide?'

'I don't think he did it himself, but he was a criminal lawyer. He probably had lots of criminal friends to do the dirty work for him. Come to think of it, he probably had quite a few crooked cops in his pocket too.'

'And who was—?'

Before he could finish the sentence, the door flew open and three people entered: the security guard that Alex had floored with that beautifully executed punch, and two of San Francisco's finest, one of them female.

'There he is!' said the security guard, evidently proud of himself for stating the obvious.

It was the female police officer who had the presence of mind to flip the light switch.

As the strip lights flickered to life over the course of three and a half seconds, Alex froze in panic. But it wasn't the cops or the security guard that sent the shivers up his spine and gave him goosebumps. It was the framed picture by Mrs Olsen's bed. That framed picture was one of Esther Olsen's wedding pictures, where the couple go round and have themselves photographed with each of the guests. Not that the sight of the young Esther or the moderately youthful Edgar Olsen sent a jolt through Alex. What shocked him to the core was the wedding guest between them with his arms round both of them.

The man was Chuck Dusenbury!

23:34 PDT

Nat had decided to take a chance and speed up after crossing the Golden Gate Bridge. He figured that the cops in Marin County wouldn't be so aggressive and pushy as those in San Francisco. He had in fact no basis for this belief other than wishful thinking. But he reasoned that if they did pull him over, he would just tell them the truth about going to the execution and hope that they would wave him on.

The problem wasn't the police, however: it was the heavy traffic. Even at this late stage, people were going to the prison to demonstrate either for or against the execution. And in addition to that more reporters were turning up. The local press had covered it since this morning, but now, as it was becoming clear that the execution was going ahead, reporters and cameramen from all over the country were converging on San Quentin. Maybe because it was likely to be one of the last executions in Dusenbury's term of office. Maybe because Dusenbury had become increasingly vociferous in his reluctance to send people to the death chamber. Or maybe because of Martine Yin's leak of Dusenbury's clemency offer.

Whatever the reason, this case had suddenly aroused a lot more interest and Nat was struggling to get to the prison in the face of this column of traffic.

He still had half an hour to go. But he was beginning to wonder if he would make it.

23:37 PDT

Slowly the realization was filtering through, seeping through into Alex's consciousness.

The politically ambitious lawyer. The man who was ready to throw the rulebook out the window and violate all protocol to grant Esther Olsen's dying wish. The man who was ready to spare Clayton Burrow from the death penalty – but only on very specific and narrow terms. It wasn't just a lame duck governor who was free to speak his mind and act his conscience. It was a man who had long loved a woman, but hadn't been free to fulfill that love.

Alex could imagine the feelings that Dusenbury must have had for Esther over the years, possibly losing contact with her as he climbed the political ladder, possibly falling out with Edgar.

He idly speculated whether Edgar would have ever found out. Certainly the man was no fool. He must have known – despite his self-denial – that none of 'his' children were actually his own: not Jimmy, not Dorothy and not Jonathan. Did he figure out the rest? Did he realize that it was his friend who had cuckolded him behind his back?

443

For a moment he entertained the way-out idea that perhaps Edgar had survived Jonathan's gunshot and been finished off by Dusenbury or his henchman. He dismissed the thought as rapidly as it arrived as just too ludicrous for words. Jonathan had seen Edgar's brains splattered all over the wall. The possibility that Dusenbury had contributed to the killing, as opposed to the cover-up, just wasn't on the cards.

But still, it was becoming clearer now to Alex what *had* occurred that day.

The two cops walked up to Alex and he rose to meet them, but he *had* to be sure.

He turned to Esther Olsen and looked into her eyes. 'It was Dusenbury, wasn't it – the old friend?'

Esther looked at Alex with pitiful eyes and moved her mouth as if she was trying to speak. She mouthed the word 'yes' and then started gasping for breath. She appeared to be trying to say something. But all the lawyer could make out was something like 'yewer.' Alex turned back to the police.

'She's hyperventilating! Call a doctor! *Now!*'

23:38 PDT

Juanita was now finding it harder to match up the shredded strips to the part of the letter that she had already reconstructed. The first strips had been easy because a handful of shredded strips had stayed together at the top of the pile. But others had got separated.

She reckoned that she had reconstructed at least a third of the letter. She could make out some parts of sentences like 'I can conf...' She could also make out fragments of dates on the letter, and she knew it was important to remember that these dates were in the British format.

But she was making too slow progress. She looked up at the clock and saw that she had only twenty-three minutes. Even if she could finish, what could she do with it? Could she send it to the governor? Would he act on it? What did it say? What did it even prove?

But there were other questions going through her mind. Like why hadn't Nat returned? Where was he now?

And what about Alex? Why didn't he call in? He had told her what the governor had said and that he was on his way to speak to Mrs Olsen. But would they let him into the hospital? And what had Esther Olsen decided? Would she ask the governor for a stay of execution on Burrow? Would the governor grant it?

Juanita had to find out.

23:40 PDT

'Look, if you'll just call the governor, he'll explain everything,' said Alex as he was led away in handcuffs by the police.

They were outside the building and he was being manhandled toward a waiting police car.

'You can call from the precinct.'

'No, you don't understand. I've got a client on death row who's due to be—'

'Wait a minute!' asked the female cop. 'Are you Clayton Burrow's lawyer?'

'Yes. And I've got new evidence. I *have to* speak to the governor.'

'I don't think you're going to speak to the governor at this time.'

This was the male cop again. But his female colleague was somewhat more sympathetic.

'Hold on a minute, Jack, I think we should let him.'

'After he burst into that old lady's room?'

Alex knew that he had to say something to swing it his way.

'The "old lady" is the mother of the victim. The governor

447

told me that he would grant a stay of execution if she asked for it.'

'So you thought you'd just barge in there and browbeat her—'

'You don't understand! *I met her this morning.* She asked me to help her. We have new evidence. *She* helped *me* to *find* the evidence.'

'Sure. And I'm Superman.'

'Look, why don't you just take my phone and call the governor?'

'Yeah, like I've got the governor's number.'

They had reached the police car now.

'The number's in my cell phone. It's on my quick-dial list. You can take it out of my pocket and call him. Please, just do it!'

The male cop exchanged glances with his female colleague again. In the end it was the female who took the iPhone from Alex's pocket and selected the name 'governor' from the contacts list.

'Hi Alex?'

'Who is this?' asked the female cop.

'This is the governor – Chuck Dusenbury. And who is *this*?'

The female cop introduced herself and told the governor what had happened. This was followed by several seconds of intense shouting in which the governor could be clearly heard to be telling the female officer to release Mr Sedaka immediately and to put him on the line. The male cop uncuffed Alex and the female officer handed him the phone.

'Sir, I've just spoken to Mrs Olsen.'

'And?'

'I couldn't ask her, sir. After I found out what I found out, she suffered a relapse. They've got her on a respirator. But I've learned something else – something I didn't know before.'

'What's that?'

Alex looked round edgily, wondering how to phrase it. He could hardly tell the cops to back off, under the circumstances. And moving away from them, out of earshot, was equally not an option. He chose his next words carefully.

'I know about Jimmy and Jonathan . . . and Edgar.'

There was an intense silence for a few seconds.

'She told you everything?' asked Dusenbury, nervously.

'Jonathan told me some of it,' said Alex, 'and Esther told me the rest. I don't know if there are any more blanks to fill in, but I think I've pretty much got the whole picture.'

'And what do you intend to do with the information?'

The governor's tone was tense.

'Do with it?' Alex was puzzled. A second or two later he understood. 'I'm not a blackmailer if *that's* what you're getting at.'

'Then what is it you want of me?'

'I'm trying to say that it's beginning to look increasingly like my client was right – about Dorothy. And there's more to it because there's evidence that my own legal intern has been up to some shenanigans.'

'What sort of shenanigans?'

'Well for a start, he had Dorothy's passport at his home. The passport showed that she entered England but never left. Also, Nat was the one who was so instrumental in getting me to take on the Burrow case. And another thing – inside the passport was a picture of a young Esther Olsen.'

'What are you talking about, Alex?'

'I'm talking about the fact that Nat seems to have taken an interest not only in Dorothy, but also in her mother. And another thing: we've been chasing up that clinic in London that Dorothy went to, and they sent us a fax. But it's beginning to look like Nat intercepted it.'

'So why don't you get them to send you a new one?'

'We've bust a gut trying. But there's a problem because of the time difference. We need to speak to an administrator and right now the only people there are the night staff.'

There was a brief pause.

'It's actually quarter of eight in the morning in England by my reckoning. Maybe one of the admin staff is an early riser. It's worth a shot.'

Alex considered asking Dusenbury to grant a stay in the meantime. That was the reason why he had made this call. But he realized that even with all the evidence they had, the governor was going to do nothing unless he had what he considered to be absolute proof.

'Okay, but you *will* be waiting for my call back?'

'I'm sitting by the phone, Alex. And I'll be waiting.'

23:45 PDT

In the high security block at San Quentin, the witnesses to the execution were filing into the special room adjoining the execution chamber. These were officials of the courts, the governor's office, the state legislature and several journalists who were there to witness the event in their capacity as the representatives of the people.

Although no photography was allowed of an actual execution, there were several press artists at work. At the moment there wasn't much they could do because the curtain was drawn across the window on the side of the execution chamber itself.

As the surviving immediate relatives of the victim, Esther and Jonathan Olsen had both been given passes to witness the execution. But even before she had been overtaken by ill health, Esther had decided not to attend. It was not revenge she wanted, it was closure. And closure for her meant not witnessing the execution of her daughter's murderer, but finding the body so that she could give her daughter a proper burial.

And this had been denied her.

Jonathan Olsen, in contrast, had yearned for the day

451

when he would see Clayton Burrow strapped down to a gurney and put to death by lethal injection. But now, when the time had come, he was nowhere to be found.

The guards at the prison didn't know what the real Jonathan Olsen looked like, so they had no way of knowing that the man who had obtained entry using Jonathan's pass was in fact Nathaniel Anderson.

23:47 PDT

'Call them right now, Juanita! Demand to speak to someone in authority and don't let up. See if you can speak to that nurse again!'

'Okay, boss! Right away!'

Alex was driving to the prison. He knew there wasn't much he could do there unless they could get a stay of execution, but he had a duty to be with his client. Even if he couldn't save him, even if he couldn't comfort him, he still had a duty to be *with* him.

It was a strange thought. Racing to the prison to comfort a man of whose innocence he was now convinced, in the event that their last-ditch efforts would fail. If there had still been time, he would have petitioned the Federal District Court to grant a stay on the grounds of the passport being found at Nat's place. But the trouble was that the only evidence he had as to where the passport was found was the word of a career criminal.

Aside from that, he didn't have time to get to the District Court now. The truth of the matter was that all he could do now was get to San Quentin and see his client for what might be the last time.

Clayton Burrow's fate was now in the hands of Juanita.

23:48 PDT

The building that housed the scanning tunneling microscope was quiet but not completely deserted. David was now more sensitive and alert to any sound in the background, despite the promise the security staff had made to be extra alert. In truth, now that the attacker had been identified – his father had phoned him and told him – he wasn't unduly worried about the possibility of a repetition.

But the survival instinct is linked more closely to the emotions than the cognitive faculty. And so every foot-step, creaking door or distant voice disturbed him. But it didn't undermine his resolve. Indeed, quite the contrary. The violent attack had made him all the more determined to find something that could help to save the life of Clayton Burrow.

He didn't know if his father had retrieved the other two platters of the hard disk from Jonathan, but at this stage there was no time to get them. For this reason he had spent the last hour or more scouring recovered files on the one remaining platter. He had looked for word processing files initially, reading just enough text to determine if a file showed any promising signs before moving on to the next.

But that had proved fruitless. So he had been pleasantly surprised when he found an MP3 file. Because of its size, it was spread over several sectors and it was painstaking work recovering it little by little using the scanning tunneling microscope. But he had persevered.

The MP3 file itself was simply called 'I cannot be.' That was enigmatic enough to have caught his attention, but that alone would not have justified the amount of work that he was putting into recovering this audio file when the clock was ticking so loudly.

The reason was that every audio file, in addition to the music or speech itself, was also accompanied by a sort of mini-file containing something called 'metadata.' Metadata was a set of fixed pieces of information about the audio file, like artist, year, genre, comment. And this one stated in the comment section: 'Poem about Daddy.'

23:49 PDT (07:49 BST)

The nursing station in the ward at the Finchley Road Medical Centre was coming to life as patients woke up. But the office staff had not yet arrived, so the calls were still being diverted to the nursing station when Juanita rang again. Nurse Michaels answered.

'Is Susan White there?'

'Look, I've already told you she's off duty. She finished at two in the morning and she's probably asleep. I don't know if you know this but we work bloody hard here.'

'I know and I'm sorry. But this is really important. I wouldn't be calling all the way from America if it wasn't.'

'All I can do is leave her a message for when she's next on duty, which'll probably be in just over two hours.'

'No, wait! There's something I need you to do.'

'What?' asked Nurse Michaels, through gritted teeth.

'Did Susan White go home?'

'Yes, a few hours ago.'

'Does she live nearby?'

'Yes.'

There was a heavy sigh at the other end of the phone.

'Okay, now listen, I wouldn't normally ask you to do this, but, like I explained before, we have a client who's going to be executed in just over ten minutes unless we can save him. From the information she's given us, we think we may be able to save him. We just need some urgent paperwork. And she seems to be the person who knows where it is.'

'But like I said, she's not here.'

'I know, and what I want you to do is call her. I wouldn't ask you to do this if it wasn't a matter of life and death. Get someone else to cover your post if necessary.'

'Leaving my post isn't the problem! I can't just wake her up because someone calls up from America and tells me about someone on death row.'

'She'd *want* you to do it!'

'What do you mean?'

'She tried to help us before. I think she even sent us something. But we have a problem with our fax machine. We need it to be sent again.'

'I thought you said last time you called that it was the Chief Administrator who sent it?'

'Well he must have authorized it. But I think *she* was the one who actually sent it. The point is she'd *want* to help us. She was *trying* to help us. She probably doesn't even know that we had a problem with our fax machine. If she knew, she'd probably be over in a flash.'

'Look . . . how do I know that you're not just bullshitting me?'

'I can't prove it. I mean, if you turn on your TV to

CNN or *Eyewitness News* you'll see about the impending execution. Either you take my word or you don't. But we have a client whose life depends on your decision.'

The nurse thought about it – but only for a moment.

23:51 PDT

Jonathan Olsen was sitting in front of the TV screen glued to the report about the impending execution. He was beginning to wonder if he had done the right thing, giving Nat the pass to witness the execution. He had waited years for the chance to see the look on Clayton Burrow's face as he breathed his last breath. It was poetic justice – the bully who had beaten him up when he was small and had subjected his sister to years of mental torture, *finally* getting what he deserved.

In a way it eased his conscience about his father. He hadn't intended to kill him. But in retrospect, that was poetic justice too. His father had also been an abuser, even if his abuse had been born of his own guilt and suffering.

He wondered what Alex would do with the knowledge. It wasn't directly relevant to Dorothy's fate, but, now that Alex knew, the knowledge was out there. Of course they couldn't prove anything. Whoever had set things up to make it look like suicide had done too good a job for that. The authorities could hardly reopen the case now.

The thing that troubled Jonathan more was that he had been too close to Dorothy. She had blamed her mother for turning a blind eye to Edgar's abusive behavior and, after that day with the mirror, had never spoken to her again.

But was she being fair?

Certainly their mother should have done more to rein in her husband's excesses. She wasn't some old-fashioned 1950s housewife who greeted her husband with a hot dinner as soon as he came home from work. She had a duty to protect her daughter.

But looking back on it now, it was never quite so clear-cut. Edgar Olsen had been an extremely forceful personality and he could be a holy terror when roused. Esther had tried to encourage Dorothy to act in a way that would placate Edgar. And when that failed, she tried to persuade Dorothy to stop. But Dorothy had a mind of her own. And their mother was definitely a junior partner in the practice. She was also constantly being put on the defensive because of her infidelity. Although technically it wasn't infidelity. The one-night stand that had brought Dorothy into the world had taken place *before* the marriage.

But that hadn't prevented Edgar Olsen from using it as a bludgeon against both Esther and Dorothy. When it was Esther he was angry with, 'whore' was the epithet that he threw. And when Dorothy crossed him, he called her a 'little mamzer' – the Jewish word for a bastard. Edgar Olsen loved to lash out verbally and cause pain to others to numb himself to the pain of guilt that he felt over the death of his three-year-old son.

461

But Jonathan now felt guilty about his unquestioning alliance with Dorothy.

Was it right to punish his mother? Was it right to snub her?

Unlike Dorothy, he had continued to speak to Esther after the incident with the mirror, but always coldly and without emotion.

The phone rang. It jolted him. He sensed that this was no ordinary call. It was something special. Perhaps it was the time. No one would call him at this time. And yet it was too early for the execution.

'Hallo?'

'Hi, is that Jonathan Olsen?' asked a man's voice.

'Yes, it is,' he said nervously.

'My name is Rodrigo Alvarez. I'm calling from the Idylwood Care Center.'

23:52 PDT (07:52 BST)

Susan White opened her eyes and tried to adjust to the light that was streaming into the room, even with the blinds half closed. The phone . . . that infernal noise . . . it wouldn't stop.

Her hand groped for the phone, eventually finding it. She managed to pick up the handset without knocking over everything on the bedside cabinet.

'Yes!' she practically shouted.

'Susan . . . Susan!'

'Wha . . . what is it?'

'Sorry to wake you. Listen. It's important.'

'Danielle?' said Susan, recognizing the voice. 'What is it?'

'We had another phone call from that woman.'

'What woman?'

'In America. At that law firm.'

'Juanita?'

'I think so.'

'What about her? Did she get it?'

Susan was now rubbing her eyes and stretching her arms.

'Get what? Wait a minute. Listen! She said that you or someone sent her something but that she didn't receive it. They were having trouble with their fax machine.'

Susan White sat bolt upright.

'*They didn't get the fax?*'

23:54 PDT

'Ladies and gentlemen, I would ask you now to take your seats. There will be no standing during the procedure and anyone who stands up or speaks while the procedure is in progress will be asked to leave. The curtain will be opened in a few minutes.'

They had filed in and taken their seats. The execution procedure had already been explained to them and there would be no further explanation of the technical side.

There had been some recent changes in the execution procedure in the State of California. It was still a three-drug procedure consisting of an initial injection of sodium thiopental, a barbiturate sedative to render the prisoner unconscious, followed by pancuronium bromide to paralyze the muscles and finally potassium chloride to stop the heart.

The spectators – witnesses on behalf of society, officially – took their seats, avoiding each other's eyes. Even among those who approved of the death penalty, there was a kind of guilty embarrassment about being part of the procedure. That was why the executioner's identity was kept secret and not – as was sometimes falsely claimed – to protect him or her from revenge at the hands of the prisoner's family.

Nat took his place at the end, positioning himself in such a way so that he was close to where he thought Burrow's head would be.

'When the curtain is opened, the death warrant will be read out and the prisoner will be allowed to make a brief final statement. Members of the press may transcribe the final statement and, depending on the prisoner's arrangements with the warden, written copies may be given out. Finally, we would ask that if any spectators experience any discomfort during the execution procedure, to leave the observation room as quietly as possible.'

23:56 PDT (07:56 BST)

'Can't you stick the pieces of it together?'

Susan White had been incredulous when Juanita told her what had happened to the letter that she had faxed over. So she had hastily thrown on the minimum clothing to comply with the laws of decency and raced down the road to the clinic.

'I've been trying,' Juanita replied. 'But we've only got four minutes. I need you to fax it over again.'

'I...'

Susan froze with fear. She could easily print out another copy. She knew that. But it was risky – in some ways riskier than the first time. At least it felt like that. She had been frightened enough yesterday. But now she was off the hook. If she printed another copy and signed it, she would be inviting trouble. It was forgery, whatever the excuse.

But still ... it was a man's life.

'Look, I didn't tell you this before ... but ...'

She looked up. Nurse Michaels was a few feet away. She didn't appear to be paying attention to the conversation, but she was still within earshot.

'Listen ... it wasn't all it seemed.'

'What wasn't?' asked Juanita. 'I don't understand.'

'The letter . . . it wasn't . . . look, it's hard to explain.'

Juanita had pieced together enough of the letter to see the signature.

'Is Stuart Lloyd there?' she asked desperately.

'Not yet. None of the admin staff is. They should arrive between eight and nine.'

'Was he there last night? When the fax was sent?'

The hesitation was slight but noticeable.

'No.'

This time the hesitation was on Juanita's end of the phone line.

'It wasn't from Stuart Lloyd, was it?' said Juanita. 'The letter you faxed over, I mean. It was from you.'

Susan White lowered her voice, realizing that the truth could be concealed no longer.

'Look, I could lose my job.'

'I'm sorry . . . but we have a man here who could lose his *life*.'

Susan White thought about it for a moment. It wasn't a case of weighing up the rights and wrongs. She was simply trying to pluck up the courage to do what she *had* to do.

'Okay, I can't get you a signed letter. But I can get you something else.'

'What?'

The nurse was thinking frantically about what she could gain access to that wasn't under lock and key.

'Dorothy's records.'

'Will it show the dates? When she was there? When she was discharged?'

'Yes. All of that.'

'Please hurry. We have only minutes.'

'All right.'

Susan White ended the call and raced over to the filing cabinets. But the files were numerical. She had to look up the name in the card index to get the file number. Then she realized that the cabinets were locked.

23:58 PDT

The staff at the fingerprint lab were taking this case very seriously – especially after what the governor had told them.

They had cut the pages out of the passport and put them in the chamber. They had filled the chamber with cyanoacrylic vapor. They had evacuated the chamber of the toxic gases. The lab technician – at twenty-two, a picture of a science nerd – thought it ironic that they were using a 'gas chamber' to decide if a man was to be spared lethal injection. He had even made a joke to that effect to the girl who worked with him. She had smiled politely, but he could tell that she didn't find it amusing.

Now the fingerprint expert at the lab – a slightly older man than the technicians – was doing the comparison, noting points of comparison one by one with the thumbprint that had been sent over electronically from the California Department of Motor Vehicles.

Most of the prints on the passport had been eliminated very quickly. But there were a couple that required a close look – those that were clearly thumbprints. And as the fingerprint expert looked, he was counting the number of points of comparison. And what he found amazed him.

After a few more seconds, he looked up as if a light bulb had gone off in his head. In the pregnant silence that followed, the sound of the three of them breathing could be heard. The others knew what he was about to say, from the look on his face.

'It's a match.'

00:00 PDT (August 15, 1997)

The curtain that covered the window between the execution chamber and the observation room was opened.

Clayton Burrow lay strapped to the gurney.

Although no one was supposed to say anything, there was a collective gasp. The guards who stood at the corners of the observation room said nothing. They knew that it was an involuntary reaction and in any case could not be heard in the execution chamber itself. The flow of sound was regulated by microphones and speakers: the glass itself was triple-glazed.

The warden of the prison began reading out from a single-page, black-bordered document. But Nathaniel Anderson was not listening. He was looking down at Burrow, now a pathetic figure, staring up at the ceiling, making no effort to look round at the spectators.

What was he thinking? Nat wondered. *Was he afraid? Did he feel guilty? Ashamed?*

The warden finished reading the warrant and then looked up, through the window.

'Mr Burrow has made a short written statement, which he has asked me to read to you:

'"There are things I have done in my life that I'm not proud of. There were things I shouldn't have done. I was a product of my upbringing. I wasn't always taught right from wrong. And I was taught to hate people for things they had no control over or for things that I thought were bad because that's the way I was brought up. But whatever wrongs I am guilty of, murder is not one of them. Dorothy Olsen suffered at my hands. I bullied her in school and I raped her. But I did not kill her. I am saying this, not in the hope of being spared the death penalty. I know it is too late for that. But simply because I want the truth to be known."'

The warden then looked down at Burrow.

'Do you want to add anything to that?'

Burrow nodded, lifted his head slightly and turned to face the spectators.

'I just want to say that I have no complaints about the justice system. I had a fair trial and everything was done that could and should be done in order to ensure that I had a fair trial and in order to ensure that justice was done.'

Then he lay back and the prison staff found two veins and inserted two needles, one for the sodium thiopental and one for the other two drugs. Then they stood back from the table. The execution was about to begin.

At that point, Clayton Burrow turned his head to face the spectators again, but this time, he tilted his head upward relative to his body, so that he could see all of them.

And then he met Nat's eyes.

00:02 PDT (08:02 BST)

Susan White had shocked the other nursing staff by running from room to room in her disarrayed clothes. But, seeing the tenacity and determination in her eyes – as well as her large girth – none of them saw fit to challenge her.

She was now frantically putting papers into the fax machine and keying in a long number. It wasn't clear what she was doing or why she was doing it. But she seemed to be having some kind of breakdown.

'Come on! Come on!' she muttered hysterically.

She was – in a very real sense – a 'woman possessed,' not by some evil spirit, but by the determination to save the man whose life should have been saved last night by Stuart Lloyd, if he had had any sort of sense of moral responsibility.

But in the face of his moral vacuity, it was now Susan's burden to save this anonymous man whose life was in her hands. She cursed herself for her cowardice yesterday as well as her carelessness and complacency.

She was painfully aware of the clock on the wall.

The time showed that in California it must be just after midnight.

Do they do the execution immediately? How quickly does the person die?

00:03 PDT

Sergeant Grace Nightingale was at her desk doing routine paperwork when the phone rang.

'Nightingale.'

'Hi, Grace? It's Lou here from the lab.'

Grace sat up abruptly.

'What have you got?'

'We've got a perfect match, that's what!'

'Wait a minute, let me get this straight.'

'A couple of thumbprints on the passport – one on a page and one on the cover – match Nathaniel Anderson's thumbprint from the CDMV. That means he handled this passport at one time or another, no question.'

'And you're sure about this?'

'One hundred percent.'

'How many points of comparison?'

'In the best print? Sixteen.'

'*Jesus* Christ! We'd better call the governor!'

00:04 PDT

Clayton Burrow was no longer lying back peacefully. He was twisting and wrenching frantically, as if he was trying to get out of his restraints and sit up. All the calm and placidity that he had shown at the start of the execution procedure was now long gone.

Sodium thiopental was now being injected into his veins, but had yet to take effect. The drug was supposed to have rendered him unconscious in preparation for the other chemicals that were to follow.

But some sort of adrenaline rush was keeping him awake. After apparently making his peace with God, instead of lying back and quietly surrendering to unconsciousness, he was now showing all the fight and bluster of a man determined to cling on to life.

It was like that poem by Dylan Thomas entitled Do Not Go Gentle Into That Good Night. But then again, neither was he raging. It looked like he was crying . . . pleading . . . begging.

However, this was no escape attempt. Rather, it looked like an attempt to communicate . . . to say some words that had been left unsaid and that now cried out to be spoken in his dying moments. He kept twisting and turning to keep his eyes on the spectators. It was like he had unfinished business in *this* world and – like one of those tormented ghosts in the horror movies – he wasn't yet ready to move on to the next. He seemed to be saying something. There was no sound coming from his lungs, or if there was, the spectators couldn't hear it through the glass. But his lips were moving and his mouth was struggling to shape words.

Although the spectators had been given strict instructions not to stand up, some of the reporters and 'citizen witnesses' were leaning forward – almost out of their seats – to catch his elusive words. Nobody could be sure what he was saying, or rather what he was *trying* to say. But one reporter thought that she could read his lips.

And what he appeared to be saying was . . . 'I'm sorry . . . I'm sorry . . . I'm sorry . . .'

00:05 PDT

Chuck Dusenbury was sitting in the library of his suite in Sacramento. His wife was sitting nearby in patient silence. She was ready to hold his hand and comfort him if necessary, but she said nothing. She knew, all too well, what was going through his mind right now. This was the first execution of his tenure – and would surely also be his last.

He had been waiting all day for that phone call from Alex Sedaka, telling him where the body was located. He had been hoping against hope to be able to give Esther Olsen the closure that she so definitely needed as her own mortality loomed ahead of her.

But he realized now that it was not to be.

Alex Sedaka had done his best. But Alex's client had been stubborn. He had denied his guilt even to the end.

Ironically, Burrow's lawyer, who had started off so skeptical of his own client's denials, had come close to believing his client as the day wore on. And even Dusenbury himself now had doubts that he hadn't entertained before.

Was Sedaka right? Had Dorothy Olsen really fled

to Britain to have an abortion? Had she really fled because she feared being implicated in the death of the man she had so long thought of as her father? That would have been the biggest irony of all, not only because he was not her father, but also because she was, in fact, in no danger of being blamed for his death.

Perhaps he had been wrong not to suspend the death warrant. Maybe there *were* unanswered questions. He had told Alex that he would stay the execution if Esther Olsen asked him to. But her relapse had precluded that.

Should I have done so anyway?

Even now, Dusenbury was haunted by doubts.

But the biggest doubt of all was over what Alex had told him about his own legal intern. Had this Nathaniel Anderson really stolen or intercepted a vital document from the medical center in England? Did he really have possession of Dorothy's passport? Alex had told him that the passport had been found at Nat's place. But the only evidence they had to support that was the word of a professional burglar – hardly the most convincing evidence.

Could it be that after all this, Nat Anderson had been Dorothy's killer and *not* Clayton Burrow?

That would explain a lot of things. But the one thing it wouldn't explain was *why*. Was he some nerdy geek at Dorothy's school who secretly loved her? Had she spurned him? Had he sought her out and killed her in England in revenge?

Or had the passport been planted on him? Maybe it was Nat who was being set up rather than Burrow.

But who would have done it? Certainly not Alex himself: he was a man of the utmost integrity.

The real question was, had Nat handled the passport? That would surely be the clincher one way or the other. If he had handled it, then that would show that Lee Kelly – career criminal though he was – was telling the truth.

Suddenly, the phone rang.

He grabbed the receiver.

'Dusenbury.'

'Hallo, Mr Governor. It's Grace Nightingale. We've got a match on the dabs lifted from the passport.'

'Whose dabs?'

'Nat Anderson! It's a sixteen-point match.'

'Holy Mary, Mother of God! Clear the line!'

00:06 PDT

Juanita was standing over the fax machine, watching a fax coming through. It was from the medical center. But the fax machine was one of those slow, lumbering inkjet machines. Alex had promised to get a faster one, but three months after the promise she was still waiting.

The phone rang.

It was on the other side of the room, but she leaped up to answer it. She couldn't make the fax come through any faster but the call might be important.

'Alex Sedaka's office.'

'Hallo,' said a voice. It sounded like a man, but she couldn't be sure. He sounded like he was crying.

'Yes?'

'My mother! She's dead.'

She realized who it was. And she realized what this meant. The man at the other end of the line – the man who was now crying pitifully – was Jonathan Olsen.

She didn't want to hurt his feelings and she empathized with his pain. But she needed to get him off the phone so that she could get back to the fax machine and see what was coming through.

Gently, she eased Jonathan off the phone and was just about to go back to the fax machine, when she thought that it might be a good idea to tell Alex. Then again, she realized that there was nothing he could do. It was this fax that might make a difference – if there was still time.

She looked up at the clock and wondered if there *was* still time.

00:07 PDT

Clayton Burrow was no longer struggling. Whatever had unsettled him, it had now been drowned out by the strength of the sodium thiopental and the paralyzing drug that had been injected into him. In the spectators' room next door, the witnesses to the execution sat back in their seats, still tense as the drugs took effect, as Burrow's breathing became labored, as his chest went into spasm, as life slipped away from him.

In the control room on the other side of the execution chamber the warden watched tensely. The execution had gone reasonably smoothly, but it had not been an easy case.

But he felt in some way surprised that it had come this far. Throughout the day, he had had this feeling that something was going to stop this execution from taking place, even *after* the temporary restraining order had been overturned.

But in the end, it had gone ahead and in a few moments it would be all over.

The hotline from the governor rang!

The jolt it sent through the warden was sharper

than a shock from an electric chair. After a momentary convulsion that was physical as well as psychological, he grabbed the phone.

'San Quentin.'

'It's the governor! Pull the plug! He's innocent.'

'*Shit!*'

Not waiting for anyone else to act, the warden leaped out of his chair to hit the abort button. Then he ran into the chamber, personally ripping the needles out of Burrow's arms. The spectators' section erupted into pandemonium.

00:08 PDT

Alex Sedaka arrived in the reception area just as the spectators were being herded out. He had been allowed into the high security section because of his pass. But they had told him that he couldn't go into the spectators' section because the procedure had already started. He cursed himself. He had wanted to give Burrow some comfort.

Now the doors to the spectators' section had been thrown open – somewhat earlier than expected and people were positively *charging* out in a state bordering on hysteria. This was not the usual press stampede to phone in their stories. These people were in a state of shock – as if something untoward had happened.

'What is it?' he asked frantically as one man barged past him.

He had heard of things going wrong with executions before, especially with the electric chair: heads catching fire, frothing at the mouth and going into spasm from lethal gas. But this was a lethal injection procedure. The worst thing that could go wrong was the prisoner regaining consciousness before the other drugs had taken effect. And that was supposed to have been precluded by the new execution protocol.

The hysteria all round him was such that he almost forgot his recent discovery, not to mention his concerns about Nat.

But what he saw next brought it all flooding back to him. For the last person to emerge from the spectators' room was Nat. He looked completely unfazed even as he walked up to Alex. There appeared to be not just an air of calm about him, but almost an air of relief, as if a great burden had been lifted from his shoulders.

'We found Dorothy's passport.'

Surprise flipped across Nat's face, followed by fear . . . followed by a smug calm.

'Oh really?'

'Yes. And the picture of Esther when she was younger.'

'And what conclusions have you drawn?'

'I . . . I'm not sure. I know that you've had an obsession with this case for some time. And maybe even an obsession with the Olsen family. The passport shows that she went to England but never came back here or entered another country.'

'But you still don't know what to make of it,' Nat taunted.

'No.'

'And presumably it was your burglar friend Lee who found the passport and picture?'

'Yes. Lee.'

'I should've guessed. I should have searched him.'

'I also know about Dusenbury and Jimmy . . . and Jonathan.'

Nat smiled.

'You really *have* been doing your homework.'

'But I still don't understand the rest, what you did . . . the why and the wherefore.'

'Does it really matter now? Isn't it more important that the man who tormented Dorothy has finally got what he deserved?'

'Do you mean Clayton Burrow or Edgar Olsen?'

Nat shrugged.

'Both, I guess.'

'To be perfectly honest, Nat, that's *not* what concerns me right now. What concerns me is you. I want to know what *your* interest in this case is.'

'My . . . interest?'

'Oh come on, let's not play games, Nat. You badgered your way into my office, battering down my defenses with flattery. You set your sights on working for me and you made it happen. You went about it like a military campaign. You also made sure that I got the Clayton Burrow case. You were working with the Public Defender's office and you got some con to recommend me to Burrow. Hell, I wouldn't even be surprised if you persuaded the other law firm to drop the case.'

'Oh no, that I didn't do. That was just luck. They wanted out and I saw my opportunity. If they hadn't dropped out, I'd've probably gone to work for them. Although I must confess I liked it a whole lot more this way. I liked the irony of defending the man who was found guilty of killing Dorothy.'

'Except that he didn't kill her, did he?'

'No,' replied Nat, swallowing nervously. 'I did.'

00:09 PDT

Juanita was waiting for the second page of the fax to come through. But there seemed to be a problem. The machine was making frantic noises like it was making valiant efforts to print the page, but it wasn't happening. After a few more seconds, the machine fell silent and it flashed a message on the LCD display: 'Black toner empty.'

'Damn!' she cursed.

She raced to the office supply cupboard and found another, angrily ripping the box open and tearing the wrapping off the cartridge. There was a frantic haste in her movements as she opened the fax machine and removed the old cartridge, tossed it aside, pulled off the tape that covered the flow-hole of the cartridge and slotted it into the machine.

Then came the long wait for the machine to restart. The motor cranked to life and started huffing and puffing like an aging locomotive struggling up a high-grade track to the top of a hill. Even then it wasn't over: the LCD display invited her to choose 'Y' or 'N' for whether she had changed each of the four cartridges. And even then, after more cranking and wheezing, the LCD announced: 'Cleaning.'

Every time! she thought to herself. *Every fucking time!*

00:10 PDT

'I had a feeling that you were going to say that,' said Alex, meeting Nat's eyes unflinchingly. 'I assume you were one of her classmates. I don't remember your picture in the yearbook. Which one were you?'

'It doesn't matter,' said Nat.

'Is he dead?' asked one of the crowd of people, a reporter.

'The doctor's still checking.'

'Why was it called off?' asked the reporter.

'They got a call from the governor,' said another reporter.

For a moment, Alex and Nat had got distracted by the exchange. But now they looked at each other again.

'Okay,' said Alex. 'I don't need to know the minutiae now. But I want to understand why. Why did you kill her? What had she done to you?'

'You really don't get it, do you?' asked Nat with a sneer in his voice. 'I was doing her a favor.'

'A favor?'

'Yeah, you know . . . like in that movie – *They Shoot Horses, Don't They?*'

Alex was beginning to understand. 'You wanted to put her out of her misery?'

Nat nodded.

'Think about it. An abusive father. An indifferent mother who turned a blind eye to what her father was doing to her. Bullying in school, not just at the hands of Clayton Burrow but most of her class. Burrow was just the ringleader, but how do you think the rest of them reacted to a cross-dressing bull-dyke?'

'So what was it? A mercy killing?'

'You could call it that. I know that's not a defense in law, but it's the truth.'

'But when did you do it?'

'What do you mean, when?'

'Well it wasn't round about the time she vanished. We know that she went to London and had an abortion. We know that she never came back. You had her passport at your place and it didn't have any exit stamp from England. What happened, Nat? Did you go over to England and kill her there?'

'I had to. It was hard. To do something like that is never easy. But I had to. I finally killed her when she was over there.'

'What do you mean "finally"? Had you been trying before?'

'Oh, I'd been trying to kill her for a long time.'

00:11 PDT

Looking at the clock on the wall, Juanita was frantic. The fax machine was taking ages to go through its self-cleaning routine. She shifted uncomfortably, waiting for it to finish and start printing again.

But what was the point? Looking at the clock on the wall, she realized that it was too late. Unless they had taken a long time reading out the warrant or Clayton had made a particularly long final statement, he had to be dead by now.

While she waited, she remembered Jonathan's call about his mother. She thought she should tell Alex. But when she called, it went straight to his voicemail. She decided to send him a quick, tersely-worded text.

Finally the machine finished its routine, the chugging sound gave way to a rapid high-pitched whirring and the printing started up again.

Juanita's heart leaped into her mouth as she waited for the machine to spit out the next sheet of paper.

00:12 PDT

David had finally recovered the MP3 file. He wasn't sure
if the recovery process was bit perfect, but even if there
were a few inaudible or distorted parts, they would still
have the bulk of it.

He had copied it over to a PC in the lab; now he had
to run it and listen to it. But the PC didn't have any
speakers, it was built as a high-spec functional machine,
not a games machine – so, although it had a sound card,
it had no speakers.

He wandered off in search of another computer that
he could borrow. The trouble was, most of the offices were
locked, making it impossible to check them out. The offices
that *were* open told the same story: no speakers.

Finally, on a hunch, he decided to check the drawers in
some of the offices and labs that were open. He eventually found what he was looking for: a set of headphones.

He raced back to the lab and plugged the speakers
into the PC. Then he put them on and played the MP3
file, listening to the voice of a girl who may or may not
have been dead, addressing her daddy.

00:13 PDT

'So you killed her in England?' asked Alex.

He was still facing Nat. In the background, several other people seemed to be taking an interest in them.

'Yes.'

'And what about the body? What did you do with it? Why was it never found?'

'He's dead!' said a reporter in the background.

Alex and Nat half turned.

'Are you sure?' asked another.

'Yeah, they've just confirmed it.'

'Why did they try to halt it?'

'The warrant was withdrawn.'

'Procedural or substantive?'

Some of the reporters were looking at Alex from a few yards away, as if hoping for a reaction from him.

'God knows.'

Alex, for his part, kept his eyes locked on Nat.

'So what did you do with the body?'

'I buried her.'

'Where?'

'Somewhere deep.'

Nat hadn't noticed the uniformed men who came up behind him, until Alex motioned to them with his eyes. When Nat did eventually look to his side he noticed them – a slightly fat older one of just below average height and a lean younger one, maybe two inches taller. They were wearing the uniform of Marin County Deputies.

'Nathaniel Anderson?'

'Yes.'

'We have a warrant for your arrest for obstruction of justice.'

One them flashed the warrant in front of him, while the other clamped his hands behind his back and hand-cuffed him. Nat offered no resistance and made no attempt to run. As he was about to be led away, he smiled at Alex.

As Alex watched them leading Nat away, he switched his iPhone back on. As soon as it came on, a message came through. He looked at it.

Had call from Jonathan. Esther Olsen died.

As he walked out into the corridor toward the entrance area and the exit from the prison, Alex felt the pain in the pit of his stomach. He had been moved by the death of Clayton Burrow. But it was nothing compared to the gut-wrenching feeling that ripped at him now. This poor woman, who had wanted only to bring happiness to her daughter, had instead alienated her and lost her love forever. This woman who had tried to ease her husband's pain and guilt as best she knew how, had lost him – and lost her daughter trying to keep him. This woman who had gone to unimaginable lengths to give her tormented husband a son, had lost the son's affection and love. This woman who had sacrificed everything and let other people walk all over her for the sake of those she loved had died alone . . . unloved.

He remembered what Nat had told him about how he had expressed himself so forcefully to Sally Burrow, criticizing her hands-off parenting technique that had left her son Clayton bereft of any sort of moral guidance. At the time, he had chided Nat – albeit mildly – for his loose tongue and lack of tact. But now when he thought about it again he realized that Nat was right – that there is a time to speak out and tell the other person what one really thinks of them . . . and why.

He could still see Nat ahead of him, accompanied by the two county deputies, and was determined to have his say. He wanted Nat to know what he thought of him. It was a futile, fruitless gesture, but he was determined to go through with it.

He hastened his steps, lengthening his stride to close down the distance between them. By the time he reached the entrance area, he had caught up with them. But he didn't want a scene inside the prison gates. Instead he waited until the entrance security staff had let them out into the floodlit courtyard, where the two groups of demonstrators were still assembled, kept apart by lines of law enforcement officers. Then, as the deputies escorted Nat to the waiting police car, Alex strode up to them.

Sensing his approach, all three turned to face him.

The two cops bridled at his proximity. Only Nat remained calm.

'I just want you to know that not only have you deprived an innocent man of his life, you've also deprived a mother of peace and resolution of her grief.'

'What are you talking about?' Nat scoffed. 'If Clayton was innocent, then he couldn't have told her where the body was in any case.'

'No, but you could.'

'Maybe I still can.'

'No, you can't. Esther Olsen died half an hour ago.'

Alex didn't understand why of all the things he had said to Nat in this confrontation, this was the first thing to really touch him.

There was an uncomfortable twitching on Nat's face and then the man who had been so arrogant only moments before broke down in tears, crying like a baby, his nose running pathetically. The arresting officers looked embarrassed and the older one took pity on him and unlocked the handcuffs so that he could reach for his handkerchief, while the younger officer opened the driver's door. This was strictly against the rules, but Nat had been passive until now and his comparatively small size made him look unthreatening.

But the cop had misread the situation. For in a second, Nathaniel's grief had turned to rage. His knee shot out like lightning, catching the older officer square in the groin.

But Nat wasn't finished yet, for he followed up with a vicious left hook and right uppercut, sending the officer spinning away. Alex, who had been about to act to restrain Nat, feared that the officer would be injured further if he hit the ground in that state, so he moved to catch him.

By this stage, the younger cop had reacted, hearing the commotion behind him. He turned and, assessing the situation, realized that Nat was too keyed up to be taken down by physical restraint alone. So he reached for his gun. But as his hand moved to his holster, Nat closed the gap between them in one leaping stride. Even at this stage, the cop could have contained him if he had remembered his training. But in the heat of the moment, and in shock over what had just happened to his partner, all the training went out the window.

So he was still reaching for the gun when Nat grabbed his ears and pulled his head forward. Too late he realized that Nat was lowering his own head to deliver a vicious headbutt. By the time he felt it, he was just about able to mentally prepare for the pain that was to follow. This mental adjustment kept him conscious. But the force of the impact left him weak and dazed.

So when he felt Nat reaching for his holster and yanking out the gun he was powerless to stop him. He slumped to the ground as Nat gripped the handle of the sidearm, effectively leaving the gun in Nat's hands.

Alex had now released the injured older officer and turned to see what Nat was doing. He was just in time to see Nat swinging the gun in his direction. He realized in that moment that he still didn't know what Nat's motives had been and therefore what his current intentions were. For a split second he thought that he was doomed, as if Nat had some grievance with him too.

But Nat just smiled.

'We're taking a ride,' said the intern.

'They'll never let you get away with it. They'll scramble a helicopter!'

Nat took a step forward and brandished the gun in Alex's face.

'I said, let's go.'

And with that, he grabbed Alex's arm and hustled him into the driver's side of the police car. He zipped round and got in the other side, pointing the gun at Alex through the windshield to make sure that the lawyer didn't get any smart ideas.

The keys were in the ignition, where the young cop had just put them. But Alex hesitated.

'Are you sure you want to do this, Nat?'

Outside the car, the officers were on the ground and the prison guards had now reacted, some of them racing toward the car from the prison gates.

Nat raised the barrel of the gun to Alex's temple.

'Move!' he barked.

Alex knew that now was not the time to argue. He gunned the engine and drove off.

00:14 PDT

The second sheet of paper had come out of the machine and the third was now printing. Juanita had read the first page, but all it contained was a brief summary of Dorothy's abortion, how the patient had consulted two doctors, signed a consent form and how the procedure had gone smoothly.

The second sheet had been a psychiatric evaluation of Dorothy's mental state, referring to the fact that she had arrived at the center in a state of hysteria, but how this was not evidence of any sort of psychosis, but rather a consequence of the trauma of being raped and the further trauma of the pregnancy resulting from it.

The page also contained an analysis of Dorothy's overall mental state and concluded that she was fully compos mentis and generally mentally stable, notwithstanding the depression which the report described as 'non-clinical' and resulting from her 'underlying circumstances.'

The report continued discussing such questions as 'eligibility.' It further stated that she was a 'suitable candidate' for a 'one-year assessment.'

The language was highly technical and arcane and, although Juanita was streetwise, computer literate and legally savvy, she was hard pressed to understand this medical language.

The third page came out of the machine. She picked it up and started reading it. But when she stumbled across a phrase she recognized, she got the shock of her life.

00:16 PDT

Alex was turning left into the well-lit Sir Frances Drake Boulevard as Nat kept the gun leveled at his head. The muzzle wasn't up against his temple now. Instead Nat held the gun close to himself in his right hand, supporting his right elbow in his left hand to keep the gun steady. But there was no doubt where it was aimed.

Alex couldn't yet hear the sirens of the Marin County Sheriff's Department, but he knew it was only a matter of time. Pretty soon they'd have State Troopers on their tail too.

But that was not what was troubling Alex now. He knew they wouldn't try anything precipitate. They would know from what the deputies would have told them that this was a hostage situation: that Alex was an innocent man being held at gunpoint and forced to drive. Yes, they would call out a SWAT team and scramble a helicopter. But they would do nothing to endanger his life. They might try to stop the car with a PIT maneuver – or even try to blow out the tires on a flat stretch if no other vehicles were about

– but there was no way they'd open fire on the car itself.

What troubled Alex right now was Nat himself. What was he doing? What was he hoping to achieve? He was too intelligent to think that he could get away. In modern police chases, once a vehicle was marked, there was no getting away. They could probably track the police car via satnav. But even if they couldn't, they could track it through aerial observation. Perhaps, if Nat could make it to a wooded area, he could get away on foot and hide under foliage thick enough to be opaque to thermal imaging. But they were too far from any such foliage. Escape was impossible.

Did this mean that this was going to be Nat's last stand? And if so, what fate, Alex wondered, did Nat have in store for him?

And there was still that other lingering elusive question: *why?*

The motive remained as elusive as ever. It was almost as if Nat couldn't explain his own actions. Then again, this was not so unusual. Even Clayton Burrow had only the vaguest insight as to why he had chosen Dorothy as the target for his bullying – and he had had seven years in the shadow of death to contemplate his motives as well as his fate. Self-awareness was not a virtue with which all people were blessed. And generally those who possessed it least were those most inclined toward crime in general, and violence in particular.

But Nathaniel Anderson was no violent criminal. He was not one of those people who stood only a moment from violence at every turn. Such people might lash out at their wives or their children or get into fights with their neighbours. But Nat was not like that. Today was the first time Alex had seen any hint of Nat having a capacity for violence, let alone a propensity.

Maybe he's a psychopath or a sociopath or whatever the current buzzword is today.

But that was no explanation either. Even practical questions like the disposal of the body had gone unanswered.

His thoughts were interrupted by a call on his iPhone. Alex looked at Nat, unsure of what to do.

Nat reached into Alex's pocket, pulled out the phone and looked at the display.

'It's from David,' he said, as if inviting Alex to say what he wanted to do. But Alex knew that he was in no position to decide. Nat was holding the gun as well as the phone. Alex couldn't hold the phone to talk and he daren't challenge the gun.

'I'll put it on speaker.'

And with that Nat answered.

'Hi, David.'

'Nat?' He sounded confused.

'Yes. Your father's right here. He can't hold the phone 'cause he's driving. I'll put you on speaker.'

Nat put the phone on speaker and nodded toward Alex.

'Hi, David.'

'Hi, Dad. Listen, I've just recovered an MP3 file from the disk.'

Alex didn't want to hear this right now. By this stage

anything David could find would almost certainly be irrelevant. But on the other hand, he didn't want to tell David that all their efforts had been in vain.

'What, you mean like a *song*?'

'No. It's speech. It's Dorothy. She's talking.'

'Talking?'

'Yes.'

'What was she talking about?'

'It's that poem . . . the one I kept finding extracts from. The one inspired by Sylvia Plath's "Daddy."'

'But as an MP3 file this time?'

'Yes. She's reading it aloud.'

'Can you play it over the phone?'

It was a silly request. He didn't know why he had asked.

'Well the sound quality won't be all that good. But I can email it to you as an attachment.'

'How long will that take?'

'Less than a minute.'

'I'm driving.'

'It can wait till you get back home or to the office.'

'Send it now and then go home and get some sleep. I'll listen when I can.'

'Home?'

David sounded tense at the word.

Alex let the air out of his lungs. He wasn't going to let his son in on his current predicament, but the best way to stop him tuning in to the radio to catch the news was to tell him the outcome with Burrow.

'It's over, David.'

The line went silent for a few seconds.

'I'm sorry, Dad.'

'You did your best . . . we all did.'

'I know. I just wish we could have done more.'

'Get some rest. Goodnight, David.'

'Goodnight, Dad.'

Alex looked over at Nat, as if to ask him if he was proud of himself. Nat ignored him and ended the call.

'Take the ramp,' ordered Nat. 'Get onto Interstate 101 South.'

Alex obeyed, noticing that while he was doing so, Nat was playing with the iPhone.

'What are you doing?'

Nat smiled.

'Downloading the poem. Don't you want to hear it? It might be kind of cute.'

Alex felt anger at Nat's callousness. But he kept it in check.

'We may as well . . . I guess.'

While Alex kept his eyes on the road, Nat logged on to his email to download the MP3 file to Alex's iPhone.

'Shall I play it?'

Alex swallowed.

'Yes,' he muttered.

Nat touched the area of the screen that started the MP3 file playing.

Dorothy's voice came over the phone's speaker. The irony that she was addressing Edgar as 'Daddy' was not lost on Alex as he divided his concentration between Dorothy's words and the road ahead.

I cannot be, can never be
What I thought you wanted me
To be, to be, or so it seemed
When I didn't understand
What a fool I was, tee hee

Daddy, I know I am guilty
Though someone killed you first
I killed you as surely as if
I had pulled the trigger myself
Bang Bang! All over

And now I have to cross the Atlantic
Because I have to flee
Across the ocean, safe and sound
To where they'll never find me
You see

At that point, Alex's concentration was broken by the
sound of a helicopter overhead.

00:19 PDT

Juanita was in shock at what she had just read. She called Alex. She had got the busy signal before. But she had to tell him.

In her haste, she kept fumbling the digits and having to go back and start over. Finally she got through. It rang for a few seconds.

'Hi, Juanita. Listen, I'm kind of busy right n—'

'I just got the fax about Dorothy from the London clinic.'

'And?'

'You're not gonna believe this, boss. It says she had hormone treatment.'

'Hormone treatment?'

'*And* gender re-assignment surgery.'

There was a gasp at the other end.

'Gender re-assignment?'

'*Yes! She had a fuckin' sex change!*'

00:22 PDT

'I wish I'd known, Nat,' said Alex gently as he left Silva Island behind him.

They'd been sitting in silence for over a minute as Alex drove along the I-101 overpass just past the Planet Day Care and Activity Center. Alex had switched off the MP3 and they'd sat there tensely, each waiting for the other to speak. Alex's mind was still reeling from what he had just heard. But he sensed that Nat didn't yet trust his voice, now that the truth was out.

It changed . . . *everything*.

And yet he wasn't sure how to get through to Nat even now. At this moment, Nat was fleeing for his life and you didn't argue with a man who feels cornered. Neither could you reason with a man who felt betrayed. All Alex could do was bide his time. To try and break the ice would be suicide. But perhaps he could thaw it slowly.

'I wish—'

'Take the North Exit to Highway 1,' said Nat, breaking his silence. 'We'll head toward Stinson Beach.'

While Alex was still struggling to take it all in, a change seemed to have come over Nat. Now he looked almost relieved that he no longer had to keep it all bottled up inside.

'I can get you a good lawyer,' said Alex. 'I know most of the defense attorneys in the Bay area and I can get you the best.'

'I'm not going to spend my life behind bars,' Nat replied tensely. 'I've lived most of my life in fear. Fear of the man I thought was my father, when I was a kid. Fear of bullies in high school. Fear when I got pregnant and then fear of being found out these last few years.'

Alex thought about the fact that this last fear was of Nat's own making. If he hadn't framed Burrow for murder, the problem need never have arisen. But now was not the time to discuss ethics.

'You can't get away. They won't let you. But you can fight it through the system. Do it the smart way.'

'I need to think.'

'It's too late for that, you must—'

'Look, *shut up*!'

Alex knew when *not* to push the point.

He let the silence settle between them. In a way he was grateful for this opportunity. It could be the last.

'So what happened when you went to England?'

Nat took a deep breath.

'Well first of all, I sold a diamond ring to raise some cash to open a bank account. Then I sold the rest of the jewelry to other jewelers and dealers in London and got the money paid into my bank account. So now I had a bank account and I could function, but at the same time there was no trace of the money being transferred from my US account so there was no trail for the FBI or anyone else to follow. They didn't know if I was dead or missing, but as far as they knew I could have been either. Turn left at Highway 1.'

Alex complied, trying to ignore the helicopter overhead and the police cars on their tail. He prayed that the cops wouldn't challenge them on this narrow two-lane road. It wasn't that he feared death. It was just that he wanted – needed – to know the rest.

'And what about the medical center? I mean the abortion and the . . .'

For some reason he found it hard to say the words.

'Well I was able to have the abortion immediately. They just needed to get me assessed by two doctors, and they were able to do that in one day. But the gender re-assignment was more complicated because it has various major legal requirements. One of the formalities is that you have to live for a year in the new gender role to make sure that you're comfortable with it and really want to go through with it. It's part of the assessment process.'

'So you waited a year just for the procedure?'

Nat looked uncomfortable with the question.

'Not exactly. I was desperate to escape from the woman's body that I was trapped in. So I convinced the Chief Administrator to alter the records to make it look as if I'd been living as a man in America. That way I was able to shorten the waiting time for the start of the procedure to seven months.'

'When you say you convinced him . . .'

'As in, greased his palm.'

'That would explain the large sums of money going out of Dorothy's – of *your* – account.'

'Actually, no. Most of that money was for the procedure. Hell, it's an expensive procedure any way you look at it.'

'So how did they do it? I mean, how did they fiddle the paperwork?'

'Basically they exploited the fact that January can be written as J-A-N and June as J-U-N. And we also took advantage of the different date formats when they use numbers. In England they put the day first, instead of the month. They wrote 06-01-98 instead of 01-06-98. That made it look as if I'd been living as a man since January 6, 1998 instead of June first. If anyone had caught it, they would have hidden behind the excuse that there was a mix-up about the dates.'

Alex thought about this. That would explain why the medical center had been so reticent about confirming Dorothy's stay there: it might open a whole can of worms regarding their breach of protocol, not to mention the law.

'And in all that time since you came back, you never once contacted Jonathan?'

'I couldn't afford to. Turn left! All it needed was for one message to be traced.'

'You thought he was being watched?'

'No, of course not. But I didn't know what had happened at Edgar's place. I knew they thought it was suicide. But I didn't know why. To me it was like a timebomb that could explode any time.'

00:26 PDT

'They're sticking to CA-1!' said the helicopter observer to his ground controller, watching the white moving rectangle in the heads-up display.

'That means they're probably headed for tree cover.'

'Affirmative, Joe,' said the observer. 'But they've still got a couple of miles before that. Any chance of CHIPS taking them out with Stop Sticks?'

Nowadays, most California Highway Patrol units were equipped with devices that stop fleeing vehicles with spikes that puncture the tires. The devices were designed in such a way as to cause the tires to deflate gradually rather than suddenly – thus avoiding the danger of a blow-out at high speed. The problem was that at this time of year, California roads got so hot that tires could blow out at the slightest stimulus.

However, it was now night time and, despite the heat wave, the roads had cooled somewhat.

'That's a negative, Larry – at least not till they come out the other side of Tamalpais.'

'But if they make it to the Valley then he can ditch the car and run for tree cover.'

'Come off it, Larry, people show up on thermal imaging better than cars. He won't get far.'

'Okay, but I haven't enough fuel to stay up here all night.'

The ground controller seemed to ponder this for a few seconds.

'He probably knows we've got thermal imaging. My guess is he's trying to make it to the coastline.'

Larry laughed.

'You think he's gonna try and swim the Pacific Ocean?'

'I don't know *what* he's gonna do. I don't think he's really too sure either. My best guess is he's going to try and make it to Stinson Beach or Bolinas and then blend in with the locals at dawn.'

'So why not get CHIPS to stop him?'

'We can't set up the Stop Sticks in time. Not before Muir Beach. We haven't got a unit close enough.'

'Okay, well try and stop him at Muir Beach, 'cause if he makes it to Stinson or Bolinas he might take other hostages.'

'Ten-four.'

'And let's pray he doesn't get out on foot at Tamalpais.'

'If he does, it'll mean he's killed the hostage. Either that or abandoned him. He won't take him at gunpoint if he's hiding in the trees.'

'What's that got to do with it?'

'It means we can send in a SWAT team and take the bastard out.'

00:27 PDT

'Okay, so you had hormone treatment to change your features and genital reconstruction?'

'Yes. And I had my breasts removed.'

Nat was more relaxed now, and Alex knew that if he could keep him talking, there was a chance that they could end this peacefully. He could see the cops in the rearview mirror. And the ever-present humming of the helicopter's rotor blades still rumbled in the night sky overhead.

'So how come they let you keep the breast tissue?' Alex prompted. 'That's kind of unusual, isn't it?'

'One of the good things about having the Chief Administrator in your pocket is that you can get away with things that you wouldn't normally. I told them I wanted it and they gave it to me – in a refrigerated bag. You have to remember that they were kind of vulnerable. They'd broken the law by doing the gender re-assignment. I hadn't broken any law by having it done.'

'And then you used the breast tissue to frame Burrow.'

'That's right. I went back to his place, broke in easily enough and planted the breast tissue at the back of the freezer. You know people never look in the back of their own freezer. They leave stuff there for years.'

'But once in a while they clean it out.'

'But not very often – especially trailer trash like Burrow.'

'And what about the panties and the knife?'

'I'd kept the panties from the rape because I was originally considering going to the police.'

'And the blood on the knife?'

'It's no big deal to get a small amount of one's own blood.'

'But how *did* you get back? I mean, you couldn't have used your old passport anyway – not once you'd had the sex change.'

'I had enough money left over to pay for a forged passport. With modern computers and printing technology it's a lot cheaper than it used to be.'

'That's why there was no return stamp in your passport.'

'That's right. I got a new passport in my new name. Turn left. I want to stay on Highway 1.'

'Any particular reason for that name – Nathaniel?'

Nat smiled.

'What do you mean?'

'Well I was just thinking. After Esther told me about my name – "Sedaka" – meaning charity or righteousness, I found this website where you can look up the meaning of names. I started looking up names with a view to working out what Dorothy might be calling herself. I noticed that Jonathan – from the Hebrew Yonatan – means "God gave." And Dorothy comes from Doro Thea. That's Greek for "God's gift." It's like Theodore in reverse. I thought there might be some significance in that.'

'And?' prompted Nat smiling.

'Well I also noticed that Nathaniel also means God's gift – in Hebrew. It uses another of God's Hebrew names: El. Natan-El, God gave. At the time I thought it was just a coincidence that you had a name with the same meaning as both Dorothy and Jonathan and didn't give it a second thought. I was too busy thinking about what Dorothy might be calling herself if she was still alive. Only now I'm wondering . . .'

'It was partly that. But it was also a tribute to an author I very much admire. But that's another story. Anyway, you're on the right track. Mom gave both of us names that mean "God's gift." To her, I guess, we *were* gifts from God – especially when you consider that the old man was infertile. Dorothy had the Greek name. But I was the one from the Greeks bearing a gift – the gift that Dad – that . . . Edgar didn't want to touch . . .'

They shared a weak smile at the irony.

'And what about Anderson?'

'Another bit of Greek. Andros means man. I was the son of man – even if I didn't know at the time *which* man.'

'When did you find out that Edgar wasn't your father?'

'I'd known from an early age that Edgar wasn't my real father. I'd heard it in arguments before I was even old enough to understand these things. He'd get into drunken rages and then she was the "whore" who'd slept with another man on the eve of the wedding. I was the "little mamzer" who wasn't even his daughter. I had it drummed into me even when I was a child. Then I found the picture.'

00:28

'He turned left. They're going round the Valley.'

'Copy that, Larry. Any sign of slowing down?'

Slowing down would have been an indicator that someone was planning to make a run from the car on foot. The controller doubted this, but Larry had raised the possibility and they were now coming up to the big test of the fugitive's intentions.

'That's a negative. Suspect vehicle is still maintaining speed.'

'Looks like you were wrong, Larry.'

'Let's not get our hopes up. They're still a minute away from the trees.'

'You want to make a bet on it?'

'Yeah, two tickets to the World Series.'

'You've gotta be kidding!'

'Okay, one of the games.'

'You're on.'

'By the way, if he does go for cover, you'll have to send in a relief crew. I've only got enough fuel for another hour.'

00:29 PDT

'The picture of your mother?'

'No, the one I found with it.'

'What was that?'

'I'd been rummaging round in the closet in my parents' bedroom, looking for my dad's clothes to try on – I mean, Edgar's.'

Nat wiped a tear from his eyes. Alex realized how hard it was to distance himself from thinking about Edgar Olsen as his father, even though he had known for such a long time.

'Go on.'

'I think I must have been about twelve or thirteen at the time. And I found these pictures of this young man and woman. They were in an old shoe box with a pile of old pictures, not exactly hidden away, but pushed right to the back of the closet, as if it was like buried away. You know, burying the past and all that.'

Alex nodded, signaling Nat to continue.

'And I recognized my mom, but I didn't know who the man was. So I just took the pictures and then I waited until I could find a suitable moment to ask Mom.'

'And did you?'

'Yes. She told me about the party and the one-night stand and all that. And I could tell by the way she was talking to me that there was more to it. So I asked her – point blank – if the man was my father. And she said yes.'

'And she let you keep the picture? She didn't try and take it back?'

'No, I asked her if I could keep it. With all the shit in my life I needed something to cling on to, like my real father. And she saw the look in my eyes and . . . I think . . .' He was struggling against the threat of tears once again. 'I think . . . that she knew how I felt, how strongly I wanted it. So she said I could keep it. And I've kept it ever since.'

'But did you ask her who it was? Did she even know the name?'

'That's the funny thing. She said she didn't. She always said that it was just someone she met at a party. But I think she did. I really think she did.'

'And did *you* find out?'

'Eventually. It was shortly after I came back, after I'd framed Burrow. It helped me find a sense of purpose. You see, I had a new identity and was all set to start a new life. But I didn't have any sense of direction. I was drifting aimlessly. You know, like that poem by Stevie Smith.'

'"Daddy"?'

'No that was Sylvia Plath. The Stevie Smith poem was called "Not waving but drowning."'

'"Not waving but drowning"?'

521

'That's the title. It's about a man who was left to drown when people on the shore thought he was just waving. He was signaling for help, but they thought he was just clowning round. It was meant as a metaphor for life. We laugh to hide the fear.'

'And is that how you felt?'

The voice was gentle.

'Yes. Until then. But then I decided to become a lawyer. I did my SATs and got into college. I studied English Lit for my AB 'cause I really loved the subject. I got that from . . . my mother . . . from Mom. And then I studied law.'

'And then?'

'I'm not really sure. I mean, even after I planted the evidence on Burrow, I still wanted closure.'

'What sort of closure?'

'That was the problem. It was still too confused in my own mind. I wanted Burrow to pay for all the years of misery and torment he'd put me through.'

'And you got Burrow to ask me to represent him by going through another prisoner and using him to influence Burrow.'

'Yes. In my last year of studies I was doing my first year of internship with the Public Defender's office. I was working with quite a lot of cons and one of them was in the high security unit at San Quentin. He wasn't on death row, but he still had some contact with Burrow through the prisoners' grapevine. It's quite sophisticated, you know. It was round about the time of the Sanchez case and you'd hired me and I was just finishing my term with the PD.'

'And you got him to recommend me on the strength of Sanchez and, because Burrow was looking for someone, he ended up with me.'

'Right.'

'Very clever.'

'Thanks.'

'And was that why you didn't want to meet Burrow face to face? Because you were afraid that he'd recognize you?'

'Exact—'

They were approaching Muir Beach and looming up ahead of them was a police road block: two cars and a wagon, covering both lanes. It would be easy enough to avoid. They could just swerve round it onto the grass on either side. But the question was . . . how would the police react?

They must know I'm a hostage, Alex thought. *They won't shoot into the car when there's a chance I'll be hit.*

Of course they might try to take out the tires. But that would be dangerous too. The road hugged the cliff on this next stretch. Any damage to the tires and they might lose traction and skid over the edge.

He prayed that the cops wouldn't do anything stupid. It was too much to hope that Nat wouldn't.

'Run it,' snapped Nat, as if to confirm Alex's worst fear.

00:32 PDT

'Yes, Mr Governor, I understand, but they're approaching.'

The State Trooper in charge of the road block at Muir Beach had received a frantic phone call from his captain. The next thing he knew, Governor Dusenbury had been patched through and was telling him that under no circumstances was he to take any action that might endanger the lives of either person in the stolen police car.

'Okay, sir, we won't open fire . . . yes, sir, we won't even return fire.'

'Not even at the tires!' the governor added for good measure.

'We weren't planning on shooting at the tires. We've got the road fully blocked and we've planted Stop Sticks on the grass verges by the side, in case they try and give us the sli—'

'Are you crazy? Do you know what Stop Sticks'll do to their tires?'

'Yes, sir, but that's the point. It won't shred the tires. It'll let their air out gradually.'

'But they're gonna be hugging the cliff on a two-laner,

you jackass! Do you know what'll happen if they skid on a bend on that stretch?'

'Yes, sir, but it's too late! We can't move the Sticks now, it's not safe. Oh my God, they're swerving! They've gone over the Sticks. Shit!'

00:33 PDT

'Goddamn! What was that!' shouted Nat.

'I don't know, I think we went over something.'

Nat was looking back frantically.

'Are they following?'

'I don't think so.'

'That doesn't make sense. They usually have cars ready to pursue if the road block gets run.'

Alex was now more tense than before.

Why would they just let them run the road block and do nothing? Did that mean they had something else ahead?

'Fuck 'em,' said Nat. 'We made it.'

'For now,' Alex replied, hoping that Nat would catch the fatalism in his tone.

'We'll get to Stinson Beach and run the car off the cliff.'

'And then what?'

Nat was silent; they both knew why. He didn't know what he was going to do afterward. There was no getting away. Stinson Beach wasn't so big. Even if he could force his way into someone's house, the cops would make house to house searches. And if he stayed out in the open he could be tracked by thermal imaging. It was night and not many people were about.

However, that was Nat's worry. Alex's worry was keeping the car on the road. The cliff wasn't too steep here. But it would get steeper as they approached Stinson Beach. And there were some sharp bends in the road too. The worst part was the stretch approaching Gull Rock.

And the car was already not holding as steady as he would have liked.

'What about the meeting with Dusenbury?' asked Alex, trying to engage Nat in friendly conversation once more. 'Why were you so anxious to avoid him?'

'It wasn't him I was trying to avoid. It was my mother.'

'You *knew* she'd be there?'

'Let's just say I had a feeling. Dusenbury is an old family friend and I knew that Mom had cancer. I may have ended up hating her, but at one time we were very close and I knew how her mind worked.'

'And you knew she was going to try and persuade Dusenbury to offer clemency?'

'I had a feeling she'd meet him because of their past relationship. I didn't know if anything would come out of such a meeting.'

'And you hated her so much that you couldn't bring yourself to tell her that you were alive?'

'I didn't, I don't think. I mean, I hated her when she turned a blind eye to the way Edgar treated me. But . . . toward the end . . . I think I'd forgiven her.'

'Then why didn't you go to her? Tell her . . . tell her that you'd forgiven her?'

Alex had been hesitant to ask this. He was afraid that Nat would break completely if he had to confront the fact that he too had inflicted torment on Esther, just as Edgar and Burrow had on him. But Nat held it together and even smiled.

'Have you ever read the story "Wakefield"?'

'"Wakefield"?'

'By another Nathaniel. Nathaniel Hawthorne. He's the author I was talking about before – the one my name is a tribute to.'

'No, I haven't read it. Wasn't he the guy who wrote *The Scarlet Letter*?'

Nat smiled at the almost philistine way Alex had put it.

'Yes, he was the guy who wrote *The Scarlet Letter*. Anyway, "Wakefield" was a story about a man who left his wife for no discernible reason, stayed away for years with no contact whatsoever, and then went back.'

'I don't understand.'

'Neither do I. I mean, I do, but barely. I couldn't possibly do justice to it. You'll have to read it to understand it. But the point is by that stage I no longer knew *why* I was doing it. I just was. Yes, I blamed her for letting Edgar abuse me. But more importantly I wanted to make *Burrow* pay. And for that I had to stay hidden from public view. I couldn't admit my identity to anyone . . . just in case word got out and blew my cover.'

Alex was making a sharp right followed by a sharp left as the road took them across a small gully. Alex felt the vehicle shake awkwardly and realized in that moment that the tires were losing pressure – had *already* lost a lot of pressure. He realized what must have happened at

528

the road block. The cops had used Stop Sticks. That's what he had gone over when he swerved onto the grass verge at the last second.

'It's a pity you had to stay away like that,' said Alex. 'If you'd met Burrow – toward the end – you might have seen him differently.' Alex saw the pained look on Nat's face. 'I'm not trying to mitigate what he did to you. But he had changed.'

'I know. I suppose that living in fear of death was punishment enough for him. But it's like . . . in that moment when he raped me . . . I swore that he'd pay with his life. And even though I mellowed over the years, I didn't mellow enough to let him live.'

'And what about Jonathan? You didn't tell him either.'

'No, but he found out. That's why he came to the office yesterday.'

'How *did* he find out, by the way?'

'They showed some footage of the two of us coming out of the Supreme Court after the certiorari hearing. That was when they were reporting Dusenbury's offer.'

'Which you leaked.'

'Which I leaked. He thought he recognized me, but he wasn't sure. That's why he came to the office. He wanted to see me in person to make sure. But I wasn't there so he hung round and ambushed Juanita when she went out for lunch. Then he walked her back to the office and that's when he saw me. That was when he knew for sure.'

'Did he say anything?'

'No, but we locked eyes and I knew that he knew and he knew that I knew.'

'And is that how you got the spectator's pass?'

'Exactly. Later during the day he tried to call me. He didn't have my cell phone number so he called the office. But Juanita kept answering, so he kept hanging up. She thought it was a crank caller, so I said I'd answer. When I did, he spoke. He told me that we had to meet.'

'And is that why you had to go out?'

'Yes. We spoke again before that. I couldn't talk to him when Juanita was round, but she went out a couple of times after that. We arranged that I'd come round at some point. I was actually outside, watching, when you left his place.'

'What, after he told me about killing Edgar?'

'Exactly. After you left, I went in and we talked over old times. And I . . .'

Nat had to stop. His eyes were welling up with tears again.

'It was like the burden of all the years was lifted off my shoulders. By that stage I was ready to tell Mom.' His voice was cracking now. 'But I stupidly – *stupidly* – waited. I wanted to wait till after the execution.' He could only dam up the tears long enough to add one more sentence. '*And now it's too late!*'

Alex tried to offer some words of comfort.

'I'm so . . . sorry. I wish . . .'

He trailed off. It was foolish to wish. You can't take back what's already happened. Life doesn't offer many second chances.

And he knew that in life – once you make a choice at the fork in the road – you can never go back. He had learned that from Melody – and Nat had learned it from just about every major event in his troubled, painful life.

But the other thing that Alex had learned was that if it's a mistake to make a snap decision on what to do, it's an even bigger mistake to rush to judgement over a fellow human being.

'There's one thing I still don't understand. You didn't just get me to take on the Clayton Burrow case. You badgered your way into my office *before* that . . . *before I got the case*. Why did you do that? Why didn't you just try to get a job with the law firm that already *had* the case? They were a much bigger law firm. They were more likely to have a vacant position. Did you try them as well? Didn't they have a vacancy? Or did you mailshot a load of firms and just strike it lucky with me?'

Through his tears, Nat turned slightly in Alex's direction and opened his mouth to speak.

Then it happened.

Alex was at the curve that overlooked Gull Rock. He had to make a sharp right turn to take him away from the cliff face and then a hairpin turn to the left to take him back to the cliff face, which was shallower from then on.

But he never even made it to the hairpin turn. It may have been the tires. It may have been oil on the road. But when he made the sharp right turn he lost control of the car and it skidded off the road and onto a steep decline. At this point, the cliff was bare of foliage that might offer traction or friction.

Nat screamed, while Alex struggled frantically to regain control as he saw the car heading for that sheer drop onto the rocks below. Somehow he managed to hold it together for a split second, so they missed the sheer drop.

They skidded sideways onto a slightly shallower drop where some foliage offered a trace of resistance, but then the car bounced and started tumbling sideways down into a steep gully, bouncing every time the roof or wheels hit the foliage beneath them.

Their seat belts held them in place but, even before they hit the bottom, Alex could see blood oozing from Nat's head from the impacts.

And then – completely inverted – they hit rock bottom amid a shattering of glass. The rocks and the ocean waves lapping away at them and water flooding into the vehicle.

Alex looked round and saw in the dim light that Nat was unconscious, or at least dazed into that semi-conscious twilight world that made even the most basic life-preserving actions impossible.

He quickly unfastened his own seat belt, falling out of his seat in the process and then frantically struggled to unfasten Nat's. He caught Nat to stop him falling and hitting his head. Then it was an even more frantic struggle to open a door and effect an escape before they were fully submerged. He would have preferred to get out through the driver's door, on the side closest to the rocks, where there was still a thin sliver of land to offer them temporary safety. But it would have been hard to pull Nat past the steering wheel.

He considered getting out on the driver's side and then swimming round to the passenger side to rescue Nat. But he wasn't sure if he would make it. And the thought of leaving Nat, even temporarily, seemed like cowardice. So instead he leaned past Nat, opened the door and then pushed Nat out, following immediately.

In the rough waves of the Pacific Ocean, he couldn't tell if the tide was coming in or going out. But he knew that he had to get himself and Nat onto the rock-strewn foot of the cliff as quickly as possible. The water was still shallow enough to stand in and keep his chin above water. But he didn't know how long it would stay that way and the waves were too rough to keep his balance for long.

So he got behind Nat, held him and leaned back into the classic life-saving position, kicking to propel himself round the car and toward the sliver of land at the foot of the cliff that offered their only hope of salvation. He noticed a stirring in his arms and he realized that Nat was regaining consciousness.

Then an almighty wave swept them onto the precious strip of land, Alex's back crashing into the wall of the cliff with some considerable force. He realized that nothing was broken, but realized too that he had been lucky. For an instant he let go of Nat to rub his back and soothe the pain. But then, as Nat pulled himself up onto a rock and struggled to his feet in a state bordering on sleepwalking, the undertow took hold. While Alex in his half-seated position close to the cliff face was able to hold his position, Nat, who was standing a yard or so further out, was caught by the undertow and swept off his feet. Before he was able to grab on to the rock that he had used to get into a standing position, he was dragged out to sea.

He screamed again as he twisted his body to face Alex and reached out with his arms like a child desperate to be held. And despite the dim light, Alex was able to discern that the look of fear in Nat's eyes was also like that of a child.

Or was it a look of sadness?

Whatever it was, it remained frozen in Alex's memory as the tidal current – evidently going out – pulled Nat away from him.

He didn't see Nat go under at any time. All he saw was a head bobbing up and down on the turbulent surface, drifting further and further away. And all he heard was a voice crying out indiscernibly from the distance.

09:55 PDT

It wasn't Melody. It wasn't his wife whose beautiful face smiled down at him when he opened his eyes.

But it was another beautiful angel.

He didn't know her name. But she had a young, innocent, fresh face and the clear complexion of one who has a long life ahead of her and everything to live for.

Is this heaven?

Was she his guide to paradise?

He wanted to ask her. But he didn't trust his mouth to speak.

Then he felt a plastercast on his leg and he realized that he wasn't in heaven. He was in a hospital. They had saved him.

Someone had saved him.

He couldn't remember. He remembered the car crash and the waves – and he remembered trying to save Nat. But that was all. After that it was a blank.

'Mr Sedaka.'

Alex nodded weakly.

'There's someone who'd like to have word with you.'

Alex was confused, but not frightened. After everything

he'd been through yesterday, there was very little that could frighten him.

He nodded, still weak, but gaining strength.

He felt the upper half of his body being raised.

I'm being raised from the dead like a Freemason, he thought, with ironic humor. Eventually a man came into view. It took a few seconds for Alex's eyes to refocus on the face of the man who stood further back than the nurse. But there was no mistaking that ample girth.

The governor smiled.

'Mr Sedaka.'

The tone was polite, friendly. Alex nodded for Dusenbury to continue.

'It's been quite a roller-coaster for you, Alex, this past twenty-four hours.'

'Quite,' said Alex, stiffly, the first word he'd used since regaining consciousness. He wasn't altogether comfortable with this situation.

'I feel bad about what happened to Burrow.'

Alex was tempted to say 'and well you should.' But this time he resisted the temptation to give voice to his emotions.

The truth of the matter was that he no longer knew *what* he felt. Burrow was innocent of murder and by all accounts a wretched figure in the end. But he had still been the bully who had made Dorothy's youth a living hell – the rapist who had violated her when she was already suffering a tortured life.

Nat had obstructed justice – to the point of sending an innocent man to the death chamber. But he had had the excuse of having been subjected to the most excruciating mental torture not only at the hands of Clayton Burrow, but also at the hands of Edgar Olsen.

How could Alex express outrage or indignation, when his own moral compass had been sent haywire by the turbulent force-field that raged round him?

'I'd like to make up for it, in some way,' said the governor.

'How?' asked Alex, skeptically. He hadn't meant it to sound cold, but that was the way it came out, as if he was brushing off Dusenbury's offer before he even knew what it was.

'I can grant David an amnesty on the computer hacking charges.'

'I thought those charges are federal?'

'Okay, but I can protect him against Section 484 charges—'

'He's not going down on a State 484 'cause there was no pecuniary gain. The only thing I'm worried about is a US 1030.'

'Well I can't help you there 'cause that's federal. But I'm pretty sure you can get him a good lawyer. In any case, I don't think he has too much to worry about. He can always cite the fact that he was trying to save an innocent man's life.'

'That's not a defense in law.'

'No!' the governor's voice boomed into life. 'But it'll make one hell of a plea in mitigation!'

Alex could see that the governor was just trying to be helpful. There was no reason to fight him.

'I guess you're right.'

'Besides,' Dusenbury continued, 'I have a feeling the

feds won't be too anxious to bring the case to trial. It'll throw a spotlight on the execution of an innocent man and give too much impetus to the anti-capital punishment lobby. There's a big debate over that right now. New Jersey's getting rid of it. They had that big amnesty in Illinois. And this great state of ours has a backlog so long that even if we execute five people a month it'll take eleven years just to clear up the backlog!'

'What happened to Nat?'

'We don't know. Some clothes washed ashore at Maintop Island, but no body.'

Alex felt saddened by this, in some inexplicable way.

'They think he's dead?'

'They assume it,' said the governor. 'But it's not yet official.'

'Is he classified as a fugitive?'

'Technically he's a wanted man . . . obstruction of justice. But in reality we're just waiting for his body to turn up.'

Alex remembered the famous case of the three prisoners who escaped from Alactraz. Only one body ever turned up – and it was so badly decomposed that they couldn't be sure if it was one of the escapees – but it was widely assumed that all three of them had drowned. Even though bodies tend to float after a few days, on the Pacific coast a body could be swept out to sea and never found unless it had a chance encounter with ship or boat.

And as for the clothes, the body of the Alcatraz escapee that turned up weeks later was naked. A body could be stripped of its clothes by the currents and decomposition.

It did not imply intent or volitional action by the person who wore the clothes or indeed anyone else.

In a moment of intense longing, Alex tried to sit up, managing to raise his torso a few inches from the mattress. But his strength deserted him and he slumped back to the mattress, a smile of resignation breaking out across his face.

'How did they find me?'

Alex realized that he was looking up at the ceiling when he said this. He could have looked at the governor, but somehow he felt uncomfortable doing so. In any case what he really wanted to do was close his eyes altogether. He was still tired and all he really wanted to do was sleep the sleep of the innocent.

'The patrol helo saw the car leave the cliff and radioed in for some emergency relief from the coastguard.'

Even through the haze of confusion and the intense desire for sleep, Alex noted that Dusenbury had used the military term 'helo' rather than the civilian term 'chopper.' He resolved to ask him about this . . . some time.

'I think maybe it's time for me to go,' said the governor. 'There are a couple of people here to see you.'

For a moment, Alex thought Dusenbury meant the police. But he was pleasantly surprised when David entered the room with Debbie in tow.

Debbie!

She had come all the way out here from New York to be with him. He looked at her and gave her a welcoming smile. She returned it, but even through her gentle smile, Alex could see the hard person beneath it.

In some ways she and Nat were kindred spirits: both conceived during wild unprotected sex by alcohol-fueled students, both very determined people who could set their sights on an objective and then go for it with an almost ruthless tenacity.

Not that Debbie would send an innocent man to his death.

It was ironic that while Debbie had gone to work in New York to put some distance between herself and Alex, Nat had actively sought Alex out as an employer.

He had asked Nat, in the car, about why he had pushed so hard to work for him. But the accident had denied Nat the chance to answer the question.

Alex felt a cold chill as he thought about it now and the first traces of an answer began to form in his mind.

Dorothy's Poem

I cannot be, can never be
What I thought you wanted me
To be, to be, or so it seemed
When I didn't understand
What a fool I was, tee hee

Daddy, I know I am guilty
Though someone killed you first
I killed you as surely as if
I had pulled the trigger myself
Bang Bang! All over

And now I have to cross the Atlantic
Because I have to flee
Across the ocean, safe and sound
To where they'll never find me
You see

I never knew much about
The little boy you had before me

The son who died
The one you loved so much
That you couldn't let him go

I knew his name was Jimmy
And he died when he was three
In a car accident, with you at the wheel
No wonder you felt guilty
You never spoke about him

I tried to ask you when I was older
Tiptoeing delicately round the subject
But you gave me a look that warned me off
And I knew so well already
The anger you were capable of

But it was that poor dead toddler
Who cast a pall over me
A lightning rod for your anger
I started trying to be a he
I thought you wanted a he

Just act like a boy, that's what Mom suggested
And that would make you happy
It would give you back the thing you had lost
The son you always wanted back
We thought that you wanted a he

But all these efforts to win your love
They only backfired on me

They brought out your suppressed guilt
And your latent misery
Killer, Killer, that's what you are!

Not by malice but by reckless disregard
Then covering it up like a bully
With a wall of anger against others
As if they were to blame
So you could feel less guilty

You dragged me before the mirror
And ripped the clothes off of me
Forcing me to face the fact
That I am not, that I am not
The thing that you want me to be

You crushed the hope out of me
Not in cold blood, but angrily
And only when you died
Did I resolve the mystery
Of your vicious assault on my dignity

Because I was too young to understand
You were only trying to set me free
You didn't really want to change me
You wanted an alternative reality
You wanted to turn back the clock

And resurrect a child of three
But I saw things differently

My needs were shaped more selfishly
I had to escape my cell, I had to escape my shell
And find my own path to liberty

Now I must kill the little girl I used to be
But that won't be the end of me
Like some shapeshifting creature
Like Fantomas, like the Phoenix
I'll be reborn in the flames

I cannot slay my inner demons
For they are stronger than me
So instead, I will bury them deeply
Lay them to rest subconsciously
Daddy, Daddy, only then will I be free.

Loved MERCY? Then read on for an exclusive peek at the new David Kessler novel, coming soon

Prologue

It was only a set of fingers flying across a keyboard, yet they could work so much malice.

She watched in awe as her work appeared before her, the letters on the screen keeping pace with her fingers. What was so amazing was how little she had to change to have such a major effect. All she had to do to alter the behavior of an entire computer program was make minor alterations to just two of the lines of the program and then switch two of the other lines around. Hackers and computer nerds would laugh at the absurd simplicity of it. Some of them might even have been mildly amused by the sheer audacity of it. But few of them would have condoned her objectives. Most hackers tended to be free-wheeling libertarians, not embittered racists. And she wasn't even trained as a computer programmer, apart from one short online course she had taken recently.

But the irony went deeper than that.

Everyone knew the old cliché that you can radically change the interpretation of a contract by an ambiguous pronoun or the meaning of a statute by a harmless-looking punctuation mark. In England, a diplomat and humanitarian called Roger Casement was said to have been 'hanged by a comma' after he was found guilty of treason under a medieval statute. *But who would have believed that the same was true of a computer program?* And the biggest irony of all was that she couldn't tell anyone — like the criminal who commits the perfect crime and wants to brag about it to others, but can't.

But so what?

She wasn't doing it for fame or glory. She was doing it for justice — plain, old-fashioned justice.

As she continued her work, she glanced up a couple of times and looked out through the window. In the distance she could see the flickering lights of the nocturnal city. It reminded her that there was a world out there beyond her private domain of vengeance. But she forced herself to ignore the distraction. Her fingers continued to dance across the keyboard in the small pool of halogen light that fell upon the desk. The rest of the room was in darkness.

After a few more seconds, she paused, satisfied with the results of her labors. Then, with a couple of clicks of the mouse, she selected a menu item called 'build.' This action inaugurated a two-stage process known to computer programmers as 'compiling' and 'linking.' It was this process that actually created the finished computer program. By the time forty-eight seconds had elapsed, she had created a *new* version of the program.

And what a new version!

She thought about it now, almost wistfully. Getting the original source code had been tricky. She'd had to use some of her old contacts to break down the bureaucratic barriers. But finding out which courts used that particular jury selection program was somewhat easier. Many states had public records or freedom of information laws. She wished that she could infiltrate the altered program *everywhere*. That would be something of a coup. But she had to be realistic.

When she first started out, she had no idea that she would even be able to do it. It was more idle curiosity than a firm agenda that had prompted her to explore the possibility. But when she studied the documentation and asked a few questions of a professor to understand how the software worked, it suddenly dawned on her just how easy it would be.

Of course slipping it in *undetected* would be the hardest part. There were various ways she could do it. One way was to hack into the 'server' computers via broadband phone lines and upload the new program. But that was risky. Although most modern courts ran online servers hosting their jury selection software – so that jurors could check up on their status and whether they were on call that day – those computers almost invariably had strong firewalls to prevent outsiders from modifying the content.

There was, however, another way to infiltrate the new version of the software that didn't involve the internet at all. That way was to *get the systems administrators to install it themselves*. The key to this method was to make it seem as if it were a modification of the current program from *Legal Soft,* the company that had developed the software in the first place. By packaging the program complete with forged letterhead and multicolour process-printed documentation, and sending it out by special courier, she could trick their Systems Administrators into installing the new version under the erroneous assumption that they were getting an upgrade from the software company.

It would be the ultimate hack followed by the ultimate in 'social engineering.'

But what *was* the new program? It was *not* one of those so-called 'Trojan horses'. Neither was it a virus that could replicate itself. Nor was it a trap-door that would enable her to get into the system later. Indeed, once inserted into the system, it would simply do its work.

And now she was going to make those people pay!

Friday, 5 June 2009 – 7:30

Bethel was 19 – too young to remember the sixties and too bored to care about her grandparents' reminiscences, like how her mother was conceived at the Woodstock festival.

Pathetic!

But the sound of Buffalo Springfield's 'For What it's Worth' was ringing through her head, via the earphones of her iPod, as she stood by the roadside, waiting for help.

She knew little of the context of the song and nothing about the closing of the Pandora's Box nightclub or the Sunset Strip Curfew Riots. But the voice was haunting. It was easy to sleep through high school Civics classes – even to sleepwalk through the assignments and exams. She knew a bit about the Vietnam War and the civil rights struggles of the sixties. But it was all superficial academic knowledge, of the kind she picked up almost by default while daydreaming about the football team quarterback.

It stayed in her mind, not as a coherent picture but as a collection of soundbites: 'We shall overcome,' 'I have a dream,' 'Power to the People,' 'Burn baby burn!' The voice of anger still echoed across the decades. But it echoed faintly. A time-gulf separated Bethel from the turbulence that had almost ripped her country apart. And the time-gulf was ever widening, so all that was left of the ringing timbre of history's voices were the fading reverberations of barely-remembered heroes. Rosa Parks, Martin Luther King, Malcolm X, the Chicago Eight. Names and slogans to Bethel, but no substance . . . except, perhaps, the occasional substances she used to take her mind off the boredom of academic learning.

But she liked the song.

It had a pleasant hook to it that made it stick in her mind. What really sent shivers up her spine was that haunting phrase at the end of chorus, urging the young listeners to pause and assess the situation. She had no more than the merest inkling of what it meant. Whatever it was, had 'gone down' already.

It doesn't really matter, she told herself. It belonged to her grandparents' generation anyway. She belonged to another generation, the one that was more concerned with finding a job than changing the world. But with job security and guaranteed prosperity a thing of the past, the footing of Middle America was not so secure. And charity was beginning to end at home.

Bethel had known her own personal share of hardship in life, but it had been an exceptional episode and not something that affected others of her generation. She still bore the scars to her psyche, but she wasn't going to let it drag her down.

Her full name was Bethel Georgia Newton and she

was a mixed bag of human elements. In the looks department she was all bleached blonde and classic cheerleader figure: a carefully cultivated complexion and polished-tooth smile. Neither svelte nor-buxom, a kind of perfect 'in-between' for her 5'6", athletic, but in that soft, not-overdone way, with well-toned leg muscles, but not rippling ones. On the socio-economic side she was middle class and far removed from the culture of the street, the stoop or the 'hood. Yet when it came to experience of life she wasn't entirely naïve. She might not exactly have been streetwise, but she had tasted the bitter side of life. She knew what pain was . . . and humiliation.

She was also a rape survivor – they used the word 'survivor' these days, not 'victim'.

It had happened when she was still in high school, at the hands of a guy she knew and thought she could trust. In fact, the breach of trust had been the most painful part of the experience. It had thrown her mind into a whirlpool of confusion and self-doubt at the time.

But she had found a way to turn it around. Over the course of time, she had come to regard sex as a rigorous body workout from which she expected a modicum of physical pleasure but no real intimacy. By denying herself any expectation of enjoyment from the act, she succeeded in turning it into a weapon that she could use to get what she wanted. And most of the time, she didn't even have to give it out. She could just hold out the promise. As long as she was in control she could accept the small sacrifice of abandoning the prospect of getting any direct pleasure from the experience.

And yet she sometimes felt as if she was missing something.

She stood by the roadside in her white tight-fitting T-shirt and shorts that showed every curve of her firm body, holding out her thumb every time a car went by. She thought it would be easy hitching a ride, with her breasts thrusting out in front, straining against her T-shirt, and the perfect ripe complexion of her thighs showing like silk in the California sunshine.

But people were paranoid, she realized now, afraid of giving a ride to a girl hitchhiking on her own, for fear of what they might be accused of. She couldn't really blame them after what she had been through herself. And for all they knew, she might have been a lot less than her nineteen years.

A few yards away, her car had broken down and she couldn't even call for help because the battery of her cell phone was flat. She had made a half-hearted effort to fix the car herself, but she didn't really have a clue when it came to car engines. So all she could do was flag down a Good Samaritan and ask them to take her to a garage where she could get proper help.

Secretly she was hoping that some good-looking man with technical skills and a cool family fortune would stop and rescue her, not just from the roadside but from the aimless drifting boredom that seemed to have engulfed her life lately. But she would settle for an elderly couple taking her down the road to a pay phone if necessary. Only she wasn't even getting *that*.

Life was unfair.

And then her luck changed.

An aquamarine Mercedes slowed down as it approached her. A recent model and from the upmarket end of the European car industry. The owner was clearly affluent and probably young. By the time it had pulled over by the roadside, she could see that the driver was a black man.

The knee-jerk reaction and years of social conditioning made her fearful as she took this on board. But the feeling of guilt that followed swept away the fear. Besides, as he leaned out smiling and asked if she needed help, she could tell from his confident voice that this was no low-life creep. Also, she was drawn to his youthful good looks and quiet, cool self-confidence. She could tell from his car that this was a man who was going places and she warmed to him instantly, even if his diction still showed traces of the 'hood.

He might be a drug dealer, she thought in a moment of paranoia. But this thought, too, she dismissed under a wave of guilt.

He took a look under the hood and after a minute shook his head and said, 'I'm not really all that good with engines. I'm better with people.' He won her over with that line and a disarming smile. Two minutes later she was in the Mercedes and they were rolling along down the road, getting to know each other better. She didn't notice that, somewhere along the line, he had turned off the main road.

Friday, 5 June 2009 – 8:50

'I've got butterflies in my stomach Gene,' said Andi as the car snaked its way through the streets of Los Angeles. A sharp turn later and the car began slowing down as the office building loomed up ahead.

'It's too late to go back now.'

They both laughed. This was becoming a bit of an in-joke between them. They had both been nervous about leaving the Big Apple and crossing the continent to a new life on the West Coast. But Andi's career had demanded it.

Andi Phoenix, sitting silently and brooding nervously, was in her late thirties. She had kept her looks through healthy eating, regular workouts and a bit of cosmetic surgery. Her breasts had been enhanced from 34B to 36D with silicone implants and she had taken a botox injection to remove the first lines of age. But the rest was from hard work and healthy living. The blonde hair came from a bottle; the original had been a decent but boring mousy brown. Changing the color had been a form of therapy after the rough ride of her youth, but the enhancements as a whole carried with them the payload of attention from men that she could well do without. She was a few inches shorter than the black woman who sat next to her, and some ways felt in her shadow.

Gene touched Andi's forearm gently.

'Just remember this honey. *They* don't know *you* either. But they were ready to take a chance on you.'

In the driver's seat, in more ways than one, was Eugenia Vance, the six foot, muscular, black woman who had playfully wrestled with her in bed that morning – and won – as always.

They had met over twenty years ago, when Andi was still in her teens. Gene had helped Andi through her teenage crisis years, and they'd been together ever since. In all the time they had known each other, they never used the word 'lesbian' to describe their relationship. It wasn't denial. It was just that their every instinct railed against categorization. Neither Gene nor Andi loved 'women'; they simply loved each other.

'I'm just wondering if this whole thing is a big mistake.'

Gene snorted her mockery at Andi's self-pity.

'You've picked a *hell* of a time to start wondering girl!'

Here in California, Andi's specialty was much in demand. She had majored in psychology before going on to get her Juris Doctor degree from the Northeastern University School of Law, where she thrived amidst its progressive atmosphere that encouraged social responsibility. But after graduation she had found the law to be an irritating environment in which to work. Most of her criminal work involved plea-bargaining rather than trial work and usually that meant helping criminals plead guilty to lesser charges – hardly the service of justice and way off from the ideals that had driven her into the legal profession in the first place.

Matters had come to a head after she contracted pneumonia, forcing her to take a prolonged leave of absence from the law firm that had initially hired her and held out so much hope and promise. But when she went back to work, she found herself welcomed with less than open arms. She was protected by labor laws from outright dismissal, but found herself increasingly sidelined. She joined another firm but then spent the next eight months playing catch-up.

It was in this period that her interest in the subject changed. Although there were innocent people out there needing to be helped, criminal law meant – for the most part – helping the guilty. And that was not something she particularly enjoyed doing. So she did the old 'poacher turned gamekeeper' routine and got herself a job with the DA's office, in the domestic violence unit, where she thrived for a while. Starting at the bottom of the ladder meant she didn't get to do much courtroom work. Most of it involved working directly with victims, reading reports and collating evidence. But she was happy to do this. It gave her a sense of purpose.

Paradoxically, it was only when promotion gave her more courtroom work that disillusion set in for a second time. Because she found herself doing exactly the same thing as she was doing before, but from the opposite side of the table: plea-bargaining with criminals. She found their lawyers to be vile, for the most part, and she realized how vile she must have seemed to the DA in her earlier days as a defense attorney.

At the same time, she had developed another interest: crime victim litigation. There was a growing industry involving the pursuit of civil remedies for crime victims and she very much wanted to be part of it. The only trouble was that it was more developed on the West Coast than on the East.

So she got a job working in that fledgling field for a large law firm, but realized very soon that she had hit the glass ceiling. However, her employers were far from displeased with her performance and wanted to keep her on. They made it very clear that there were more prospects of upward mobility on the West Coast and if she wanted it, there was a job waiting for her at their Los Angeles office.

She wasn't altogether comfortable about moving but that was where the work opportunity took her.

'And what if I don't make the grade?' asked Andi, still seeking reassurance.

'*Hey, listen,*' said Gene firmly, 'I don't want to hear any of that. There's nothing to stop you except fear – and if you let that get to you, I'll be right behind you, ready to take a paddle to that cute little butt of yours.'

'My butt's not so little,' said Andi, but this time with humor rather than self-pity.

In truth, Andi's butt was fine, as any red-blooded male would have been only too happy to testify.

There was a hard side to Gene – hard enough to have given up a child. But there was a soft side too – soft enough to be haunted by it for years thereafter. To this day she wondered if she had done the right thing.

Andi knew about the child, but not about the self-doubt.

What Andi loved about Gene was that she was always so confident, never having doubts about anything, or at least never showing it if she did. On all the important matters, it was Gene who decided for both of them. It was Gene who had decided that they would come to live out here in California after Andi told her about the work opportunity. Andi would never have demanded it for herself. But she still lacked the self-confidence to stand up to Gene – to the world yes, but not to Gene. And Gene herself knew that Andi needed to make the move for her career. It wasn't in Gene's personal interests to make the move, but she cared too much for Andi to let that stand in their way.

So when it came to the crunch, Gene was ready to uproot herself and start again on the other side of the country.

It's only a sacrifice if you give up the greater value for the lesser one, she told herself, remembering the philosophy that had given her so much strength when she really needed it. *Andi's happiness means more to me than my two-bit career. So it isn't really a sacrifice.*

What Gene loved about Andi was that she was gentle and soft on the outside, yet fiery and determined when her sense of injustice was aroused. It was a paradox that was expressed as eloquently in Andi's eyes as in her words. The eyes had a kind of magic that was as frightening as it was fascinating: those eyes could look both menacing and vulnerable at the same time. It was Andi's eyes that Gene had originally fallen in love with. When Gene looked into Andi's eyes the first time they met, the beseeching, helpless look quickly dissolved into anger . . . no, not anger . . . tenacity.

The law was a natural field of endeavor for her. But it had to be the right sort of law. She was a crusader for justice and she became passionate to the point of ferocity when confronted by injustice in any of its countless forms. Gene had always found it strange that Andi had been ready to work as a defense lawyer for so long. She may have bitched about it, but she still did it – even though it was evident that it was causing her pain and leaving her unfulfilled. But Andi had made her choice and Gene was a firm believer in people making their own choices.

As the car slowed down, Gene gave Andi an encouraging smile and then looked around at the office buildings of the town Center. Andi smiled back, encouraged by Gene's contagious confidence.

'Looks like we're here,' said Gene, with an air of finality.

The car pulled up to a halt in front of a large office building. Andi unfastened her seat belt and opened the front passenger door.

'Wish me luck,' she said, taking a deep breath.

Gene looked at her with all the firmness of a strict parent still living in the mid-Victorian era. But the voice was strangely gentle.

'I won't do that honey, cause you don't need luck.'

Gene slid her left hand behind Andi's head, leaned over and kissed Andi on the lips. She had a way of making Andi feel good whenever the fear and self-doubt threatened to get the better of her. She had many ways in fact of massaging Andi's ego. This was only one of them.

That's why I love you Gene, thought Andi, closing her eyes. But she didn't say it. She just held on a moment longer than Gene did, almost clinging like a child, before letting go and getting out of the car. She wanted to stay something, but the jitters were still with her and she knew that Gene could sense it.

'Get in there and knock 'em dead honey!'

Andi closed the door and walked towards the building. Ignoring the names of the countless law and accountancy firms on the nameplates, she walked into the building and presented her ID to security.

Outside, Gene watched Andi enter the building like a mother watching her tearful K-grader vanish into the crowd of other children on her first day at kindergarden. Then she brought the engine to life with a roar, made an aggressive U-turn and drove back the way she came. She knew it was going to be a tough day for Andi – first days always are.

These thoughts were cut short by her cell phone. It was a call from the rape crisis center.

'Hallo,' said Gene, pressing the button of the handsfree set.

'Gene, we've just had a call from Riley.'

Bridget Riley was the head of the sex crimes unit in the local police. And a call from Bridget Riley probably meant one thing: another woman had been raped.

Friday, 5 June 2009 – 10:15

White.

The room was cold, clinical white. It was supposed to be relaxing as well as hygienic and useful for showing up any evidence samples that might be inadvertently dropped. But stepping into it had the aura of entering something out of a science fiction novel.

'Okay now just hold still,' said Doctor Weiner, holding the third swab between Bethel's legs.

Bethel held still and forced her mind not to think about what was happening or what had happened. But the harder she fought to avoid it, the more painful the memories that flooded back.

'I don't understand,' said Bethel fighting back the tears. 'How many swabs do you need?'

'We try to take several,' said Bridget, who was standing with her back to the wall a few feet away.

'But why?'

Bridget could hear in Bethel's voice, the inner strength that the girl was trying to draw on to dam up the flood of tears that was aching to burst.

'Because sometimes the whole sample gets used up

in the test and we may need to do back-up tests or give a sample to the defense in case they want to run their own independent tests.'

By this stage, Bethel Newton had been photographed from all angles, examined by a female doctor and had vaginal swabs and nail clippings taken. They had intended to take combing from her pubic hair, but she was shaven. They had also taken buccal swabs to use as reference samples. Bethel's body was now – in police investigative terminology – a 'crime scene'. And the vaginal swabs and nail clippings constituted 'crime-scene samples' – samples which had come into contact with the rapist and were potentially contaminated by his own DNA.

Any DNA in the crime-scene samples that could not be matched to the victim's own DNA were presumed, in the absence of any alternative explanation, to have come from the perpetrator of the crime. If there was enough of this foreign material – and if they found a suspect whose DNA matched it – then there was a good chance that they could secure a guilty verdict.

'I don't see what good this'll do,' said Bethel. 'He used a rubber.' She remembered how deftly he had held her down with the weight of his body while putting it on, before he penetrated her. It was like he knew exactly what he was doing – like he had done it before. Some men are experts with bra straps. This man was an expert at rape – and an expert at minimizing the trail of evidence that he left behind. He was what criminal investigators call 'forensically aware.'

'We don't expect to find any identifiable sperm in the vaginal swab,' explained Bridget. 'But we have to check anyway.'

Bethel shuddered, but kept her mouth shut. It hadn't been like this the first time. She had come to them much later, three days after the event, and all they did was take a statement.

'You scratched him too, don't forget,' Bridget added. 'That could give us a skin sample or even a blood sample and that in turn will give us his DNA. Also we might find traces of the rubber itself. He might have thrown it away nearby.'

'And how does that help?'

'Oh, in a variety of ways. For example, rubbers are made of a variety of materials, and contain substances known as exchangeable traces, like lubricants, spermicides and powders to stop the rolled up rubber from sticking to itself.'

'So what?' said Bethel, bitterly. 'How does that help you catch him in the first place?'

Bridget took in her breath and spoke gently.

'Okay, well let's say we find an empty condom packet by the road on the route from where it happened, and if it has fingerprints on it, and if he has a criminal record, we'll be able to identify him and issue a warrant. And let's say we find some exchangeable traces in the swabs we took from you, we can compare them for chemical similarities to any rubbers we find on the suspect or for that matter any chemical traces in any condom that he discarded nearby. Or if he discarded the packet, we can analyze the exchangeable traces in them and compare them to your crime-scene sample.'

'So what'll that prove?' Bethel spat out contemptuously. 'That he has the same type of rubbers?'

Bridget put a comforting hand on Bethel's shoulder.

'Evidence is like a jigsaw puzzle, Bethel. If we can put enough pieces together we can nail him. Fingerprints on a discarded packet or condom can link the condom to the suspect. Semen in the discarded condom can link it to the suspect. Matching trace chemicals between the condom and your samples can link the condom to you. The DNA evidence can then strengthen the case against him considerably. And if we can match his DNA to the DNA from those other crimes then before you know it he's going down on multiple counts of rape! And *you'd* be the one who can claim the credit for stopping him.'

Bethel knew that the flattery was part of a well-meaning game. Still, she warmed to the complement and nodded, pretending to accept Bridget's logic.

In fact, a bond was beginning to form between them. This was only natural. From the moment Bethel had staggered into the police station, Detective Bridget Riley had accompanied her.

Bethel had been reluctant to go through the whole rape examination procedure. Several times she had almost backed out of it, fearing that if they ever caught the bastard he would claim that she had consented. But Bridget had convinced her to go through with it, pointing out that the bruises and internal injuries showed that the rapist had used considerable force.

'There's virtually no danger he'll be able to argue

consent,' Bridget assured her. 'They sometimes get away with that in date-rape cases, but unless we goof-up badly, there's no way he can use it here.'

'But I don't know who *did* it?' Bethel had whined. 'If I don't know who it *was* then how can you arrest him?'

It was an old story. Some victims like to forget about the whole thing. But Bethel demanded explanations. She understood rape well enough. But she wanted to understand what was happening now.

'The DNA is only part of it,' Bridget explained patiently. We'll also do an artist's impression for a possible facial identification. If we catch some one, the DNA is for confirmation. And believe me, DNA is rock-solid evidence in court these days.'

'It didn't help the prosecution against O. J. Simpson!' she spat out bitterly.

'That was an exception. The cops were sloppy about how they handled the evidence. That gave the defense a window of opportunity to make it look like there was reasonable doubt. Remember the jurors were still angry over the Rodney King fiasco. But it couldn't happen again.'

Bethel was by now looking a bit more hopeful.

'Can't you check the DNA against some sort of database of sex offenders?'

'We'll check it against the California SDIS, and the NDIS in Washington.'

'What's that?'

'It's the National DNA Index System.'

'And what if he isn't in it?' asked Bethel, whining.

'If we can catch him from the artist's impression, the

we can take a blood sample from him and use DNA to *prove* that he's guilty.'

But then Bethel said something that struck Bridget as rather strange.

'But I still think he might try and say I consented?'